*For Jean,
who dreams the dream.
Anything is possible.*

*(For you, I'll even pretend the
epilogue doesn't exist…shh.)*

The true king sits
On the throne at last
A short-lived peace
Which passes fast

Months at best
'Til the scale tips
The kingdom has
Until the first eclipse

What's dead is alive
What's alive is dead
The veil has thinned
In places shred

To mend what's broken
Three must travel
Scour the Plains
Or worlds unravel

The Bringer of Life, the King,
The One Who Failed
Find the Heart of Death
Through much travail

CHAOS BOUND

A NOVEL BY
L. RYAN STORMS

Published by RaineStorms Press, 2022.

The paperback edition has been catalogued as follows:
Name: Storms, L. Ryan, author
Title: Chaos Bound / by L. Ryan Storms
Description: Electronic file (eService)
Series: The Tarrowburn Prophecies; Volume 3
Summary: Finally, the Chaos Wielder's identity has been revealed, but Quinn is gone, and Reina and Alesh have little time to save their world from an eternity of chaos and ruin. But not all is as it seems in these lands, and those who die don't always stay dead.
ISBN 978-1-7328492-4-2 (paperback)
ISBN 978-1-7328492-5-9 (ebook)
Subjects: | YFC: Children's / Teenage fiction: Action & adventure stories | YFH: Children's / Teenage fiction: Fantasy & magical realism | YFB: Children's /Teenage: general interest | BISAC: YOUNG ADULT FICTION / Fantasy / General | YOUNG ADULT FICTION / Action & Adventure / General | YOUNG ADULT FICTION / General

www.lryanstorms.com
Cover art by AK Westerman, more at www.akorganicabstracts.com

Only in Death
Can balance restore
For a time at least
'Til the next great war

For the Chaos Wielder
Has allowed
The balance to slip
Too long, too proud

That Liron may fall
To darkness and mayhem
When the power rests
In the stone of the diadem

To fix forever
Chaos bound
Only then
Balance found

CHAPTER ONE

Haunted by Memory
Reina

I ran, hard and fast, pretending the unfamiliar terrain and the darkness didn't bother me. Then my boot slipped in the slick mud, and I hit the ground, teeth clacking together, palms stinging with the brunt of the impact. I rolled with the momentum, stood, and took off sprinting again. In the dark, it was impossible to see which direction I was headed, but I ran anyway.

Getting caught wasn't an option. I flung a crimson-black tendril of power into the base of the abandoned structure as I passed but didn't stop to watch its effects. A rumble sounded as the walls crumbled behind me, and I gave an out-of-breath smile. I wasn't half-bad at learning to control the power of death, after all. Death had a different feel, a different taste on the palate, but its power was every bit as robust as life.

A wall of greenery sprung from the ground, shooting skyward and flinging dirt just ahead. I deadened a section in the center of it, creating a doorway of dried, dead vines I plowed through effortlessly.

I turned to see my pursuer dodge a half-dead tree whose roots I had weakened. The giant trunk fell through the air, reaching with leafless limbs. He took a nimble leap out of its way, and the tree crashed, useless, to the ground.

Before I could spring another tendril of death on him, I went sprawling downward headfirst, my boot snared in a root that had grown upward to encircle my ankle.

I lay stunned for a moment, trying to catch the breath knocked from my lungs in the fall. Then Alesh stood over me, grinning like a madman.

"Cunning," I said, working my foot free from the trap, breath coming in puffs as I tried to recover.

"I am still faster than you," he said, bright white teeth visible in the moonlight. His breath came heavily, but he wasn't winded, not even after a chase. Where did he store his energy? He was more than twice my age, for Saints' sake. He offered a hand and I took it, allowing him to pull me to my feet.

"As a reminder, only one of us was bit by a Gohmi viper but a few days ago. Besides, if I had my horse, I promise you wouldn't be faster." I brushed dirt from my breeches, then tucked the talisman back beneath my tunic. I missed Aeros. I missed—

No.

I shut down the thought. I would see Quinn again. He wasn't dead, no matter what the world beneath Kufataba would have me believe.

With less than thirty days until the eclipse, Alesh and I traveled southward on foot, covering as much ground as we could, training with our swapped magic as much as we dared. I learned much faster with Alesh as a teacher than I could ever have hoped to learn on my own. I only prayed I was half as useful to him in aiding his understanding of the power of life. Given that he usually won our sparring sessions, I needn't have worried.

We never strayed far from camp during our training, unwilling to leave our few possessions unguarded for very long, even if we hadn't seen another soul since our encounter with the Chaos Wielder.

Alesh was a good companion, as good as I could hope for under the circumstances, and we'd gotten close to the outskirts of the Elorin Empire's capital over the last few days. Though he hadn't opened the Map to Balance again, he hinted we might reach the city tomorrow. Unfamiliar with anything in this part of the world, I took him at his word.

On one hand, I would be thrilled to get as far from the snake-infested grasslands as possible. Despite both of us working together to isolate the venom in my veins, there was still an ache in my leg, not to mention a sense of impending doom that the poison-filled capsules floating in my body might eventually grow too weak to contain the poison. The idea of the venom being released into my blood at any time was enough to make my stomach turn and my knees weak.

On the other hand, getting closer to the capital meant getting closer to the Chaos Wielder and having to face her again. Even training with Alesh hadn't increased my confidence in our ability to defeat her. Not with her mental state.

The girl wasn't lucid. I thought back to her attack on the plains less than a week ago, about the raw power she contained with the stone in her diadem. She hadn't lied about her power being stronger than either of ours. Chaos was bigger than life and death, if only because of its sheer unpredictability.

I'd felt her heart beating in her chest that day. I could have ended this all then. At least, Alesh believed so, but…I wasn't so sure. I'd begun to suspect she would have found a way to halt me in my tracks had I tried to touch her with death's tendrils. Life and death were rigid in definition. I had aged Bruenner to his death months ago, and Alesh's father had used the power of death to give life to Alesh, but we couldn't set things aflame, start vicious, unpredictable windstorms, or take the form of other people.

"You are stuck in your head again." Alesh tapped me lightly on the shoulder as we returned to camp.

"I usually am." I sat beside my bag and laid out my bed roll, which called to me with enticing invitations of a dreamless sleep.

"Tomorrow, we reach Ivirreh. No worries until then."

Easier said than done. I sighed as I climbed beneath the blanket and rested my head on an arm. What would we find in Ivirreh? Would there be more trouble? Were the people of the Elorin Empire subject to the Chaos Wielder's same whims?

If so, perhaps we would find assistance. It was more than possible they, too, were tired of being plagued by the undead. I held to the hope that Alesh and I wouldn't have to face the crazy young girl alone again, however unlikely the true prospect of help might be.

And then my thoughts drifted to Quinn.

I couldn't fall asleep without thinking of him, couldn't see the stars without wondering where he was, if he was alive. I ran a finger over the little pink shell he'd made into a necklace for me. I kept the shell in my pocket now since the rope had burned in the Chaos Wielder's madness that night on the plains. But I still had the shell and the memory of Quinn with it.

Because of the strength of my ability with the talisman and the fact that I could still summon the magic—even if the magic was death—some days I convinced myself Quinn lived. I'd never had such power without his presence. But then, my ability had never been about death before, either.

More than once, Alesh had gone on, often to the point of exhaustion, attempting to dissuade me of the desperate notion that Quinn could have somehow survived the journey beneath Kufataba. By now, I almost believed him.

It wasn't that I'd given up hope. I couldn't give up hope. I'd just begun to accept Alesh's logic on the matter. It seemed…well…logical.

Of course my ability would work without Quinn once he was no longer living. The White Sorceress, Bringer of Life, wouldn't lose the ability to channel the talisman's power just because she was meant to use it in protecting the king of Castilles. If the king of Castilles died, there was no one left to protect with her power, and no one she needed to keep in check…at least, not until a new ruler was named. Her power became hers to use at will.

Which meant I had more power at my fingertips than I

could ever have had when Quinn was alive.

However much I wanted to deny that Quinn was—

Dead. Say the word, Reina. He's dead. Accept it.

—dead, I couldn't deny that Alesh was likely right. I'd seen Quinn disappear into the blue abyss with my own eyes. The mountain swallowed him whole. A person didn't survive that kind of horror, whatever that kind of horror was.

I swiped at the sudden wetness on my cheeks with a palm and ignored the weight in my chest. I would go on. I'd go on because it's what Quinn would want me to do. He…died so I could live. He forfeited his life so Alesh and I could defeat the Chaos Wielder. If nothing else, I owed him that at least. I owed that honor to his memory.

I'm still trying, Quinn.

"Ye're still trying, aren't you?"

I whipped my head upward, absorbing with mild confusion the library around me and the piles of books on the thick oak table where I sat. Since the official move to Irzan, I'd taken to spending any and all free time in the castle library. Dark and dreary to most, I found the library a comforting place filled with books that were a wealth of information, some more so than others.

I pushed aside the tome on the benefits of consuming goat stomach. That was one book we no longer needed to maintain in the royal library. Always good to make space.

"Trying what?" I asked Quinn.

He looked the way he always had, nearly black hair slightly unkempt as though he'd shoved a hand through it more than once, shadowed jaw dark with stubble, eyes as intense and curious as always as he viewed me. His tunic stretched over his shoulders in a way that reminded me entirely too much of how those shoulders looked when he wore no tunic at all.

I furrowed my brow.

This wasn't…right. Why was Quinn wearing a tunic in the castle? Should he not have been in royal robes and with his advisors at this very moment? I sat back, the legs of the chair protesting against the stone floor as I pushed the chair from the table.

"Still trying what?" I asked again, standing.

"Ye're still trying to find a way to bring me back. Researching even in your sleep."

My sharp inhale was audible in the surrounding silence. I looked from Quinn and the library shelves to the oil sconces and the thick stone walls. The library. The castle. We were in Irzan. Of course Quinn was…

Sympathy flashed in his eyes as he read the sudden understanding in mine.

"'Tis not possible, Reina."

"If we're in the castle, it means we haven't yet gone. There's a chance. I could—"

I could what? What could I change along the way?

He extended a hand, and I recoiled, staring at those strong, capable fingers as though touching them might remind me he no longer drew breath, that none of this was real.

I looked from his hand to his face, my eyes filling with tears as I met his gaze.

"You're dead."

A gentle shake of my shoulder sent me sitting bolt upright. I woke with a gasp, my heart in my throat, my pulse racing in my veins, an ache in my soul so deep I thought I might never breathe without pain again.

"A dream. You are safe." Alesh's warm voice was as disorienting as it was comforting. Concerned eyes took in my frazzled awakening and waited for me to catch my breath.

I nodded and swallowed with a cough, my tongue sticking to the back of my throat. Alesh reached for the water skin. He didn't speak again until after I'd taken a long drink, but I could feel the weight of his stare in the weak light of the fire's embers, the words he wanted to say.

"Thank you," I said, handing the skin back to him once more.

He set it on the ground by his side, then settled back into his own makeshift bed on the ground, having given me the remaining bedroll from the supplies we hadn't left behind in Kufataba.

"It will not last forever." His words were gentle, soft to cushion the sting of their blow.

"I know." It was the only response I could manage.

I did know. My mother's death was still clear in my mind, though she had died four years ago. And yet, sometimes I felt as though she'd been gone for a decade or more. Time could be both cruel and kind to the human heart. Quinn's death, new and raw, was a wound from which I would never fully heal. And yet, as painful as that wound was, I wouldn't bleed out from it.

I would never be granted such mercy.

I lived in fear of the future to come, waiting with dread for the day I would eventually forget Quinn's voice. The sparkle in his eyes when he teased me and the way he'd shake his head when I was so involved in the formulation of my remedies that I didn't hear him speak. Those memories would fade from my mind. I wanted to cry with the pain of it.

Someday, I would no longer remember the shapes of the scars that lined his back, and the way I let my fingers linger over them when he finally allowed me to touch. My mind would forget the familiar smell of him that grounded me home wherever we might be.

There were things about my mother I had forgotten in the years since she'd been killed. I knew her voice, and I could remember the way it made me feel, but I could no longer *hear* it in my head. Years without hearing her voice aloud had erased the sound from my mind.

She'd always smelled of the herbs she compounded daily, of dirt and earth and green, growing plants and leaves, but I'd be pressed to name which herbs were hers. Since inheriting the role as Healer in Barnham, I'd resumed the compounding. More days than not, I smelled of all the same herbs and remedies myself. Without my permission, my mind had reclaimed those scents and reassigned them a monotonous, daily presence in my life, a life no longer associated with Esmé di Bianco.

An unwelcome tear slid down my face. I placed a hand to

my cheek to find it already wet. When had I started crying?

Don't cry, she would have said. But even now, I felt as though that wasn't quite right. She would have said something else, something more personal. Something we shared between the two of us.

And it was gone. Whatever it was, I had let my mind forget.

"You had something special, the two of you," Alesh said. "It is good to cry for missing him, but do not cry for him. He is with the sky. He is free from pain, free from harm."

I sniffed. "I know, Alesh. It just… Losing Quinn"— my voice broke over his name, but I plowed on— "so unexpectedly was a reminder of how I lost my mother. It's overwhelming, I fear." I blew out a breath at having spoken aloud the words stuck in my throat.

"Ah," he said gently.

I suspected Alesh had lost a number of people throughout the years, more than his father, who had given his own life to heal Alesh as a young man. At twice my age, he had likely lost many a friend and family member in his time. I wondered how he coped with the loss, how he dealt with continuing to live and breathe while others he loved did not. I wondered if having power over death helped one accept it better.

"Your mother," Alesh began. "You were close. She loved you very much."

I nodded as I stared at the unfamiliar stars in the sky, reminding myself I was still on Liron. Everything here was so different from Castilles—the land, the stars, life.

"I mean," Alesh began again. "You were a young her."

I glanced to Alesh, wiping the last of the tears from my cheeks, and struggling to pull myself back together. Quinn would never have allowed himself to fall apart in this way. I shouldn't spend my time crying, either.

"Yes, I was very much like my mother."

Alesh shook his head in frustration. "No, you *were* a young her."

I furrowed my brow.

"A 'Little Me.'"

Don't cry, Little Me.

The words rang like thunder in my ears. Little Me. *That* was what my mother would have said. Little Me. So suddenly full of emotion, my chest felt as though it might break open just to relieve the pressure that welled inside. That must have been what the mountain had taken from me.

"Alesh." My voice cracked. "Thank you. I felt…lost. I've lost so much of her. Thank you."

"It is right. He said he would tell you, and you should know. Kufataba took it from you, the memory. And it might take the memory, but it cannot take the words."

New tears slid down my cheeks again, but I smiled this time.

Little Me. My mother was still with me. I strengthened the resolve in my heart. She would always be with me.

I would hold Quinn just as close.

CHAPTER TWO

Ivirreh's Secrets
Reina

A vivid southern sun gleamed off the whitewashed sides of Ivirreh's buildings, the blinding glare making it painful to stare too long in that direction. My first view of Ivirreh was far in the distance, but the city was built one structure atop the next. The entire place appeared no more than one enormous white palace with glimmering golden roofs and colored glass windows.

It was…breathtaking.

Up close, Ivirreh was no less impressive. How an entire city could stay so pristine was beyond comprehension. Here, tens of thousands of people lived and worked every day, and yet there was no sign of the dirt or filth that normally accompanied human occupation. No mud in the cobbled streets, no smell of manure—horse or human—in the air, no ash from fires or chimney soot stains on the rooftops. It defied logic.

"This place is very busy." Alesh gestured to the flurry of activity around us.

Vendors sold wares in the confusing maze of alleys leading to the city's center and calls rang out with boisterous claims of each stall's superior goods.

My stomach grumbled in response to mouth-watering aromas. Dozens of fruits, vegetables, and nuts in every kind of bowl and barrel, wrapped in paper and cloth, lined the borders of each stall. One stall offered neatly wrapped packages of rice and beans in sticky, oiled grape leaves twice the size as the biggest wraps I'd seen back home. They lay stacked in a tempting display that set my mouth aching, and I gazed at them longingly as we moved past. At every stall, people milled and bartered, attempting to get the best price on eggs, flour, cheese, and many foods I couldn't identify.

A place like this should have been worn down by the sheer number of people alone, but it wasn't. Every stall shone, scrubbed and clean, as if set up brand new yesterday. Counters showed no sign of wear. Blue, green, and sunflower yellow canopies that shaded the crowds from the heat of the day were sprinkled with varying stripes, damask print, gold stars, and large floral swirls of every color. Not a single swath of fabric overhead was faded by the sun's wrath or frayed by years of wind. Yet surely this market had been here for years, if not decades.

"What exactly are we doing here?"

"As I said, we are discovering the Elorin people."

Alesh said he wanted to mix with the Elorins before finding the Chaos Wielder, but I didn't fully understand what he hoped to gain by it. None of the people here were dressed as regally as the Wielder herself had been. Why should they know much—if anything—about who she might be?

We'd have to scour the wealthier circles to find the girl.

I hoped she wasn't the daughter of a noble family who was just as wretched as she. I couldn't handle going up against one, let alone an entire family of maniacal lunatics.

Still, the sooner we found the wealthier districts, the sooner we'd be able to locate her. I wasn't keen on wasting time. I especially wasn't keen on torturing myself with the increasingly appetizing smells of the marketplace. My stomach growled again. Amid the crowd, the grumbles couldn't be heard, but my insides twisted, nonetheless.

"Here." Alesh offered me a handful of coins from a pocket on the side of the pack he carried, the pack that had once been Quinn's. "Get food for us. I will see what the people have to say."

He couldn't have heard my stomach's complaints, but my face flushed anyway. Still, I didn't need to be told twice. I took the coins and made for the stall with the grape leaf wraps.

The language barrier wasn't difficult to overcome. I stood in line until I reached the counter of the stall, pointed to the grape leaves with a smile and held up two fingers to the dark-skinned stall owner with the broad smile and kind eyes. I paid for the food, then pocketed the change and accepted the two paper-wrapped bundles. I scanned the market for Alesh, finding him a few stalls away.

He was deep in conversation with one of the women behind the counter and didn't immediately notice I'd returned. When he saw me, he raised his eyebrows and held a finger in the air, never breaking stride in his conversation. I didn't mind waiting. It gave me time to study the people around me.

In the Southern Plains, which were north of the Elorin Empire, the people were dark-skinned. The shades of their skin ranged from light brown to skin so dark it nearly shone indigo, but all the people I'd encountered were dark-skinned. By contrast, Castilles, farther to the north where the weather could sometimes be bitter cold, was home to light-skinned people with light eyes and fair hair. There were those in Castilles with dark hair and eyes, of course, but none with dark skin. At least, none so far as I had seen, though I surely had not come close to seeing the entire kingdom.

Here, in the Elorin Empire, the diversity was astonishing. It was as though someone had taken half the people of Castilles and half the people of the Southern Plains and dropped them all together in one place. How had such a variety of people come to be?

Alesh stepped beside me, tearing me from my ponderings, and I handed him one of the wrapped grape leaves.

"You had no trouble?" he asked.

"Trouble? No. Why would I have trouble?" I dug into my pocket for the change and handed it to Alesh.

He studied it, met my eyes, and nodded.

"Not everyone is honest in a market. Some sellers will cheat. I sent you to buy as a test."

I unwrapped the rolled package and inhaled the scent of oils and spices before biting into my stuffed grape leaves and rolling my eyes in bliss. The last time I'd eaten a hot, prepared meal that wasn't partially scavenged or grown with Alesh's power was in the inn back in Lower South Trellington.

When Quinn—

I swallowed, the sticky morsel seeming larger as it glued itself to the back of my throat. I swallowed again and forced another bite, clearing my mind of such thoughts.

"What did you learn?" I gestured to the woman Alesh had spoken to. She'd returned to selling dried legumes and something that looked a bit like callogh, but orange.

"Ah. Life here is good," he said. "The emperor's family suffered a terrible accident some months ago, but they have seen no sign of chaos here. No horror, no storms, no fires. And no *acaffilé*."

No undead. That was a very good thing. The Chaos Wielder didn't like to stir problems in her homeland. I imagine the emperor, whoever he was, wouldn't take kindly to such disturbances, and he'd have to travel a much shorter distance than we had to put an end to her meddling. The thought of having someone nearby with that kind of authority was comforting.

I stuffed the last of the wrap into my mouth, chewing slowly to savor the taste, and crumpled the paper into a ball before depositing it into a nearby waste bin as an ear-piercing metallic clang cut through the air.

The sound originated somewhere out of sight, toward the far end of the street. I turned my gaze to the din, examining the faces of the people around me as I did. No one appeared overly alarmed to hear the noise, so I didn't panic even though the clanging set my nerves on edge.

When the last peal of the bell faded, a voice called out, shouting for all to hear. I looked to Alesh for a translation, studying his expression, attempting to read whether this news was good or bad. His brow furrowed in concentration as he listened.

"There will be a public announcement. The emperor, I think. I do not know all the words." Alesh hissed in frustration, his hands on his hips. "An hour."

He might not have understood everything, but without Alesh, I would understand nothing at all. I was grateful for his ability to connect Castilles with both the Elorin Empire and the Southern Plains.

A fortunate turn of events that the emperor would be outside the palace today. We'd been told it was impossible to arrange an appointment inside the palace walls. At least this way, we could attempt to meet with him if we could manage to gain his ear. Alesh insisted he would be discreet in garnering the emperor's attention. I wasn't sure how such a thing was possible, given that there were bound to be many who wished to speak with him.

An hour later, a herald called out above the sound of the people. His voice was louder than it should be, and I couldn't pinpoint how such amplification was accomplished. I squinted, examining him as he spoke. Alesh translated.

"Presenting her Imperial Majesty, Emperor Elodie Gehtanan, fourth of her name, savior and sole survivor of the Gehtanan line."

The crowd erupted into wild cheers.

A woman, then. I hadn't expected a woman as the emperor.

She emerged from the midst of a dozen guards and

climbed the stairs to the platform, holding her layered gown in one hand so as not to step on the hem. I craned my neck, struggling to see better, but the crowd had grown thick, and I caught only glimpses between the heads and shoulders of taller men and women.

Alesh and I sifted through the people, to get close enough to be noticed when the time came, but the crowd was stubborn in their devotion to their emperor. People gave us disapproving glances, outright glaring, as we nudged and elbowed our way forward. I slid past a tall, pale man, his gray beard grown down to his chest. His hands were high in the air, clapping as he hollered, his head shaking, eyes closed as he agreed with whatever the emperor was saying. Then, finally, we found a spot where Alesh and I might see the emperor as well as hear her. I turned my gaze to the stage, raising a hand to shield my eyes from the sun overhead.

Then I suppressed a vulgar curse.

The emperor would *not* be helping us.

The emperor was the Chaos Wielder, the same shrew who tried to kill us a week ago. Alesh's hand tightened on my arm. I met his gaze and nodded, dread firmly building in my stomach.

The brand on my chest itched something fierce, as though her very presence reminded my skin of the damage she'd done to it. I fought the urge to press a hand to my heart, instead gripping the shell in my pocket to ground myself. I forced myself to think of Quinn.

"My people," Alesh translated. "I am always delighted to see how the empire prospers with your spirit and dedication."

Cheers erupted from the crowd in response. I scowled.

"While troubles and war plague other nations around Liron, the Elorin Empire remains strong and untouched. Despite the recent tragedy that has befallen my family, despite the loss I have suffered, I, like my mother before me, will do everything in my power to ensure the empire and all who reside here will prosper in these uncertain times."

"Oh, I bet you will," I muttered, my words swallowed by another cheer of the crowd.

When the cheers died, she resumed speaking.

"While our great empire is a land to be desired, this is not the reason I have called for a public address today."

"God bless you, Holy One!"

Alesh translated the words of the woman who had shouted from the crowd, too, and I sucked in a breath. This was bad. If her followers adored her as a holy relic, she would be a far more difficult target than I could have imagined.

"And may He bless you, too. All of you. But the real reason I have asked you to gather today is because our great land is in danger. *I* am in danger. There are enemies from afar who would do me harm and take the empire for themselves."

The crowd gasped collectively.

"Fear not." She smiled as she gazed out, a subdued smile compared with the leer I'd seen on her features in our last meeting. "I will not succumb so easily to the whims of lesser beings. You know me. You know my family and what we've always stood for. You know my strength. But I will require something of you. All of you. I ask that you be alert, aware of…" Alesh faltered, unsure of the translation. "I think," he said. "I think she's asking them to watch for any who might be her enemy."

Wonderful. She would turn the entire empire into a den of paranoia. This would make our task much more difficult. Unless…

I reached into the talisman, into the dark power of death. I could do it now. I might hate myself for the rest of my days, but I could take her life. The magnitude of Quinn's self-loathing swept through me all at once, with power near enough to knock me to my knees. Would that agony be worth the kill if it meant no one would ever be hurt by the Chaos Wielder's madness again?

I couldn't be sure, but I thought…just maybe, it might. I'd never understood that side of Quinn, but everything he'd once said about justified killing suddenly grew crystal clear.

My chest pounded with every beat of my heart as I reached deep into the talisman's reserve. I would have to be swift. There must be no question. I couldn't risk giving her a chance to protect herself. I couldn't risk her throwing the people around us into danger.

Alesh looked on, aware, encouraging. He gave a nod.

"End it. Now," he said.

So I did.

At least, I tried.

In the very moment I readied to release the deadly power into the Chaos Wielder's body, she stood, spine rigid, alert, as though my tapping into the magic of the talisman had sent her an announcement of impending danger. Her head snapped in my direction, frantic, wide eyes searching the audience for the source of the disturbance.

Fiermi. She knows.

The magic faded into nothingness as I bent it to my will, and I grabbed Alesh's arm to drag him back through the crowd, away from the stage. He hurried behind me, not asking why we were running. The people around us throughout the crowd didn't realize anything was amiss. They continued to cheer for their emperor, showering her in well wishes for good health and prosperity.

I risked one look over a shoulder, making eye contact with the Chaos Wielder across the distance. Then her figure disappeared behind a swell of the crowd. Alesh and I wove through the masses with increasing speed, changing our location as quickly as possible. By the time we emerged at the back of the crowd, the Chaos Wielder was exiting the stage, no longer searching the audience for us, but her hurried gait did nothing to reassure me.

She knew I was here. She'd felt the magic and, somehow, she'd extinguished it.

I watched, narrowing my eyes, wishing for a moment I could unleash the deadly magic and close her throat. Then, as she neared the steps at the edge of the platform, she slipped, her arms windmilling wildly. Was it wrong I wanted to see her fall?

One of her guardsmen steadied her with a quick hand, and she remained upright. She looked down at whatever had caused her misstep, then masked a downright murderous glare with a smile as she turned her attention to her people again. She smoothed her gown, then waved to her nearest followers as she descended the last two steps and stepped into a carriage headed by four black horses that would presumably take her back to the palace.

By this time, Alesh and I were well-concealed behind hundreds of people as well as the overhang of a nearby building. The Chaos Wielder had lost sight of us, but I didn't think for a moment she'd forgotten we were here.

"Why did you not do it?" Alesh asked. "It could be over."

"I…tried. She *took* the magic from me, Alesh!"

He shook his head. "No. That is not possible."

"Apparently, it is. She's strong, even with the gemstone cracked. If she can feel the magic before I have the chance to use it, we stand no chance."

Alesh kicked the corner of the building in an uncharacteristic show of frustration. I sympathized. Nothing about this situation was easy, but this new development made taking the Chaos Wielder's life a thousand times more difficult. Now, not only had she set the dispersing crowd into a panic about foreigners who wanted to see her dead, but she was also well-aware when I engaged in the talisman's magic.

I stared at the empty platform where the Chaos Wielder had given her address and thought.

"Alesh," I said absently, an idea slowly forming. "We'll have to reach her while she sleeps. We'll have to find a way into the—"

I stopped and squinted at the platform steps, where a child was squeezing out from the space beneath the stage. She glanced left, then right, though the crowd in the center was now no more than the regular flow of people coming and going from wherever it was they normally would at this time.

Once extracted from the space, the girl stood and dusted the knees of her trousers. She was dressed as a boy, though her long hair was hastily braided to keep out of her face. Alesh followed my gaze.

"Curious. An ardent follower of the emperor or a small maker of trouble?"

I suppressed a grin. "I'd bet anything on a troublemaker. Come."

I cut across the pavilion toward the stage and followed the young girl, who had disappeared down one alley and was already turning a corner into another.

My boots hit the ground with hardly a sound as I ran along the narrow back alleys, trying to keep from alerting the girl to my presence, but my efforts were wasted. As soon as I turned the corner, I faced a long, empty alleyway, squat buildings pressed up against one another for blocks, boxes and bins and trash receptacles near almost all the buildings' back doors.

Had she gone inside one of the homes or shops? Or hidden behind a bin?

I let the magic of the talisman locate a tiny fast-beating heart, feeling out its rhythm, seeking its owner.

I found the girl behind the third trash bin, her little pulse beating faster than a rabbit's. She wasn't breathing—no, wait, that wasn't right. She was holding her breath.

So she knew I had followed her.

Clever child.

Alesh drew beside me. He would have to translate.

"Hello," I said. "Don't be afraid."

Alesh translated, but the girl didn't move. Maybe she thought if she were still enough, we would think she had gone.

"I'd like to talk to you. About the emperor." I made my voice as small and sweet as I could, talking to her almost as I would have to Aeros.

Her feet shifted—the slightest movement, just enough to send vibrations rippling through the talisman.

Alesh translated again.

I waited a long moment, giving her time to consider.

Finally, she peered around the corner of the bin with one uncertain blue eye.

I smiled, standing ever so still.

Then she stepped out from behind the trash receptacle and stood in the middle of the alleyway, hands on her hips. She spat on the ground and met my eye.

"If by the emperor, you mean the rogue imposter in the palace, I have no desire to speak on the subject."

I reeled.

"You speak my language," I said.

"I speak many languages."

She was either older than she looked or a very, *very* intelligent child. She might be standing here speaking to us, but she wasn't happy about it. Her eyes remained guarded, feet ready to bolt.

I kneeled in the alley, bits of gravel biting into my knees through the fabric of my pants. "My name is Reina, and my friend is Alesh. We've traveled a long way to reach the Elorin Empire. We'd like to know more about what happened to the emperor's family. Please, do you have a name?"

Her eyes grew glassy for an instant before she scowled and regained her steel composure. She jutted a small chin, her lips pressed together.

"I'm Abigayle. Call me Abi."

"It's nice to meet you, Abi. Do you live nearby?"

"I live in the palace," she said. "Or I did until my imbalanced sister murdered the rest of our family."

My lips parted. Alesh coughed.

The girl curtsied and smiled.

"Abigayle Gehtanan, youngest of the Gehtanan Imperial line and sole survivor of her sister's wrath. Nice to meet you."

CHAPTER THREE

Family Ties
Reina

"You're her sister!" I couldn't hide my surprise.

"I am, and don't be fooled. Just because I'm alive doesn't mean she loves me any more than she did the rest of the family. She tried to have me killed, too. If she knew I was here, she'd set her chaos on me in a heartbeat."

Chaos.

Abi knew her sister was the Chaos Wielder. What else did she know?

The girl glanced to the darkened windows of the buildings around us, her lips forming a pout.

"I have to go. I said too much."

"Wait!" I cried. I didn't attempt to hide the desperation from my voice. "We need your help."

"There's nothing I can help you with." Her words said one thing, but her eyes said otherwise. The guarded expression on her features said she knew much more than she was willing to let on.

She turned to dart away, but before she could, Alesh angled his staff across her chest, preventing her from dashing off, keeping our only viable chance to gain any useful information from escaping.

The girl flashed an annoyed glare at him but allowed herself to be stopped. She ran one hand over the staff, as though examining it. I waited for her to push it away and run.

"You are alone," Alesh said.

She scowled. "You're only alone if you don't care for your own company."

Alesh grinned, his mouth breaking into a wide smile. "Yes. This is true. But we"—he motioned between the two of us with his free hand, his smile fading— "are also alone. And we cannot do what needs to be done without knowing more about what your sister can do. People are dying." He paused before adding, "At your sister's hand."

Abi swallowed, turning her gaze to the staff in front of her. I held my breath as she examined the head of the staff with probing fingers, running them across the gnarled wood that encircled the ruby within.

Her eyes didn't leave the stone when she spoke. "We can't talk here. If you want to know more, you'll have to come with me."

I glanced to Alesh. He nodded.

"We will come with you," he said. "I think you have much to teach an old man like me."

I shook my head with a smile. Alesh wasn't old, but to a girl as young as Abi, he might as well be ancient. We followed Abi turn by turn through narrow alleys and cobbled streets, and I prayed she wasn't leading us with the intent of stranding us in the middle of an intricate urban maze. There was no chance of finding my way to the square again after all the turns we'd taken.

Given the girl's secretive nature and reluctance to help, I wasn't entirely sure she *wasn't* going to leave us, which may have been why my feet hurried and my eyes strained to keep her in view. If I had to, I'd guess she'd disappeared from plain sight more than once in her time around the capital.

So I was half-surprised when she led us down a set of stairs, through a short tunnel, down a second set of stairs, and through a niche in a wall that opened into a long-discarded storeroom of whatever business had once occupied the abandoned building.

The room was equipped with a wooden trunk, a chair and low table, on which sat a pile of books and an oil lamp, and what could best be described as a nest of blankets in one corner of the room.

"You live here," I said.

Abi nodded once. "Among other places. I don't stay in one place too long."

"How old are you, Abi?"

"Eleven," she said, sticking her chin out again as though daring us to accuse her of being too young to be on her own.

She *was* too young to be on her own, but I wasn't about to tell her that. Her sister had murdered the rest of their family and claimed the title of emperor for herself. Where else should Abi have gone? That a young girl who had lived in a palace all her life, being cared for day in and day out, could survive on her own at all told me all I need to know about her.

Abi had grit.

The kind of grit that might be what we needed.

"This is a fine home," Alesh said, knocking the dirt floor once with his staff and admiring the four walls around us. "You have done well, Abi Gehtanan. Where I come from, a person must provide for themselves to be judged worthy. You are worthier than most."

Abi beamed in response.

"What were you doing beneath the stage?" I asked.

She gave a sideways smirk that reminded me of the younger boys in Barnham after they'd hidden a toad in one of the girls' aprons. I suspected Alesh and I were onto something when we labeled her a troublemaker.

"I threw a river squid on the first step so Elodie might slip and fall on her rear. I was hoping she'd show everyone how horrible she is. She's not the best with self-control when she's mad."

I didn't mean to, but I laughed. The fact that the imp in front of us would think to play a prank on the Chaos Wielder—arguably the most powerful human alive—and get away with it was more than I could comprehend.

"But Lieutenant Cronan caught her when she slipped, and she didn't fall." Abi's lips formed a scowl.

"She looked plenty angry to me. I'd say you succeeded," I said.

Alesh nodded in agreement.

I took the girl's hands in my own and gave them a squeeze, hesitating a moment before speaking. It wasn't fair to ask an eleven-year-old to help us, and yet doing so would give us an incredible advantage if she were willing to make our cause her own.

"Abi, I know this may be difficult, but we need to know more about your sister and what happened to your family. Alesh and I are from far north of here. Your sister is wreaking havoc throughout our lands by destroying the living and raising the dead. We've traveled a long way to stop her. With your help, I think we have a chance."

Abi heaved a giant sigh. "It figures. She's trying to make the Elorin Empire the finest place on all of Liron. I mean, it *is*, but it figures that she would make everyone else's lives that much worse everywhere but here. It's like she can't prove we're the best unless everywhere else is worse than the worst." Abi sank into the lone chair, placed an elbow on the table, and rested her chin on a palm.

"What can you tell us about her diadem?" I asked.

"It was my mother's," she said. "My grandmother's before that. The diadem is passed to the child most worthy of keeping balance. It should have"—she swallowed, training her gaze on the far wall— "gone to Melánd. She was the most level-headed of all of us. She had Mama's cool temper. Daddy's eyes, though." She gave a sad smile that failed to reach beyond her mouth. "And his sense of humor."

The pain in Abi's expression was palpable. I wished I could heal her. A child so young shouldn't know so much pain. If only I could take the suffering away…

"Elodie knew the diadem wouldn't go to her, same as I knew it wasn't meant for me. Artur knew it wouldn't be his, and Deni and Hati knew it wouldn't be either of theirs, too. We all knew."

A large family. I hadn't suspected. She'd killed them all. So many. How could a person—a child—do such a thing?

Abi looked up. "Deni and Hati were twins. They were the oldest. Then Artur, Melánd, Elodie, and me. My father used to call us his own Imperial Circus."

A royal family of laughter and mischief, of love and delight. Imperial Circus, indeed. If I closed my eyes, if I enticed a vision to come, I could see them as Abi once saw them—dressed in their finest garments, noble and royal before their empire, and yet still managing mischievous smiles, tricks, and antics when they weren't in the public eye. My throat strained with grief.

"Abi, may I…give you a hug?"

For all that she looked like she needed a hug, the girl shook her head adamantly, fighting tears in her eyes again.

"Someday, maybe," she answered, her voice thick with emotion. "Not today."

I understood all too well. When my mother died, an unending stream of townsfolk wanted to take me in and console me, but a soul cannot be soothed before it's had time to grieve. I needed time to grieve then, and now, so did Abigayle Gehtanan.

I nodded. "When you're ready."

"This diadem," Alesh said. "What is its stone?"

The change in subject was a welcome one.

"The center stone? A yellow sapphire. Why?"

"That fits." Alesh gave a chuckle.

Abi wiped the unshed tears from her eyes, and I turned to Alesh to give her a private moment to do so. "What do you know about yellow sapphire?"

"It is said it is a help…that is, it aids in making real the will of the wearer," Alesh said as he tapped the side of his head.

"Manifesting its user's will," I mulled. "Yes, that would fit, wouldn't it?"

"Well, what happens when the user is a murderous lunatic?" Abi said, her voice once again strong and unyielding.

"We need to get the diadem out of her hands," I said.

Abi outright laughed. "Good luck with that. She's fairly got that piece woven into her scalp."

"She's got to take it off sometime."

"When she sleeps…" Alesh said. "You might be right."

"So you want me to get you into the palace," Abi said. "Is that why you chased me down?"

"Yes. And no. We hardly knew who you were when we followed you, but anyone willing to stand up to the Chaos Wielder—Elodie—is a friend in our book."

"How much help can I be? I'm *eleven.*"

"And what does age matter when the soul has a reservoir of untapped strength?" Alesh regarded Abi with an expression I'd seen him wear on more than one occasion when he and Niles were deep in conversation.

He had a gift for it. Despite all the judgments I made regarding Niles, Alesh had seen through to his true self, had coaxed good out of him even when the rest of the world had given up on him. He was doing the same for Abi now.

Abi hadn't racked up the years of self-loathing Niles had,

but she had survived where her family had not, and the kind of guilt survival brought with it was immeasurable.

"What good does any strength do against her magic?" She gestured to a palace somewhere beyond the walls of her safe haven.

Alesh smiled, his eyes crinkling with years of knowledge, understanding, and determination.

"Ah, but magic alone doesn't determine an outcome," he said. "You have fortitude, Abigayle Gehtanan. You have soul. And you have friends—in us. I have seen much in my life, but what I have seen in this last month is beyond anything I could have imagined. It was my new friends who brought me through, and I who brought them through."

Abi was rapt with attention now.

My eyes filled with tears. Alesh was right in so many ways, but friendship alone couldn't overtake magic as strong as this. It wasn't fair of him to paint that kind of picture, not to a young girl who couldn't know any better.

And not all of us had made it *through*, as he'd said. I was torn between encouraging Abi to aid us and spilling the truth about where some of our friends had truly ended up on this journey.

Brigantino—severely injured—and Ywelo, his love and caretaker, were still somewhere far behind us in the lovely seaside town of Aberly, where the sand glittered as the waves lapped the shore, and the trees reached for the sea with the very curve of their trunks. Was Brigantino yet recovered? Had Ywelo kept him from returning to the road to fulfill his duty and serve his king?

Then my thoughts drifted to Niles and Quinn—both dead, thanks to Kufataba. My heart gave an extra bump, threatening a fit of palpitations, but I ignored it, instead pressing one hand to the Chaos Wielder's brand on my chest.

Niles, who had unintentionally sacrificed his life so we might succeed in stopping the Chaos Wielder. Niles, who hadn't believed in his own self-worth, and yet, who had proven himself anyway.

And Quinn.

Quinn D'Arturio, who tortured himself time and again with the dark things he'd done in his service to the Order of the Southern Cross, but who never saw the light he brought into the world. Quinn, who'd fully, intentionally sacrificed his life so we might succeed in stopping the Chaos Wielder. Quinn, who I loved—and would always love—fiercely, and with every fiber of my being.

"Are you all right?" Abi's voice sent my thoughts tumbling, scattering to the wind.

"I…"

Was I all right?

"Yes," I answered belatedly. "I was thinking of the friends I've loved and lost on our journey to stop your sister from throwing the world into chaos. Remembering is… difficult sometimes."

"You had that look about you," Abi said softly. "The one I get whenever thoughts of my family creep in, like you wanted to hug a ghost."

I swallowed hard, fighting the lump in my throat.

"You're very perceptive, Abi. Has anyone ever told

you that?"

"Deni used to say that. He said I'd be a good ambassador someday because I like to watch people."

"Sounds like Deni was a smart young man."

She nodded, one blond lock coming loose from her braid.

She reached up with a hand, tucking it firmly behind one ear, her expression shifting to sheer determination.

"I'll help."

CHAPTER FOUR

Drifting Souls
A Man with No Name

Lost. He was lost in pain and self-loathing, drowning in it, smothered by it, so much so that he didn't hear the voice. Days. Weeks. An eternity. So much pain, the least of which was physical.

No, the real pain lay in the onslaught of memories, the lives he'd taken, whispers from the dead who would never have a chance to live their stolen lives. They lived now. In his head, forever reminding him how he'd failed.

Was this hell? If so, it was surely nothing less than what he deserved.

Then, a scene he remembered all too well. Innocent, wide eyes staring up at him, dead. They were all dead.

He'd been stationed somewhere. Briefly. On…a mission. He hadn't been there very long. It was…there were secrets he was supposed to keep. It was why he couldn't stop the slaughter.

The slaughter.

He remembered the screams, the crying, women begging for their children's lives to be spared. The slashing and gurgles, the sound of death. So much death. So much blood.

And he hadn't stopped any of it from happening.

Glassy, unseeing eyes stared at him from the wooden planks of the tavern's floor. He remembered it well now. The Resistance militia had collected the women and children of officers in the King's Army. They'd locked themselves inside the tavern with the hostages, then summoned the officers to meet them, but it wasn't the officers who arrived. It was a small battalion of King's Army soldiers instead.

His battalion.

When the battalion refused to surrender to the whims of the untrained Resistance soldiers, the hostages were eliminated, one by one. Slowly. Excruciatingly.

They hadn't known.

The militia inside the tavern's walls hadn't known the soldiers outside were not the officers requested. They hadn't known the men standing outside were not the family and loved ones of those trapped within. They didn't understand why the soldiers outside refused to comply with their order, or why they were all too willing to let their innocent loved ones die.

And what was there left for them to do but kill the hostages when the King's Army refused to back down?

He could have stopped it.

He could have thrown off the cloak of his secret identity and charged into the tavern alone, demanding to speak with the commanding officer. He could have halted it all.

But he hadn't.

He'd stayed in place, rooted to the spot his own battalion leader had assigned him. Blowing his cover would mean the information he'd gleaned would no longer be useful to the Order. The short assignment was almost complete. He was days from being sent southward again. He'd been chosen for this assignment because of his age, because he looked the part they wanted him to play—an angry, disgruntled soldier all too happy to sign up with the King's Army if it meant seeing death and glory.

The echoes of the children's cries would never leave his skull. The screams were seared in the hollows of his ears, and the images of innocent, tear-stained faces imprinted beneath his eyelids.

And now they spoke to him. Dozens of them glowing in the darkness, surrounding him, angry eyes assaulting him with their accusations. Children and women. Dead children and dead women.

"You let it happen."

"Ye're the reason we've died."

"Monster."

"Wicked savage."

"All you had to do was step forward."

Their words burned into his skin, as though each syllable were being branded into the very fabric of his flesh.

"We aren't the only ones, either, are we?"

"You've blood on your hands."

"D'Arturio."

"Murderer."

"Could have saved my child, but you didn't."

"LOOK AT MY BABY'S THROAT! LOOK WHAT YOU DID."

He closed his eyes and screamed, tried to drown out the voices, the painful accusations of his past inaction. He'd been obeying orders. His identity. He was to maintain his identity. Giving up his identity was unacceptable. The Order had said so, they'd told him…

"D'Arturio!"

He yelled louder, holding hands over his ears, crumpling downward, his knees buckling until he lay upon the floor—if the darkness had a floor—and curled into himself like a child.

"All you had to do was say something."

"All you had to do was intervene."

"You could have saved us all."

"You wanted us to die."

"D'ARTURIO!"

CHAPTER FIVE

Through the Fog
Quinn

The single word shattered me. The silence that followed was absolute. It was a name. D'Arturio. A name I knew once. I…I *was* D'Arturio. Something…something D'Arturio.

"Bloody hell, D'Arturio, you're even more cracked than I was."

The voice was familiar, almost. And yet, my stomach turned at the sound.

"Who are you?" I croaked, opening my eyes a stitch, waiting for the *other* voices to return.

My own voice was almost unrecognizable, even to myself. The screaming had marked my throat, leaving it raw and damaged.

"A friend," the voice in the darkness answered. "The closest thing to a friend you've got at the moment anyway, all the more unfortunate for you, truly."

I pulled myself to a sitting position, letting my hands fall to my lap. The burning sensation across my skin had calmed. The voice had stopped it somehow.

"Where did they go?" I asked. "How did you stop them?"

There was no sign of the dead children or women who'd

hovered over me moments ago.

"*I* didn't stop them. You did. Took a long enough time to get out of your own mind, though. I knew you were hard-headed, but, honestly, I had no idea how thick that skull of yours really is. I must have called your name a half-dozen times before you began to hear."

The darkness began to ease, letting in just enough light so my eyes could focus upon the lone figure standing beside me. The figure wasn't illuminated, which was already a relief to my sensitive eyes, still haunted by the vision of glowing, dead children.

"Do I…know you?" I squinted at the man beside me, then pushed myself off the ground and stood.

"Getting up, that's a start. Walk with me, D'Arturio."

I obeyed even though I wasn't sure where the two of us could walk in the surrounding gray.

I was silent for long moments, waiting for the man to speak again, waiting to know who he was and why he was here. There was something familiar about him, but I couldn't say what exactly. I wasn't sure if I wanted to throw a fist at him or hug him, though I surprisingly felt the urge to do both.

The man had blond hair, neatly combed back, and a swagger that irked, but he'd been kind enough to scare away the dead and keep me from being attacked, so I could forgive an arrogant swagger, couldn't I?

"Do I know you?" I repeated.

"You did. When I was alive anyway."

I inhaled sharply.

"Ingram." The name fell from my lips even though I didn't understand the urge to say it.

"Impressive. The mountain hasn't fried your mind yet. That's something, I suppose."

"I'm dead," I said. It wasn't a question.

Ingram outright laughed, stirring irritation in my chest. I did not like being laughed at by this man.

"No," Ingram said. "You're not."

None of this made sense. Ingram was dead. I knew it. I… remembered it.

He'd been crushed by an enormous stone. Crushed after holding the mountain passage open for all of us. Crushed when my body had failed me, and I hadn't been able to hold it any longer.

I swallowed.

"But you're dead."

"Observant." He gave a dry smile.

"So I must be dead, too."

"Not quite. Think of this as an in-between state."

"But you're—"

"Dead, yes, and thank you for bringing that up yet again. I do so love being reminded of it."

"So—"

"All right, look, D'Arturio. If you want any sort of explanation from me, you *will* have to shut your mouth and listen for a bit instead of asking questions. How about we save the interrogation for the end of our time together, hmm?"

I fumed but said nothing. I remembered full well why

Ingram irked me, and I definitely, definitely wanted to throw a fist at him now.

The gray fog lightened, revealing looming shadows in the distance. I couldn't make out what they might be or where we were headed, but I kept my mouth shut, determined not to give Ingram another reason to goad me.

"You're not dead," Ingram began. "This place is a sort of…holding cell, for lack of a better word. You arrived here voluntarily, and until you complete what's required of you here, you will not be released."

"A holding cell." I narrowed my eyes at him as we walked. The ground beneath my feet had grown firmer. I was almost certain of it.

"Which is why I'm here."

I waited. Dammit, I hated waiting for Ingram to speak. He paused on purpose, of course. His only goal in life—and death, apparently—was to remain a perpetual thorn in my side.

"I was given a choice," he said. "An unexpected one. Apparently, the Higher Ones believe in second chances when one's final act of living is to save the lives of others."

"And what was the choice offered to you?"

He sniffed. "I could remain where I was, or I could retrieve you from your self-made torment."

I turned his words over in my mind. Niles Ingram wasn't the charitable type.

Niles, that's his name.

"And what's the *true* motivation?" I asked.

He scoffed.

I worked my sore jaw into a scowl. Everything ached, but the memories of the burning and the dead and the accusations were already fading from my mind, like a nightmare I might have had long ago and only just remembered.

"Fine. I admit there was more to it than good will. I was told I could stay and pay for the wrongs I had committed in my life, or I could retrieve you, and I would ultimately be granted a clean slate. It wasn't much of a choice. What else was I to do? Besides, at least this way, I get to rub in that I saved your hide."

My instant reaction was to deny that he had saved me at all, but the reality was something I didn't care to admit. I shivered, the accusing voices still echoing in my ears.

"So you get redemption."

"Only if I succeed." Ingram eyed me as though he wasn't entirely sure I was worth the trouble. "And let's face it," he added, gaze flicking disapprovingly. "I'm not sure you're going to allow that to happen."

"But you got rid of the voices," I said. "Isn't that enough?"

He laughed again. I hated that laugh.

"Saints, no, D'Arturio. I have to do far more than get rid of the voices. I have to get you to forgive yourself."

"What?"

"Mm. That's what I thought. You don't even comprehend the concept."

"What are you talking about?"

"We get to review each and every one of the atrocities you believe is your fault, and I get to convince you why they aren't."

I stopped dead in my tracks.

"Oh, hell. No."

Ingram was the *last* person, dead or alive, I would talk to about the acts I'd committed in my life.

I shook my head in sudden remembrance and turned to face him, blinking.

"Wait a damn minute. *You're* the reason those women and children are dead! The voices, those innocent victims, you gave the command to have them murdered."

Ingram paled and swallowed once as though he'd rather not be reminded of the orders he gave long ago. He cleared his throat.

"See? I told you I was here to help convince you of your innocence."

I snorted. "I'm not innocent."

"That may be, but it doesn't mean you get to drown yourself in your own guilt forever, not with so much riding on…well, that's more than I can say."

"Riding on this? What's riding on this?" I demanded.

"I can't tell you."

His eyes widened in shock as I grabbed him by his collar and pulled him close.

"Don't play games with me, Ingram," I growled.

If my teeth clenched together any harder, they would crack. He spread his arms outward.

"I can't say! If I even thought about it, my shot at redemption is gone. Do you think I'm about to risk that? Do your worst, D'Arturio. I'm *already* dead."

I let go of his shirt and pushed him away, shaking

the clouded fog from my brain. There were dozens of unreachable memories floating in a haze near the edges of my mind. So many of them I could *almost* grasp, but when I reached to recall them, they slipped away as though coated in oil. Fiermi. There was something I wasn't remembering, something big.

Not the deaths. Not the pain. That came all too easily…

"Stop fighting so hard," he said to me.

"What are you talking about?"

He smoothed his tunic and gave a sigh, as though he was about to explain something to a child. That alone would normally have angered me, but I was too distracted by my own evasive thoughts to be properly frustrated with him.

"Look around you, Quinn."

He rarely used my first name. The sound of it startled me.

"I'm serious. Look around."

I did, shocked to find the gray fog around us had lifted to reveal a clear green meadow dotted with hundreds of thousands of tiny, white wildflowers. I suppressed the unexpected urge to pick a handful and weave them into a crown.

What a strange thought.

A dusky purple mountain range far in the distance sat on the horizon, a deep crimson sunset setting the peaks afire. I hadn't seen anything so beautiful in…I didn't know how long.

"How long have I been trapped here?"

"I'm not the best estimate of time, being dead and all. I do know time is of the essence, so the sooner we can move through this process, the better. Have a seat."

"In the grass?"

"No, on that." Ingram pointed to a large oak bench, wildly out of place.

"Where did that come from?"

The bench wasn't there a moment ago. I would have seen it.

"You should know," he replied. When I didn't respond, he gave an exasperated sigh and held his hands out wide. "All of this is yours, D'Arturio."

"You mean Irzan?"

Irzan. What was Irzan?

I *owned* Irzan or—I frowned—something along those lines. The name was familiar anyway.

"No, you clod. This place. It's your creation." He tapped the side of his temple.

I moved to the bench and put a hand on the carved surface. It felt real enough, the grain of the wood smooth beneath my palm. I sighed as I slid onto the bench. Everything here was confusing. I didn't like confusion.

The air smelled right, though. And if I was dreaming, if all of this was in my head, could the air have an odor? Could it smell of grass and dirt, worms and wildflowers, delicious, crisp, early evening air? How could that be in my head?

"Don't overthink it."

"Could you stop doing that?"

"Doing what?"

I gestured to him.

"All of that. Everything. Being my conscience."

He sat beside me and let his gaze fall over the swaying grass but said nothing. Instead, I let the silence extend.

"Look," I finally said. "I don't know what you want from me."

"Me? I want nothing. I'm here to help you. As I've already explained."

"If you can't tell me anything, you're not much help, and so far, every time I've asked you a question, you've found a way to avoid answering it."

He grinned and, for a second, I could almost see something genuine in him.

"Come now. Would you expect anything less from me?"

So much for genuine.

"How did I end up here? Can you answer that?"

"I can."

"Ingram." A warning tone. I was losing my patience with him, even if he *had* made the voices disappear.

"Well, you didn't say please."

"Don't make me take down a dead man."

He huffed. "Fine. You're here of your own volition. You volunteered as payment. For what, I can't say, but you're here because you offered yourself."

It sounded like something I would do, and I thought I might have even remembered falling into a deep blue pool at one point—the entranceway to this bizarre world.

"And how do I leave?"

"I told you before. You need to come to terms with the… things you've done."

I scoffed again. The things I'd done. The things I'd done

could never be forgotten, could never be forgiven. They were the only memories in my head that weren't plagued by fog and dust in the corners of my mind.

"You need to forgive yourself."

"I've done unforgivable things, Ingram. Things even you can't imagine."

"Well," he said as he extended an arm over the back of the bench and leaned. "Then it's a good thing I'm not going anywhere. You can tell me all about it."

CHAPTER SIX

The Problem with Being Poor
Reina

With the Chaos Wielder's followers on alert for anything out of the norm in Ivirreh, Abi insisted we stay somewhere less likely to be noticed. As such, we were in the immigrants' quarter—a section of the city with a diverse array of customs, dress, food, and language.

Essentially, we were residing where we wouldn't stand out as the obvious strangers we were. The three of us shared a room at a small inn Abi said was one of the best places to stay anonymous. On the second night, we switched inns to keep from remaining in one place for too long. I suspected moving every night or two would become habit. How many inns resided in the immigrants' quarter? How many times would we move in the coming days and weeks?

"You won't be able to take the diadem from her," Abi said as we shared our lunch in the room. "Not even when she's sleeping. She'll have it guarded."

"I can handle guardsmen," Alesh said, a sly grin spreading across his face.

Memories of Alesh blinding Quinn in the sand ring and stealing the breath from his lungs ran through my mind. Yes,

Alesh could certainly "handle" a guardsman or two.

Abi shook her head. "It's not guarded by a person. That would be too easy."

"What guards it, then?"

Abi grabbed a long batter-dipped, fried bean from one of the many plates laid out upon the desk, and took a bite, giving a satisfied sigh as the spices touched her tongue. Given how much the girl had eaten in the days since she'd been with us, I guessed food hadn't been easy to come by during her time on her own.

"She guards the diadem with magic."

"Of course she does." I rubbed my eyes.

How silly to have assumed otherwise. Magic might be something I had learned and Alesh had grown up with, but to the Chaos Wielder, magic wasn't just a part of life; it *was* life. It was the reason she had gained control…and the reason she feared losing it. Naturally, she would use every ounce of that same magic to keep it safely in her hands.

Alesh massaged his jaw, deep in thought, his eyes shifting toward the dark ceiling of our room.

"What if we make another diadem," he said. "We find a jeweler who can craft a…a…"

"A replica," I said, my mind churning with the idea and the possibilities.

"Yes."

"But no goldsmith is going to be able to give our fake diadem the powers of the original." I frowned. "So if we tried to pull off this trick at all, it would have to be fast. She'll know there's no magic in the replacement the minute she touches it, maybe even before then."

"Unless…" The word came out sounding more like "unwess" since Abi's mouth was full of grilled potato wedges. As if suddenly remembering her manners, she held up a finger, took her time chewing, then swallowed. She licked butter from the tip of one finger. "Unless we get someone to charm it. It still won't give Elodie the kind of power the real diadem contains, but she'll feel the magic, and won't suspect it's been swapped. At least, not right away. Until she attempts to use it."

"Charm it?" I couldn't shake the odd words from my head.

Was it possible to turn a non-magical object magical? How could an object be charmed? My head began to throb. Less than a year ago, I hadn't believed in magic at all, and now I possessed a magic-filled talisman, had traveled through an enchanted mountain, and ventured to a land where apparently anything could be charmed at will. It was almost enough to make me laugh. Almost.

"Sure," Abi said. "It won't be serious magic, but it might fool her long enough."

"Right," I said. "I understood that part. I meant the charming bit. You can *charm* an object?"

I took some comfort in the expression on Alesh's face and the surprise in his eyes. This strange phenomenon wasn't familiar to him, either.

"Oh, sure!" she replied. "Well, *I* can't charm anything, but there are a few spellbinders in the gold quarter who can charm anything you bring them. When I turned eight, Artur hired one to charm an orange paper butterfly he made me. It turned from plain orange paper into a real-looking butterfly of orange and black. It even had white spots at the edges of its wings. Once it was charmed, it fluttered all around the shop and everything."

"That is very nice for a brother to do," Alesh said.

Abi's mouth twisted to one side. "It was, but then I let it go outside even though he told me not to, and it flew away. I guess I wanted to see if it would fly like the real butterflies I sometimes see in the summer. Artur was pretty mad. He said he'd saved for a month to pay for that charm, but he never worked a day in his life, so he was definitely lying." She shrugged.

"Maybe it's still out there somewhere," I said. "Flying over an ocean or a faraway land."

Abi raised her brows at me, giving me a look of disbelief, as though I might have forgotten she was eleven and not six.

"It was made of *paper*," she said. "It'd fall apart at the first rain."

My cheeks grew warm. Of course paper would never last. I gave a small smile. "I guess the idea makes me hopeful. If paper can be charmed to fly, who's to say it can't also hold up to a bit of water?"

Abi pressed her lips together but didn't argue.

Alesh cleared his throat. "So, we find one of these spellbinders, then?"

"And hire them with what money? Charms can't be cheap." I put my hands out to the dismal room around me. "Renting this room uses up almost all our reserve. Now we need to hire a goldsmith *and* a spellbinder?"

Alesh's brows drew together as he thought, forming a deep groove in the dark skin between his eyes. Abi's gaze darted back and forth between us.

"I could raid the treasury," Abi offered. "I was always good at sneaking in and out of the palace unseen."

"No," Alesh and I said in unison.

The very thought of Abi in her sister's grasp sent my pulse leaping. We couldn't put her in danger. Not in any *more* danger anyway.

"The market." Alesh tapped a finger on his staff, then pointed to me. "We will grow the foods they have not seen here, then sell them."

"We can't just show up at the market. We have no stall, no provisions, and no space to set up in. Everyone there will be *looking* for unfamiliar faces."

"I could go," Abi countered.

"No," I said firmly.

If Abi were recognized, and word got out that the Chaos Wielder *wasn't* the only surviving member of her family, the murderous harpy would be all too happy to arrange an accident for her younger sibling, I was sure.

Abi crossed her arms and glared at me but said nothing.

"None of us are going to the market," I said.

"Then hire someone from the immigrants' quarter for a portion of the earnings," Abi said. "No one here would think twice about taking the opportunity. None of them are wanted criminals, *and* you'll get your wares—whatever they are— to the market for sale."

I nodded. "That's a possibility…and no one said we were criminals."

She grinned. "You will be once you steal a diadem."

I grimaced and shook my head.

"All right. We're going to need a cart, an open space with plenty of soil, and the cover of darkness if we're to do this at all."

"Lucky for you, I know where there's lots of land and where we can *borrow* a cart for the evening. As for night, that should be here soon anyway." She picked up another potato wedge, dipped it in a thick cheese sauce dotted with herbs, and shoved the dripping mess into her mouth.

Alesh rose from the stiff, wooden chair, and pushed it across the floor with a scrape. "I will find someone to sell for us at the market tomorrow."

I nodded. "Be back by nightfall. You're our grower now."

He smiled, pulled a cloak over his shoulders, and headed out the door.

"What did he mean by tomorrow?" Abi asked. "It will take weeks to grow anything, even if you have the best seeds. You'll never be able to go to market tomorrow!"

Now it was my turn to give Abi a sly smile.

"You'll have an answer to your question in a few hours," I told her. "Think you can be patient until then?"

"I might be persuaded into patience if we were to… say…order a citrus tart?"

I laughed but stuck out a hand. "You drive a hard bargain, but I think we can arrange that…as long as I get a few bites."

She grinned and eagerly shook my hand.

Abi fell asleep in the bed we shared after I promised her no fewer than three times that Alesh and I wouldn't leave without her. She had me swear by locking our fingers together, as though that somehow made my promise more official.

I kept my word, though, and now she stood beside me in the midst of a field that moments before had hosted weeds and wildflowers.

Empty no longer, the field around us was full of vegetables, nuts, tubers, and vines upon vines heavy with berries we'd need to harvest before the sun came up. I was grateful for the light of both moons tonight.

"How…how"—Abi shook her head and turned in a slow circle, taking in Alesh's newly grown bounty— "I mean, *how* is this possible?"

Even knowing about the diadem's power, she hadn't anticipated there existed a magic to rival it.

"Like the diadem, the talisman and the staff contain wells of magic that call forth both life and death."

Abi's face lit when she made the connection. "Life, death, and chaos!"

"Yes."

She drew puzzled brows down for a moment and looked between Alesh and me. "But, if he rules life, that must mean you rule death."

I nodded.

"I don't…wish to sound mean, but you don't look very deadly."

I stifled a laugh while Alesh answered. "Looks can be deceiving."

"You'll see what I can do after we harvest all this. So, come, let's get to work."

The night crept on into the small hours of the morning, my back and fingertips growing sore with the work. As the sun's rays extended over the horizon, we picked the last of the ripe, purple berries and the remaining bright yellow squash I'd never seen before, but Alesh insisted would fetch a good price. It would take all three of us to pull the fully loaded cart. True to her word, Abi had stayed up all night, picking and hauling, reaching the lower branches of each plant and clearing them all of their fruits.

The dark smudges beneath her eyes were partly due to fatigue, and partly from rubbing tired eyes with dirt-covered fingers throughout the night. She'd been raised in a palace, but she hadn't once complained about a night of physical labor.

"Now we prepare the field for tomorrow night," I said.

I closed my eyes, took a breath, and fell into the deadly power of the talisman, seeing without seeing, destroying every green thing Alesh had grown hours earlier, sending death across the veins of leaves, wilting them until they folded in on themselves, blackened, then turned to ash that would nourish the soil again. When at last I opened my eyes, the field was bare dirt, not a single green sprout or shoot left to be seen.

I turned my gaze to Abi. Her eyes were wide. Slowly she turned her attention from the empty field to me.

"Can you…do that to people?" she asked.

"I'm a healer. While I *could* use the power to stop human life, I've taken an oath never to harm." I pushed the memory of what I'd once done to Bruenner to the back of my mind, trying hard not to remember.

The girl pushed out her lips, looking more confused.

"Death is not the power she is meant to have," Alesh elaborated. "That power was mine. When your sister tampered with magic, our powers were changed. Mine for hers, hers for mine."

Abi's brows relaxed in understanding as she nodded. "Ohhhh, that makes *much* more sense, actually."

"It's been a bit of a challenge, unlearning what was instinct, but we've been training as we traveled," I said.

"Don't you think you should grow a little something so the field looks as it did before, like weeds and such?" Abi asked.

Alesh didn't break eye contact with Abi but waved a hand in the general direction of the field, and, in seconds, straggly grass and wildflowers filled the space once more.

"Braggart," I muttered.

Our plan couldn't have worked better. Alesh hired a muscled Yonheli man named Ito to take the cart into town and sell the produce to the food vendors in the area. The man had come to Ivirreh to sell his own wares and didn't mind the additional task for the pay promised. Given his size, he had little trouble with the heavy cart.

The vendors' reception to the novel produce was overwhelming. Everyone was eager to try something no one else had offered before. Food stalls used the produce to experiment with new dishes they could sell, and customers flocked to be the first to try them.

At the end of the day, we had enough coin in hand for a down payment on a diadem. We needed only to find the right goldsmith to craft it. Ito confirmed that no one had been particularly interested in how he'd obtained the goods, and he agreed to pull the cart for us three more times over the next week.

Now, in bed and attempting to get some sleep before another night of work, my back and arms ached just thinking of the harvesting that would need to be done. My mind kept counting the days. Twenty-two. It seemed near-impossible that we could commission a goldsmith to make the diadem, hire a spellbinder to charm it, craft a reliable plan to steal the real diadem, destroy it, and grow enough rare produce to pay for it all in twenty-two days.

And yet, if there was one person in the whole world who could have done it, who wouldn't have doubted even for a moment it *could* be done, it would have been Quinn D'Arturio. Saints, I missed him.

I missed him so much, it hurt to breathe if I thought about him too long or too deep. I missed his stubborn protectiveness and his subtle charm. I missed his arms around me, the look in his eyes when he spoke of our future, the way he watched me when he thought I wasn't looking. I missed his scent, the fresh air and pine that was home. *He* was home.

And now I was a ship at sea, rudderless, lost, tossing on the waves, no longer sure which way was home.

I wiped a single tear from one eye and rolled onto my side, trying to settle in the bed in the room that somehow seemed more claustrophobic without Quinn's arms around me than it would have with. Abi snored softly beside me, and Alesh slept soundly on the floor despite the clank of glassware and the raucous voices carrying from the inn's dining room below.

Golden light from the late afternoon sun filled the shuttered window. I closed my eyes against it, tried to pretend I was in Irzan, in the castle, in Quinn's bed, by Quinn's side. When that didn't work, I pretended I was tucked in my bed in my cottage back in Barnham, on the farm I'd last seen a lifetime ago, but that didn't help to lure sleep either.

Every bone in my body ached with fatigue. My eyes burned from exhaustion, and still I fought to find sleep. I pushed aside my thoughts of Quinn, the feelings I hadn't yet dealt with, the feelings I needed to deal with, the ones I *would* deal with…when this was all over.

For now, Quinn needed to stay locked tight in my heart and far from my mind. Like a drug, thoughts of him would serve to dull my senses—a luxury I couldn't afford, now more than ever.

CHAPTER SEVEN

The Pain Behind the Past
Quinn

Niles Ingram was a pain in my arse.

He was a ghost whose sole purpose was to ensure I remained as miserable as possible. A perpetual shadow to remind me that, even in death, he wouldn't leave me alone.

"Stop following me, Ingram."

"I quite literally have nothing else to do, Quinn." His tone was far too light, making a mockery of my anguish in his company.

I'd walked the meadow and the land beyond until I reached the purple mountains I'd seen from a distance. Up close and in daylight, the mountains weren't purple at all. They were gray, craggy, rocky, and probably difficult as hell to climb.

Which is why I was going to scale them.

Let Niles follow me then. If he insisted on parroting my every move, he could enjoy a nice trek across the mountains to whatever lay beyond.

In this new world, I felt no thirst or hunger, which I attributed to being dead even though Niles insisted I wasn't. There was still a nagging fatigue, but who wouldn't be fatigued in Ingram's constant company?

Still, every moment that passed pushed the darkness and the pain farther into the recesses of my mind. My body had begun to feel mine again, the searing pain from earlier hardly more than a memory now.

"If you think climbing a mountain is going to get rid of me, you're sorely mistaken." Niles watched me as I assessed the looming rocks and boulders, hands on my hips.

I cleared my throat, dried my hands on my pants, and climbed the first low overhang.

"I can certainly try," I replied.

I didn't wait for him as I continued to climb upward, moving methodically, letting the muscles in my arms and legs direct me along the path that required the least amount of effort. Climbing felt good. Climbing for the joy of climbing and not because I was required to was a novelty.

Ingram followed silently behind me.

When I reached the first decent ledge where I had a moment to rest, I sat and dangled my legs over the edge. The world below—whatever world this was—was silent save for the breeze in my ears. Sunlight played across the long grasses in the distance, dappling the white flowers in shadow and light. From here, the meadow almost looked like an ocean with gently rippling waves.

I'd seen an ocean recently. I'd been on a ship. There was…a storm. No gentle waves. It was…it was—

Puffing and out of breath, Niles pulled himself over the ridge and practically threw himself to the flattest portion of the rock floor. I thought I heard him curse as he lay, catching his breath.

"I plan to keep climbing," I said.

My statement wouldn't deter him, but at least I could make him as miserable as he made me. Were heights still a problem for him now that he was no longer alive?

He didn't immediately reply to the taunt. Finally, he pulled himself to a sitting position and turned to me.

"I expected no less," he replied.

I bristled. I'd been hoping for a better response, some sign of his discomfort. Letting loose a long sigh, I leaned back on my hands, closed my eyes, and listened to the sound of the wind in my ears again.

"You're going to have to talk at some point, you know."

His words buzzed in my skull, breaking the peaceful quiet of wind and the sun. I'd be happy if I never heard that voice again. And yet, even dead, he was *still* talking.

After a few moments, I stood, gave a stretch, then looked upward to the path I intended to follow, tracing with my eyes the hand and footholds I would utilize, planning ahead. The face of the mountain wasn't sheer, and the ascent was part hike and part rock-climb. It was enjoyable exercise, exertion my body sorely needed after its time in the torturous dark.

More importantly, it got me away from Niles and his insistence that I had to remember all the horrible things I'd ever done in order to leave here.

This place wasn't so bad.

Once I got rid of the voices and the accusations and the burning and the pain, I began to feel that this might be a place I could stay for quite some time.

I outpaced Niles, scaling rocks and boulders with ease, breaking at each ridge to regain my breath. Niles caught up as I sat on the next ledge, again reminding me of his presence.

"You know you're going to run out of mountain eventually, right?" he asked.

I ignored him and began climbing again.

Not long after I reached the next ledge, he caught up. I stood from my resting spot and searched for a suitable path to the next ledge before climbing forward, once more leaving him without a word.

"All right, good, we'll talk when we reach the top then," he said, bent over and short of breath.

My boots found sturdy footing with each step, and my hands never tired of pulling forward. An energy welled in my veins, so much energy. I almost felt as though if I cupped my hands together and focused, I might create whatever I wanted between my palms.

Godlike.

I didn't care for the comparison, but it was the only word I could think that described the way my body felt. If I took a leap off the mountain to the land below, would I die? *Could* I die here?

Thoughts swirled through my head as I gained altitude. I didn't wait for Niles to catch up before tackling the next section of mountain, or the section after that. All the while, he climbed behind me, an occasional curse from below evidence that I wasn't alone.

When I reached the summit, I was almost surprised Niles was still climbing. I hadn't expected perseverance. He reached the top ridge and sat down amidst the gravel and dirt, practically falling onto the ground.

"You'd think the fact that I'm dead would make this climb easier."

"I would have thought being dead would mean you'd no longer speak, but clearly, that's not the case either."

He didn't reply.

A breeze cooled the sweat that gathered on my temples and along the back of my neck. I took a seat against the base of a lone tree I wasn't sure had existed here a half-hour ago. I hadn't seen it from down below. Was it like the oak bench—a product of my mind, created for my comfort? I tilted my head back, resting it against the trunk, closed my eyes, and sighed.

If I stayed here, on the mountaintop, would I be at peace?

The silence extended into minutes, hours. It may have been the longest stretch of time Ingram had ever kept his mouth shut.

Out of curiosity, I opened one eye to glance his way, then sat up abruptly, both eyes open wide. I was alone on the mountaintop. Ingram had gone.

I got to my feet and searched the area, peering behind boulders and down the leeward side of the mountain. Nothing. Not a sign of him anywhere. There weren't many places to hide, not that Ingram would play games anyway. No one down below, either.

Where could a dead man have gone?

Finally, I sat against the tree once more and closed my eyes. Wherever he was, he was sure to return, so I should enjoy the silence while I was blessed with it. The base of the tree was perfect, the most comfortable resting spot I'd ever known, and I sank into it, letting the wind in my ears lull me into an otherworldly sense of calm.

Before long, a sound roused me from sleep, a sound I wasn't sure I'd actually heard. It very well could have been part of a dream, which would have made more sense since I was still alone on the mountain, but still, it had awakened me, and now that I was awake, all senses were on alert.

I pushed myself up, sitting, scanning the area. How had I fallen asleep? Even here, I shouldn't have felt secure enough to sleep. Agents didn't fall asleep on duty.

Agents.

I was an agent. At least, I had been an agent.

An agent of...of...something.

I cursed. The memories were spotty, my mind like aged cheese filled with mold and holes.

The sound resumed, a clicking that pulled my attention to the rocks below somewhere on my left. That must have been the sound that woke me. I stood, sudden memories of the undead in my head.

Undead. I'd seen them once.

Before I came here...wherever here was. The vivid image of what they looked like returned to my mind's eye all too well. The empty eyes, the half-hinged jaws, the blackened, decaying skin, and shreds of clothing hanging from decimated frames. I suppressed a shiver and moved with purpose.

Moving toward the ledge, I crept forward, crouching, all

the while holding my breath, praying I wouldn't see sightless eyes and flesh and bones over the mountain's edge.

What I saw was almost worse.

There was nothing but air and empty space.

Then the clicking resumed behind me. I whirled on my feet to face…nothing.

Click. Click.

Was it in my head? Had I lost my mind?

It sounded like…the tapping of a cane. Someone walking.

Like the old man I killed.

The blood drained from my face, a light-headedness taking its place. I crouched, letting the moment pass, breathing in through my nose and out through my mouth, trying to maintain a shred of sanity.

I'd killed the old man long ago, a freelance-scout-turned-double-agent for the right price whenever it suited him. He…he'd found out my identity and planned to sell the information to the King's Army. He would have sold my life away, my secrets, the Order's secrets. The Order.

I was an Agent of the Order of the Southern Cross. And I'd killed the old man to keep the secrets from being told. Saints, have mercy.

I drew a ragged breath as the clicking grew closer. The mountain around me turned gray, foggy with a darkness I feared. I knew what happened in the darkness here.

How had I thought I might be at peace? How had I imagined I was free?

I would pay for everything I'd done, every life I'd taken, Order or not.

The old man. He was someone's grandfather. Someone loved him once. Someone missed him. And I had drained the blood from his body with a single slice across the neck. He never even knew it was I who had killed him. Like a coward, I'd done it from behind.

It was the first—and last—time I'd killed from behind.

Click, click.

I pulled into myself, curling into a tight ball on the ground I could no longer see.

"I told you you'd pay," a voice said. "I know all your secrets now."

Over two years had passed, yet the old man's voice was exactly as I remembered—smoky with age, a hint of the southern accent.

My skin began to burn.

Oh, God, help me.

CHAPTER EIGHT

Questionable Business
Reina

I opened my eyes to blinding sunlight, implicitly aware something was amiss. Surrounded by a green meadow in all directions with a mountain chain somewhere in the distance, I couldn't help but feel as though I'd woken in a place I didn't belong. The vibrant grass was dotted with wildflowers the likes of which I'd never seen before, white-petaled flowers that held smaller white flowers in their center.

I spun in a circle, attempting to orient myself, to gain some awareness of where I was and what I might be doing here, but my mind encountered a blank wall. When I turned back again, a pathetic whimper escaped my throat. Quinn stood before me, strong, tall, and healthy.

"Reina." The sound of his voice sent violent shocks through my body.

He grasped my hands in his. Saints, his skin. The calluses on his palms, the warmth of his muscle, the blood running through his veins!

"But you're...dead," I whispered.

"I fear your imagination has gotten the best of you."

I searched his dark eyes for some hint of the cruel trick

that was surely being played on me. Then I took a step back and pulled my hands from his, already missing his warmth, already desperate to run to his arms, to fall into his embrace. My empty fingers tingled.

"'Tis a dream." My voice stretched thin.

"If so, surely we should never wake."

Long ago, once before, in the waking world, he'd said something similar to me. I shook my head, my unbound hair tumbling forward over my shoulders.

"I have no time for dreams," I replied.

His eyes lost some of their shine as he gave a single nod. His mouth pressed into a line, angled jaw covered with a dark stubble my fingertips itched to touch. I clenched my hand at my side.

"Perhaps not."

This, whatever *this* was, felt as real as anything I'd ever known. I wanted to grab his hand again, to press it to my cheek and feel its warmth.

And yet, I knew I couldn't be here in this meadowy paradise, that Quinn couldn't be standing in front of me, that his death was absolute, and this twisted version of a vision wasn't real.

"I miss you," The words came involuntarily, my eyes welling with tears.

"But I'm right here."

Gasping, I sat up. In the too-warm room in the too-soft bed, my pulse thrummed, the dingy walls of the inn slowly coming into focus as the dream in my mind's eye faded. My hair was plastered to my forehead and the back of my neck, held in place by the perspiration that drenched my skin.

I piled the damp mass on top of my head, letting stale air cool my neck as I steadied my heartbeat. 'Twas no more than a dream. I let out a long, slow breath.

Not a vision. Not an omen. Not a sign that Quinn was alive.

A dream.

With Quinn still in my mind, I pulled the little pink shell from the nightstand, kissed it once, and cradled it in my palm. I leaned back onto the mattress slowly so as not to wake Abi and waited for the light to fade and my companions to wake for the night of work ahead of us.

Three days later, Alesh and I followed the road we'd been told to find, a clean cobblestone path swept free of all traces of dirt. Jeweler's Row demanded the eye be drawn to the sparkling displays behind the glass storefronts. Dirt would never do.

Finding the right goldsmith for the task wouldn't be easy…as though anything about our current scenario were easy. We'd need a goldsmith who was talented enough to craft an exact replica of the diadem, but also one who wouldn't raise questions about why such an item was required.

A fine balance between talent and integrity.

Abi was good at pointing out the goldsmiths we wanted to steer clear of and had suggestions as to one or two who might be of some help, but it wasn't like we could ask outright for a replica of the diadem.

Unless we asked outright for a replica of the diadem.

Maybe being bold was better for throwing off suspicion entirely. The idea wasn't without merit. Who would suspect us of attempting to steal the real diadem? Who would be daft enough to take a magical object from a magic-wielding emperor of an entire land? Such an endeavor would be madness.

"What about that one?" Alesh pointed to the wooden shingle over the door of a goldsmith shop.

I looked down, scanning the list Abi had made for us.

"That one is on our 'definitely not' list. Abi says that jeweler—he works in *all* materials, not just gold—is one of Elodie's most devout followers. Thinks she's the chosen one since she somehow survived the family massacre."

In response, Alesh gave a disapproving *mmm*, his lips pressed firmly together, just shy of scowling. Jeweler's Row offered dozens of options, but neither of the two goldsmiths on Abi's list would be found here.

"Follow the road to the end of Jeweler's Row. You'll see an alley that looks like it's an invitation to thieves and brigands. That's the place. Turn left down the alley, and you'll find the goldsmith we need."

That's what Abi had said, so although Alesh looked as though he wanted nothing more than to set foot in one of the fancy shops with their shiny, gilt shingles, we hadn't yet reached our destination.

I tugged at the neckline of my long, peach-colored gown.

It chaffed around the neck, despite the clothier claiming it fit me perfectly. I wasn't used to having a collar so tight, and the fabric was scratchier than anything I'd known—some sort of false silk. Abi had provided the dress, too. Not directly, of course. But she'd given us instructions on where to find clothing to better blend with anyone shopping in a place like Jeweler's Row.

I suppose I looked a regular southern noblewoman now. Sheer, almost white sleeves were sliced on the outsides so that when I bent my arms, the material fell from my elbow entirely. As strange as I found the style, there was something to be said for the flow of air such a cut allowed within the garment itself. In the heat of the Elorin Empire, any way to stay cool was welcome.

Alesh looked as uncomfortable in his own clothes as I felt in mine, but he matched the local style now, a half-buttoned, green silk shirt that exposed his dark chest, black trousers, and black leather boots shined to near blinding. The shoes were what "made a man" here, or so the clothier told us. Most of the men here wore a similar style, so she must have been telling the truth, although how they retained such a shine was beyond comprehension. They must buff their shoes every night after the evening meal or beg their wives or daughters to do it.

I tugged at my collar again. At least the high collar meant I could keep the talisman on and hidden. Alesh no longer carried his staff in public. It made him far too easy to identify, so he'd left it with Abi in our room. Abi promised she'd guard it with her life. I'd suppressed a laugh at the earnest look in her eye when she uttered the words. Entirely serious in her devotion, she wouldn't have appreciated my making light of the situation, even if she *was* too young to defend against someone intent on stealing a jewel-topped staff.

Like the talisman, the staff chose its owner, so Alesh wasn't concerned that Abi might be tempted to try to grow a garden in the small room, even if she *had* appreciated the number of new fruits she'd gotten to taste since we'd taken to our nightly gardening ritual.

When Alesh and I reached the end of Jeweler's Row, I turned left, stopped, and gave a reluctant sigh. The sight in front of me was exactly what Abi had said we should expect—the kind of place one might think to be robbed.

A narrow, cobbled alley with a high stone wall on one side and a row of run-down shops along the other greeted us. These cobbles were covered in a layer of grime that made it clear the pathway hadn't been swept in quite some time. The cleanliness that extended to most of the city stopped here.

The stone wall was mostly hidden by a mess of vicious-looking vines that twisted together, their strange, arrow-shaped leaves hiding from sight the thorns that would rip apart any hands that dared climb them. I might like to take a cutting for a sample one day. When this was all over. When I could study plants again.

"Anyone here might take our money and give us nothing at all," Alesh muttered, breaking me from my thoughts.

My instincts agreed, but I pushed the hesitation from my mind.

"Looks can be deceiving. You've said so yourself. Besides, Abi said we would find what we need here."

"She is a child." Alesh's voice was soft, but the words hit where he intended. She *was* a child. Had we put too much faith in her because she was our only link to the Elorin Empire and the Chaos Wielder? With her, we had a plan, however ludicrous it might be. Without her, we were back to no plan at all.

"She's a Gehtanan. She knows more about this city than you or I could hope to glean in a month. Come."

With that, I stepped forward into the deserted alley, Alesh close at my side. I followed Abi's instructions, stopping at the fourth shop, a wooden door with cracked paint. The door was once blue beneath the layers of white that peeled away. It had been some time since the wood had seen a fresh coat of any color. The window beside the door was dark, and it took me a moment to realize it wasn't because the shop itself was dark, but rather because a thick, black cloth had been draped over it, concealing the inside of the shop from view.

Why sacrifice natural light and spend more on oil to keep lamps burning inside? I put a hand to the worn doorknob, intending to turn it, but was met with resistance. Locked. I stepped back in surprise, then knocked.

We waited several long moments, a stiff breeze rustling the leaves on the vines behind us. I counted the doors again, checking to ensure I had the right one, then I knocked again, harder this time.

"No one is here." Alesh pointed to the darkened window.

I stepped back from the door, reluctant to try the other

goldsmith on Abi's short list. He wasn't Abi's top choice, but he would have to do. I hoped he was home.

We had just turned to leave when a soft click sounded, the door opened, and one distrusting, narrowed eye peered through the crack.

"De natro á zirka?" The woman's voice was rough, sandpaper and smoke.

Alesh hesitated a moment too long before answering. Maybe he was as surprised as I that the door had opened at all.

"You have an appointment?" she said.

She spoke the northern tongue. I let out a sigh of relief and smiled.

"No, but—"

I winced when the door slammed in my face, the sound echoing off the wall and through the alley.

Blinking, stunned, I turned to Alesh, who somehow didn't appear surprised at all.

"I guess she does not want to talk." He shrugged his shoulders.

I pressed my lips together and gave Alesh a look—the kind of look that told him he wasn't particularly amusing. Then I stepped to the door again and did what Quinn would do. I rapped on the wood. When there was no reply, I rapped harder. I knocked on the door until there were complaints from the windows of neighboring tenants, until my knuckles grew red, until I could no longer feel my fingers.

Then I knocked with the other hand.

Finally, the door opened a crack once more, anger on the

sliver of the face in view.

"You will stop."

"How do I make an appointment?" I asked.

"I have no appointments available." She made to close the door again, but I slid a foot forward and wedged my boot between the door and the jamb.

She looked up sharply, surprised someone dressed so fine would act in such a manner, no doubt. I held a hand out behind me to Alesh, never letting my gaze leave hers. That's what Quinn would have done, stared her down. I needed to *be* Quinn. That's how I would get through all of this. Afterwards? Afterwards, I could go back to being me.

Alesh dropped the coin purse into my hand, the weight of it filling my palm. I brought my hand forward to show our goldsmith what we offered.

"I don't suppose this might help gain me an appointment?"

One eye narrowed. Then the door opened to reveal a flourishing smile on her face.

"I think an appointment might have opened," she said with a half-bow. "Come."

I glanced back to Alesh as I stepped through the doorway, allowing myself a smirk of satisfaction. Old Reina never would have bribed a goldsmith. New Reina would channel Quinn D'Arturio in all things until she defeated the Chaos Wielder and could go home.

Once we entered the shop, the woman clicked the lock of the door behind us, then took one quick peek into the alleyway behind the black cloth. What—or who—was she so wary of?

"You come highly recommended to us," I said.

In return, the woman gave a snort and turned up the oil lamp to brighten the space around us. She crossed her arms and leaned against a workbench covered with an array of tools and jewelry in pieces.

Was she…taking apart existing jewelry?

Noticing my stare, she threw a cloth over the jewels, hiding the work from view. I cleared my throat and returned my focus to her again. It didn't matter what she was doing, or what she'd done in the past. All that mattered was her ability to create what we needed.

The woman was neither noticeably young nor old, but somewhere in between, her smooth, even brown skin making it more difficult to see any sign of wrinkles that might have otherwise given away her age. She wore coarse, black hair pulled back into a thick braid that fell to the small of her back, a scrap of gold and turquoise cloth tied around her forehead.

The turquoise wrap matched the print of the tool-filled work apron around her waist. A nub of a charcoal pencil was tucked behind one ear. Had her eyes been welcoming and her mouth quick to smile, I might have thought her attractive, but between her frayed apron and her frayed patience, I found it difficult to imagine anything other than a scowl and her irritation at our unexpected visit.

Alesh stepped forward to stand beside me. "We need a very specific item," he said. "And we were told you are one of the few craftsmen who can make such an item."

"Craftswoman," she corrected with an upward tilt of

her chin.

He nodded. "My name is Aleshkatel Bhalehi. My companion is Moreina di Bianco. I hope you will do us the pleasure of considering our request."

Honeyed words. I regarded Alesh with interest. A few moments ago, he hadn't even wanted to venture into the alley. Now he was plying our goldsmith with sweetness as though it might win her over. I suppose it couldn't do harm...

"Call me Djana."

"Djana," I said. "Thank you for seeing us."

She motioned to the coin purse in my hand. "I do not see you out of the goodness of my heart. You have something *I* need, and I have a skill *you* need, so let us get on with it, yes?"

"Very well. We require a replica of the emperor's diadem." I studied her face as I said the words, assessing for any sign she might take issue with morality behind crafting such an item. "There's a young girl, you see, who admires the emperor so—"

She held up a hand. "I do not care why you need the item. I craft. I need to know nothing more than materials and design."

I nodded. Well, at least I wouldn't need to embellish the lie about a nonexistent younger sister who desperately wanted a crown like the one Elodie Gehtanan wore. I was almost disappointed I'd spent any time coming up with it.

"How accurate?" Djana asked.

"As close as possible to the real diadem," Alesh answered.

"Indistinguishable," I added.

She looked at the bag full of coins in my hand, then back and forth between our faces.

"It will cost more than that." She nodded at the bag in my hand.

I nodded and offered the bag. "We're prepared to pay in full when it's ready."

She accepted the satchel and dumped the coins onto the uncovered corner of her workbench. Her fingers moved over the coins swiftly, stacking them neatly as though by magic. When she'd counted to her satisfaction, she swiped the coins back into the bag, then made the bag disappear into her apron.

"When?" she asked.

"Two weeks."

"I'll require three more of those."

"Three!" We would never grow and sell enough produce to provide three more bags of coins before the eclipse.

"What you ask requires great intricacy, great detail. It means I will take no other customers, and that costs me. You wish the job done?"

I turned to look at Alesh.

He nodded. "We will see what the other can offer," he said.

Djana's brows drew together. "There is no other who can craft what I can in that time *and* keep their lips sealed. Not in these parts."

My breath caught. She knew we weren't creating a diadem for a young girl, fictional or not. What might she do with the knowledge that someone was seeking to create a replica of the emperor's diadem?

Alesh was careful not to let emotion show on his face. "Is that so? My source tells me Baarti is as good, if not better." Alesh was nearly as practiced a liar as Quinn.

Abi had told us to look for Djana first, and Baarti as a last resort. She suspected Djana might give us trouble, but she said Baarti was "older than Liron" and might not craft the diadem before the *next* full eclipse…which was a hundred-fifty years away.

Djana balked. "Baarti Tawin? Never! The old man can't see past his own nose any longer," she said. "And he's slow."

"Craft this for us, and you will get two more bags of coin," Alesh said.

Djana pressed her lips together and narrowed her eyes, contemplating her options.

"And, like you, our lips will also remain sealed," I added.

I pushed aside thoughts of how my life had changed so much in the last year. The girl I once was would never have thought to bribe anyone even if her own life had depended on it. And now? I'd resorted to bribery twice in one day…

"What? I have nothing—" She followed my gaze to the cloth-covered workbench, then clamped her mouth shut, a nervous tic working in her cheek.

"Very well," she conceded. "Two bags of coin, and I shall have what you need two weeks from today. You have the specifications?"

Alesh pulled Abi's detailed drawing from his bag and handed it to me. I unfolded it carefully, then handed it to Djana.

"Every detail you need should be found here."

The general shape and size of the diadem was well-known throughout the Empire, but only Abi would have knowledge of the intricacies of the swirls of gold and dripping pearls, and only Abi would know the exact size and shape of the yellow sapphire clasped at the diadem's center. Anyone else who might have once possessed such knowledge was no longer living.

Djana examined the drawing with its measurements, scanning the paper for the details she needed. I held my breath as long moments passed. Finally, satisfied with what she found, she nodded.

"The stone will not be the same," she said.

"The crack is essential." We couldn't exchange a broken stone for a whole one. It wouldn't fool the Chaos Wielder for a moment, charmed or not.

"Not the crack," she said, much to my relief. "That, I can create. It will be difficult and may not be exact, but it will be close, close enough that no one will know. But as for the stone itself, I will not find yellow sapphire here."

Knowing nothing about jewels or gemstones, I asked, "Is there a substitute? Something similar?"

She rubbed three fingers across her chin and over her lips as she thought, then laid Abi's drawing atop the cloth on the workbench.

"Topaz is similar in hardness, but the optics won't match, not that anyone would notice up close, but topaz is expensive, nearly as expensive as yellow sapphire. Citrine. Could use citrine. It's more affordable, anyway. Optics will be better suited." She narrowed her eyes, then seemed to remember Alesh and I were still here. "Won't be as hard," she said, tapping on bench. "The stone will be softer. Sapphire is too hard. I won't be able to match the hardness and the color."

"I do not think that will be a problem," Alesh reassured her.

"Whatever it takes to get as close as possible, visually, in the time provided," I said. "I trust you know worlds more about such things than I."

"Indeed. Very well. Come back in two weeks."

"If you need to reach us, we reside at the inn on the corner of Crushalhe and Dharta," Alesh said. I guessed we'd no longer be changing inns, at least for now.

Djana turned from us and pulled the pencil from over her ear, already making detailed notes on Abi's drawing and mumbling to herself.

"So, we'll just…" I motioned to the door.

Djana looked up briefly, as though we'd become a distraction.

"Yes, yes, I'll lock it when you're out. Come back in two weeks, mid-day."

When we returned to the alley again and the latch on the door sounded behind us, I turned to face Alesh and ran my thumb across the pads of my fingertips.

"We've got a lot of harvesting to do."

CHAPTER NINE

Saints Above
Quinn

The darkness drove me to pain, to tears, to pleas for mercy. I'd never begged in life the way I begged now, but the onslaught was relentless. In my head, beneath my skin, the searing pain bubbled everywhere.

I'd killed the old man, murdered him. It was my fault he was dead. Because of me, his family, whoever they were, endured the pain of losing a loved one to a wretched street death. They'd never know why he died or who killed him. He'd been doing his best to care for them. Selling information was his life, the only way he knew to provide for his family, and I'd killed him for it.

"You would have done the same if you had no choice, as I had no choice," he said, leaning close, his voice burning in my ears, echoing in my head. "Lucky you to not be body-broken and poverty-stricken. Lucky you to provide for loved ones without dipping into the dangers of selling information to those who would pay. And yet, you judged me, judged my livelihood, then pretended you were better than I. How did that work out for you, boy?" A harsh laugh followed, and a new pain seared my legs as he whipped his cane across my calves.

I screamed.

The scent of scalded flesh filled the air, the cane a brand on my skin.

He would watch me burn.

The old man would watch me burn, and he would enjoy it.

I deserved it.

Tears squeezed from the corners of eyes I shut against the glowing form of his long hair and grizzled beard in the dark. I deserved the pain. Oh, God, what had I done?

"I swear to God, D'Arturio…"

A voice. Another voice. Not the old man.

I swallowed and latched onto the voice, clutching it to me as a man gone overboard grasps at a life ring, panicked and desperate.

I knew this voice. It had rid me of the blackness once before. This voice chased away the angry dead who wished to see me repay the suffering I'd once exacted from them. It could do the same now. I needed to focus on the voice instead of the old man. I strained my ears in the darkness.

"Give it up, already!" The voice sounded irritated.

I raised my head, and seeing nothing in the dark, I issued a cry of relief. The old man was gone. The pain he'd inflicted was already receding. My head fell back to the ground and I panted in relief.

"I cannot be-*lieve* I have to do this again," the voice grumbled. "Why does it take you so long to hear me? This is bloody ridiculous. Half a dozen times now. How many more do you need, D'Arturio? D'Arturio. D'Arturio!"

A gray haze began to form around my body, slowly expanding, then illuminating the annoyed figure. Niles Ingram, I remembered. Niles Ingram, whom I loathed with every fiber of my being. Niles Ingram, whom I would do anything to keep nearby if it meant the accusing dead and their blistering pain stayed at bay.

I coughed as I dragged myself to my feet.

"You got rid of them," I said, grateful and embarrassed at once. "Again."

He shoved his hands into the pockets of his tunic and rolled his eyes.

"I already explained this to you once, Quinn. I have nothing to do with it. The sooner you accept that, the sooner we can get on with it. I know how you love to torture yourself, but really, this is getting quite old, and we don't have the time."

Anger flared in my veins. Who was he to assume to know my mind? Who was he to believe for a moment he knew my being? I opened my mouth.

"Ah," he said, holding up a hand. "Before you start on a tirade, let me remind you that my time here may be limited." He didn't wait for my response. "Let's walk."

We didn't go far this time before the mountaintop beneath my feet came into focus, the meadow far below, a light breeze stirring. The backs of my calves still burned from the cane, but every step relieved me of the sensation a little more. I wiped at the tear stains damp on my face, hoping Niles hadn't noticed their presence. Niles Ingram did not need to know I had shed tears.

"Where did you go?" I asked. "You left."

He cleared his throat and pursed his lips as he looked around, thinking on his response.

"I didn't leave by choice."

My response was automatic. "I didn't think you would."

Of course I assumed he'd left by choice. What better payback for making him follow me up an entire mountainside?

"The Higher Ones called. I had no choice but to answer."

"You mentioned them before. Who are these Higher Ones?"

"There's not much I can say on them save for the fact that you invoke their mercy on a fairly regular basis."

"I—"

"Well, to be fair, just about everyone does."

"For Saints' sake, do you have to be so cryptic?"

He responded with an amused tilt of the head, eyebrows raised, lips pressed together in a concealed laugh, waiting for me to figure something out. I reeled, the implication hitting me like a stone to the head.

"The…Saints?"

He gave no reply, but the look in his eye said I was an idiot for not figuring it out sooner.

"They're…real?"

"Bloody hell, Quinn. Didn't you attend services as a child?"

My mind spun. Nothing made sense. Again, I grasped at the lingering threads of logic quickly slipping away.

"Well, what do they want with me?"

"Oh, don't be so self-absorbed. This is far bigger than you."

I clenched my jaw, took a deep breath, and released it. "Let me rephrase. What do they want?"

"The Saints? They want to see the success of a prophecy already set in motion."

"What prophecy? And how can I help them with a prophecy?"

"Too many questions, D'Arturio."

Dark clouds collected far in the distance, threatening to overtake the blue sky as though the tiny bit of peace I'd found here had offered up a white flag, surrendering to new horrors that had yet to reveal themselves. A low rumble of thunder rolled on and on across the gathering gray masses. An ominous sign.

There would be more horrors to face.

I swallowed.

I couldn't do what Ingram wanted me to do. How could I forgive myself for the atrocities committed? For the many lives taken? For even more lives destroyed? How could *anyone* forgive such a thing? Agents made that sacrifice. They gave their souls for the good of the cause, so the White Sorceress could be found. They sacrificed their peace of mind, their innocence, their right to a future.

So how could I turn around and believe I had any chance at redemption, at reconciling my actions? How could I consider for a moment there was peace in my future? Agents didn't get peace, and they rarely got a future.

As though sensing the direction of my thoughts, Ingram

said, "Allow me to pose a question. I sense you're at odds with yourself."

Warily, I nodded.

"Your friend, Captain Brigantino"—Niles shifted awkwardly as though the mere mention of Brigantino made him uncomfortable— "is considerably older than you and has undoubtedly conducted far, far more nefarious deeds than you, yourself, have committed. You agree?"

I didn't want to agree, but Niles was right, so I nodded again.

"Do you consider Brigantino to be a good person?"

A trick question. Brigantino was one of the best men I'd ever known. He was dedicated, loyal, and would do anything to protect those around him. Of course he was a good person.

But Brigantino was an agent. An agent who'd been undercover in the King's Army for far longer than I had. A man who'd been feared in the King's Army not only by his enemy, but by those in his own command unit. What did that say of the things he must have done? What acts had he committed to render such a fear in his own men?

"It's not a difficult question, D'Arturio."

I hesitated.

"Yes, Brigantino is a good person and a good man."

"Ah, good. And Brigantino—wait…I must ask, does that man have a first name or is that another of the Order's well-guarded secrets?"

I made a sound that was more snort than laugh.

"Piero."

"You're kidding."

"I'm not."

"Hm. What are the chances? I had an Uncle Piero. Or maybe he was my mother's uncle. Not a common name. Anyway, Brigantino. You say he's a good man."

"The best."

"And yet you know what the Order required of him."

I fidgeted with the end of my belt.

"I'll take that as a yes. So, allow me to pose a question. If Brigantino committed so many awful deeds in his time as an agent, does he then deserve his happiness with Ywelo?"

Ywelo. I remembered. Brigantino and Ywelo were on the ship. Ywelo was Brigantino's love, the woman he left behind years ago so he could continue in the Order. They were…dammit, where were they? Left behind somewhere.

"Ywelo," I said. "Dark skin, fierce eyes, gold cuffs around her arms."

"That's the one. Look at her the wrong way and she might put a knife in your middle. Good match for our little Piero, she is. So, does he deserve his happiness with her?"

I struggled, finally forcing out, "Of course he does. He's worked his whole life, given up everything. He has a chance at happiness. He deserves every moment of it."

Niles's eyes lit as though I'd handed him the key to a treasure chest full of gold and jewels.

"Right then. Do you suppose Brigantino would, for a moment, even consider missing the opportunity he has with Ywelo now? Do you think he would berate and strong-arm himself into believing he didn't deserve her?"

Damn. I *had* handed Niles a key. It wouldn't unlock any

treasure, but it was a key, nonetheless. He'd gotten to the heart of the matter quicker than I would have thought he could.

"You know the answer. Spit it out, D'Arturio. Don't be a stubborn boar."

"Brigantino doesn't allow himself to dwell on the past."

"Then why do you?"

I slammed a fist into a tree with a frustrated growl, scraping my knuckles raw against the bark, relishing the pain. Pain was good. This kind of pain was pain I could focus on, pain I could deal with. This kind of pain was better than the kind inside my head.

"Because I should know better!" I finally answered, my words echoing through the distance.

Niles gave me a long, hard look. I didn't miss what he said with that look. How could I claim to know better than someone more than twice my age who was smarter, braver, and sacrificed more than I could ever imagine? Professing I knew better implied Brigantino didn't.

'Twas an insult to a great man.

"Are you done being an imbecilic martyr now? Are you ready to face yourself?"

Thunder sounded in the distance again, and I turned my eyes to the incoming clouds. The wind pushed the grasses across the meadow, stripping the flowers and sending white petals flying into the air.

A storm. I could weather a storm. Let the world outside rage the same as my thoughts inside.

I turned to face Niles. "Go throw a stone."

The look he gave me before his form disappeared into thin air was equal parts disappointment and amusement.

When the rain began to soak my skin, I was glad for the excuse to hide my tears. It wouldn't be long before the dead came back to haunt me. I deserved it.

Didn't I?

CHAPTER TEN

Artful Visions
Reina

Once again, I was in the midst of the strange, sunlit meadow, pulling the tall strands of grass between my fingertips, letting the fuzzy tips of each blade fall apart as I rubbed them between the pads of my fingers. A floral aroma carried on the breeze, carrying with it a hint of rain, the musty scent of charged air that sent a fierce longing for Barnham's coastal storms aching through my limbs.

I startled at a touch on my shoulder—a familiar touch, a familiar hand.

Quinn.

I turned to better view him, to drink in his features, like a parched desert mouse happening upon an oasis. Quinn *was* my water. In a world that tried to kill me every day, Quinn was the elixir of life, the reason for my being.

Without a word, he slid his hand from my shoulder down my arm until he was holding my hand and teasing my palm with his fingertips, his eyes glinting playfully the way they once had when we'd first settled in the castle at Irzan, his gaze never leaving mine. A smile tugged on his lips, as though he was withholding some secret.

My breath grew shallow, pulse quickening beneath the lightness of his touch. He pulled my hand to his mouth, warm lips brushing the back of my knuckles. His breath kissed my skin, warming it, bringing me alive. Saints help me, but I was lost without him. I squeezed my eyes shut, letting the moment take me, feeling the delicious closeness of the boy I'd once known, the friend I'd always had in my heart, the man I loved.

He pulled me close, lips traveling upwards, leaving a trail of kisses along my arm, my shoulder, and across my collarbone. Unbidden, a small sound escaped my throat. A whimper, perhaps, but more likely a cry for more. He smelled like Barnham, like sea and pine and home.

When I opened my eyes again, he was there, eyes locked on mine, lips a hairsbreadth from my own, teasing. Then he leaned down—

My eyes flew open to a view of our room, blood hammering through my veins from the sensual version of Quinn I'd been enjoying a moment before. A frustrated growl slipped from my throat. Traitorous self. When would I learn? When would my mind let him go?

I swallowed, pushing thoughts of Quinn far to the back of my mind. Again.

One day, Quinn. I will give myself time to grieve, time to remember, time to hold you close again, but I can't do it if I want to hold myself together. And right now, I can't afford to fall apart.

I missed him so damned much.

I sat, swiveling to rest my feet on the floor. Groaning, I

attempted to work the kinks from my neck and shoulders. My arms ached. My back burned. I'd never been so keenly aware of every muscle in my body, not even when I was studying the medical texts from my mother's shelves and quizzing myself on each muscle group and their corresponding ligaments. At least the complete and utter fatigue made it easier to sleep through the street noise of the late afternoon.

Which was why I hadn't heard Alesh slip back into the room after his meeting with Ito. It wasn't until the door latched behind him that I realized he'd returned. His face was a mask of worry and concern, a deep line etched between his brows.

"What is it?" I whispered, all too aware of Abi sleeping soundly beside me.

I slid from the bed, careful to tuck the covers back around Abi, then Alesh and I convened at the table in the corner of the room.

"He is dead."

I stopped mid-stretch. "What do you mean he's dead? The Yonheli? Ito?"

Alesh nodded.

I couldn't suppress a gasp. "What happened?"

I slid into the seat beside him, running my fingers across the table.

"Murdered. They found him hanging from a post in the alley."

My gaze traveled over the wood grain in the table, following each knot and whorl. Our seller was dead. A man had lost his life. Because of us.

"There are rumors. They say others were wanting his success."

"Jealousy," I said softly. "They were jealous of his sudden success." But the explanation didn't sit well with me.

"I do not think this is what happened." Apparently, the rumors failed to sit well with Alesh, too. "She knows something. She does not know what, or we would also be dead, but she knows."

He didn't have to elaborate. I knew exactly who *she* was.

The murderous, cunning imposter.

She might not have killed Ito outright as she had her own family, but she'd hired someone else to do it. I rubbed my chest, the marked flesh still irritated under my tunic. Beneath my ribs, my heart ached a little for the man who'd been trying to make a life for himself and his family, who'd accepted our job offer with excitement towards what the future might bring for him. His death was one more weighing on my soul, one more that was my fault for not having killed the Chaos Wielder when I had the chance.

"We can't raise the money to pay Djana without selling our produce. And we can't sell produce without pulling someone else into this tangled web. We can't, Alesh. We cannot be the cause of death for another innocent man, woman, or child. Not one."

Alesh gave a nod, his gaze lowered, his brows pushed together in concentration. I hoped he had another idea. I hoped he might think of another route, some other way we could fix this plan we'd put into motion. And yet…for all the world, I couldn't think of a single suitable alternative. I swiped an angry tear before it could crest the rim of my eye.

"So I get to raid the treasury now?"

I turned in my seat to find Abi sitting alert in the bed, her face bright, blond hair mussed from sleep, pillow lines across one cheek. How long had she been awake? How much had she heard?

I wanted to say no. I wanted to shout it. I wanted Abi safe from harm's way, out of her sister's clutches, away from any and all danger.

Instead, Alesh and I shared a look, and he said, "I think we have no other choice."

Abi clapped and bounced once on the bed. "Yes! I *knew* I could help. When do I go? Tonight? Say tonight!"

We sent Abi into the treasury that night, my nerves alight with anxiety and fear. There was so much riding on the success of her mission I couldn't consider what we might do if she failed. I should have been more concerned with the fate of the world, with chaos reigning over all, with Liron falling into disorder.

Instead, I feared for Abi's life.

The precocious young girl reminded me of another young girl I knew long ago, though at eleven years old, I was helping my mother deliver babies and diagnose ailments. Still, Abi's insistence that she could be of use, that she didn't fear what might lie ahead, was a potent reminder of my own childhood. My mother had believed in me when no one else had.

Now the positions had reversed. I'd been left behind, pacing the room at the inn, wearing the fibers of the threadbare throw rug thinner with each pass of my bare feet, while Alesh escorted Abi to the palace grounds through the cover of dark. I hated being here when they were there. I loathed feeling powerless to do anything, to contribute in some useful way.

I paused in my pacing, once again feeling as though I finally understood Quinn's mind, and how he'd felt when I left him behind to discover the talisman's powers on my own.

I pulled the teardrop-shaped stone from beneath my tunic top and studied it, absently caressing the cabochon's surface. Once, not so long ago, the talisman had been foreign to me, shocking relentlessly, echoing the turmoil in my own mind if I had to guess. Now, it hummed at my fingertips, ready for use—almost *begging* for its power to be released.

"Not today, my friend. You may be more reliable now than you were weeks ago, but I have no need for the power of death right now."

The aqua shifted in the depths of the gemstone in response.

I halted mid-pace. While I couldn't use the talisman's magic, there was no reason I couldn't use the kind of magic I'd known all my life, the second sight I'd known long before the talisman's magic came into my life, the gift I'd once preferred to pretend wasn't a part of me at all. My heart raced as I sat on the bed, then reclined, and tried to even my breathing.

I focused on the truth I needed to see, on whatever might help me find a way to defeat the Chaos Wielder, even if I couldn't use the talisman's magic to do it. Information. I needed information. I pushed my will into the sheets beneath my body, into the floorboards below, into the very soil of Liron.

Give me something I can use.

Then, I relaxed my eyes and followed the grain of the wood in the large square beams in the ceiling above, allowing my mind to clear, and my breathing to slow. Before long, the sweet taste of a vision touched my tongue.

A flash of a marketplace. Different than the one I'd visited with Alesh, and not the one in streets of the immigrants' quarter outside our inn. Smaller, but just as crowded. The buildings were not the pristine white of those at the center of Ivirreh. The outer walls of these buildings were cracked with age, but still clean as though well-cared for, even if not freshly painted. Here, the buildings were older, more lived in, as though more feet had worn their floors and polished their steps in passing.

Then an alley. On one wall, a mural drew my eye. In the vision, the larger-than-life painting depicted a scene that had no business being in Ivirreh…or in the Elorin Empire at all. Three silhouetted figures stood over a circle with landmasses and oceans, an image that was clearly meant to be a depiction of Liron.

On the head of the center figure was the Chaos Wielder's diadem, its bright center stone painted a faded yellow. To either side of the Chaos Wielder, though, stood representations of figures I knew well, for one of the dark figures held a staff with a ruby gemstone surrounded by carved, gnarled wood while the other wore a necklace with a teardrop-shaped cabochon in hues of blues and greens.

I searched for anything in the mural that might help me make sense of what I was seeing. There were other images within the mural, but they were hazy in my sight, seen through a fog.

My eye was drawn to a spot where heavy boughs of thick ivy clung to the side of the building, shadowing the side of the mural from view. Placing one foot in front of the other until I stood before the giant mass of ivy, I gently pulled the greenery from the wall, attempting to see the hidden images. Removing the ivy revealed—

Abruptly, I was pulled from the vision as the door to our room opened, and Abi tumbled in, futilely attempting to suppress giggles behind her hands. I sat up, rubbed my eyes, and held the vision in my mind to mull over later.

"What time is it?" I asked, as though it mattered.

"Half past three." Abi jumped on the bed beside me.

I heaved a sigh of relief to see her face. They had returned, unharmed.

"You sound like you didn't think we would succeed," Abi said, narrowing her eyes at me.

"I was…sleeping. And did you? Succeed, I mean." My voice was thick with hope. They hadn't been detained or killed, so I wanted to assume everything had gone according to plan, but more often than not, we'd been forced to change our plans at every turn.

"Well, of course!"

Alesh offered a wide, sincere smile of relief in my direction, white teeth seeming brighter in the light of the dim lantern on the table.

"Our Abigayle Gehtanan is resourceful."

"Is she, now?" There was likely more to the story than I could have imagined.

In response, Abi gave an enormous yawn and rubbed at tired eyes. She nodded her head and grinned at me.

Alesh pulled a seat from beneath the table and turned it to face where Abi seated herself on the bed beside me. They were prepared to tell me a harrowing tale of theft and mischief, no doubt. A swell of emotion surged beneath my chest, and I fought not to let show my sudden desire to hug them both tightly. These two had come to mean so much to me in so short a time.

Abi held out a hand to Alesh, and he placed the strap of his worn satchel in her grasp. Then she held open the flap, turned the satchel upside down, and a cache of coins and paper treasury notes spilled onto the bed, the coins jingling together in musical relief to my ears.

My gaze shot from the pile on the bed to Abi's wide grin. The coins, I expected, but…

"Treasury notes?"

Signed, treasury notes were easily worth ten to a hundred times what coin could buy. But these would be no use to us, unless… I plucked a note from the pile, testing the paper's satiny texture beneath my fingertips.

The treasurer's signature was scrawled across the bottom in official purple ink. The note was signed. As was every note in the pile.

"How?"

"You don't think I lived in the palace all my life and didn't know how to visit the treasury undetected, do you?" Abi gave another grin, this time laced with wicked mischief.

Speechless, I stared.

"Artur never saved money. That's why he was mad when I let the charmed paper butterfly go that day. He wasn't as clever at getting the treasury notes signed as Hati and I were."

"Hati…" I couldn't remember which of Abi's siblings bore the name.

"One of the twins. The oldest. She showed me where to find the stamp. Artur never knew about it, which was for the best, as he would have emptied the entire treasury overnight."

"A stamp?"

She nodded. Of course there was a stamp. The treasurer couldn't sign every single note in circulation by hand. He'd never have time for anything else. I turned my attention back to the notes and coins on the bed.

"You stamped all of these?"

She nodded.

"She would have stayed all night had I allowed it." Alesh leaned forward in his chair, elbows on his knees, hands clasped.

"Not *all* night. I just wanted to provide enough to prove my worth!"

Alesh shook his head.

"Abi." I clasped her hands between mine. "You're everything good in this world, and there's no need to prove your worth to anyone, least of all to us. You're worth more than a million of these notes combined—no, a hundred million."

She looked away sheepishly. "I want to be able to help. You—the two of you—have no idea what you're up against with Elodie. And I do. I want you to succeed. Because…" Abi's eyes grew glassy with tears, and she swallowed, fighting to keep them from falling. "Because no one else would dare act against her. No one else knows what she's done. They revere her. They don't know the monster inside. But you do."

I squeezed her hands tight and gave her a sad, sincere smile. "Thank you for doing what you did tonight. I'm so glad we have you on our side."

I meant it.

CHAPTER ELEVEN

The Price of Guilt
Quinn

I never experienced a darkness so desolate, a blackness so complete, or a terror so consuming. Breath, difficult in coming, resisted being pulled into my chest at all. I gasped, a fish without water, the air turned molasses. I would suffocate and burn at the same time.

The voices grew in volume, slashing hot blades through my mind, searing with their accusations, exposing raw welts in their wake, again and again, until I broke. Rough, unseen hands grabbed furiously at my clothes, my face, my hair, seeking to rip and tear apart the monster who'd destroyed their lives and taken their futures. There was no escaping. Not this time.

I was stupid. So daft.

If I thought for a second I might get a moment of reprieve by not having to see their ghostly forms, I'd be wrong. It didn't matter that these ghosts were not illuminated, that the darkness devoured all. They made their anguish known.

The dead hurled insults into my ears and lashed out until I was on my knees, lost in sea of torment and grief—an ocean of the suffering I'd caused. It came in waves upon waves, suffocating, choking, assaulting me until I quaked like a newborn left in the cold.

Thunder roared overhead, shaking my teeth, vibrating the world inside and out, but no lightning relieved me from the darkness of my prison. Fat droplets fell from the unseen sky, a few at first, until a deluge soaked my hair and clothes, the rain lashing at my skin. I waited for the water to soothe away the scorching sensation, but every drop sliced new lacerations into my skin, needles of pain, stabbing with each drip.

A storm.

I thought I could weather a storm.

I was wrong.

So wrong.

The torture lasted hours, days, *weeks*. Without light and dark, there was no way to gauge the passing of time. And through it all, the thunder taunted.

Strong, bony fingers gripped my wrist, piercing my forearm with a shooting pain, and I screamed, the scent of burning flesh fresh in my nostrils. I wrenched my arm away, but the grip tightened, and I no longer had the strength to fight. Exhaustion succumbed to madness, for who could remain lucid in such circumstances?

I knew. I knew I deserved the pain, but, Saints, how I wanted it to stop. The things I'd done in my life for the Order…they were horrifying. Unthinkable. I would never fully recover from them, not really. But oh, how I was sorry for having done them.

I sobbed.

"I'm sorry." My choked words were hardly more than a hoarse whisper.

The resounding silence that followed was deafening. Every nerve throbbed in time with the pounding of my heart, my body suddenly free from the deliverance of new pain. The wounds I'd already been dealt pulsed almost numbly. I didn't know why the assault had stopped, only that it had.

With a final sob, I collapsed and let the blackness swallow my mind as well as my body. For a moment, at least, oblivion was my friend, and I fell into its embrace.

"Sorry's a start."

I groaned and rolled onto my back, my skin prickling with the memory of pain. Sitting slowly, I pushed off on one elbow, every scrap of my body stiff from torture, and blinked in the dull gray surroundings. Ingram sat alert on a tree stump, far too alert for my current state of mind.

"I—" A coughing fit seized me, and I doubled over. The burn in my lungs made me wonder if the ghosts had attacked my insides, too. Long minutes passed before I tried to speak again.

"I've always been sorry," I croaked. I cleared my throat again.

That I was openly admitting this to Ingram was a true

testament to my state of mind. I didn't have the energy to deny it—to him, or to anyone.

"Well, then. Saying it aloud is a start." He examined the nails on one hand as though bored with the conversation, and maybe he was. He had some nerve, looking polished and put-together when I felt like I'd been rolled over a dozen times by a fully stocked supply cart.

I touched fingers to my swollen eyes, examining the tender skin. Had I been crying? For how long?

My skin tingled, but there was not a single mark on my arms other than those placed there by my time in the Order. The hand around my wrist…it'd felt so real. How could it leave no mark? If I closed my eyes, I could still feel the sting of bony fingers on my skin, smell the stench of seared flesh.

"Thank you," I said to him, my words low, but genuine.

"For what?"

"For stopping them."

"Saints, but you're hard-headed, D'Arturio. I don't know how many times I must tell you this. *I* didn't do anything."

So he said, but I wasn't sure I believed him. The ghosts disappeared when Niles showed up. It was difficult to believe the two actions were unrelated.

Niles sensed my disbelief.

"You did it yourself," he said. "I've been waiting to talk to you for days, but they wouldn't let me near you until you tortured yourself long enough, apparently."

I gave a hoarse cough that could have been a laugh. The gray fog muted the sound. "Tortured myself? *Tortured myself*? Did you not see? You think I did that to myself?"

He gave a tired sigh.

"Quinn, you—no, wait. I need to phrase this in a way you can understand since my current explanation doesn't seem to be enough." He stood and blew out a long, frustrated breath before continuing. "When did the torture stop?"

"If you were here, you know when they finally released me. I don't have the faintest idea. I wasn't exactly right in the head if you hadn't noticed."

"I don't mean the time of day. I mean at what point did you get reprieve? What did you do to gain that stay?"

Agitated, I flung my arms outwards. "Nothing. I did nothing!"

"Oh, come now. You genuinely believe that, do you?"

Being spoken to condescendingly by Niles Ingram was not on the list of pleasantries I'd hoped for today, or any other day for that matter, even if it was marginally better than being abused by ghosts.

"You spoke the words!" he bellowed. "Say them again."

"I'm…sorry."

"Yes!"

I swallowed. "You're telling me because I said I was sorry, the ghosts stopped pulling me apart inside and out?"

It seemed too easy.

Those things that seemed too easy usually were. I narrowed my eyes.

"I already told you. I've always been sorry. That hasn't changed."

"D'Arturio, try to follow along. Communication means more than just thinking something. You need to at least attempt to let another being understand your thoughts by forming words, and indeed full sentences, aloud."

"But…they're ghosts."

"And?"

I sat back, my hands in the dirt, or what I assumed was dirt. Beneath the gray haze, I couldn't see much. The storm had moved on. Despite the soaking it had given me, the ground did not appear to be wet. This place was stranger than anything I'd ever imagined.

"They'll be back, you know."

Cold tendrils slid down my spine, coating every organ with ice. My breath quickened. I leaned forward again, resting my arms on my knees, and let my head hang.

"What do I need to do?"

"Forgive yourself."

"Yes, you've said that, Ingram." I gritted my teeth. "How?"

"I wouldn't think this is difficult to understand."

The puffiness around my eyes was fading, but a splitting headache was quickly taking its place. Of all the dead people who could have been sent to help me, it figured I would end up with Niles Ingram. Was he intentionally obtuse?

"Do I have to say it out loud? If I shout to the dead that I forgive myself for the atrocities I committed, am I free to go? Will they leave me alone?"

He had the nerve to laugh.

"I don't think it's quite that simple, but if saying so aloud makes it easier for you to work through all you've been through, you can start by talking to me. That is, after all, why I'm here."

I swallowed. This was the point in the conversation where I would normally tell Niles to throw a stone. Every bone in my body resisted the idea of asking forgiveness from him. My muscles tightened in dread at the thought of his judgment. After all the times I'd judged *him* over the years…

"I'm not here to judge."

"Blast it! Will you stop that?"

"Stop what?" He stepped back, palms raised in the air, eyes wide as though to prove his innocence.

"Reading my mind! It's unnerving."

"I can't read your mind, D'Arturio. But your face doesn't hide much these days. That must be the ghosts' doing."

I carefully plastered a mask of indifference on my features. I wouldn't let Niles meddle with my head.

"Oh, much better. Now I surely cannot see how disgruntled you are by my company. Well done."

I closed my eyes, took a deep breath through my nose. *He will not get to me. I will not let him get to me.*

"In all seriousness, let's start with the most recent memories that haunt you and work backwards. The sooner you address your past, the sooner you can move forward, and there's, well, a lot riding on this, as you know."

I turned away and stared into the gray unknown, tapping a finger against my leg as I swallowed again. I didn't have the strength in me to tell Niles off, nor the heart to resist. I only wished I had to confess to anyone but Niles.

"Fine."

"Excellent! Where do we begin?"

"How about with your death?"

CHAPTER TWELVE

Calculated Risk
Reina

When Abi and Alesh finished recounting their heroics and had finally fallen asleep, and rays of morning sun began to crest the rooftops, I slipped from the bed without a sound. I hadn't necessarily been waiting for them to sleep, but not having to explain where I was going or why was a convenience. I'd return before they awoke anyway. Abi shifted in the bed as I stood, a low murmur leaving her lips.

I froze, counting to twenty before moving again to ensure I hadn't woken her. Her mussed, honey blond hair was stuck to one cheek, a sweet face normally so animated now relaxed in sleep. When she didn't rouse, I dressed quickly, then crept past where Alesh slept on the floor, and snuck out the door, careful to avoid the squeak at the threshold.

It wasn't difficult to find the oldest quarter of Ivirreh. In fact, the marketplace wasn't far from our own inn, so all I had to do was follow the flow of people as a new day of trades and bartering began.

As the sun rose and the day grew warm, the flow of people surrounding me was almost overwhelming without Alesh or Abi's comforting presence. I shouldn't have gone out without at least Alesh by my side as company and translator if needed, but the mural was something I needed to see alone.

Besides, they had both worked long hours through the night. Who was I to steal their well-earned rest?

The crowds carried me forward as I wound my way through the streets, taking in the walls of the buildings, searching for some familiarity from my vision, all the while my thoughts tumbling round and round through my mind.

The mural had to be of some significance to have appeared in my vision last night. I'd focused on answers when I fell into my vision state. I'd searched for the truth behind what we were doing and why, and how we could succeed. There must be something more beneath the ivy.

Several of the buildings in this part of the city were adorned with murals, but nothing like what I'd *seen*, nothing that showed any hint of the talisman, the diadem, or the staff. On one, birds and butterflies sprang from a meadow, taking flight into a cloudless blue sky. On another, two snakes dueled in a flourish of fangs and color. I couldn't help but notice neither was a Gohmi viper, the snake I'd encountered shortly after leaving Kufataba behind. A shudder passed through me with the reminder of the venom that still lived inside my body, waiting to be released again—my own personal looming reminder of mortality.

Some of the larger murals paid homage to the imperial family, each family member outlined in light and celebrated in one way or another. In many of them, Elodie and Abigayle were easy to recognize. I tried hard not to study the remaining faces, not to allow myself to linger on the members of the Gehtanan family who hadn't survived Elodie's wrath.

One mural was made entirely from bits of colored glass stuck to the wall in a mosaic that showed a sunrise over Ivirreh, the glittering white pieces as pristine as the city itself. I ran a hand along the rough edges of the pretty glass pieces and their mortar edges, my fingers trailing along the oddly satisfying texture until I reached the corner of the building.

The crowds thinned as I drew farther from the marketplace, leaving the pressing bodies and the noise behind. When I rounded the corner to a lesser used street, I turned a slow circle, examining both directions. This street. I would find the mural I sought here.

I closed my eyes a moment, focused on the mural, and followed my feet as they lured me left, down the increasingly narrow street to a section of the city that hummed with the quiet of solitude compared with the perpetual commotion blocks away.

I walked until my shin ached where I had been bitten by the viper, until I was reminded yet again that I shouldn't be alive, that I could, in fact, die at any moment. The bite hadn't bothered me before, not since I'd first been bitten anyway. Perhaps today was the day I'd join Quinn, my mother, and the Saints above.

I gave a frustrated groan at the direction of my thoughts and bent to rub my leg beneath the gown, clutching the fabric in one fist and holding it up to better examine the skin below. The marks from the Gohmi viper's fangs were a welted purple-red, despite having healed weeks ago. I'd always bear the mark. What was one more scar to add to my growing collection? I was turning into Quinn in more ways than one.

I muttered a curse under my breath at the thought, let the skirts of my dress fall to the ground once more and continued walking. The venom might take me, but I'd be damned if I would let it take me today. I had things to do.

Such thoughts were a comforting distraction, a convenient lie I might tell myself, as though I had a choice when death might come to claim me and the Saints might take my soul. Quinn hadn't been given a choice.

I cleared my throat, thick with emotion. Quinn *had* been given a choice. He chose death.

So you would live, you ninny.

The conviction didn't console me, even if it was true. He chose death so I could live.

So caught in my thoughts of Quinn and death, I almost passed the building with the mural entirely. The sight of ivy stopped me in my tracks, the abundant green leaves spilling over the side of the building and across adjoining walls.

I took a tentative step closer to the mural, my lips parted in surprise even though I shouldn't have been shocked to see the reality of the image before me. And yet, I *was* surprised because no matter how I had prepared to see this painting that depicted the three figures with the talisman, the staff, and the diadem, I couldn't prepare for the fact that such an image should never have been placed here at all.

I scoured the painting, taking in every detail, my eyes drinking in the sight of the reality before me. I studied the strokes, the colors, the subject—the three silhouetted figures, the planet, the three individual magical objects. Who had painted this mural? And when?

What did it mean that three figures stood over Liron as though watching from above? What did it mean that the figures were painted larger than the planet itself? I wanted to believe this somehow proved those who wielded magic were meant to keep the balance on Liron, to protect the planet and all who lived and died here, but there was nothing in this image that gave such comfort beyond my own desperate desire.

The paint was not as vibrant as it might have once been. Cracked in places, the surface revealed peeling layers beneath. The mural had been maintained throughout the years, carefully repainted by hand—more than once, by the looks of it. Who was the original artist? How many times had someone repainted it since the first time the wall saw paint?

How could they have known about the necklace and the staff? Less than a year ago, the talisman necklace had been hidden away for a millennium at Magnus Tarrowburn's instruction. To my knowledge, Tarrowburn was the only person to have referenced all three items in his writings, and he'd hailed from Castilles. Tarrowburn had lived a thousand years ago—so long ago that no one alive today knew much beyond his surname and the prophecies he'd left behind. This mural had no business being in Ivirreh.

Finally, I took a resolute step toward the wall and carefully tugged at the clinging vines so as not to chip the paint in my intense desire to satiate my curiosity in revealing the hidden parts of the mural. The suckers let loose from the painted plaster reluctantly, clinging to the wall as though the ivy itself wished to hide the full image from my prying eyes, as if its sole purpose was the keep the mural hidden from inquisitive onlookers.

When at last I had the ivy in piles on the ground, and the rest of the mural was uncovered, I was no closer to understanding the meaning behind the images than I had been moments ago. I stood, blinking, brow creased in confusion, trying to piece together the disjointed story before my eyes.

"Who is the artist?"

I whirled to face the familiar voice behind me.

"Alesh!" My heart leaped into my throat. "What are you doing here?"

Unconcerned, Alesh stood, his head tilted back as he viewed the mural I'd uncovered, his hands resting on his waist, dark cheeks gleaming in the sun as he bit a lip in thought. His eyes were ringed red with fatigue, but they were the only indication he'd been creeping about into the small hours of the morning. A warm breeze ruffled the sleeves of his half-buttoned shirt.

"Did you follow me?"

He gave a distracted nod, his attention never leaving the mural. "Abi woke me. She worries for you."

I *had* woken her.

"Why didn't you make yourself known sooner?"

"I did not want to burden you, to, ah…"

When it was clear he couldn't think of the word he

wanted to say, I offered, "Intrude?"

"Yes, intrude. I did not want to intrude on your solitude." His gaze flicked to me for a moment as he nodded before returning to the mural.

I bit my lip to keep from smiling. The way Alesh had spoken the word, it sounded like "silly-tude."

I waved a hand at him. "Nonsense. I'm always glad for your company. After your outing last night, I didn't want to wake you." I didn't tell him I'd seen the image before, that I'd gone for a very deliberate walk, looking for it.

"You have found quite the mystery."

I sighed as I turned to the wall again. "Indeed. What are your thoughts? You're better suited to decipher its code than I."

He shook his head. "It is strange, no? In my years, I knew of other powers in this world, but I did not know what they looked like. That the artist should know all the stones—my staff, your necklace, and the diadem…it is strange."

It didn't escape my notice that he avoided acknowledging Elodie's possession of the diadem. The stone never should have ended up in her hands, and it wouldn't have if she hadn't made sure she was the only one left alive capable of wielding it. Minus Abi, of course, but it was safe to say the Chaos Wielder didn't know her sister had survived.

"And what are these, to the left?" Alesh pointed to the side of the mural, where I'd pulled the ivy from obscuring the rest of the image.

"I've been puzzling over that, too."

The center mural featured the three silhouetted figures

with each of the three talismans, and they were arranged over a depiction of Liron, but to the left…well, I wasn't quite sure *what* I was seeing.

Stars. Another planet far away that looked like a duplicate of Liron, smaller and with different land masses, though it was difficult to tell after so much of the paint had been peeled away by the determined ivy. Between the two planets, Liron and the other, there was a third circular object. A third planet? But this circle was entirely black, devoid of any features of land or sea. I wondered if there had once been more detail, but the paint had chipped away over time. Still, the rest of the mural had been well-maintained. Why let one portion fall into disrepair?

"This is curious," Alesh said as he stepped close to the wall. He pointed one long finger to two irregular, elongated shapes between Liron and the black circle.

"Those aren't just chipped bits?" I raised a brow.

"I do not think so."

I shook my head. I could make no sense of the scene on the left of the mural. Planets and stars and elongated vessels with no more significance than chipped paint to me.

"What about the other side?"

He swiveled to examine the rightmost part of the mural, a scene that made little more sense than the one on the left. Alesh shook his head, as baffled as I.

To the right, three figures appeared again—this time all three were clearly women, even though they were still silhouetted. The size of the mural on the right was smaller compared with the three silhouettes in the center, so they were of lesser immediate importance somehow. There was no sign of any of the three stones or…of much else, really. The silhouetted women were outlined by a shining white light and no more.

I didn't know what I was supposed to glean from this information. Was this some indication of what would happen, or what had happened? Had the stones originated with the three women? Were they the first sorceresses to walk Liron? Had Tarrowburn known of their existence?

"Useless," I muttered with a shake of my head. "Utterly useless."

I startled as bells clanged throughout the city, their peals deafening. I looked to Alesh. The last time we'd heard the bells, an announcement had followed. Sure enough, when the ringing stopped, a disembodied voice carried on the wind. How *did* they do that?

Alesh translated, "A show of unity. The emperor invites a single member of all households to the palace."

"A meeting?"

"A…celebration, I think." He listened to the words again before translating. "The night of the eclipse."

"Open gates to the palace?"

Alesh chewed the inside of his cheek, contemplating. "There is no better way to reach her."

"She knows we're here. She's alerted others to our presence. Is it not the perfect trap?"

"That is a risk we may have to take."

CHAPTER THIRTEEN

What Love Remembered
Quinn

Once I began speaking my endless regrets, all the times I wished I had acted differently, all the people I wished I could have saved instead of hurt, it was as though the floodgates of my life had opened. Reining the words in was no longer an option. Confessions kept coming, emotions I'd long shoved away flowing, as though resolved to make it past my mouth before I changed my mind and locked them away once more.

But when I finally finished, when at last the words grew sparse, the silence that followed was overwhelming.

"Is that all?" Niles asked.

"Truly, Ingram? Your first instinct is to mock me?" Anger flared in every muscle.

Niles closed his eyes for a moment, then folded his hands together, looking every bit as frustrated as I would have imagined, given our situation. He examined the ground before speaking. "I do not intend to mock. I just mean to ask, are you *sure* there's nothing else?"

"Of course there's nothing else. I would know if there were something more, no?" And yet, *blast it*. His intense stare forced me to sort through the memories once more, searching for something I must have somehow forgotten.

I couldn't fight the nagging sensation there *was* something I was missing. But what?

"Since you clearly know something I do not, I don't suppose the Saints would allow you to bestow a favor and give me a hint?"

Niles rubbed his forehead, looking pained. "I truly wish I could, but if you cannot remember her—"

Niles disappeared. No slow fading. No indication that he knew he was about to leave, that the Higher Ones were calling him. I blinked, and then he was…gone.

If you cannot remember her. If you cannot…remember… her.

Who? Who was I not—

Dark hair. A single white streak.

Bright eyes. Lips I longed to touch.

The next breath stabbed through my chest as I remembered who I'd forgotten. I remembered everything. In a torrent. A flood of memories with Reina's face, Reina's laugh, Reina's tears. Oh, God. Reina. The pain I'd caused her.

Her pain brought any chance at forgiveness to an entirely new plane. Where was she now? What was she doing? How much time had passed? The eclipse. The Chaos Wielder.

I jumped from where I'd been sitting and screamed into the empty blue sky above. Could the Saints even hear me past the confines of Kufataba?

"Send me back! Send me back *now!*" I kicked at the ground. I threw fists at a tree. I howled and roared like a child scolded for eating too many sweets. Then I pleaded.

"She needs me! Don't you understand?"

No one responded. I hadn't expected a response, but the resounding silence still stung. They wanted me to forgive myself, to allow myself the chance to live again, but I was a prisoner in this Saints-forsaken place, with no way of knowing how much time had passed and if Reina lived.

"I'm sorry," I finally said aloud. I sank to my knees. "I'm so sorry. I should have told her all of it. I should have confided in her when she asked. I should have been there for her."

No sooner had I said the words aloud than a furious windstorm swept from nowhere, the ground around me spitting chunks of grass and dirt upward as though the sky itself had demanded a tribute from the earth.

I pulled the neck of my tunic over my nose, covering my face so I might keep from being suffocated, then closed my eyes against the flying debris, stumbling as I tried to crouch and run to safety.

There was no safety to be had. As the ground fell apart, I tripped, feet scrambling for purchase as everything solid slipped away beneath me. Then I was falling into nothingness, into nowhere, into the blackness where I'd first become conscious of myself again.

The blackness where the ghosts lived.

Primal fear licked like fire through my veins.

Niles had said forgiveness was key. And I'd believed him.

What a cursed fool.

The ghosts never came. I waited in darkness, but the torture I expected, the pain I convinced myself was inevitable, never came.

After a small eternity waiting for *something* to happen, for Niles to return, for some light source to reappear, I began to suspect this was a new test. Finally, I pushed myself upright, my balance unsteady in the utter blackness. The dark was so complete, phantom colors and shapes began to swim across my vision. I forced my eyes closed, remembering how I'd been trained to fight blind. If I could fight blind, I could walk blind.

Slowly, I placed one foot forward, toeing my way through the darkness, fighting to keep my hands by my sides, to not grasp for physical boundaries in my reach. Reaching would serve to throw me off balance, especially if there was nothing to hold onto.

I closed my eyes and I walked, pace increasing slowly as I grew surer of my feet, steadier in my belief that this was what I was intended to be doing, that I was meant to push forward, to find my own way from the darkness.

All the while, it was Reina I saw behind closed eyes. Reina, who I had failed… My chest tightened. I hadn't failed her. I hadn't. Not yet. Not if there was still time. And if Niles was working to help me leave wherever this Saints-forsaken place was, then there was still time for something to be done. Hope was not lost. I had not failed her, my Reina.

When next I dared to open my eyes, the quality of the darkness surrounding me had changed. Still complete, yes, but no longer without boundaries. There was a sense of an echo in the space I now occupied, of walls and a floor. If I flung out an arm, I suspected I would feel cold stone beneath my fingers. I kept my hands by my sides. If I was still being tested, I would continue as was expected of me. Regardless, I closed my eyes again and walked forward, following the path I *felt* in front of me, focusing on Reina with every breath, every thought.

Reina was my compass. Do right by her. Do right by myself.

The thought shocked me. It was the first time I'd considered my own feelings without Niles's prompting. Of all the skills I'd been taught in the Order, exploring my emotions was not one of them. Now, as I traveled the path forward, I wondered how much time I'd wasted beneath Kufataba with stubborn declarations that what I wanted didn't matter.

It did. It mattered. *I* mattered.

The thought gave me an odd sort of comfort, like an internal warmth beneath my ribs. I almost felt that if I opened my eyes, I would see—

—exactly what I saw.

Eyes wide, I swallowed, a strange, desperate noise coming from my throat in the process. There was light… everywhere. I was surrounded by it, bathed in it; it was *in* me, originating from me.

There was no explanation for such a thing, but then, there

was no explanation for many of the things I had encountered in the last few days. Weeks? I couldn't say how long I'd been trapped.

I held my hand eye-level and turned it, watching the light swim beneath my skin, shimmer below the surface, and pulse in a glow from my fingertips.

"What does this mean?" I asked aloud, stunned.

I didn't expect an answer, but one echoed in my head regardless. A familiar voice.

I knew that voice. I'd heard it before.

The being of Kufataba.

Sacrifice made. Payment accepted. What are your requirements?

I spun, looking for the source of the voice, trying to locate its origin, but my attempt was useless. Like the first time I'd heard it, the voice spoke within my own mind.

"Requirements for what?" I asked.

Departure.

Requirements for departure? I was leaving, and I was to give Kufataba my requirements?

"I don't understand."

What do you require for your journey?

My journey. Kufataba was going to let me leave. I had been waiting for this moment for so long, but until this very moment, I wasn't sure I'd actually believed the cursed mountain would let me go.

"I could use a few weeks of my time back," I muttered to myself.

Denied.

"Right. I figured." I ran a luminescent hand across the back of my glowing neck and rubbed the tension from my muscles.

Yes, I was full of light and warmth in this strange cave, but oddly, I was much more aware of my body now than I had been before. I was hungry, tired, and every muscle ached as though I'd been back in my initial training for the Order.

What do you require for your journey? Three items.

"What are you able to supply?" I asked.

The mountain didn't reply. I ran scenarios through my head one after the next. What would I need? I had no way of knowing what the lands on the other side of the mountain would look like, how far away I was from Reina and Alesh, what they were now planning, or even if they were alive at all. How could I plan without knowing a single variable? Sure, I had gone on many an assignment with next to no provisions, but this was a far more important task than the Order had ever sent me on. This was the very fate of the world.

"I suggest a horse." I jumped at Niles's voice.

"Blazes, man! Give some warning!"

He had the audacity to smirk in amusement. "There was a time I never could have snuck up on you." He paused, seeming to consider whether to continue, before adding, "Not without a distraction, anyway."

Surely, he referred to the time he'd had an arrow pointed at my heart. Because I'd been preoccupied with Reina, I definitely had not heard him sneak up on us.

"Times have changed, I suppose. It helps that you're

dead and make no sound," I answered. "What are you doing here? I thought…"

I thought what? That he'd been punished? That he'd angered the Saints and would never return? That they'd somehow eliminated his very soul?

"They weren't happy. I didn't mean to mention her, but… it jogged your memory, and that was enough. I did what was needed." He took a breath, released it slowly. There was more he wanted to say, more he *couldn't* say. I knew the signs, his reluctance to meet my eyes, his roundabout manner of speaking that let on there was more to his words than what he was saying.

I didn't push. I didn't want to lose my…friend? Dare I call Niles Ingram a friend? How things had changed, indeed.

"Self-forgiveness looks good on you, D'Arturio. You clean up well."

I glanced back to my glowing form, illuminating the space around us, and grunted in reply.

Undeterred, Niles continued. "You need a horse. A fast one. You've got hundreds of miles to cover and not much time to do it." These were words I knew, words that contained one meaning, words that made sense. I preferred these kinds of words.

I nodded in understanding.

"Reina's medicine bag, with all its powders and concoctions."

I nodded again.

Then Niles opened his mouth and hesitated, at war with himself.

"You can't tell me the last item I need, can you?"

He shook his head, misery written across his features. If he didn't tell me the final item I needed, we risked losing all of Liron to chaos—not that it should matter to Niles as he was already dead. If he told me the final item I needed, he risked angering the Saints and losing his eternal soul.

The world or his soul? Which was more important?

Niles's eyes shifted to the walls around us, as though judging whether the mountain might hear him. He opened his mouth and took a breath as though to speak, then shook his head and pressed his lips tight again. Then he began to mime, his lips forming silent words as his hands crafted giant, erratic circles in the air.

I shook my head in confusion, brows drawn in concentration, trying to read what he was wildly attempting to convey with no luck.

Sculpture? Wind? Whirlwind?

I focused less on his arm movements, and more on the word he was mouthing.

Kay. Kay who? Kay—

No. Not Kay. Chaos. Chaos.

I glanced to the walls, unsure if I was allowed to speak the words he was trying to relay.

Chaos, I mouthed. *What about it?*

He nodded and held up a hand. Then he grew rigid and wrapped both hands around his abdomen and torso as though he'd been tied in rope.

I must tie up the Chaos Wielder?

Niles shook his head vehemently to my mouthed question

and mouthed back one word, then repeated it.

Mine—no, mind.

Mind? His mind?

Exasperated, he shook his head again and resumed mouthing the same word.

I growled.

What do you require for your journey? the mountain prompted again.

"I'm still thinking," I said, hoping the being who ran the mountain would buy that I needed more time and not grow suspicious that Niles was attempting to aid me when he wasn't permitted to do so.

Growing frustrated, Niles began to draw in the air with a finger.

B - I - N - D

Bind?

He nodded, then continued.

C - H - A - O - S

"You'll need something that will…" he prompted.

"I need something to bind the chaos," I said aloud, half a question to Niles, half a request to the mountain surrounding me.

Granted. What do you require on your journey? Two items.

Niles slumped with relief, leaning with hands on his knees, he let his head hang. If I had to guess, he suspected he would be punished again for the help he had given me, but what good was an eternal soul without the peace of mind brought about by saving Liron? What was there to do in eternity if the world you knew was forever lost to the horrors of chaos?

I spoke again, this time with more force, gaining confidence that I was making the correct decisions, taking the right steps.

"I need Moreina di Bianco's medicine supplies. Her fully stocked bag."

Granted. What do you require on your journey? One item.

I swallowed. A horse. Not any horse. A fast horse, Niles said. One horse came to mind. "I need Aeros, Moreina di Bianco's dapple mare who rides like the wind even if she acts a yearling. The horse was left in the stables in—"

Granted. Requests fulfilled.

I should have known I wouldn't need to specify where the horse had been left. The odds that Aeros remained there were slim, regardless.

With my requests granted, the light from my body began to fade—at least I would no longer be a human lantern—but a new light shone ahead. Dim, persistent, I could make out what I only assumed was an exit to the cave in which I stood.

"Niles?"

But no answer came.

I wondered at the curious pang in my chest. Was it possible to miss the ghost of a man I'd despised for so many years? I shook my head at the absurdity, placed one foot in front of the other, and move forward.

Where would I get the items I'd requested? Would someone deliver them to me? Would I find them in the next village? Were there villages beyond the mountain? How did any of this make sense?

When, at last, I made it to the mouth of the cave, steady moonlight illuminated miles of swaying grassland not unlike the meadow of my prison. The grasses here were longer, unadorned with flowers, but the resemblance was there.

Tears pricked the corners of my eyes at the sight. I hadn't thought to see life outside my prison—or anywhere—again. I'd thought…well, I'd thought I was doomed to be tormented forever.

Worse? I believed I deserved it.

I searched for the familiar crushing weight of guilt I'd carried in my chest for so long, but instead of finding it, I found a lightness—an understanding that I was human, that I'd done human things, that I deserved a chance, that I could still make a difference.

Thank the Saints for Niles and his persistence. I hoped he'd been welcomed into the afterlife with open arms. I hoped he was cele—

"Standing there like a daft mule isn't going to get you to Reina any faster."

I jumped. "Blast it! Stop sneaking up on me, Ingram."

Out here, Niles looked almost alive. Only the slight glow of his skin made it clear he was still in ghostly form.

"I thought you were done with me."

He scoffed. "And rob you of my company just when you were beginning to enjoy it? Never."

"I didn't say anything about enjoying your company."

"You don't have to. It's written all over your face."

Had I begun to think of Niles as a friend, for however brief a time? I fought the urge to punch the smirk off his face. If he was an apparition, I'd only end up on the ground without having laid a finger on him. I scowled, but somehow I didn't feel like my expression contained the intensity I normally reserved for Niles.

Finally, I countered, "Stop reading my face."

Niles gave a laugh. "Come. Your gifts are beyond the cavern walls."

Indeed, they were. Reina's bag stocked full of her medicines—powders, liquids, pastes in dozens of vials of all shapes and sizes, and the note I'd left for her when I left her behind at Irzan those weeks ago. I'd have to make sure she saw that later. The bag sat on the ground beside the horse I'd watched Reina adore nearly all her life. Aeros nickered as I approached, arching her neck around to nuzzle my shoulder as I stroked her withers.

"It's really her."

"I don't think the mountain deals in duplicates," Niles answered.

I ran a hand over a coin-sized spot on Aeros's mane that no longer grew thanks to an accident she'd had in the paddock when she was five. I pushed aside the thick gray hair to better see the white skin of the scar it hid.

Reina had arrived at my house out of breath that day, almost unable to speak. She'd flung open the front door without so much as a knock, grabbed my hand, pulled me from where I'd been helping to bring in the firewood, and hauled me back out into the street. She hadn't let go until we'd reached the paddock.

Then I'd spent the next twenty minutes working the mare's neck free from the gate while Reina kept her calm and plied her with applikens and brown sugar. The gash had run deep but was narrow and healed easily once Reina and her mother were able to tend to it. Still, Aeros was left with a scar that kept her mane from growing in that one spot.

And here Aeros stood, the same horse, the same scar. I rubbed her withers lightly, feeling a connection to Reina simply by standing beside an animal she loved almost unnaturally. Reina had always had a connection with the world around her, plant and animal alike.

"I'd give anything to hear about your journey here, horse. I can imagine the tales you'd have." I stroked her neck again, and she nudged my shoulder when I stopped. "Don't worry," I murmured. "You'll care for me, and I'll care for you. Isn't that what she always said, that girl of yours?"

"Are you going to hug the horse all night or can we maybe…" Niles motioned both hands forward as though he might urge me on by sheer will alone.

"Now I'm tempted to hug the horse all night just to irk you." I put my face to Aeros's side and breathed in the musty scent of horse and earth.

Niles extended hands outward and turned. "I should have known. I really should have. I taught you poorly. You're picking up my habits."

I laughed—a real laugh, a sound I hadn't made in a long time. "Come," I said. "I yield. Let's get to Reina."

And for once, hope lighter than a bird filled my chest. I

had Aeros. I had Reina's bag.

"Ingram, wait. Where's the third item? The way to bind the chaos?"

Niles peered beside the open bag, then shoved his hands in the pockets of his tunic and shrugged. "I suspect it'll turn up when you need it."

"You suspect?!"

"What shall we do? Go back through Kufataba? Tell the mountain to pay up?"

I shuddered at the thought, the air on my back instantly cold with the remembrance that the mountain lay behind me.

"Onward, then," I agreed, but I spared Nile's an extra glance. What wasn't he telling me?

I cinched Reina's bag shut, then pulled it over my shoulders and tightened the straps. How had someone so slight carried so much weight? Had her bag been packed with stones?

Then I turned back to Aeros, who had begun to lazily mouth the long strands of grass.

"Fiermi."

"What now?" Niles said, exasperated.

I pinched the bridge of my nose, already anticipating the pain the upcoming days would bring. I spoke my next words slowly and clearly. "Why didn't you think to specify I'd need a bridled, saddled horse?"

CHAPTER FOURTEEN

The Visitor
Reina

Abi agreed the celebration at the palace would offer our best chance to gain entrance to the palace, but I still wasn't so sure. It felt like the exact kind of opportunity the Chaos Wielder would take to make certain she had us cornered in her own home, and too much a coincidence that her event would occur on the night of the eclipse.

"But she doesn't know we're after the diadem," Abi countered when I brought up my concerns. "So even if she thinks you'll be at the palace, she's going to expect you to try to destroy her, not steal her crown."

"If we're there during waking hours, how are we supposed to take anything from her? Wasn't the plan to go in while she's sleeping, the *only* time the diadem isn't on her head?" I rubbed my left temple and the spot over my eye. I was working on what quickly wanted to become a wretched half-headache. I'd need to see if I could find basil and lavender oils before the day was out.

"We go *into* the palace for the celebration. Then we wait until night. There is a place to hide, yes? Surely Abi must know." Alesh watched Abi, waiting for her eyes to light with the possibilities.

Abi nodded enthusiastically. "There's at least a dozen hiding spots I can think of off the top of my head. The stable has a tack room that smells like dried alfalfa and capsicol nuplums. No one really goes in there, especially at night, and there's a direct entrance to the palace through an underground tunnel, but it leads to the throne room where the biggest part of the celebration will be. Which…is the opposite side of the palace from the royal chambers. So, you might not want to hide there unless you have a good reason to travel the halls after dark. The guards will be on the lookout for anything suspicious, especially after any sort of ball."

"A ball? I thought—"

"Oh, for sure. Elodie wouldn't miss a chance to have a party. If she's calling for a celebration, you can bet it will be a ball with lots of food and music and dancing."

I heaved a sigh.

Abi tapped her fingers as she tallied the other hiding places. "If you don't want to hide in the stable, there's the weapons room, the artist's loft, the pantry closet, the second pantry—and that one's got a giant cold room where Chef keeps all the meats, the royal dress room, and the library. Actually, the library might be a good place. It's closer to the royal chambers and there are plenty of nooks to hide in." Abi paused to stare at me a moment. "Are you all right? You look pale."

I put additional pressure on my temple. "This is turning into a full-scale intelligence operation worthy of the Order."

"The what?"

I shook my head. "Nothing. It's just quickly turning into a plan with a lot of details is all."

There was, indeed, to be a ball. The streets practically sang with excitement. Merchants were out by the hundreds, the marketplace having extended the length of the city overnight in anticipation of the purchases that would soon be made.

Alesh and I returned to Abi and the inn after a brief visit with Djana, who was *not* pleased at our unexpected appearance, and who made it known she was not yet done crafting the diadem. I wasn't sure Djana could complete the project. Behind her narrowed eyes and frequent scowls, she'd taken insult I might suggest she couldn't finish the work on time. Shining financial incentive from the gold in the treasury helped brighten her attitude, even if she still hissed in displeasure about the time constraints.

I stood at the window of our room, looking down at the street below, letting a breeze cool the perspiration from my skin. I was glad to be out from the crowds. The whole of Ivirreh was in the streets today, preparing for the emperor's big event.

Maybe it was the crowded street, or the fact that my attention had been drawn to a number of merchants setting up stalls directly across from the inn, but I didn't hear the first tap on our door right away. When it sounded again, Alesh, Abi, and I exchanged looks of confusion. With the three of us *in* the room, who could be at the door?

My hand went to the talisman beneath the neckline of my dress, a small comfort, even if I wouldn't use it. Relying on its inexplicable warmth had become a habit. The smooth stone was no less comforting now. Alesh opened the door with confidence and a smile, no sign of the hesitation that hung heavy in the air.

A man leaned against the thick wood of the door jamb, his height and bulk taking up the entirety of its frame, the light in his hazel eyes and the smirk on his face filling in whatever space his body hadn't. Thick brown hair looked recently hand-tousled and a carefully sculpted beard glinted with gold on his square jaw. Mid-twenties, if I had to guess, though a solid air of arrogance made him seem older.

He wore the same style clothing most of the local men wore, tight breeches over toned thighs, a loose, white shirt half-open, revealing a muscled chest as tan as his face, lightly covered with golden curls that instantly reminded me to keep my eyes pinned to his face. One might have thought I'd be used to the style by now, but one would be wrong.

"Yes? How can I help you?" Alesh asked.

"I think, my friend, the question is not so much how you can help me, but much more how *I* can help you." His drawl was a practiced tone, thick with notes of honeyed manipulation.

He pushed off the jamb and stood, moving past Alesh, entering our room without so much as an invitation, the shine of his boots emphasizing his full swagger.

"Excuse me. You cannot be in our room, sir!" I exclaimed,

feigning exaggerated insult.

My act didn't need much exaggeration. That a man would strut into a room that wasn't his without even a semblance of an invitation was outright offensive.

Already near the desk, he turned, placed one hand in his pocket, then leaned against the desktop for support. "Ah, and yet, here I stand!"

Alesh took a hard look at him, eyes narrowing, his dark face scowling in resentment at being taken advantage of all too easily. He grabbed the staff by the bedside, with thoughts to wield its magic or to look more intimidating, I couldn't be sure.

As though sensing Alesh's mood, the stranger raised his hand in deference. "All right, old man. I mean no harm. The name's Mical Raumati, and I believe I can be of assistance."

Abi stood beside me, quiet as she watched the exchange. She was still dressed in the clothes she wore whenever we were out—a loose top, dirty and pants torn at one knee, with her blond locks shoved beneath a cap. I put a protective hand around her shoulder.

"We are not in need of assistance," Alesh said.

"On the contrary, from what I've seen, you are. Your hauler is dead, and you need someone who can bring your goods to market covertly. Just so happens, I can be very covert when the need arises." He winked—had the audacity to wink—at me.

"You killed him." The words escaped my lips without a thought.

Mical had the good sense to look offended as he recoiled,

face a mask of horror. "Saints, no, I didn't kill him! I'm all for making coin in…non-traditional ways, but killing isn't on my list of approved methods to attaining riches."

"Then how did you know he was dead? And how did you know he was working with us?" I challenged.

"Anyone with a pair of eyes could see what was going on."

We'd been secretive in our arrangements, stealthy in operation, which meant he was lying. I narrowed my eyes at him.

Alesh intervened, attempting to squelch the conversation before it could go further. He stepped forward and gestured toward the door. "Again, my niece, her son, and I have no need of your assistance. We will see you out now."

Mical ignored Alesh's invitation to leave, instead choosing to cross his arms as the desk groaned under the shifting of his weight.

"Look, I can see how you might be skeptical, but I make a point of knowing what takes place on a regular basis around here. I keep watch, and when I see an opportunity, I take it. You lot have been *very* interesting to watch. I'm not sure what your end goal is, but you're making a lot of money getting goods to market no one else seems to be able to get ahold of. There's quite the stir at the marketplace, and the produce you once provided is sorely missed these last few days.

"Now, I'm not saying I need to know where it comes from, or your methods of getting it into the empire, but if you need a new go-between, I'm your man."

"That's extortion!" Abigayle exclaimed, cheeks flushed with anger.

"Easy, boy. I'm not exactly threatening to hand you over to the authorities now, am I?" He barely offered her a glance.

"I think you did just that, right now," Alesh said.

Mical lifted his eyebrows. "Not what I meant, I assure you."

As if assurances from a perfect stranger meant anything at all. Now that he mentioned he'd been watching us, his face was familiar. I'd seen him in the inn's dining room more than once, but had never given much thought to him, figuring he was no more than another of the inn's guests staying in one of the numerous rooms for rent.

"We have no more need of a hauler, and we're out of the produce business." I did not elaborate on why, no mention of our raiding the treasury and attaining all the funds we could possibly need.

Mical furrowed his brows. "Forgive me for saying so, but I'm not entirely sure I believe you."

"Believe me or don't. It makes no difference. You'll be leaving now, or I'll be talking with the proprietor about exactly what kind of rabble she allows on her premises." I carefully coated my words with ice. Quinn would be proud. Shocked, but proud.

Instead of looking alarmed, Mical threw his head back and laughed. "Oh, she already knows! You can believe that." He rubbed a hand over his short beard before conceding. "All right. All right. Plucky, I see. I'm leaving. But should you need my services in the future"—he winked at me again as he pushed off the desk— "my offer stands. Tabra, the barkeep, knows how to contact me."

"Don't expect us to come calling anytime soon," I replied.

"Or ever," Abi added.

Mical smirked over his shoulder. "Point made, young sir. I'm leaving."

When he crossed the threshold to the hall again, Alesh closed the door softly behind him. I would have made a point of slamming it, but Alesh was far more reserved than I, or he wanted to avoid *more* attention.

My blood heated with anger. If not for the crowded streets below, I might have walked to cool my nerves. Alesh held up a finger as he leaned against the door, waiting silently as if counting long moments in his head to ensure no prying ears remained close enough to our door to hear his words.

Finally, he said, "We cannot stay here. I will find a new room today."

"You won't have any luck." Abi threw her cap to the bed, her hair tumbling down her back with the motion. "Not since the ball has been announced. There will be people coming from every part of the empire to take part."

Blazes, she was right.

"I will try," Alesh said. He met my eye. "Lock the door, slide the desk over it when I am gone. I do not trust him."

"You're looking for a new inn now? Immediately?"

"You won't find one. It's already too late," Abi quipped.

"If he has been watching us, who else has been watching? Who else might know something? We cannot risk it." The worry on Alesh's brow had my stomach lurching. "I do not trust him, this Mical. I do not like that he knows where to find us."

I nodded. "Be safe, Alesh."

Abi picked up one of her books from where she'd piled them on the floor and flopped on the bed. Her nose was already buried in the pages when she said, "Be safe, Great-Uncle Alesh."

He grinned at her, eyes crinkled with lines. "Be on your best behavior, young man!"

She giggled, then Alesh was gone, and I moved the desk into place behind the locked door to wait for his return.

Why hadn't I *seen* Mical's appearance in our lives? I couldn't help but wonder why whatever force that drove my second sight hadn't deemed that bit of information worth relaying, why a mural that relayed nothing worth knowing should be more important.

Hours passed in Alesh's absence, during which Abi and I played cards, nibbled on snacks and fruits we'd bought in the market earlier that morning, and dozed in the stagnant heat of the afternoon.

When Alesh returned, to both his relief and ours, we'd seen no sign of Mical or anyone else who might have taken an interest in us while he was gone.

As anticipated, there were no rooms to be had, not in the immigrants' quarter and not in the more affluent parts of Ivirreh. It was as though the city's population had doubled overnight.

Abi shrugged. "I told you you'd find nothing. It's not

every day the palace doors open, so when they do, there's always a push to see who will be let in first. Families that are supposed to send one member of the household will often try to send two or three to gain influence."

Alesh sighed as he took a seat by the desk and sat. He bent and ran both hands over his more-gray-than-black kinked hair.

"If you see him again—either of you—we leave, room or no room."

CHAPTER FIFTEEN

Cunning New Recruit
Reina

We did not see Mical Raumati again. Not in the hallway, not in the dining room, and not on the streets. A small relief, but knowing he was out there somewhere, watching us unseen, had me on edge.

So the last thing I expected was for Abi to suggest seeking him out.

"I've been thinking." She didn't look up from her book as she pulled another dried stone fruit from the plate beside her on the bed and popped it into her mouth, chewing carefully before spitting out the pit and slipping it back to the plate.

"Have you?" I asked, almost amused. I uncapped a glass bottle from the local apothecary and sniffed at it, wincing at the aromatic bite of something the locals called *neemet*, which was supposed to be good for helping to dispel toxins from the body.

It wasn't that I thought Alesh and I wouldn't succeed once our magic was swapped back to normal, but the growing ache had moved from my shin to my thigh, and I was on edge, becoming steadily more uneasy as the days wore on. It couldn't hurt to use the neemet in an attempt to break up the snake venom lurking somewhere in my body.

I gave a long sigh.

We'd been doing too much sitting in the room, too much waiting—waiting for time to pass, waiting on our diadem, waiting on the ball attire we'd ordered, waiting for the ball itself, waiting for the eclipse. Sometimes I wondered if we were waiting to lose and for the world to fall into complete and utter chaos.

I remained convinced I would go mad if I had to wait for one more thing.

"I think we should find that Mical."

I turned sharply to Abi, pulled from my thoughts of snake venom and chaos.

"Are you mad?"

"Hear me out."

I raised a brow. "I'm listening."

Abi sat up on the bed, pushing her book aside. "We need a way into the palace for the celebration. One member per household, yes, but which households won't be going at all? We need to know. I mean, if you get to the gates and pronounce you're representing the Gyllhren family, what happens if one of the Gyllhrens is already inside? Probably nothing. Probably, they'll turn you away, but what if they don't? What if that's part of Elodie's plan and the guards take that opportunity to investigate the second members of households? We could get caught over something very, very stupid."

I chewed my lower lip in thought. "And how could Mical help with that? We don't know him. Or where his loyalties lie."

"Well. I did some…investigating."

"Investigating" was Abi's way of saying she slipped out and snuck around the city while Alesh and I checked in the with goldsmith, retrieved food, or any number of other tasks that sent us out.

I frowned, putting all my energy into looking at her as my own mother once would have to me. I didn't often break the rules back then, but when I did, there was always *that* look, the one I hoped I was giving Abi now.

"Why would you leave the safety of the inn?"

She swung her arms into the air. "What difference does it make? He knows where we are anyway!"

She had a point, but it didn't make me feel any better.

"I thought I recognized him. Not right away, but later. I started thinking about why he looked so familiar to me. And then I remembered."

She glowed as she sat straight, obviously satisfied with herself that she'd made the connection.

"He used to work at the palace. Not one of the close guards, but he was in the alternate rotation, and he'd show up for some of the less important positions. Until he got sacked anyway."

I coughed suddenly, half in surprise at Abi's words, half choking on my own saliva as I swallowed.

"Gambling. Papa didn't allow anyone in the guard to gamble. Too much trouble, he said. Too easy to be bribed if you went into debt, and he said he needed to make sure the palace guard was un-bribable."

Somehow, Mical's history as a gambler fit perfectly with the image of the swaggering figure that sought us out days ago.

"Why on Liron do you know so much about the guard at eleven years of age?" I asked.

Abi shrugged and cast her eyes to the bed. She pulled at a loose thread in the woven blanket. "I liked learning about the empire. I liked knowing the reasons for the things my parents did and why. I mean, I knew I wouldn't be in charge, but I always dreamed of helping somehow, of being useful."

Oh, but Abi *would* be in charge. At least, if we succeeded.

"I have a difficult time imagining you not being useful," I said, letting a genuine smile cross my lips. "I swear, some days, I think the Saints themselves sent you to us."

Abi's face lit.

"So how would Mical, the notorious gambler, help us?" I prompted.

"Oh, well, he *must* still know some of the guard, right? So he's got to know some way we can get in without being turned away or interrogated. I imagine he can get the lists of households who have already replied with their acceptance and households who have declined. There won't be many who decline, but there're bound to be a few."

Her words clicked into place. "You want us to use those names. Names from households that have declined?"

"Exactly. But he'll have to get the response changed on the palace end, too, so those families will show as accepting instead of declining."

"Hmm."

It wasn't a bad idea. But I didn't trust Mical. My first instinct when he had shown up in our room was to throw him out. He was a pompous cad who thought he could turn a quick coin by taking advantage of others. I didn't relish being the end that was taken advantage of.

And yet…

"Hmm? What does that mean?" Abi's eyes were bright. She leaned in as though to decipher my body language.

"We'll run it past Alesh," I agreed.

"Yes!" She pumped a fist in the air.

"Curb your enthusiasm," I warned. "It's a good plan—an exceptionally good one, but it's not foolproof. We'll discuss it further."

"I know, I know. But I'm *helping*. And after the last few months, that feels really good."

Naturally, Alesh agreed that Abi's idea had merit. Naturally, too, I was sent to the bartender to ask for Mical.

"He is more likely to respond quickly if the pretty young woman requests his presence," Alesh had said. I returned the sentiment with a scowl, but I saw his point.

Tabra, the inn's barkeep and proprietor, was a tall woman with a mop of dark curls pinned to the top of her head, and sleeves folded neatly to her elbows. Always in motion regardless of how busy or idle the dining room was, she was not easy to catch inconspicuously.

When I finally managed to pin her down during the

dining room's emptiest hours, she hovered over a checklist at the bar, a pencil in one hand, comparing figures to a slip of paper in her other hand.

She mumbled to herself with a shake of the head, not seeming to notice me. If I had to guess by the frantic scrawling on her paper, she'd probably muttered something about the latest shipment of ale or wine being too expensive. It was always the way of things.

"Excuse me," I said, as I pushed closer, sliding into a seat at the bar.

"Och, yeah? Northerner, then. What'll you have?" she said, matching my tongue right away.

"Oh, um, I'm not…" I'd intended to turn her down, but I hadn't had a drink in forever. Saints knew I could use one. "Surprise me."

She gave a husky chuckle, swiped the papers and pencil off the bar, and filled a glass with a vibrant purple liquid before handing it to me.

"I like a challenge. You seem like a queballah wine type of woman if ever I saw one. That'll be two-forty."

I slid the coins across the worn wood of the bar top and nodded my thanks. Gingerly, I sniffed the liquid before sipping at it, even as Tabra watched to gauge my reaction.

I took a mouthful and swallowed, the queballah setting fire to my insides as it slid to my stomach, a warmth that passed to my muscles almost immediately.

"That's…quite good." And it was. The drink had been mulled with a handful of spices and nuts, so many subtle notes of flavors I couldn't begin to pick out, but it was delicious and the first unnecessary pleasure I'd allowed myself in as long as I could remember.

"Queballah sunwine, a southern specialty. You can't get this up north, so it's always a welcome surprise when someone from the far north comes for a visit." Tabra returned to the glasses behind the bar, inspecting them for chips, wiping the insides, and placing them back on the shelf again.

I raised my glass in a toast to her and took another sip, then focused on the purpose to my visit at the bar. "I understand you know Mical Raumati?"

Tabra set the glass she held onto the bar, crossed her arms, and leaned forward on her elbows. She licked her lips and smiled.

"I know Mical as well as anyone can know him. Are you looking for…?" One thick, dark eyebrow rose as she smirked and cleared her throat. "I mean…" She pushed a sleeve off one shoulder, gave her shoulder two shakes, and ran her tongue across her teeth.

Heat flooded my cheeks when I realized the meaning behind her actions.

"Oh! Oh, Saints, no! I just need to talk to him. He said… he said you would know how to get ahold of him."

Tabra let loose a wide smile and an open laugh, a deep, husky bark made louder by the closeness of the wooden beams on the ceiling and the floor.

"Shame, that. He's…well, he's well-liked. And he knows his way. If you change your mind."

"I won't."

"Very well. Who should I tell him asks?"

"Room 2B. He'll know."

She gave another knowing smile, as though she was quite sure I was looking for Mical for all the reasons she thought and not for reasons of my own. Then she disappeared behind a swinging, wooden door into a room somewhere behind the dining room, leaving me to my drink and my imagination.

Sitting at the bar, drinking my queballah sunwine, my thoughts drifted to Quinn. Was it because Tabra had insinuated certain things about Mical? Or was it because I was alone at the bar in the empty dining room in a time when I was so rarely alone these days? There always seemed to be something to do since we'd arrived in Ivirreh and, other than the time I'd slipped out to see the mural, I hadn't been alone outside of room 2B in forever.

I rubbed my eyes. I hadn't even been alone when I'd gone to see the mural, either, had I? No, Alesh had followed me even then. Saints, I missed solitude. I missed home. I think I even missed Irzan at this point. But mostly? Mostly, I missed Quinn.

Quinn had known what to say and when to say it. I smiled at the thought. Maybe not always how. Quinn struggled with words, but he always knew what I needed, even if he didn't communicate it well.

Once, when I was twelve, I'd unexpectedly started my flow during lessons at school. Having assisted my mother on so many of her calls, I knew well what it was, and I'd expected it someday, if not exactly then. Nevertheless, I didn't know how to take care of it, and so I ended up trying to hide the blood staining my skirts until I could go home.

In the meantime, Theodor Gerr noticed and tortured me mercilessly until Quinn stepped in and punched him square in the jaw, knocking him to the ground in one go. It was the one time I'd seen Quinn fight before he left Barnham at sixteen. Perhaps it was a premonition of the fighter he would become.

Then he gave me his coat to tie around my waist and walked me home. My cheeks burned in embarrassment the whole way, but Quinn, at thirteen, with his voice only yet half-dropped, had insisted it was nothing to be embarrassed of and that his mother had always suffered something awful each month, so he was plenty familiar with what was going on.

When I got home, my mother welcomed me with open arms, drew a warm bath, and treated me to cheese-stuffed sweet peppers for supper and spiced applikens for dessert. I didn't return to school for three days.

Quinn, in the meantime, stopped by every day with scraps of cinnamon bread from the bakery and his mother's homemade sweet cheese spread to top them with. He'd stand on the doorstep of our cottage beneath the kissing blooms, shuffle his feet awkwardly, hand me the warm, delicious-smelling bundle, and give me a list of what I missed at school before ducking his head and turning around for home again. Quinn D'Arturio had always known what to do to make things better.

I cleared the thickness gathering in my throat and the tear threatening to crest the rim of my eye. Quinn would have already had a plan for removing the Chaos Wielder from the throne. He might have even already done it, had he still been with us. But he wasn't with us. And instead of fighting to keep him, I'd let him sacrifice himself to please the vengeful Kufataba gods. I hadn't even fought. I could have—should have—done more.

Absently, I rubbed at the scar the Chaos Wielder had branded into my chest just above my heart. It still itched. I'd done what I could to keep the skin from scarring horribly, but it was still there, tight, pink skin unhappy with the mess that had been made of it. Someday, when I regained my powers of life, I would get rid of that scar. I might keep every other scar in my growing collection, but that one would go.

I hadn't expected my words to reach Mical quickly, so when the solid bulk of his body slid onto the barstool beside me, I almost drew back in surprise. He was clothed in a different shirt, a midnight blue silk this time, but the front was still left open, exposing his broad chest covered in light, downy curls. Inwardly, I cursed for letting his chest catch my eye, then reminded myself it was merely the southern style that threw me.

"When Tabra said there was a raven-haired beauty at the bar asking for me, I hoped it would be you."

Though I shouldn't have let his words surprise me, they did. I struggled for a response.

"I had a feeling I'd hear from you sooner or later," he said, revealing a wide grin as he leaned one arm on the bar. His eyes dropped briefly, making me feel a bit like a lamb at auction, before meeting my gaze once more. He cocked his head to one side. "I must admit, I'm rather glad it was sooner."

I stared at him through bored, half-lidded eyes, hoping they looked unamused rather than inviting. Finally, I found the only words I could think to say. "Don't flatter yourself."

A hearty laugh rumbled in his barrel of a chest. "I like you."

Then he gave a quick wave and a nod to Tabra, who had returned to the bar, though she was keeping her distance, allowing us some semblance of privacy for the conversation at hand. Without a word, she nodded, filled a glass twice the size of mine with a foamy orange brew, placed it in front of him, then left once again.

"Yell if you need me," she said before disappearing through the door again.

"You're here rather quickly. Did you camp on the roof?" I took a sip of the queballah, enjoying how it loosened my muscles ever so slightly.

Mical took a long swig from his glass, careful to keep the foam from coating his mustache or beard. "I'd love to take credit for a brilliant idea such as setting up camp on the inn's roof, but I cannot say I did. I'm never far, though."

"So you live close."

He squinted his eyes and wobbled one hand in the air. "I live where the work is. Sometimes close."

"Well, it turns out my…uncle and I might have need of your services after all."

Mical grinned again, nearly bouncing in his seat at the prospect of lining his pockets with coin.

"I knew you'd call. I mean, I couldn't *know,* but I hoped

it might be the case. Which is why I introduced myself that day, of course."

"Was that an introduction?" I scoffed. "It was a truly terrible first impression."

"I agree. I could have done better. I left without even managing to get your name. And me? Mical Raumati? Not catching the name of a beautiful young woman? Unheard of."

I resisted rolling my eyes as I stared at him. Was this the person Abigayle thought we could trust despite his history of gambling and questionable service? He was a shameless flirt. Worse even than Niles Ingram certainly more confident.

Mical was like Niles and Brigantino rolled into one. Large, imposing, confident, and entirely too charming for his own good. It didn't sit well.

I debated giving a pseudonym, but the moment passed, and it made no sense to give a potential ally a false name.

"Reina," I said. "My name is Reina."

He gave a half bow from his seat, locks of chestnut hair swaying forward with the motion. "It is, as ever, a pleasure to meet you, Reina…"

"Don't push your luck. Reina is as much as you'll get." I took another sip of my wine.

"Then I shall have to guess a surname. How delightful. Reina Bella. It fits, no?"

I shook my head. I was not going to pursue this ridiculous conversation. "Do you wish to know what the job entails or not?"

"All work, I see. Hmm. So Reina Somber, then."

I slid from my barstool, standing. "This was a mistake. I should have known."

Mical put a hand on my forearm and gave a gentle squeeze. "No, please. I jest. It's what I do. I want to hear about the job. I swear to you I'm good for it. Whatever it is."

I paused, letting his words talk me out of my instinct to flee, to forget him, to make our own way into the ball. If he could provide us with the information Abi thought he could attain, he was, indeed, an asset. But was he not also a risk? He was flippant and unfocused, more intent on wooing me than gaining the details of the job he claimed to want so badly.

Reluctantly, I sat once more, rearranging the layers of skirts over my legs again. "I've been told you've a contact at the palace, that you once worked there."

He paused in his next sip, stilling, then putting the glass down, sip untaken. He turned to face me, all humor gone from his features. He no longer reminded me of Niles. The seriousness that had replaced his jesting now reminded me instead of Quinn.

"Your task involves the palace?"

My heart leaped. I swallowed, forcing myself not to run back to the room, pack up, and leave. This was where Mical realized the opportunity he had to turn us in for a reward, wasn't it? A man who looked to fill his pockets would also look for whoever might help him fill them overflowing, and if he'd heard the announcements given by the emperor, it shouldn't take long for him to suspect we were the foreigners she wanted captured or dead. Quinn would take a measure of the man before committing to working together. Quinn would ensure he could trust an ally.

I licked my lips, hesitating. "If I say yes, will you run to the emperor now, or wait a week to ensure you first get paid by us and then again by the emperor?"

"You misread me." Offended, Mical pulled back, dark brows drawn over eyes that no longer danced with amusement, lips pulled into a frown.

"Do I?" I pushed. "Truly? If a man thinks it appropriate to seek out employment in…less than savory ways such as you did when you came to us to begin with, what else might he consider for coin?"

"Bollocks, I don't need the job this badly." He swallowed the remainder of his ale in one go, placed the glass with a thud that should have shattered it back on the bar, then stood and gave a single nod. "Good luck with whatever your plans might be. Sounds like you'll need it."

This was the reaction I'd hoped to see. I played the game the way I thought Quinn might, taking measure of a man before truly offering him the job. Mical had passed.

"Mical," I said before he could turn. "Wait."

He stood silent, a raw energy pulsing within his veins. For a moment, I could see what Tabra saw in him, what she assumed every woman saw. Mical reminded me of the Ishkal gray cougars that roamed the very northern borders of Castilles—sleek, powerful, refined. Like most cats, he was easily offended, but he operated by his own code, his own morals. I could work with someone of morals.

A muscle twitched in his jaw, his teeth clenched as though

to keep himself from insulting me the way he probably wanted to.

"I'm sorry," I said. "It was… a test."

He turned his gaze on me, smoldering eyes glittering as they assessed the truth behind my words. I fought the urge to shrink beneath those eyes, and forced myself to sit straighter, be taller, be who I needed to be, who he needed me to be in order to make this work.

Finally, he said, "A test."

"How were we to know if we could trust you? Even you must admit the way you chose to introduce yourself was rather unconventional. So, yes, to take the measure of the man inside, I goaded you to see what you might find offensive."

Something in his expression softened as he viewed me. He leaned against the barstool but did not sit. Instead, he crossed his arms to his broad chest, a chest now at eye-level. Then he gave a slow, deliberate smile, and I realized my eyes had strayed there again.

"You know, there are better ways to take a measure of a man." He nodded toward the door where Tabra had disappeared. "Tabra could tell you."

This time, I addressed the obvious flirtation instead of ignoring it. "Try elsewhere. My heart is taken. Are you interested in the job?"

A grin split his face, dissipating the tension. "I am. But unless you want Tabra and the entirety of the pub to know as well, I suggest we take this conversation elsewhere. The evening rush is coming."

CHAPTER SIXTEEN

Looking for Signs
Quinn

Riding was a lot easier once I stole a saddle. I wasn't proud of myself, and I didn't like that I'd taken something from someone without payment in return.

But times were desperate, and the mountain hadn't been generous enough to put coin or food inside Reina's fully stocked medicine bag, so I was on my own. Even so, my thighs burned from the days I'd gone without stirrups or a bridle, and I was an expert horseman. Thank the Saints for it.

Niles continued to needle me about my actions regardless of their necessity. "Do you think their daughter will be crushed in the morning when she discovers her palfrey's saddle missing?"

The sun had just crested the horizon, sending rays into my bleary eyes. So far, Aeros hadn't minded pushing both late into the night and in the early hours before the sun rose, but Niles was on a mission to make sure I knew *he* minded.

"I mean, it's a beautiful morning when most honest people would still be sleeping, or at the very least milking their goats and collecting eggs and preparing for the day. But you, you're already flying across the land on a mare with stolen tack."

"You won't make me feel poorly about this."

Niles's lip curled in amusement. He alternated between walking and simply showing up wherever it was I paused at times. "Are you so sure?"

"Yes. Not all of us can wish ourselves where we need to be."

At that, he glowered a little. "It's not like I prefer it this way."

I laughed. "What's it like to be dead anyhow? Is it like under the mountain? Is it like what I felt?"

"I couldn't say," he said dryly. "It's not as if I can see inside your head to measure your experience."

Aeros flung her head in a circle, annoyed with Niles's sudden appearance near her face. His ghostly presence kept the horse on edge. She didn't mind his figure at a distance, but whenever he got too close, she'd dance beneath me and throw her head upwards, eyes rolling back in their sockets.

"Could you *please* stop making the horse nervous? I swear you're doing it intentionally."

He dropped back. "I'm not doing it on purpose. If you'll remember, that horse never liked me anyway."

For good reason, I wanted to reply. Instead, I clamped my jaw and shook my head. "How much farther have we to travel?"

"The Empire capital is a few days' ride yet."

I glanced to the quickly lightening sky. "And the eclipse?"

"I'm no astronomer. Your best bet will be to speak to someone in one of the cities. There's bound to be celebrations planned around the event. Superstitions galore."

It would be more difficult to gain information this far south without someone to interpret, but I held out hope I might find someone who knew the northern tongue or even Ndoyo. Cities all around Liron were good for that at least. The diversity found within usually made it easy to blend in and disappear. Hiding in plain sight. Brigantino was excellent at applying the technique.

I wondered where he was now, and if he'd yet healed from his injury. If Ywelo was fighting tooth and nail to keep him from coming after us again. He would insist. And yet, I suspected, in a fight against her, he would lose. It was enough to bring a smile to my face and a longing to my heart.

I'd see them again. I just needed to get to Reina and Alesh. I took a single glance at Niles trailing slightly behind and nudged Aeros into a canter.

We reached the city of Emborid hours later. At least, Niles said it was the city of Emborid. As I had no map and knew nothing about the Elorin Empire, I took his word for it. Since being dead, he seemed to be more honest, all things considered.

The sun was high in the sky when we first set foot in the city, beads of sweat gathering at my temples as the air grew warmer through the course of the morning. The city was squat, with small clay buildings that appeared to have sprung up from the ground itself. The grassland gave way to a thick red dirt from which the buildings had been crafted, brick by sunbaked brick. The people were much like I expected, dark-skinned, dark-eyed, wary of a stranger, but welcoming despite their hesitation.

If there was one thing that surprised me most about the city of Emborid, it was that no one spoke the northern tongue. Not a single person. Still, through hand gestures and stick drawings in the dirt, I was at least able to determine the date…and I didn't like what I discovered.

First, we'd gone entirely too far in the wrong direction. When Niles had said we needed to travel south, what'd he'd neglected to specify was that south should have been south-west. As a result, we were now two extra days from the heart of the Empire.

Second, there was less than a week until the eclipse. Six days and thirteen hours until Andra lined up behind Stellon, and both were cast behind Liron's shadow. If we didn't bind the chaos—whatever that meant—before that time, we would lose. Everything.

I wanted to hope I was being overly dramatic, that I'd spent too much time in Niles's company and developed a penchant for drama, but that wasn't it. We were closer to our deadline than I cared to admit, and I no longer had a plan that could get us to Reina and Alesh with time to figure out what came next.

If only I'd figured out how to forgive myself sooner.

"Do you prefer to sit here and feel sorry for yourself until the eclipse, or would you care to find a way to right the situation?"

Niles's voice pricked my thoughts, hitting all the sensitive spots. He had some nerve, goading me, when he was responsible for sending us in the wrong direction.

"I'm attempting to work out some way we can get there in time when we're currently two and a half days behind," I answered, keeping my voice intentionally emotionless. "I'll have even less time to scour an entire city for two people. If I don't find them…"

"Well, while you're making plans, I have someone to see."

I shifted in the saddle so suddenly I spooked Aeros who gave a small sideways hop as I turned to stare Niles down.

"You have *someone* to see?"

"Business to attend to."

"*Business* to attend to?"

"Do you plan to repeat everything I say, D'Arturio?"

"You lead us two days in the wrong direction, giving me no inclination that you're doing so in the process, we get here, and now you've got *someone* to see?" I tried—and failed—to fight the rising temperature in my blood.

"I don't expect—" Niles disappeared, yanked once more into wherever it was he went when he wasn't here with me.

It took the better part of the day and night before the fury no longer left me blind with rage. I'd steered Aeros out of Emborid and into the grasslands again only a few hours after we'd first arrived, turning west and hoping no mighty river or canyon separated us from where we needed to be.

When at last I gave the horse a break, I slid out of the saddle, legs and back so weary I thought I might fall into the grass before I could fashion any sort of bed. The people in Emborid had been willing to trade food for a coin I had stolen when I'd taken the saddle and bridle, and I relished the juices in my mouth as I bit into a meat pie. I neither knew nor cared what kind of meat was folded into the flaky crust, but I savored every last morsel, every buttery crumb.

Then, I licked my fingers clean when I was done, delighting in having food in my stomach for the first time since I'd gone beneath the mountain.

I wasn't overly concerned that I hadn't seen Niles again, not right away at least. It wasn't until two days without a single sighting of him that I'd stopped being angry with his navigation mishap and started worrying that whatever power let him continue to communicate with me had decided we no longer needed such communication.

And did I need Niles?

No.

Of course not.

I'd gone years without someone to talk to, and missions in the Order were often one-person affairs. Up until recently, Reina had really been the only true friend I'd had, though I'd found one in Brigantino, too. I suppose even Alesh and Ywelo could be counted as recent additions to my growing list of friends.

But Niles?

And anyway, Niles no more wanted to be my friend than I wanted him to. He'd stayed with me out of his duty to some higher power, out of a promise he'd made to the Saints to save his own soul. It wasn't as though he actually cared about me, or my soul, or the outcome of this whole blasted situation.

Still, I couldn't fight the image of Niles's face when he thought about the future, about whatever he wasn't supposed to tell me, the worry lines between his brows, and the concern flashing in his eyes.

Fine.

Maybe he had begun to care. A little.

So when I closed in on where the Emborid people had directed me to go, I suspected I'd finally reached the empire's capitol. Gleaming spires atop pristine white buildings towered above the land. Even the "small" buildings were enormous and bright. The entirety of the city seemed built from whitewashed stone and polished daily.

If the red clay buildings from Emborid had sprung from the very ground surrounding them, Ivirreh had been chiseled from a shining, granite mountain. Aeros snorted, her nostrils flaring as she scented something in the air. Grain, probably. After a grass diet and little water, it was no wonder the horse would be pleased to return to civilization.

I surveyed the city before us, hoping—nay, praying— Reina was somewhere within its walls.

"All right, horse. Let's go find our girl."

I nudged her ahead with a squeeze of my calves, and we joined the road that led to the city's gates. I wished there were a better way to enter the city. Had I more time, I would have found a way to enter undetected, but with a horse and no knowledge of what lay before us, I had to use the more direct route.

It wasn't as though the Chaos Wielder knew I was here. Saints, he probably didn't even know who I was. I wasn't the one he'd appeared to time and again. No, he was hunting Reina, tormenting her for sport. If he continued to do so after our journey through Kufataba, then he'd already noticed my absence, which meant he thought I was dead.

Which meant I had the element of surprise.

As long as I didn't draw attention to myself within Ivirreh, I could find a way to blend in and locate Reina covertly.

Four days.

We still had four days.

I prayed she and Alesh had a plan already in motion.

Because I sure as hell didn't.

Planning became exponentially more difficult without resources, allies, any idea where I was or where I was going, and no knowledge of my opponent.

A thousand scenarios had run through my head as Aeros and I journeyed to get here, but without any solid knowledge, I couldn't formulate a reliable plan. Instead, my only plan became to find Reina and Alesh.

Once I was through the lightly guarded city gates, I realized exactly how futile such an attempt might be. This city was easily twenty times the size of Irzan. Two hundred and twenty times the size of Barnham. My heart sank as I steered Aeros through the streets. Too many people. Too many streets. Too many buildings.

Aeros herself was a bit of an attention-grabber. In the Southern Plains, nudromedaries were the preferred mount in the desert lands, but this far south, horses had once again become the popular method of travel. As I garnered more than one stare, though, I realized I hadn't seen a single horse a color other than brown. Chestnut, bay, dark bay, even, but not a single white, roan, paint, or dappled gray.

The people, however, were diverse even where the horses were not. The city was as I expected. Skin tones of every color, people of every size and shape. I didn't stand out here as I had in Emborid. One mark in my favor. Finally.

The biggest relief of Ivirreh was not its diversity, but rather the array of languages spoken throughout the streets, the northern tongue carrying delightfully to my ear here and there. A consolation. I walked the cobbled streets, leading Aeros behind me. It was too crowded to ride and even the mare could use a break from my weight on her back.

My first task? Find the largest market. The one thing I hoped Reina would have learned from her time with me was that the easiest way to hide was not to hide at all, especially in a city like this. She'd never been in such a place. Would she have thought of it? Or was she, even now, camped out somewhere on the plains instead?

"Sir, excuse me. Could you point me in the direction of the largest market?"

I spoke to a heavyset man with a crown of short black hair around his head and a well-trimmed black beard across his cheeks and chin. He packed up his empty cart, pulling down the colorful awning and folding in the cart's wooden sides.

The look in his eyes was one of honesty, a refreshing change in any city marketplace. If he was already packing for the day, he couldn't fault me for asking about another market instead of buying his wares.

The man laughed, an open-mouthed grin wide on his face. "The largest market? The whole city is a market, boy! Have you not noticed?"

I had, actually. But that wouldn't bring me any closer to Reina.

"Well, yes, but I was hoping for the most notable one. I haven't been long in the city, and I'm not familiar with the streets or the wares."

He grinned again as he looked up from tying the fabric awning across the empty cart. He pulled a knot tight, the laces tightening with a *zip* as the fabric slid against itself. "Here for the celebration, are you?"

"Of course," I answered. "Who wouldn't be?"

What I really wanted to say was, "What celebration?"

"So, the biggest market starts on the corner of Crushalhe and Dharta, but most of the biggest vendors are blocks and blocks eastward. Can't miss them, really. The vendor carts extend fourteen blocks in three directions. And that's when there's *not* an event scheduled at the palace."

"Thank you," I said to him. "I appreciate it."

"Of course, of course."

"About that celebration…"

He gave a hearty laugh. "Between you and me? Don't waste your time trying to get into the palace if you've already got a family representative who's been picked. The guard won't bend, and you'll never get in."

I fought confusion as I processed the information. A celebration. At the palace. A family representative. One per family. Guards to ensure the rules were followed.

"I'm not much for celebration, simply curious about the event that's got everyone excited. I thank you for the advice, though. It looks like you've done well today. I wish you well in your sales tomorrow, too."

"Luck! Luck has nothing to do with it. Having the right produce does. I did well even before I sold those new roots I got my hands on a few weeks ago, but with those? Oh, the fortune I could make. What I wouldn't give to find more of *that*. Scarcity runs the world, I suppose."

I tilted my head as I observed him. "A root? What kind of root?"

"I don't even know what it was called! A seller came through a couple weeks back with piles of produce we'd never seen around here before. I picked out a purple root that looked versatile, made a small fortune selling cakes and breads my Hildi made with it."

A purple root.

Purple? Callogh?

"You're from the north, right? I mean, you speak it and all. You ever see anything like that?" he asked, his eyes bright with hope.

Aeros nudged my shoulder, taking the opportunity to try to chew the sleeve of my tunic. Distracted, I gently pushed her muzzle away, then placed my hands apart to about the size of a typical callogh root. "I might. Is it about this big and kind of round, maybe a bit more oblong? Lumpy? A strange blue-purple when it's raw, but a thorough deep purple when it's cooked through?"

His eyes lit with excitement. "Yes! That's it!"

"I thought that might be. It's called callogh. It needs damp, cold climates to thrive, and you'll probably never see it here again."

His shoulders fell as his expression deflated. "I had hoped… Well, I guess it's back to business as usual, but I had really hoped it was something we might see more of. You're sure, this callogh? It couldn't be grown here, in our soil?"

I thought a moment. "Warm weather plants can grow in cold climates. If you've a greenhouse, it's easy enough to do, but cold weather plants in extensive heat? Unlikely."

"Well, at least I know what it's called. I suppose that's something, right? I'll convince Hildi to make a voyage north with me a few times a year. The money to be made…"

I nodded absently, thinking about advising him to stay away from Kufataba, which was a pointless piece of advice, given that he would probably never go north at all, not for callogh root alone. I thanked him and made my way through the crowded streets, Aeros trailing behind as I held the reins in one hand.

Callogh. Where would he have gotten callogh? I could think of only one way it might have made its way this far south, and it would be just like Reina to use magic to make enough money to survive on. She'd never resort to stealing as I had. She hadn't a dishonest bone in her body. A smile found its way across my lips.

Reina was here. Alive. And well.

At least she was a week ago.

CHAPTER SEVENTEEN

The Measure of Trust
Reina

"Are you sure this is a good idea?"

I didn't mind Alesh altering my appearance—or his—but I was uncomfortable with not knowing how permanent the changes might be.

"She knows your face. She knows mine. It is best we look different for the ball."

I examined my new cheekbones in the mirror. They were sharper than my rounded cheeks. The nose he'd given me was also sharp, narrower, though not unflattering. He'd altered my brows and my hair, lightening them so they were golden. Alesh had wanted to add to my height, but I outright refused.

The changes he'd wrought were painful enough. I didn't want to imagine how my bones might protest the extra length. And, if I was honest, I was also concerned about what might happen to the snake venom still floating somewhere in my body if he accidentally altered that, too.

I reached down and rubbed a calf absently as a sharp pain shot through the muscle. A cramp. Not snake venom. Just a cramp.

"I liked you better before," Abi said from beside me, her intense blue eyes scrutinizing me in the mirror. "I mean, you're still pretty, but you…"

She scratched a shoulder.

"But what?" Alesh asked, near offended by her opinion.

"Well, it's just that you look like everyone else now. The same kind of face every woman covets around here. Same cheeks, same chin." She shrugged. "I liked the way you looked before better."

I leaned into her, placing an arm around her and squeezing. "Then I thank you for the words because I prefer to look like me, too. And using the magic to grow a new face is not something I would have thought of." I glared at Alesh. "I'm much more content with healing."

"I do only what needs to be done."

"Hiding in plain sight does make things easier," I agreed.

I knew Alesh's work on my appearance was a clever idea, but it didn't change the fact that I was now less comfortable in my own skin than I'd ever been. Was I even the same girl Quinn had always loved? My only consolation was that so long as I kept from using the magic in her presence, Elodie wouldn't recognize me.

In less than a month, Alesh had mastered the power of life far beyond what I could have imagined was possible. His skills were both impressive and terrifying. If I thought there was a chance he might rid me of the venom with the power of life, I'd ask him to try, but Alesh had been extremely specific when we'd sealed the poison in isolated veins that he needed the power of death to do it. There was no choice but to wait.

"What is it? You are troubled."

I smiled in return. "Nothing, I… Well, I can't help but feel more than a little inadequate when it comes to magic. Your skill is phenomenal, almost beyond belief. You changed my entire look in less than a minute."

"Yes, but I have been taught magic. I have used it all my life, yes? You have not."

He'd said as much before. It still didn't ease the sting of how quickly he'd learned to master the power of life after so many years working with death.

He patted my knee. "It will come."

"Will you do me next?" Abi asked, her eyes aglow with excitement.

"No. You are too important. You must look like you."

The hopeful grin fell from Abi's face. "But I'm the *most* recognizable to her!"

I placed a hand over Abi's. "While that's true, we still don't know whether we'll be able to reverse the changes we've made."

"We will." Alesh sounded so certain. What was it like to always be so certain of one's abilities?

"Anyway," I continued. "The last thing we need to do is make you unrecognizable to the entire empire."

Especially if we were going to rely on her being Elodie's successor, not that we had yet shared that with her. I rubbed my thigh. The ache that had been in my calf moments ago had grown.

"I need to walk," I said. "I'll go purchase our dinner from the market tonight. Any requests?"

"Something sweet!" Abigayle said, momentarily forgetting her desire to be someone else.

I rolled my eyes. The girl thrived on sugar.

"I'll see what I can find."

The streets were as crowded as ever—more so, if I judged correctly. I had never seen so many people. And horses. Now that we were mere days from the emperor's ball, citizens from the Empire's farthest reaches had arrived, filling the streets with clammer and noise, odors both pleasant and unpleasant, and an inescapable warmth no matter the time of day or night.

In the pocket of the gown I'd donned, I ran my fingers over the scallops of the little pink shell from the shores of Aberly. I was still the same person. Changing my looks had not changed who I was inside. I pulled my thoughts from Aberly, and my identity, and Quinn—who was always there, in the background—and focused on following my nose to a stall that would provide dinner.

I stopped at a vendor selling spiced dishes, cooked beans and rice and cheese, and requested three servings to take back to the inn, my mouth already watering in anticipation of the flavors. As I waited for the vendor to count my change, my gaze wandered.

Then my breath hitched as though I'd been punched in the gut.

For a second—really an instant—I swore I saw a shock of dark hair and broad shoulders, a familiar stubbled jawline. And a dappled hind end of a horse. In a blink, both were gone. If I hadn't been waiting on the vendor, I might have raced down the street.

Quinn. I'd seen Quinn. It was—

Saints, get ahold of yourself, Reina.

I put a hand to my eyes, pressing my fingers into my eyelids until I no longer felt as though I would cry. Quinn was dead. No amount of wishing would bring him back.

"Missá."

I returned my hands to my sides, keeping my eyes downcast, and muttering my thanks as I accepted my change, shoving the coins into my pocket, then took the wrapped packages from the vendor.

I spared one last glance down the corridor of the street, hoping to see the man and horse, hoping to verify it was *not* who I thought I'd seen. It might help, to know I'd seen someone real and living, not a ghost of my past, but a passing resemblance to someone I'd known and loved, but there was no sign of man or horse. Nor any sign of a ghost who resembled Quinn.

When I returned to the room, Mical had joined our party.

"Had I known you were coming, I would have brought extra food." I passed a container to Alesh and another to Abi.

"Had I known he was coming, I would have asked *him* to get the food," Alesh said. "Better him than you."

Mical didn't seem overly surprised at my new façade. I supposed Alesh and Abi had filled him in before I'd gotten back. Still…

"I am well aware I no longer look myself, but must you stare?" I didn't look at him as I spoke, instead concentrating on the food in front of me, on getting it into my mouth, on not being distracted by the foreign, honey-blond locks to the sides of my vision.

"I don't mean to. Truly. It's… Well, you look so much like a lover I had once." Mical said the words with the nonchalance of someone who'd said I looked like a sister, or an aunt.

I choked on the bite of hot rice, sputtering, reaching for a water skin as I coughed. I drank, coughed, then drank again. Minutes passed before I could speak, during which Mical was delighted to continue his conversation.

"Sorry."

Was he? He grinned, his gaze passing over me, assessing what felt like every curve, every feature.

"She was a fabulous lover—passionate, considerate, and very, very good with her—"

"I do not think we need to know more," Alesh broke through, giving a deliberate look in Abi's direction.

Mical shrugged. "Suit yourself. We don't shy from such things here in the Empire." Then he grinned directly at Abi. "Right, boy? You've probably stolen your fair share of kisses already. And what are you, a scrawny ten years of age?"

Abi shoveled another spoonful of a beans and melted cheese into her mouth and shrugged her shoulders, seeming indifferent to Mical's words.

"Why are you here, Mical? Have you names for us?"

My questions had the desired effect. He brightened. "Ah, yes. I've contacted a guardsman who owes me a favor or two. Here are the identities you are to present when you arrive for the celebration."

He handed me a palm-sized piece of parchment. I read over the names, then handed the list to Alesh without comment, who took it with interest. I took the name meant to be mine as an omen we'd be able to pull off this foolish scheme. It seemed fitting. Abi stood and leaned over Alesh's shoulder, mouthing the names as she read.

"That won't work. You can't be Nhuli Jerrok," she said with certainty, pointing to a name on the list.

Alesh turned his head to look at her. "And why not?"

"He's been banned from the palace for two years. Any guard there would know that. He was a notorious drinker on every occasion and always had to be escorted off the premises."

Alesh's gaze whipped to Mical, who immediately held up his palms. "Now, wait. I'm just the messenger. I didn't know… And what does the boy know about it, anyway?"

I stood, pinning my gaze on Mical. "You worked at the palace. You knew that name. Why would you give us a name that won't work?"

Mical paced the room like a caged cougar, running his hands through his hair. "I didn't know Jerrok was banned. I swear it. My source gave me three names to use, so I added the fourth."

"It doesn't matter," I snapped. "We only need three names. You're no longer coming with us." I reached into my pocket, pulling a handful of coins and two treasury notes from within, offering them to him. "Payment for your services and for your silence."

He stared at the money, but didn't take it, his face a mix

of displeasure and offense. "Now wait. Just a minute. I can do more to help. Let me raid the palace with you. I'm good for the work."

"We aren't *raiding* the palace," I hissed, pushing the money into his hand. "I've already told you that."

"That may be so, but you haven't told me what you *are* doing, so I must make my own assumptions." He forcefully closed my fingers around the money, pushing my hands and their offering from him.

"You have proven you cannot be trusted," Alesh said, stepping forward.

Even though Mical towered over Alesh, he stuttered backwards two steps. "No. Listen. I wouldn't have let you use that name. I just needed time to find the name of someone else that would have worked, and then I planned to return and let you know of the change."

"Then why come at all?" I challenged. "Why not wait until you had the four names we needed, Mical? You talk of honesty, but I have yet to see an honest side to your words!"

Finally, he growled. "Fine. I came because I…wanted to see you again? Because I have not stopped thinking of you?"

I recoiled, eyes wide with surprise.

"Was that a question?" Abi asked.

Mical looked to her, then to Alesh, then back at me again. He shoved his hands in the pockets of his sleek, black breeches, letting his shoulders droop as he took interest in the wooden floorboards below his feet.

"Yes. No. I don't know."

A long moment passed before anyone spoke. When Abi

finally did, it was out of sheer discomfort for the moment.

"You're very indecisive," Abi noted.

Mical looked to her with a tired smile as he rubbed a hand over his face. "God, I don't know. Maybe I've had too much—" Mical paused, his gaze fixed on Abi, his brows drawn as he cocked his head to the side.

Abi's eyes shifted nervously from Alesh to me.

"You're the youngest Gehtanan."

A roaring sounded in my ears. He wasn't supposed to know. We'd agreed to collaborate with him, but Mical was never supposed to know Abi's true identity.

"Am not."

"You most certainly are. I should have seen it sooner." He let out a low whistle from between his teeth. "Abigayle Gehtanan lives."

Abi gave a husky boy-laugh. "Go on! You're raving mad."

Mical turned, eyes flashing as he faced Alesh. "You're planning a coup."

I shook my head.

"Yes, you are. You're planning a coup to put the youngest Gehtanan on the throne."

I gave a nervous laugh. "You *are* insane."

"Maybe, but I'm also correct." He pinned me with a steady gaze. "Before, I wanted in on whatever it was you were doing because I could use the coin, but now? Now I want in to get that bitch out of the palace."

My jaw dropped in shock. The wrath that came from Mical's lips was more than I could have anticipated. I had no reply.

"She's the reason half my friends are dead. No doubt the reason her own family is dead. I'll do whatever it takes, whatever you ask. I'll wring her pretty little neck myself if that's what you want." He turned to examine Abi again and shook his head in wonder. "How'd you survive?"

Abi looked to me again as though asking for permission to drop the ruse. I gave a slow sigh, closed my eyes, and nodded. She removed the cap and let her pale blond locks fall past her shoulders. Then she met his gaze.

In front of her, Mical knelt, sliding one knee to the floor and bowing his head reverently.

"Forgive what I said earlier. I beg you, please. My behavior was horribly inappropriate."

Abi looked my way, a half-grin, half-frown on her face. *He's a lunatic*, those eyes said.

He wasn't. Not really. She was too young to realize the hope she gave to anyone who *wasn't* squarely in Elodie's coffers.

"Erm, there's nothing to forgive, sir. I've been around worse."

"Still, I shouldn't have spoken that way in front of a member of the imperial family."

"You had no way of knowing." Desperate, her eyes darted to me again.

"Mical, stand up," I ordered. "She said there's nothing to forgive. Move on. And don't let *me* hear you speak with such vulgarities again. She may not mind, but I do."

Alesh gave a firm nod and a proud smile.

Mical rose slowly, his head remaining bowed until he reached his full height.

"I swear to serve you, Abigayle Gehtanan, rightful heir to the throne. In whatever capacity, however I may be of service, by my life or by my death." He placed an open hand over his heart.

After a moment of silence, Abi finally replied. "I hate to break it to you, but I'm not really the one in charge here." She motioned to Alesh with a single nod of her head. "He is. And Reina. I just get them what they need."

Mical looked to Alesh, then to me for confirmation.

"She discredits herself," Alesh said.

Another silence fell before Mical licked his lips, hesitating. "You *are* throwing a coup."

I answered. "If we don't, there won't be an empire, or a Liron, left for *anyone* to rule."

Mical leaned against the table, the wood creaking as his knuckles gripped the edges. "Tell me," he said.

So I did.

CHAPTER EIGHTEEN

The Tragedy of History
Quinn

The problem with arriving in Ivirreh at this very moment was that almost everyone else in the entire empire was *also* arriving, which meant lodging was nowhere to be found, even once I'd stolen enough coin to pay for it.

I wasn't proud of my continued thievery, but if I could forgive my past self for destroying so many lives, I supposed I could manage additional forgiveness when it came to swiping coin from the exceptionally well-to-do patrons and vendors in the city.

I hadn't taken from anyone whose jewels weren't openly on display or whose polished boots didn't give off a blinding shine. I would take only from those who could afford the losses, from those who, in fact, wouldn't even notice the losses.

Niles had not appeared. Three days had passed since he'd last shown himself, and I wondered if he ever would. I'd begun to worry for my companion ghost. My anger over his sending us in the wrong direction had long since flared out. I was instead left wondering if he was facing consequences of the actions he never should have taken. Perhaps he was never meant to leave Kufataba by my side. Perhaps the Saints were taking out their anger on him at this very moment.

I stared at the stars as I lay against Aeros's side. The horse had settled on the ground quickly and with a groan, as fatigued as I. She wrapped her long neck around to rest her soft muzzle in my lap. I stroked one dappled cheek absently, speaking nonsense words to her as I did.

I'd found a hollowed-out building barely more than three walls on the outskirts of Ivirreh, far from the eyes of men, and Aeros seemed as happy to settle here as any stable. She'd eaten her fill of the grasses and taken a long drink from the nearby stream that was no more than a freshwater trickle.

"She's here, your girl, isn't she? Do you think you could find her if you tried?"

The horse gave no response.

"You could probably scent her. That's a useful skill. You'd make a good agent with an extra skill like that."

Aeros shoved her head into my palm, obviously annoyed that I'd stopped stroking her face. I resumed with a smile.

"Saints above! You've taken to speaking to horses in my absence. I'm not sure whether I should laugh or cry. On one hand, it's quite amusing. On the other, it's rather sad my company can be exchanged so easily."

Aeros stiffened at Niles's voice.

I know the feeling, girl.

Regardless, she stayed on the ground with me, as though more annoyed by his presence than fearful.

"Good of you to return, Niles. I thought you'd left for good."

"And make your life so easy? I think not."

I laughed. Niles's form glowed with the moonlight. He sat across from me, unwilling to get too close to Aeros. Or perhaps he sat away so as not to startle her. I had begun to question all of Niles's motives throughout our time together.

"It's good to see you," I said, surprising myself. "With the way you left, I…didn't know if you'd be back, if *they*"—I pointed to the sky— "would let you come back."

"I missed you, too."

I noticed it then, Niles's subdued attitude. Shoulders lowered, anxious fingers working against the ethereal fabric of one pant leg.

"Are you all right?"

He swallowed. "Fine. Sorry I left when I did. It was… unavoidable."

"What did they do to you?"

"They? The Saints, you mean?"

I nodded.

"Nothing. I was called by…well, something *else*."

I waited, hoping against reason for further explanation.

"And?" I finally prompted.

"And I know how to bind the chaos, so when the time comes, we won't fail."

Relief flooded my veins. Despite the mountain reassuring me that my request was "granted," I wondered time and again how I could bind the chaos and when I would know what needed to be done.

"That's fantastic. Well done, man. Tell me."

He frowned, then quickly masked it with an air of

indifference, leaving me to wonder if I'd seen the frown at all.

"If I tell you now, you'll have no more use for me, and I'll never know if you've succeeded or not. Can't let you get *all* the glory, D'Arturio." He grinned, his teeth glowing whiter in the moonlight.

I squinted at him. There was something he wasn't telling me.

"Very well," I said. "But what if you disappear on me at a most…inopportune time?"

"Fear not. I don't think the Saints will call while I'm in the midst of helping to save the entire world. Otherwise, why would they have sent me at all?"

"But you said—"

"I'm tired, D'Arturio, and I'm not even the one who rode hard this last week. Close your eyes and let yourself sleep for once. I'll keep watch."

I wanted to argue, to remind him he just told me the Saints weren't the ones who called him when he'd disappeared for three days. Instead, I closed my eyes, leaned against Aeros's warm belly with the weight of her head in my lap, and slept as though I hadn't slept in a year.

I spent the better part of the next day winding my way around the crowded streets, speaking with anyone who looked as though they might understand the northern tongue or the Ndoyo tongue. What I learned throughout the day was that people matching Alesh and Reina's descriptions had been seen several times over the last few weeks.

In fact, they'd even been seen regularly at the intersection of Crushalhe and Dharta which left me standing outside an inn called Porenskahal, gazing at the shuttered windows above, and wondering if I could be so lucky to have found them so quickly.

I took a spot at the bar in the dining room and ordered an ale, or whatever passed for it, from the barkeep, a burly man with thick, tattooed forearms and a dark beard halfway down his chest.

I paid him in coin, left a hefty tip, and sipped as I studied my surroundings. Mid-sized establishment. Not a place where trouble might brew easily, but neither was it a place where high-end coin would flow.

Long bar, small dining area. Men came to drink more than to eat, but there were enough tables to lead me to believe the food here must be half-decent. Several seats at the bar were occupied, two by a pair of men younger than I, both of whom kept turning to ogle the rear of the server behind them as she took orders from the one occupied table. Typical.

At the opposite end of the bar was a large man who might have been inconspicuous if not for the way he kept watch around the room and beyond. A guard out of uniform? His eyes swept the room and the entranceway beyond, as well as the staircase that led upwards to where I assumed the inn's rooms were located. He was careful not to meet my gaze as I made my own observations.

"Can I get you another?" The barkeep's voice broke me

from my thoughts.

"No, thank you. I'm still working on this one. Good brew. Excellent quality."

He gave a wide grin and nodded.

It never hurt to shower with compliments those from which I hoped to gain information.

"I wonder if you might help. I'm looking for a couple of friends of mine," I said. "I suspect they're staying in this part of the city, but I have no way of knowing exactly where. Can you tell me if a dark-haired young woman about this tall"—I held my hand about to Reina's height— "and dark-skinned man with a walking stick have been through here?"

"Ah." He scratched his head for a moment as he thought, then crossed enormous arms over his chest and frowned in concentration. "I don't recall seeing anyone like that around here, but I haven't been working the bar very long. I'm usually in the kitchen." He thumbed toward the door at the end of the bar. "Tabra's out tonight. She's the one you'll want to talk to as she's usually out front and keeps track of all the patrons coming and going."

"You don't, by any chance, have a room available, do you?"

He laughed. "Saints, no! You won't find a room. Not until after the celebration, anyway. It's not often the emperor opens the palace to the regular folk. It's the first time the new emperor has done so since she came into power."

"I've heard about this celebration. What's the occasion?"

"Eclipse, supposedly. The emperor has invited a representative from each household to join her at the palace for the evening. The palace has viewing scopes on the lawns. Any remarkable celestial event usually leads to a public invitation."

"That's intriguing. Any event?"

"Well, the big ones anyway. Eclipses, the regular star showers, planetary alignments, and such. But this one is a big deal. It's the first celebration at the palace since most of the imperial family was lost."

I didn't bother to hide my surprise. "What happened?"

"About six months ago, there was an accident. Some say the family was in the wrong place at the wrong time. Some say it wasn't an accident at all. Either way, the result was the same. Every member of the Gehtanan family perished, save for one. Elodie Gehtanan. The grief that girl must have dealt with throughout these months. I'll tell you. Breaks my heart for her."

"That's truly awful." Thoughts swirled in my head as I took another sip of the bitter ale. "How did she survive?"

"That's the thing! No one knows. She should have been dead, too. It's a miracle. We thank the Saints every day to still have her in the palace."

Something about this story didn't sit right. I had no reason to believe the barkeep was telling anything but the truth, but…

I chalked up my disbelief to my experience in the Order. Something didn't add up.

"Forgive my curiosity, but…what exactly happened to the family?"

The barkeep grew somber, eyes downcast as though

speaking the story aloud might curse his future. He lowered his voice when he answered. "Terrible carriage accident at night. No one knows how it happened. There was a broken lantern involved. The oil must have sent the flames spreading quickly. Few of the guards that night made it. The emperor made sure the families received lifetime pay for their losses.

"Anyway, when the remains were discovered, the fire had destroyed everything. It was naught but charred bones, ash, and pieces of rubble." He paused, lending an air of reverence to his tale. "Except for her. Elodie Gehtanan stood, pristine, untouched amidst it all. A figure in white, they said, like a saint herself. Glowing.

"We've had six months of mourning for the family. For the first month, the remains—not that there were many— were on display in glass cases in the palace rose gardens for the families who wished to say their farewells."

I nodded. "A tragic tale," I agreed. And one ripe with discrepancies, but now was not the time to push, and the barkeep was the only source of information I currently had. "I'm sorry to hear it."

"I'm infinitely relieved one member survived. Emperor Elodie Gehtanan has shown fortitude when others might collapse into grief, mercy where some would lash out with anger, and compassion where others might not have any at all. The Elorin Empire is lucky, indeed."

I nodded again, then raised my glass in a silent toast. It seemed the wisest way to answer. I wondered if the Chaos Wielder had been behind the murdered imperial family and the burned carriage, and why he had spared this Elodie. His love? Or his accomplice?

I'd seen enough chaos in my travels through Castilles and the Southern Plains to know the Chaos Wielder's mark. This reeked of it.

"Anyway, I've got to get back to it," the barkeep said as a handful of patrons trickled through the front door. "Let me know if you need another pint."

I nodded and thanked him again.

I spent the better part of the afternoon at the bar, even ordering food to keep from being conspicuous, but I saw no sign of Reina or Alesh. Dozens of people came and went throughout the afternoon and into the early evening hours. Men, women, children—the establishment buzzed with activity. Even the man who'd reminded me of an off-duty guard at the end of the bar had relinquished his seat some time ago.

As daylight began to wane, I finally stood, left a tip, and made for the door. I'd left Aeros outside the city, where she could graze to her heart's content. Niles promised to keep an eye on her, though I didn't know what he thought he'd be able to do if she decided to break free and bolt.

I reached the edge of the dining room when I had the sudden urge to glance to the stairs. A woman was climbing them, her pale pink gown swishing with each step. She wasn't anyone I could have known, wasn't anyone I'd seen in the streets or in the inn's dining room, but there was something familiar about her. I blinked and tried to place her.

Long, blond curls fell halfway down her back. In one hand she held a canvas bag with goods from vendors outside, the edge of one container and part of a loaf of bread visible at the top. Her other hand fiddled with something at her neck. It occurred to me then why she seemed familiar. Reina was forever fiddling with the talisman at her neck.

I almost called up the stairs to the unknown woman, to ask if she'd seen anyone who looked like Reina or Alesh, but guests had their own business to tend to and weren't generally useful sources of information. What reason would she have for knowing anything about other guests' business? I'd be better off waiting to speak with Tabra tomorrow. With that, I turned and left the inn.

I was nearly outside the city when another thought clicked into place. The woman on the stairs—the air she'd moved through, the space she'd left behind her, had *smelled* like Reina. I hadn't realized it right away. With the overwhelming aroma of food and drink and sweat from the heat of the day, I hadn't registered the anomaly, but now, as the stars began to show in the sky, my mind belatedly identified the scent.

Something Reina used in her hair. A flower or an herb. I wished I knew the name and if it was readily available here in the Elorin Empire. Could it have been a coincidence? Or had Reina passed through that space earlier and I'd sensed her only afterwards? I gave a frustrated growl as I returned to where Aeros was tied.

Niles glanced at me with what could have been amusement. "No luck then?"

"I feel as though I'm losing my mind."

He opened his mouth to respond, but I held up a hand. "Don't say whatever it is you're about to say."

Niles gave a hearty laugh. "All right, then. I won't. What did you learn?"

So I told Niles about the vendor and the callogh root, about how two people matching Reina and Alesh's descriptions were spotted frequently on the corner of one of the busiest markets, and how there happened to be an inn at that same corner.

I did *not* tell him about the woman who smelled like Reina, lest he think me mad. He'd most certainly accuse me of being a lovesick pup, and true though that might be, I felt no need to have the obvious shoved in my face.

"Tell me about the ale," Niles said. "You sat in the tavern, had a drink. What was it like?" Eyes full of longing accompanied his wistful tone.

"You couldn't have had a drink even if you'd been alive, Ingram. You'd let go of drink, remember?"

"Yes, well, it doesn't mean I can't remember the taste fondly."

I sat in silence for a moment before answering. "It was a bitter brew, but in a skilled sort of way, the kind of ale that intrigues the senses enough to make you want another taste."

"The dangerous sort, then," he said with a snort.

"Indeed. Honestly, though? I prefer the brew back home." I positioned myself in the grass, stretching out to view the glittering sky above. "And what did you do while I was gone? Did you make amends with Aeros? She seems unaffected by your presence now."

"I had my own errands to attend to, but fear not, I checked in on Reina's mare throughout the day. She told me she's enjoying her day off, and she would like very much if you and I would go throw a stone somewhere and leave her to this grassland paradise."

I laughed at the image but didn't miss the part about Niles's having errands. He might have tried to bury those words in his tale about Aeros's feelings, but I couldn't let them slip by unnoticed.

"What errands?" I asked.

"Hmm?"

"What errands did you attend to?"

"Ghostly ones."

"Mmph." I should have known better than to expect a straight answer.

"Well, ghostly errands are infinitely better than ghastly errands," Niles quipped. "So I have that in my favor at the very least."

I didn't bother arguing.

CHAPTER NINETEEN

On the Trail
Quinn

Finally. Something I could follow. According to a local street vendor, a man matching Alesh's description had been seen in the jeweler's quarter of the city, a tidy little piece of the city that shined both in looks and in wares.

I rode Aeros deliberately through the streets here, relying on her unusual color to prove that I, too, was worthy of being on this street, amongst these shops, even if I hardly looked the part. My hair had grown longer, and I sported what was dangerously close to a full beard. I'd have to remedy it soon, the itch along my neck had grown irritating, particularly in the heat.

The people perusing the storefronts here oozed money. From the quantity of jewels already adorning trinkets, pins, chokers, and hair combs to the quality of the silk and the brilliant shine of boots, there was no doubt the money exchanging hands here did so in abundance.

The storefronts were immaculate, the walls whitewashed and clean, the dark wood of the window frames free from grime, and the glass windows themselves polished to a high shine. The large display windows were full of raw and cut gems, many jewels in settings and some without. Each window featured a prominent piece of jewelry—a necklace, a diadem, a bracelet—exquisite in artistry and sparkling beneath the sun's rays.

The smaller windows were made of translucent colored glass that lent a fairytale feel to the entire row of shops. Some of the windows pictured objects or scenes, like flowers or jewels around a graceful neck, but others were no more than a splash and swirl of color against the white of the buildings they were nestled within.

Riding Aeros into the city had been a good wager. I never would have fit in here had I come on foot, but on such a magnificent animal, I was a wealthy nobleman who was simply worn ragged from my time on the road.

Of course.

Or perhaps I was being optimistic. The stares from patrons and shop owners had more of an edge than pity for travel-weary nobility might earn. Still, no one was outright hostile, and none had the gall to tell me I didn't belong, so I continued on my way.

What I hadn't yet figured out was why Alesh had been spotted here, in this part of the city, among shops that had nothing to offer him or Reina.

The obvious answer, naturally, was that there *was* something of importance here. I needed only to work harder to figure out what. I examined each shop as I navigated Aeros down the cobbled street, read the names painted in gold across the shingles at the doors, tried to figure out which of these shops was home to more than a simple jeweler. One of them must be something more, a front for something greater.

I suppressed a growl when I reached the last shop. There was nothing. I'd been chasing a ghost. Maybe it hadn't even been Alesh my vendor informant had seen at all. Facing a wall at the end of the street, I swung Aeros around to return the way I'd come, but something about the alleyway to the left caught my attention.

Aeros danced beneath me, prancing, unhappy with my change of plans as I led her toward the alley instead of back down the street. The alley was barely wide enough for a horse, and certainly not for a horse who already possessed a nervous disposition. I dismounted and took a moment to soothe Aeros, running a hand along her neck.

When she no longer quivered with anxiety, I took the reins and led her forward into the alley. With me walking in front, she was content to trail behind like a docile puppy.

"You're ridiculous, you know that, right?" I said to her. "There is clearly nothing here to be fearful of. What's bothering you? Is it the ivy?" I brushed one hand along the ivy-covered wall beside us, almost pricking a thumb on a wicked-looking thorn hidden in the tangle of greenery. The leaves sprang upwards again in my hand's wake.

Aeros pulled her head back, yanking on the reins, showing the whites of her eyes as she viewed the positively terrifying leaves beside us. I shook my head.

"It's amazing she's put up with you this long. I cannot believe she's traveled through woods and wilds with you. And you're afraid of this? Of ivy?" I yanked a leaf off the vine and placed it in front of her nose. "This?"

She gave a single snort before opening her mouth and ripping the leaf from my hand to sample its flavor. I shook my head again. "See? Food isn't scary. Can we continue now?"

Aeros trailed behind me, occasionally making a grab for more leaves at the wall, but otherwise content to follow as I moved through the alley, examining every building. The lack of upkeep on this particular part of the local neighborhood spoke volumes. The clientele browsing the street from where we'd just come wouldn't dare open their purses on this block.

Which meant, to exist at all, the few shops here were funded by a *different* clientele, and the type of person who might set up business here was probably more along the lines of someone Alesh would work with.

All right. Think.

Say Alesh had been seen, and I was not, in fact, chasing a ghost. Why would Alesh be here, and what would he be looking to purchase?

"That one."

At least Niles had the decency to appear in front of me this time and not behind Aeros.

"That one what?"

I followed where he pointed to a shop with a white door that looked like it had known paint once but hadn't seen a fresh coat in some number of years. The large shop window was dark and none of the windows above the shop showed any sign of life. If anyone worked—or lived—here, they hadn't bothered trying to impress their clientele.

I stepped closer to examine the door, putting a hand to the

knob and turning gently. Locked. Unsurprising. I stepped to the side to peer into the darkened shop window and instead faced my own reflection. A heavy black cloth nailed to the inside of the window prevented anyone from looking in.

"What's special about this one?" I asked, turning back to Niles.

"I've been inside."

I took a breath. "I imagine you've probably stuck your head inside all the shops here, so you'll have to be more specific as to what's so important about this one, Niles."

"There's something inside worth seeing. Or someone, anyway. Knock. You'll see."

Saints help me, I followed Niles's suggestion and knocked. No one came to the door.

"No one's home," I said.

"She's definitely home. And the coin pouch sitting on the corner of her desk is the same one I'm sure Alesh used to carry. The same turquoise thread in the drawstring. He's been here."

I gave a short sigh and looped Aeros's reins around the railing post. "Fine, then. The back door."

He craned his neck to examine the building. "I…don't think places like this *have* a back door. This whole block rather *is* a back door."

"Then we'll make one. Or I will. You can…float through the wall, right?"

He glared at me in response, but in a moment, he had disappeared. I slipped behind the narrow walkway between the building and the one next to it, examining the structure, placement of windows, and calculating the risk of entering on the second floor versus the first. I cursed myself for sending Niles ahead. I should have had him examine the layout of the building from the inside first. I'd grown so used to working alone, it hadn't occurred to me that I *could* depend on someone else.

Without him, I couldn't be entirely certain the second floor was connected to the shop at the front of the building. Breaking into an unsuspecting, innocent tenant's home wasn't ideal. Still, the second floor was the better option, and with the decision made, I glanced left and right, then began to climb the wall, using the edges of beams, exposed brick beneath the wall's outer façade, and the window trim to propel myself upward.

The rough edges of the bricks bit into my fingertips but climbing the wall of the building was still easier than climbing mountains, and since that's what I'd been spending much of my time doing while in my self-made Kufataba prison, I reached a second-floor balcony with little trouble. It wasn't a balcony so much as a ledge, certainly not meant to support the weight of a person.

The window, unfortunately, was stuck in place, glued shut by years of dirt and filth. It took three tries, one of which almost cost me a fall to the ground, before the glass panels slid upward, the wooden frame protesting in the humidity.

I crawled through the window headfirst, on my belly, unceremoniously dumping myself on the floor in relief. The room was stifling, a layer of dust across every surface. Of course, "every surface" was the floor. The room was empty, dust motes I'd disturbed floating through the beams of light from the window I'd opened.

I stood and crept toward the door, careful to keep the floor from squeaking beneath my weight. At least one skill I'd learned in the Order was still useful in my new life.

The doorknob turned easily in my hand, leading to an empty hall, two other closed doors, and a descending stairwell. Judging by the undisturbed dust on the stairs, no one had used them in a very long time, which meant the entire apartment was likely empty. At least I wouldn't be surprising a tenant. I took the stairs, creeping close to the wall, disturbing the dust as little as possible as I descended. Better to leave no trace if I could.

At the bottom of the stairwell was another door. I calculated the angles and the number of turns I'd taken in my head. The shop. This door would lead to the shop.

I'd have to be quick, use the element of surprise to my advantage. Niles said a woman was inside, and I should have thought to glean any additional information from him before entering. I didn't like sneaking up on a woman who might assume I was breaking in for reasons I'd rather not contemplate.

I took one breath, then opened the door and burst into the room, relying on the element of surprise to give me the advantage. I assessed the room quickly, from one point to the next, noting every potential hiding spot, every weapon, searching for the person Niles had insisted was here.

But the shop was empty.

I stepped forward, slowly, cautiously.

And was rewarded with a clunk to the back of my head that sent my vision spinning. I winced as I whirled to face a woman who must have been behind the door I'd opened. She held a large, metal pipe at arm's length, ready to strike again. I held out a hand to delay additional injury.

"Wait," I said. I pressed my other hand to the back of my head. "Please."

Her eyes shone with a fierce glow as she stared me down. She would get along well with Ywelo.

"You break into *my* home, into *my* shop and have the gall to ask *me* to wait? I should crack open your skull, northern thief."

Well, she spoke the northern tongue, at least.

"I'm not a thief."

"Breaking in is a strange way to show it."

"I knocked."

Her eyes widened with anger, or incredulity, maybe.

"You knocked? And what happened when you knocked? Was the door flung open and an invitation extended to come in? Did I say, 'Oh, please, sir, come in!'"

I kept my arm extended but shuffled back half a step. "No."

"Well, she's delightful, isn't she?"

As ever, Niles picked the worst time to make an appearance inside. I wanted to growl at him but yelling at a ghostly entity the weapon-wielding woman couldn't see or hear probably wasn't good if I wanted to convince her I wasn't, in fact, a madman and a thief.

"I need to talk to you."

"Those who need to talk to me usually know how to arrange a meeting. If you couldn't manage to do that, then you aren't someone I need to speak with."

"Please. Ten minutes of your time is all I ask."

She tilted her chin upwards and narrowed her eyes. "And what will you give me for my ten minutes?"

"If you can answer a few questions, you'll be helping to save Liron from the grasp of a lunatic who would see us all thrown into chaos."

She scoffed. "Everyone seems concerned with the end of the world these days. It won't matter much to me. I'm leaving."

"You can't escape what's coming."

Instead of recoiling, she held her pipe higher. "Is that a threat, thief?"

"No," I said softly. "It's a fact. Can you…put the pipe down? Ten minutes. I wouldn't have broken in if it wasn't important. I'm not that kind of person."

"As though I should believe you. My time for what coin?" She rubbed the fingers of the hand not holding the pipe together, miming the symbol for money.

Of course. She wanted payment.

"Fine. May I?" I nodded to my hand and pointed to a pocket before pulling out a handful of coins I hoped would be enough to ply her.

She eyed the coins in my palm. "Put them on the desk."

She lowered the pipe as I slid the coins onto the desk at my side. No, not a desk. A workbench covered in an array of tools and a cloth covering what I assumed was several pieces of work. Illicit work, by the looks of it. Which is probably why she didn't open the door when I knocked.

Noticing my stare, she said, "Sit. The chair over there, so I can keep an eye on you. You have ten minutes, not a second longer."

"Told you you'd want to see the woman inside. She's a piece of work. Talks to herself while she's working, too." Niles crossed his arms and leaned against the wall, the same wall he'd come *through* to get in. How did that work, anyway?

I ignored his voice since it was clear the woman across from me had no idea we weren't alone. I sat on the chair that wasn't much more than a stool, leaning against the low-slung fabric backing. I placed my hands on my lap.

"I'm sorry I broke in," I said.

Information was more likely to flow if the person being questioned wasn't already furious with the person doing the questioning…

"It is of no consequence, and you're down to nine-minutes and thirty-five seconds."

I nodded.

"I almost wish we weren't on the same side, D'Arturio. I rather enjoy watching someone give you a difficult time."

I ignored Niles again, and said, "I need to know if friends of mine have visited. I have reason to believe they've come to do business with you."

"It is possible. I do business with a lot of people, but unless your friends had an appointment, it is not likely I would have seen them. My appointments have been booked solid for two months' time."

"They would have arrived"—I calculated the math in my head of how long ago Reina and Alesh might have arrived and how long they'd been staying in the city— "about two to three weeks ago, so any business you might have had with them would have been recent. And urgent."

I watched her face as I said the words, measuring her reaction to my pleas of urgency. Sure enough, there was a flare of recognition in her eyes, a slight twitch in one shoulder. She'd had an urgent request for work. I was in the right place.

She'd seen Reina and Alesh, or at least Alesh.

"I have had no recent requests. I'm sorry you've wasted your time—"

I held up a hand. "Now, just wait. I paid you for *your* time and, according to your clock, I have seven minutes and forty seconds left."

Her eyes lit in amusement. Given her ferocious disposition, she probably wasn't used to anyone throwing her own words back at her.

"That clock runs slow. But very well, thief."

"I am not—"

I closed my eyes. She was trying to distract me, goad me with name-calling.

"A man, twice my age, dark skin, dark hair, about my height, but leaner. Carries a staff with a red gemstone in the center. Sound familiar at all? A woman, about my age, medium skin tone, dark hair, one white streak on the left side. Perfect cheeks, lips that always seem to frown ever so slightly, and an exquisite perfume that I can never quite identify, but that always seems to linger in the air when she's visited."

She grunted and rolled her eyes. "You will make me ill. I hope she feels the same way about you as you do her."

The corners of my lips twitched in a smile I tried, and failed, to fight. "She does."

And despite the situation, my heart warmed with the thought because, Saints above, she did, and nothing would separate us again. Not ever.

The woman stared at me for a long minute. I stayed silent, waiting, hoping, hedging my bets that love would get her to break her silence.

Unfortunately, Niles decided it was the perfect moment to speak. He grew closer to the woman, studying her face, gauging if my words had hit their target. "I cannot believe you took the emotional route, nor can I believe that it appears to be working. Intriguing."

Finally, the woman narrowed her eyes. "I saw your friends a week or so ago. They ordered a custom project that was delivered to them yesterday."

I fought the urge to stand up and hug her. Instead, I plastered a carefully neutral expression on my face and inclined my head in thanks.

"She's lying about something. It's in her eyes, isn't it?" Niles tilted his head as he viewed her. "I don't think she delivered it to them at all. It's still here somewhere, whatever it is. You should search the shop, check out whatever's beneath that cloth on the workbench."

"Thank you," I said to the woman, ignoring Niles. "I'm relieved to know they made it to the city. Do you…know where they're staying?"

"No."

Her answer came too quickly. Now she was definitely lying, probably warring with her conscience since she had no way of knowing whether Reina and Alesh were truly friends of mine or whether I was a lovesick stalker.

"But." She hesitated. "They're likely in the immigrants' quarter. I would check the inns there. It is the best place for a foreigner to stay with easy access to food and anything else one might need while spending time in the city."

"She knows exactly where they are, doesn't she? Interesting," Niles said, arms crossed as he walked around in front of her, his eyes gleaming with suspicion.

"Very well," I answered her. "I appreciate the information. One more question and then I'll leave you to your work."

"You have one minute and twenty-three seconds."

"What did you craft for them?"

"I do not share the details of work I have done for others."

I closed my eyes, opened them again, and pinched the bridge of my nose. Then I stared into her eyes, pushing every ounce of sincerity into the words my request.

"Did they ask you to craft a diadem?"

"I'm telling you, flip back that cloth on the work bench," Niles intervened.

The woman's nostrils flared. I either hit my mark, or I insulted her by asking again when she already told me she was bound to secrecy. Knowing what I knew about the Chaos

Wielder and Tarrowburn's last prophecy, a diadem must be involved. If the source of Reina's power stemmed from the talisman, and the source of Alesh's power stemmed from the staff, then I would put all bets on the Chaos Wielder's diadem being the source of his power. *Her* power?

"I already told you I have nothing more to tell you. Search the immigrants' quarter."

I stood. She tensed again, reaffixing her grip around the pipe in case I was a madman who paid to question her *before* attacking. Instead, I walked past, to the front door. I unlocked the three deadbolts in place, and swung the door open, greeted by Aeros who had migrated to the ivy-covered wall facing us and was happily munching on whatever thorn-free leaves she could grab.

"One last thing." In the doorway, I turned to face her. "How did you know I broke in?"

I'd been bothered, not just because she'd managed to get a hit in and my head still throbbed from the blow, but because she'd known I was in the building and in the stairwell, despite my efforts. I had been stealth itself, silent, a ghost of my own making, and still, she had detected my presence. How?

"My whole building is warded."

I furrowed my brow in confusion.

"It helps to know the best spellbinders in town. I was alerted as soon as you opened the window, thief. Then again when you opened the door to the hall."

"A…spellbinder, you say?"

She nodded once.

"Don't think to find a way around the wards." She palmed the coins from the desk and shoved them in a colorful work apron at her waist. "They've already reset."

CHAPTER TWENTY

The History of Tragedy
Reina

By the time we relayed the whole story to Mical, I had to convince him to unclench his fists. He practically seethed with fury.

"I knew she killed them. I just didn't know how, and I couldn't prove it."

I glanced to Abi, then back to Mical, subtly reminding him that no matter how much he loathed Elodie and what she'd done to his friends in the guard, what she'd done to her own family was that much worse, and Abi was the one who suffered the brunt of the pain.

I didn't elaborate on how Abigayle had escaped her sister's wrath. I still didn't know, and she offered nothing when we reached that portion of the tale, choosing instead to keep her mouth clamped tightly shut and her eyes downcast, feigning sudden interest in her palms.

"You have the replica diadem?"

I shook my head. "Not yet. Alesh will get it tomorrow before he…changes."

It was why he hadn't yet changed his own looks. We'd have no way to explain our sudden change in appearance to

Djana, and we couldn't risk that she might refuse to release the diadem to a hired messenger.

Mical nodded. "If I'm to go with you, if I'm to help make this happen, you'll need to change me, too. My face is too familiar to the palace guards. Not all of them, of course, but to many." He shot me a sheepish grin. "I owe a couple of them money. I'm sure they haven't forgotten."

"Very well," Alesh agreed. "But should I die or should we fail, I cannot change it back."

I swallowed, catching a glimpse of myself in the mirror. I wouldn't have to worry about staying in this form. If Alesh died or we failed, I would be dead, too, and it would hardly matter what face adorned my corpse.

"Can you do it now?" he asked.

"So eager to change." Alesh remarked.

It was Abi who stated the obvious. "He owes more than he's let on. You're in trouble, aren't you?"

Mical licked his lips. "Yes, Little Grace, I am. Your father was right to cut me from the guard. I'm a liability. I go where the money flows, which isn't necessarily a dreadful thing, unless one also happens to be a gambler, which…" He raised his hands in the air with a shrug.

"Very well. Sit." Alesh's tone signaled his displeasure with Mical's admission.

Not that any of us were pleased. Aligning with someone like Mical spoke volumes of our desperation. We didn't have the luxury of time on our side to recruit and select a reliable team. What we had was a mere handful of days, a gambling ex-guard, and an emperor-to-be who had likely not even started her first flow.

Saints, what had we gotten ourselves into?

When Alesh had finished altering him, Mical looked… more dashing than he had before.

"You could have made him ugly, you know," Abi said with a pout. I was relieved she had spoken my thoughts aloud.

"I can only work with what is already there," Alesh said, amused by Abi's words.

Mical examined himself in the mirror, turning left and right. "That is…amazing. That you can do such a thing."

"Now he'll be even *more* full of himself." Abi rolled her eyes and flopped backwards on the bed, making a point of being dramatic.

"I've always been worth looking at, Little Grace. You're simply too young to realize it."

Now, I rolled my eyes.

Still, Mical wasn't lying. Alesh had done an exquisite job of bringing out his finest features and, whereas he'd been a brawny and handsome man before, now he was also refined.

"I *am* something to behold." He turned to me and gave a smoldering stare, letting his gaze drop to my lips as he stood, stepping into my space. "I bet even you can't resist my charm now."

Ah. Refined in looks only.

"I'm afraid you'll have to direct your charm elsewhere. My heart is taken, Mical."

I swallowed, the truth in my words sticking in my throat. Alesh put a hand on my shoulder and squeezed, then directed the attention elsewhere, for which I was infinitely grateful.

"Now then. We discuss how you will get into the palace."

Over the next few days, I saw Quinn twice more in the streets below. It wasn't him. Logically, I knew this. But there was something about the shape of the shoulders and the cock of his head that had me longing for Quinn again. No horse this time. If I was honest with myself, it probably wasn't even the same man I'd seen before, just another dark-haired, broad-shouldered stranger who made my heart ache.

Maybe it was the lack of sleep finally catching up to me after months of riding and running and planning and worrying. Maybe I'd truly cracked and lost my mind entirely. Maybe Mical's advances, even in jest, made me long for what I'd had in Quinn. Whatever the case, I was now seeing Quinn in waking hours as well as my dreaming ones.

"Anything interesting happening out there?" Abi said, joining me at the window and peering down into the crowd below.

"No, nothing. The same as every day, I fear."

"We've almost done it, Reina. I know it." Wise beyond her years, Abi intuited my melancholy, but probably attributed it to our current situation and not my heartbreak over Quinn's death.

How peculiar. I could think about his death now, even say it aloud, too. Quinn was dead.

Abi took my hand from the windowsill and squeezed,

leading me back to the table in the room. "I…have something I'd like to tell you," she said. "While Alesh is away. It's not that I think he won't understand, but, well, I think you know loss like I do, and I…want to tell you about that night."

I stored away thoughts of Quinn for later, and sat, giving Abi my full attention. As she struggled to find a place to start, I shared my own grief. "Growing up, I didn't know my father. My mother was killed when I was fifteen. I had no one, save for my very best friend who had gone away for over two years, only to come back a stranger. I fell in love with that stranger." I swallowed and took a shaky breath. "Three weeks ago, he died, too."

Sadness touched the corners of Abi's eyes as she watched me speak, a sadness eyes so young shouldn't have. "I can feel it, you know. The sadness in you is like the sadness in me, too. So I knew you would understand when I wanted to tell you my story. And I think it's important, too. You should know what Elodie is capable of. Knowing…about that night might help."

I returned her sad smile with one of my own. I feared I knew all too well what Elodie was capable of. I'd seen as much in Castilles and the Southern Plains. I'd seen the dead hunt the living, bogs appear in healthy, green forest, frost in near-summer heat, storm clouds from bright blue skies, and perfectly innocent people killed at her whim. There was no doubt in my mind Elodie was content to spread chaos wherever she went. I suspected the night she gained that power would not likely change my opinion of her.

"My mother didn't wear the diadem often. She kept it

with her, always, but she preferred to keep it in this blue velvet-lined box of hers. She said power could be too tempting. It was one of the virtues she instilled in us from birth—a sense of responsibility. As the Gehtanan family, the imperial family, it was our job to guard the diadem and all the power that came with it. Really, it was her job, but she knew it wouldn't be so forever."

"Your mother sounds wise."

Abi nodded vigorously. "She was. That night, we took the large carriage, the one big enough to carry the whole family. It needed six horses to pull it. We were going to see a show, a beautiful performance with dancers that twirled on their toes and jumped through the air as though they weighed nothing at all. At least, that's what I was told." Abi's gaze fell to the table. She traced the wood planks with one finger and bit her lip. Then she took a breath as her lip trembled.

"It's all right if you'd rather not tell me, Abi." I didn't want her to relive a night of pure horror. Not for my benefit.

"No, I want to. Anyway, the performance wasn't in Ivirreh. It was half a day's journey away, but since it was an evening performance, we left mid-afternoon. By the time the sun had set, and it was winter, mind you, we were a little more than halfway to Chaltonnea. And that's"—her voice broke— "That's when it happened.

"Elodie opened the case with the diadem, which wasn't odd. We loved to look at it. Who wouldn't? It's beautiful. But then she got this strange smile on her face. Deni and Hati were asleep. They always fell asleep on long carriage rides. Melánd and Mama were knitting. She was making me a shawl, a beautiful purple one, with rainbow beads at the ends." She looked up at me, blue eyes clear as a summer's sky. "It doesn't really matter what color the beads were, does it?"

Tears crested her eyes and traced streaks down her rounded cheeks. I wanted to grab her to me and squeeze her until she was cried out. But she wasn't done talking, and she wanted to see this story through.

"Papa and Artur sat in the front with the driver. Papa liked to be seen by our people sometimes. Said it was good for them to know he was a normal person just like them. So he didn't see, and he couldn't stop her. I was the only one paying attention. I…could have stopped it all from happening."

Her chest heaved in giant gasps as she began to panic. I gripped both of her hands and forced her to look at me. "Abi, look at me. No, *look*. You must look at my eyes. There. That's it. This was *not* your fault. You couldn't have stopped Elodie. You couldn't have known what she would do."

She sobbed. "But I did. I saw it all. I knew from the glint in her eye. I *knew* she was going to place it on her head."

"Shhh. It doesn't matter. You still couldn't have known what she would do once she wore it. Abi, none of this is your fault. You cannot blame yourself for the actions of others. We make our own paths in this world, and you can only bear responsibility for those things which *you* are in control of."

She heard the words, I knew, but they did nothing to slow the river of tears that now flowed from her eyes. So, I pulled her close, hugged her, swayed with her until her tears were spent and she could speak again. I knew that pain. I knew it all too well. I swallowed away the tears threatening to form in my own eyes, the lump threatening to overtake my throat.

"I'm sorry," she finally said with a sniff, her voice weak. "I didn't mean to cry. I'm stronger than that."

"Oh, Abi! Crying doesn't mean you're weak. Crying is a sign of strength. It means you're strong enough to feel emotions and unafraid to let them show. Too many people don't cry when they should, and they end up alone and miserable. Let the tears flow and take comfort that you were brave enough to release them."

She looked up at me, head cocked, a confounded expression on her face, the edges of her hair wet from tears and plastered to her cheeks. "How do you do that?"

"Do what?"

"Know what to say to make things better? Is that your power, too?"

I smiled and swallowed once. "No, I don't think so, but you and I are so very alike. I'd even go so far as to say you're a Little Me."

"A little you?"

"Something like that. You're so much stronger than you know." I brushed the hair back from her face.

"Then I guess I should say thank you," she said.

"Oh? And why's that?"

"Because being like you is the highest praise I can think of. There's no one else I'd rather grow to be like."

I grabbed her again, pulled her tight into a hug, my cheek pressed tight against the top of her head. Then I planted a kiss there and released her.

"Tell me," I said. "I'm here. You're not alone. Tell me what you think I should know."

She took a shaky breath, nodded, and launched back into the tale of that night. "Once the diadem was on her head, it was a matter of seconds. The entire carriage was set aflame, our family…didn't stand a chance. I lived because…because I did something I shouldn't have. I ran."

"You ran?"

"I jumped from the carriage the moment she put the diadem on her head. It was stupid. I could have at least tried to save everyone. Instead, I ran and saved myself."

"Sweetheart, you couldn't have known."

"I knew Elodie. I knew her before. She was always wrong inside. Vengeful, mean. She enjoyed watching others suffer. And it infuriated her that she would never wear the diadem. Hati always said the diadem should have been locked, and only my mother should have had the key, but Mama didn't want to lock it away. She wanted to be able to use its power at a moment's notice. 'Power is no good if you take too long to use it,' she used to say. She had a lot of ideas about the magic and how it should be used. I fear Elodie has many ideas, too, but none of them involve helping others.

"Anyway, I…should have told you before." Abi's chin trembled. "She knows I'm not dead. She's known all along."

Dread swept from the top of my head to the tips of my toes as though I'd been doused with a bucket of ice water. "What do you mean?"

"Afterwards, after the fire burned and the guards behind

us were unsuccessful in their rescue—several of them were killed, too—well, afterwards, they brought Mama, Papa, Melánd, Artur, Hati, and Deni to be blessed so their souls could reach the sky. She knew I was missing. I…don't know who she killed, but…but there were remains. My size. Also burned. She…she…"

Elodie's cruelty knew no bounds.

"It's all right." I placed my hand over Abi's and squeezed. "I understand. You don't have to say more."

Elodie had burned another child Abi's size so she could claim to be the sole survivor of the Gehtanan family line, but she knew her sister lived.

Our plan suddenly became a thousand times more dangerous. Elodie must have always known her sister would come back, and she knew Alesh and I sought her out to destroy the diadem. The ball was a ruse. She'd known from the beginning. She'd always known.

"Reina? Say something." Abi's blue eyes were wide with fear, their glassy depths threatening tears again.

"Thank you for telling me. You, my dearest Abigayle, are so very brave. It's hard to share sometimes, but it's good for us to know how much Elodie knows. I expect she's been waiting for you to return for a long time."

She screwed her mouth sideways. "Maybe. She probably thinks I'm dead, though. It took me months to get back to the city on my own, and she never thought highly of me to begin with."

Saints above, Abi was stronger than even *I* could have known. I suspected child Reina very well could have been best friends with a girl like Abigayle if she hadn't been born a handful of years and a half a world away.

Then Alesh swung through the door, his pack slung low across his back, a smile on his face.

"It's done?" Abi asked, wiping the last traces of tears from her face and composing herself.

"It is." Alesh reached into the pack and withdrew an umber-colored cloth package the perfect size to contain a jewel-encrusted diadem. He set it gently on the table. When neither Abi nor I moved to unwrap it, he said, "Well, go!"

Abi met my gaze and I nodded to her. She should be the one to reveal Djana's masterpiece. With my permission, she pulled the cloth across the table and began to unwrap it corner by corner.

When at last the diadem was revealed, we shared a collective gasp. The resemblance was uncanny. Abi turned the piece sideways, then back again, tilting it upwards so the cracked citrine sparkled in the light. Djana said differences would be visible, and to a jeweler of her caliber, they could, but to my amateur eye, I could tell no difference between the piece before me and the one worn on the head of the girl who tried to destroy me. Seeing it set my nerves on edge.

"It's amazing," Abi breathed, running a finger along one smooth, gold edge. "I mean, it's not perfect, but it's really, *really* close. The gemstone is a little pale, but if you swap it in a room with low light, she'll never notice."

"That is the plan," Alesh agreed.

We would swap out the diadem while Elodie slept, but the ball was the easiest way into the palace. Once inside, we'd stay in our arranged hiding places to wait until our Chaos Wielder slept.

The plan was not without its faults. We could be caught at the gates despite the alternate identities Mical had given us. We could be allowed to pass into the palace unchallenged, then caught within the ball itself, regardless of our changed appearances. Elodie could find and kill Abigayle despite our precautions, eradicating our only chance at keeping the entire empire from an uprising. Too many things could go wrong entirely too easily.

Quinn would take the chance, I reminded myself. Quinn would do what needed to be done, and therefore, so would I.

"The size and cut of the stone are amazing. And all the pearls here," Abi ran her finger along the pearl drops at the edges, setting them swinging. "I don't know if the damage is accurate. I haven't seen the diadem up close since that night in the carriage, the night she… Well, it was still whole then."

"It's as accurate as we're going to get. It shouldn't matter anyway. With any luck, she won't see it until the morning when she wakes."

Abi sat up, alert, mouth open in a silent *oh*. "What about the spellbinder?"

Alesh shook his head. "We are out of time. We will have to go in without binding magic to the diadem."

Abi shook her head vehemently. "You can't! She'll know. She'll wake before you leave the room with the real diadem. As soon as she no longer feels the magic, she'll wake. And if she's within reach of even a tiny portion of the magic, she'll destroy you. You *have* to see a spellbinder!"

"I'll go," I offered, turning to Alesh. "While you're changing your appearance, I'll go. I'll do it now." I turned back to Abi. "Is it something that can be done quickly?"

She nodded.

I looked back at the delicate piece of jewelry again, my hopes falling as quickly as they'd risen. Who would enchant a replica diadem without suspicion? We didn't have the time to shop for the right kind of individual as we'd done with our goldsmith.

You have a plan in place. Make it happen. That's what Quinn would have said, what he would have done. I needed to do the same. I hardened my resolve.

"All right, then. Who's your spellbinder?"

CHAPTER TWENTY-ONE

Curious Consequences
Quinn

I stopped once more at the Porenskahal Inn, to inquire about Reina and Alesh, but the same barkeep was still present.

"Ach, Tabra's on shift in forty minutes if you want to stick around to ask about your friends. Can I get you a pint in the meantime?"

I ordered a pint of the Butcher's ale I'd had before, but it sat on the counter in front of me, growing warmer by the minute. Occupying the end of the bar where I might keep watch on the doorway to see who came and went, I took note of the same woman I'd seen on my last visit, this time descending the stairs and heading for the inn's front door. She wasn't worth a moment of my attention, not when Reina or Alesh could be here, but something about her pulled at me.

I tossed a couple of coins to the bar to pay for my drink, then decided to follow. I had no reason to follow her. I had no reason to be interested in her business. By my estimate, Tabra would be working the bar in another ten minutes. But Tabra would be there all night, and I could just as easily visit her later.

My gut told me to follow the blond woman in the teal gown, so that's what I did, even if it made absolutely no good sense at all. I stayed behind her on the streets, far enough to keep out of sight, not so far that I couldn't keep her in *my* sight. The bustling streets made it easy to blend in, to keep pace without being seen. I followed her turn after turn, and even when she'd gone far enough that the streets should have been empty, the vendors were still bustling, calling out sales to willing customers.

Her walk, I realized, was the same as Reina's. That was what had caught my eye. If that was what really drew my attention, I was a fool for leaving the inn behind and following a perfect stranger through the crowded streets. I was wasting time I didn't have. Still, I followed, letting instinct guide me where common sense screamed to turn back.

She arrived at a storefront with a sign I couldn't read, comprised of letters from the local tongue. I memorized the look of it, made note to ask my barkeep friend—or Tabra if she indeed existed—later. The woman passed through the open doorway and into the shop beyond, leaving my sight.

To follow, or not to follow?

I couldn't very well go into the shop without a reason. I may have stolen enough money to buy drink and ply a criminal jeweler for information, but I was certain I could not afford whatever was beyond that door.

I meandered to the giant bay window, feigning interest in the wares displayed behind the clear glass. Trinkets, baubles, wooden sculptures, handmade dolls, and glass vases sat upon a black velvet display cloth. I wasted no time focusing on them, but instead looked deeper within the shop to where the woman, her back to me, was bartering with the shopkeeper.

If only Niles were here. He could have easily gone inside and listened in on the conversation without fear of being seen. His ghost had been sparse today. I hadn't seen him since early morning, and I wondered what he was doing with his time. Perhaps nothing. Perhaps he failed to exist at all outside of his contact with me.

The shopkeeper took something from the woman's hands—a palm-sized, cloth-wrapped bundle the details of which I couldn't make out. Watching the woman speak, I couldn't shake the feeling that her hands, the way she used them to elaborate her words, seemed eerily familiar. I squinted, taking in her profile as she briefly turned her head to the side, but still, I couldn't place her.

Then the shopkeeper nodded with a smile, held a hand to his heart, and smiled.

I have a daughter the same age as your sister. She adores our emperor. What a wonderful idea. Perhaps I will take credit for your idea as my own on her next birthday.

I read his lips with uncertainty. I hadn't often needed to read lips during my time in the Order, and the task was a hundred times harder when trying to read the lips of a non-native speaker of the northern tongue. The glare from the window didn't help.

The shopkeeper placed the now unwrapped bundle—I still couldn't see what it was—on the shop counter, then returned to a spot behind the counter, pulling an array of vials and bottles from cabinets below.

Within a few moments, he'd concocted a mixture within a shallow bowl, stirred it a handful of times, then immersed the woman's offering—it was a jewel, I thought, something yellow and glittering—into the bowl with a pair of tongs.

He was speaking, words I couldn't read. I didn't think it was the northern tongue. Something about the cadence of his speech, though, was familiar. A chant. He was chanting as he worked.

I stepped back and looked again to the shop sign. What *was* this place?

Then the woman turned to the window, and I ducked around the corner, out of sight. It wasn't that I thought she would recognize me, but if she saw me here, then happened to notice me sitting at the inn's bar later…well, it would look as though I'd followed her.

Which I had.

She exited the shop a few moments later, took one look up and down the street, then turned back the way she'd come. Back to the inn now that she'd completed her task, likely.

I waited until she passed out of view before returning to the shop window. Then, I stepped back in surprise. I'd been so focused on my self-assigned mission that I'd barely given more than a cursory glance to the display items.

The trinkets and baubles gleamed as if being twirled in the light, even though the sun had grown low on the western horizon and could never produce such shine. The wooden sculpture of a jester actually *moved* despite not having joints. The wood itself morphed as the figure juggled three wooden balls. The dolls blinked and smiled as though they were living children, asking to be held. And the glass vases within the display spun in changing colors.

I stepped back as I examined them. How was such a thing possible?

A voice startled me out of my reverie. "You look like a northern man. If you're looking for a gift beyond the fantastical, you've come to the right place."

The shopkeeper stood in the open doorway, leaning against one side, a smile wide on his face as he watched the awe on mine.

"What kind of place is this?"

"Tairo Entlei, Spellbinder. It's what I do. There are others throughout the city, but none who can make a vase match the color of the room it's placed in, or the flowers within it. That's my specialty. No one's managed to duplicate it yet. Do you have a girl at home? Does she like flowers? I can charm a flower—or an entire bouquet—to spread floral scent through a whole estate."

I pointed to the wares behind the window. "You do this?"

His chest puffed with pride. "I do."

"Do you…enchant other items?"

He flustered for a moment. "I charm them, not enchant, but yes."

"Is there a difference, between charming and enchanting, I mean?"

"*Big* difference, but not one I could explain to the average layperson. You'd have to study the craft for years to understand it."

"Fascinating."

"Is there anything I can get for you? Or custom make for you?"

I debated asking him about the woman who'd been here moments ago, about what she'd had charmed and what she meant to do with it, but I couldn't think of any plausible excuse to be asking such a question.

Perhaps in forgiving myself beneath Kufataba, I'd lost my edge. Brigantino would be disappointed.

"Not today, thank you, but now that I know such a shop exists, I hope to be back again soon," I answered. I hated to give him false hope of a sale, but it seemed the kindest way out of the conversation.

"May the eye of the emperor watch over you always."

I nodded my head. "And you, as well."

I didn't see the woman again, nor did I expect to since she'd had a head start on getting back to the inn. I made it back to the inn's bar and dining room as darkness began to touch the sky. I slid into the only empty seat among the raucous crowd.

A woman was at the bar. Tabra, I assumed. By her looks, I guessed my barkeep friend to be her brother. The two were almost identical from the dark curls on their heads to the circumference of their thick arms.

"What can I get you?" she asked from halfway down the bar, her gaze meeting mine, so I assumed she was speaking to me.

"Can I get a Butcher's ale?" I really should figure out something better to order. Despite what I'd told Niles, the ale tasted like goat piss. It was better if I avoided alcohol anyway.

She filled a pint, then placed the glass in front of me. With the size of the crowd, she expected payment right away, so I slid over enough coin for the drink and a tip, then I struck up conversation.

"Is it always this busy?" I asked, shouting to be heard above the noise.

"This time of year? Usually. But right now, even more so. Too many people in the city. Day after tomorrow, they'll all be on their way," she said, as she filled another pint for a customer three seats down.

"Can I ask you a question?" I said as she leaned back to hand the drink to the customer, then turned her attention back to me.

"Depends on what the question is."

I almost laughed. I'd be willing to bet she heard all sorts of interesting questions behind the bar.

"I was hoping you could tell me if my friends are renting a room here. Moreina di Bianco and Aleshkatel Bhalehi. I suspect they arrived before most of the crowd descended on the city. We were…separated some weeks ago. I didn't expect to be able to catch up."

Tabra eyed me like a mother in search of her child's lie. Finally, she answered. "I believe they checked out two days ago."

My shoulders fell in defeat. Leaving made no sense. Where would they have gone? Why leave shelter when there was nowhere else to go in the city, especially now? Blast it. What *were* their plans?

"Do you know where they might have gone?"

She shook her head, a black curl coming loose from the twist at the top of her head. She pushed it out of one eye. "I don't."

"Might I…see the room where they stayed?" I knew she'd never consent, but I asked anyway.

"Afraid not. Someone else checked in immediately afterwards. The room is occupied."

I nodded my head and thanked her. I took a sip of my Butcher's ale, swallowed, then caught her attention once more as she had begun to turn away.

"One more question."

Tabra gave a sigh, but like any barkeep who knew the worth of a good tip, she listened.

I licked my lips. "I saw…a blond woman earlier. About this tall, high cheeks, narrow chin. She was so familiar, but I couldn't place her. Any chance you know anything about her? I know only that she's staying at the inn."

One eyebrow shot upwards. Tabra leaned back against the shelves lined with alcohol and glassware, her arms crossed, as she eyed me. I couldn't blame her. A foreign man comes into the bar asking about not one, but two separate women who'd stayed at the inn? I must have seemed a murderer searching out my next victim.

"Hmm."

I shook my head and held up one hand. "Never mind. I realize how that must sound. I just…couldn't shake the feeling I knew her from somewhere. You've already been helpful. Thank you."

Tabra nodded once and walked away, through a back door to where I presume the kitchen was located. She returned shortly afterwards, rolling new casks to replace empty ones behind the bar.

I sipped at my ale and wondered where Reina and Alesh had gone and what they planned on doing about the Chaos Wielder. I hoped they'd discovered his identity by now. I hoped they'd discovered how to defeat him. Dread filled the pit of my stomach. If they hadn't defeated him already, what were the chances they would be able to do so before the eclipse tomorrow night?

I should be with them. I should be helping them. I could—

"You're looking for a blond woman?" A man reminiscent of Brigantino's hulking size slid into the recently vacated seat beside me, his medium brown hair combed, a neat stubble on his cheeks passing for a beard.

I tilted my head as I assessed him. I had no reason to engage in conversation, but I also had nothing to lose by a friendly chat.

"Not any blond woman," I assured him. "There was a specific young woman I glimpsed earlier. She reminded me of someone. I just…couldn't place her."

The man gave a knowing smile, as though he could imagine in what kinds of ways I might be trying to place her. He nodded to Tabra as he flagged her down for a drink of his own.

"What can I get you?"

He laughed, a deep rumble from a large chest. "The usual."

She stared at him blankly. "And what's that?"

The man shook his head as though he'd forgotten something. "Sorry. White ale, shot of amber."

Tabra nodded before serving him. He plunked four coins on the counter. She pocketed them, then returned to the opposite end of the bar.

"Anyhow, I think I might know who you're looking for. A woman, about this tall"—he held his hand out to approximately the right height— "Delicate chin, high cheeks, beautiful body, perfect shape…eh, a teal dress today, I think. Yes? Sound familiar?"

I stared.

I hadn't seen the woman with anyone, and I didn't know this man, who increasingly seemed familiar enough to be her lover. It might be wise to pretend there was someone else I'd noticed instead.

"I…don't know what she was wearing today," I lied. "Could be the same person. I saw her once yesterday." Another lie.

The man stared. "Is that so?"

I nodded. "Anyway," I said with a shrug. "It's no matter. If I don't see her again, I don't. I only thought I might remember where I knew her from."

He held up his drink. "Memories, I'll drink to that."

I breathed an internal sigh of relief. Whatever suspicion I'd aroused in him had settled now.

I finished my ale, cringing at the bitter aftertaste, then bid him a good night.

"Do you have far to travel to your quarters?" he asked.

My eyebrows drew downward. "No," I lied again. "Just down the street. Perhaps I'll see you again."

"Perhaps."

I hoped not. Especially if the woman I followed today was with him.

I made for the inn's front door, exchanging the noise of the dining room and bar for the noise of the eager vendors outside, who hoped to make money before tomorrow night's festivities.

I was three blocks away when I noticed my shadow. A curse fell from my lips. It shouldn't have taken me so long to realize. My time as king had made me lazy. Had I forgotten all my training?

I slipped between two buildings, down a dark alley where no vendors or customers roamed, where I could gain an advantage over my stalker.

Only, I didn't have the chance.

The much larger man appeared out of nowhere, from behind me in the alleyway and not from the street. He had me pinned to the side of the building in minutes, my training all but useless as he held a knife to my throat.

The man I'd spoken to in the bar, the man who'd been possessive over the woman I'd been asking about stood hovering over me, his broad, angled face full of solemn gravity, tinged with anger.

I struggled to breathe, resisting the urge to fight. I'd be no use to anyone dead, and he had the clear advantage. If I could talk him into a distraction, I might be able to regain the upper hand.

"Easy, friend. This was definitely not what I meant when I said perhaps I'd see you again," I said.

He scowled and pushed me harder against the whitewashed wall behind me, thunking my head in the process, right in the same spot the goldsmith had hit me yesterday. Pain radiated through my skull.

"I am *not* your friend," he seethed. "The woman. Tell me what you know about her."

I tried to hold up my arms in a sign of innocence, but it was difficult to do so with a knife at my throat, so I managed a shrug instead.

"I know nothing," I said. "I told you already. I thought she—"

"Sure, sure. You thought she seemed familiar. So why did you follow her to the spellbinder's shop today?"

I reeled. I'd been followed. Worse, I'd been followed and hadn't even *noticed*.

I narrowed my eyes. "Who are you?"

"No, my *friend*. I have the blade. I ask the questions. Who are you?"

Lie. Lie, you daft idiot.

I swallowed. "I'm looking for friends of mine in the city. When I saw the woman, I…something compelled me to follow."

He shoved at my chest again, rattling my skull against the wall behind me. I squeezed my eyes shut. "I'm telling you the truth."

"And what did you learn by following my lady?"

The point of the knife was too close to the tender spot in

my neck. There was no way to twist myself out of his hold without losing a lot of blood in the process.

"Nothing of interest," I answered. "Just that she went to a spellbinder's shop. As dozens of people do every day."

He glared hard at me, as though trying to determine whether it would be too much trouble to kill me.

"Look," I said. "I'm sorry if it all came out wrong. I promise you, I swear, I have—"

There. The knife moved a hair. It wasn't much, but it was enough.

I grabbed his wrist with both hands, ducked out of his grasp, and twisted my body to pin him against the wall instead. He was larger, and definitely stronger, but he hadn't anticipated I might present a challenge. He'd underestimated his opponent, a mistake he wouldn't make again now that he knew I was better at a fight than I'd let on.

I slammed his wrist into the solid wall above his head once, then twice more, even while his other enormous paw was already grabbing at my shirt. One more slam against the wall, and the knife clattered to the ground.

I twisted again, pulling both of our bodies to the ground in the opposite direction, throwing him down before he could think to defend himself from the move. Applying pressure on the spot by his ear that would cause him to pass out, I attempted to give myself a chance to escape without killing him. This man, whoever he was, whatever his lot, *had* a life and I would not take it.

I pressed downward as he struggled beneath me, then a giant fist knocked into my ear with so much force the whole world went white behind my eyes, and I was flung sideways off him.

On the ground again, I struggled to regain my footing before his punches landed, but I made it only to one knee before he managed a hit to my temple.

My world was black before my head hit the ground.

I groaned, surprised to wake. Unsurprised at facing a colossal headache. I hadn't been bested in hand-to-hand combat so badly since…well, since Alesh, actually. Humiliating, really. At least this time Reina hadn't been here to witness it.

"That was something."

Of course Niles had seen it.

I rolled onto my back, staring at the sides of the buildings and the scrap of star-studded sky visible above them. I sat up slowly, rubbing my jaw, my neck, my shoulders.

"You bastard," I said. "Where were you when I needed you?"

Why was I still alive? The man had been willing to put a knife against my throat. He should have killed me once he gained the upper hand, but he hadn't.

"Me? I was where I needed to be, doing the things I needed to do. How exactly do you think I'd be able to help you in a fist fight anyway? I'm no match for *you*, let alone him." One eyebrow arched in amusement. Why did it seem as though Niles was always laughing at my expense?

I fought the dizziness in my head. A man didn't hit that hard and in *that* spot unless he knew what he was doing, unless he'd been trained to fight.

I ran a hand along a shoulder and the back of my neck. "I meant earlier today. I followed this woman. To a… spellbinder's shop."

"Why on Liron would you do such a thing? Why take an interest in anyone here at all save for Reina, Alesh, or the deranged lunatic we're trying to eradicate?"

I stood, my body almost reluctant to support my full weight. I shifted back and forth on my feet, waking myself, reminding my body parts they needed to function.

"There was something about her. I can't explain it. I had time to kill, so I followed her."

"And?"

I shrugged, then brushed dirt from my pants. "And nothing. Other than a spellbinder's shop, which is…rather phenomenal."

"I'm guessing Brigantino Jr. didn't appreciate you taking interest in his wife."

I coughed. "Something like that."

"Well. You survived."

"It would have been infinitely better if you'd been here to follow."

He shrugged. "Sorry."

Somehow, I didn't feel the sincerity in his apology.

"So what now?"

"Now? Now, I scour the rest of the inns all night and hope someone can give me *something* on Reina and Alesh.

They can't have vanished. They're here." I looked out into the street beyond the alley. "Somewhere, they're here."

CHAPTER TWENTY-TWO

Stalkers, Venoms, and Brands
Reina

"You're being followed."

Mical surprised all of us when he entered the room without so much as a knock. We'd been going over the exact timing of our plan all afternoon, into the evening, and now well past dark, running through it until I thought I might see images of the palace's layout in my very dreams.

I now knew where every guard between the grand entrance and the throne room was stationed. Plus every guard in every hall and every room along the way.

"Who follows?" Alesh asked. I still hadn't gotten used to his new appearance, hair turned white with age, thick, wiry eyebrows, a nose larger than it should have been, and an increasing number of wrinkles on his forehead.

Mical shook his head. "Not you. Her."

He pointed to me.

I swallowed as my heart thumped.

"By whom?" Alesh asked again.

It could only have occurred when I'd visited the spellbinder. The trip was the lone solo journey I'd made of any significance today. Other than ordering food from the dining room or the vendors outside, I hadn't left our room without Alesh and Abi by my side for days.

"When I saw the spellbinder?"

Mical nodded, a shining lock of hair falling over his devastatingly handsome face before he swept it back again. I wondered if the move was practiced.

"By a man who looked like trouble. And yes, when you visited the spellbinder's shop today."

I met Alesh's gaze. "The Chaos Wielder?"

He chewed his lip as he thought, his brows drawn downward over his eyes in a scowl. "I do not think she would have sent someone for you. Not this close to the eclipse."

I heard the words he didn't speak aloud. Not this close to the eclipse that would seal her fate as ruler of a world fallen to chaos.

"Maybe it *was* her," I suggested. "Like she appeared before. In the body of another."

Abi snorted. "She is *far* too busy planning the ball to be following you right now. If there's one thing I know about my sister, it's that she's unconcerned with *anyone* but herself right now. I hate to think what the palace staff is being asked to do." She gave a shudder.

"Describe this man," Alesh demanded.

Mical held a hand level with his chin, which was still well above my head. "About this tall. Dark hair, dark beard. Dressed like a northerner. Young. Twenties, maybe."

"Do you know anyone like that?" Alesh asked me.

I shook my head. "No one who would be here." I thought for a moment before asking a question I had no good reason to ask. "Did he have any scars, Mical? Any identifying marks on this man? Something that might have stood out?"

Mical's eyes lit. "He did. A thin scar. Here." He held a finger to the outside corner of his left eye.

My breath caught in my throat. I forced my eyes closed. *Don't hope. Don't. He's gone.*

Then I opened my eyes and gave a half-hearted shrug. "There must be plenty of men who match that description."

"Where is this man now?" Alesh asked.

"He's probably still knocked out in the alley where I left him. I debated bagging his head to blind him, then dragging him back here, but I didn't want to draw attention on the street."

I stared.

Somehow, it was entirely too easy to picture Mical lugging an unconscious man with a burlap sack over his head through the streets. If it weren't for our attempt at remaining low profile, he'd have done it with glee.

"You knocked him unconscious?" The healer in me fought the urge to have him lead me to the man so I could help in some way.

Mical nodded, one corner of his mouth pulling upward in a proud smirk.

Not Quinn then. Aside from the fact that he was dead, Quinn never would have allowed himself to be bested by Mical. He would have killed him outright first, then worn the guilt of taking Mical's life for the rest of his days.

Of course it's not Quinn, you dolt. Quinn is dead.

"Hopefully, that's enough to deter him," I said.

"There is one thing that bothers me," Alesh said. He'd worn a deep-in-thought scowl since the start of the conversation. "Why would anyone have reason to follow you when you are"—he held out his hands to me, waving them in the air— "changed?"

In the few days since he'd changed my looks, I'd almost forgotten entirely. I'd grown used to seeing blond wisps at the sides of my face, and the high cheeks and angular face in the mirror.

Before Alesh changed his own looks, he checked us out from the inn. Less than a minute after he left, a lovely blond woman with dark eyes and a narrow chin arrived looking for a room.

"A stroke of luck!" Tabra had said.

They'd just had a guest leave. The room was not yet freshened, but if I cared to leave a deposit, they would freshen it, and the room would be ready for me in an hour's time. It was the only time the three of us had strayed from the room together since we'd left to grow our produce to sell at the market two weeks ago.

We'd taken the opportunity to walk the immigrants' quarter, to see the local murals and The Artist's Den, a shop that set Abi beside herself as she took in the number of colored charcoal offerings. Art was something that had always drawn Abi's eye. Before her family had been killed, her mother had hired a private tutor to teach Abi the basics. She'd had all of three lessons before she'd been forced to live on the streets.

I looked forward to the day Abi was back in her home,

when she could return to the life of a child, when she could take as many charcoal lessons as her little heart desired. Soon, I prayed. Soon.

Even if Abi was the next in line to the throne, and our only chance at keeping the Empire from falling into despair, she wasn't yet old enough to rule. We'd find a regent who could watch her, teach her, and rule in her place until she came of age.

"I don't know," Mical said, bringing me back to Alesh's question as to why anyone would be following me when I looked as I currently did.

I blinked away my thoughts.

"But he was exceptionally interested in you, said you *reminded* him of someone, but he wouldn't elaborate beyond that. If you want my thoughts, that's rubbish. He made it up so I wouldn't question his motives."

"So what do we do about tomorrow?" Abi looked back and forth between the three adults in the room, the light from the oil lamp illuminating the worry in her eyes.

"We continue," Alesh said.

"Agreed," Mical answered.

"There's nothing to be done," I told her. "We must continue. We'll be vigilant, keep our eyes out for any who might wish us ill, but we're out of time. The eclipse is nearly upon us. She'd have chaos descend on us all—forever—if we don't do something about it."

I didn't want to scare Abigayle. I should have cushioned my words with promises of our success, but I couldn't. I wanted to believe we wouldn't fail, but our entire plan had increasingly begun to seem like that of a nine-year-old boy breaking into his neighbor's treehouse with neither a ladder nor a rope at his disposal. Unlikely to succeed.

I fought back the despair caught in my throat.

"And for now, we sleep," Alesh said.

Reluctantly, I agreed. We would be worthless tomorrow evening without rest tonight. Mical took his leave with an additional warning to take care, then Abi and I settled into our bed for the night, Alesh on the floor below, snoring almost immediately.

For me, sleep was difficult to find and even more difficult to seize. Every time I found myself drifting off, visions of Quinn behind my eyelids forced my eyes open again. Weeks had passed and, still, I saw him in my dreams and in my waking moments. Had I lost my mind? Had I descended into madness, my own brand of chaos? I gave a frustrated sigh, then turned to lie on my side.

Would I be conscious of myself when chaos ruled the world? Would I be aware? Or would I be as good as the *acaffilé,* trawling the land for prey? If the talisman still had magic, Elodie would enjoy using it—or making me use it—to kill all the living creatures around me. Then she'd use Alesh's staff to resurrect them. Maybe, in the midst of it all, she'd—

A sudden pain gripped my thigh. I bolted upright, near-breathless with the agony, applying pressure automatically. The venom.

Maybe I wouldn't be around to watch Liron fall to chaos at all.

I slid from the bed and crawled to the window, where the weak light from both Stellon and the vendor stalls allowed me to examine my leg. I hitched the fabric of my nightgown upward, revealing a web of darkened veins along the inside of my thigh.

Fiermi.

I debated waking Alesh. If the snake's venom had been fully released back into my body, there likely wasn't anything we might do to stop it at this point, but, had that happened, I suspected I'd feel pain far beyond one leg.

I rubbed the spot, the pain subsiding slowly, so slowly. For now, I would keep the issue to myself. I didn't want to worry Alesh or panic Abi, who knew nothing of the snake bite or the venom in my blood to begin with.

No. I'd climb back in bed, close my eyes, and dream of chaos instead.

I didn't dream of chaos. I dreamed of Quinn. Again and again and again. I dreamed of lying in a soft meadow with willowy white flowers swaying in the breeze, of kissing Quinn among the flowers. I dreamed of Quinn surrounded by dark, of Quinn letting loose strangled cries. I dreamed of mountains and valleys, snow, and desert sun. I saw myself in a runaway carriage pulled by undead horses.

When I woke in the morning, I wished I hadn't remembered my dreams, but I remembered all of them, and I felt less rested than when I'd gone to bed to begin with. In the washroom, I examined my leg. The sunlight streaming through the window was more than enough to show no evidence of the web of veins that I'd seen on my thigh last night.

I paused, pushed my lips into a pout in thought.

Had I…dreamed the pain, and the darkened web of veins, too? I sat on the edge of the cast iron tub, closed my eyes, and rubbed the back of my neck. Then I rolled my shoulders and tried hard to remember. A dream made more sense, even if the pain had been so real.

How many times had I woken as a child, convinced my mother had made chocolate briarmint bread for breakfast, or an appliken tart, only to find the same wheat bread, hard cheese, fruit, and goat's milk as every morning?

Last night had been the same. I'd dreamed I'd climbed from bed and viewed my leg by the light of the window. I must have. Besides, if the venom really had let loose in my body, rubbing my leg wouldn't have helped. If anything, the action would have sped up my circulation, increasing the blood flow and killing me faster.

With all the nightmares in my head, how surprising was it, really, that my mind had added one more about the snake venom in my blood? I released a sigh as I ran water into the tub. At least the temperatures in the Elorin Empire meant a cool bath was preferable to a hot one, which was fine as there was no way to heat the water in the washroom anyway.

I looked in the mirror, no longer surprised by the face that greeted me. The branded scar over my heart was the same. I hadn't shown Alesh, so he hadn't attempted to remove it. I was sure he would have insisted on ridding my body of the awful brand, but that half-lidded eye was a reminder to never let myself be ensnared again—by words or by force.

I hope Elodie enjoyed her evening. After tonight, she wouldn't be around to see another.

The anxiety in my gut throughout the day kept me from feeling hunger, and I wasn't alone. Even Abi, who had delighted in the sheer variety of dishes she could sample from the street fare, hadn't asked for breakfast this morning. She, too, was caught in thoughts of what this evening might bring.

I ran a hand along her back as she stood by the window, looking down below. "Don't be nervous," I said with far more confidence than I felt.

The girl's stare was far away as she bit a thumbnail.

"I'm not. Not really, but I do wonder what it will be like to be back there again. Home, in the palace, I mean. You know. Without…them."

I hadn't thought about it. Abi must think of nothing but. How strange it would be for her to return to the place she'd always known without the comfort of the familiar faces that made it home. I squeezed her shoulder.

"You won't be alone, and there will be so many who will be happy to see you, Abi. Truly, I cannot imagine the joy they'll feel after so many months believing the entire family perished. You're a blessing."

She made a small sound from her throat. I leaned over, hugged her from behind, and rested my chin on the top of her head, her soft hairs tickling my face.

"And what is that sound to mean?" I asked.

She hesitated. "I just…don't want to see Elodie dead."

"Oh, sweetheart!" I gripped her arms and turned her towards me so I might hug her. "We won't kill her." I wasn't sure my words were true. I'd had thoughts of doing otherwise. More than once. "We won't. We need only to destroy the diadem. Then, maybe we can find help for her, someone to assist her with…everything. There are doctors, healers, who can help with matters of the head as well as the body."

Abi shook her head. "She'll never let you. She'll die before she gives up power. And it's probably for the best, but she's…still…my sister." I was glad I had not changed into my gown for this evening. Abi soaked my tunic with tears.

"I know, Abigayle. I know."

I did, but I also knew we would do whatever needed to be done. Did we hope to get the diadem, destroy it, and make Elodie disappear somewhere she couldn't threaten Abigayle's position as heir? Of course, but part of me knew what Abi said was true. Elodie was mad. Destroying the diadem wouldn't be easy.

Abigayle pulled away slowly, sniffling, wiping her eyes with her palms. I wanted to hug her all over again.

She stilled, frowning.

"What's that?"

I looked down to where her eyes were fixated at my chest. It was not the talisman that had caught her attention. It was a corner of the brand her sister had marked me with a month ago. Without a word, she gripped the fabric in one fist and yanked the neckline of my tunic aside to reveal the entire brand, the half-lidded eye made of long red scars across my skin.

Horror filled her eyes as her gaze shot upwards to meet mine. Her mouth fell open. "Reina! She *marked* you."

I closed my eyes briefly and nodded. I swallowed before I spoke, taking a moment to compose myself. Getting angry all over again wouldn't help.

"I know," I said. "It was a month ago, and it's fine. It's healed over. It no longer pains me. I am—"

"No!" she cried. "You don't understand. She *marked* you." Abi waited a moment for me to reach some sort of conclusion. When I didn't, she continued. "When Mama wanted to make sure she could keep something of importance within her gaze, she would mark it with her seal—*that seal*. It meant she always knew where it was."

I felt as though I'd been punched in the gut. All this time. All this planning. All for nothing.

"You're saying…" The words trailed off.

"She knew you were here all along!" Abi let loose a groan and slid to the floor, propping herself up against the windowsill.

I sank to the bed.

"You mean to tell me she's known where to find me this entire time?"

Abi closed her eyes, brow wrinkled in distress, fingers working the hem of her own tunic as she clunked her head against the wall, then gave a barely perceptible nod.

I fought to keep from retching. There was nothing in my stomach to be rid of, but that didn't stop my body from wanting to expel my insides anyway. I rocked back and forth, eyes closed, as I attempted to reconcile this new information and what it meant.

She'd been toying with us. All this time.

She could have destroyed us at any time, could have sent her guards, or an assassin, or her *magic* to kill us, but she hadn't. Instead, she arranged the celebratory ball on the night of the eclipse as an open taunt, a dare to us to set foot in her home, to show up desperate and with the barest of hope, so she could toy with us where her power was strongest and our time the slimmest.

"Why didn't you tell me?" Abi's voice was barely more than a whisper. Her eyes bored into mine, those clear blue pools no longer threatening tears, but filled with anger instead.

I sank to the floor on my knees. "I didn't know! Abi, please believe me, I didn't know anything about the brand. I thought she'd marked me for the fun of it because she *could*. I didn't know. If I had known…"

Abi shook her head and gave a groan. "It wouldn't have mattered. There isn't anything we could have done about it anyway."

Having said all there was to say, we fell into a heavy silence. I rubbed the brand with one hand, hating it more with every breath. That was why Elodie had known I was in the crowd that day. She'd felt my magic because she had marked me, had inserted a piece of her own magic into mine.

"You can't go with us tonight," Abi said, finally breaking the quiet.

"What?"

"You can't. She'll know the plan is in motion if she detects you nearby."

"It doesn't matter, Abi. She's knows it must be tonight anyway. The eclipse is tonight. We're out of time."

"You still can't—"

The door to the washroom opened and Alesh came out, toweling his whitened hair dry, a grin on his much older face. The grin was the same, at least.

"We are ready, yes? Today, we succeed," he said as he sat on the bed. He took one look between me and Abi before the grin fell from his face and trouble worried his eyes. "What is wrong?"

"Ask her," Abi said pointedly, looking at me.

I sighed as I pulled the neckline of my tunic to the side to reveal the brand. As expected, Alesh looked horrified. He dropped the towel to the bed, then raised a hand to his jaw and shook his head.

"When was this done?" he asked.

"When we crossed the Retryant Sea. She told me I needed to make a deal to offer up my necklace to her the next time we met. I agreed. She branded me to mark our agreement, I guess."

"The necklace. That's why…"

I nodded. "That's why I offered up the necklace Quinn gave me. She never specified the talisman. She just said 'necklace.' I kept my end of the bargain. I was…afraid what her magic might allow her to do if I broke my word. Her magic is so much stronger."

"You were in pain. All that time."

I nodded. "But Alesh, the pain is not the problem. I've"—my lip trembled, unwilling to say the words— "been marked," I finally finished. "Beyond the physical brand, she's connected her magic to me, bound a piece of me to her. I didn't know. Not until Abi saw. Not until just now."

Alesh waited, quiet, thinking.

"It means she knows where I am. She's known the entire time. She knew when we first saw her in the square. She knew we never left the city, and she knows we'll come tonight."

Finally, Alesh swatted the air with one hand. "Ach. It makes no difference."

He might have said the words, but he didn't look as though he believed them. It seemed to me there was a very big difference in his mind. The worry that creased his brow had grown deeper, his eyes more distant as he worked through how tonight would likely play out.

"She shouldn't come." Abi lifted her chin as she stood.

I stood, too.

"I told you, I'm coming."

"Your presence will serve to assure Elodie that the plan's in motion," Abi said.

"Does it matter?" I cried. "Does it matter at this point? She knows! She's always known."

Alesh sniffed. "Our Abigayle Gehtanan is right. If you stay here, she will sense it. Her guard will not yet be raised.

Then Mical, Abi, and I have a chance to take the diadem without her being—" He wiggled his fingers in the air, searching for the word.

"Aware?" I supplied.

He snapped. "Yes! Aware of us. You will sound the alarm for her. We must not let that happen."

"Alesh," I begged. "She knows anyway."

"No. You will stay. It may be the only advantage we get tonight."

"I can't stay. I can't sit here all night, waiting for the end of the world. I can't!"

CHAPTER TWENTY-THREE

Strange Bedfellows and Unlikely Allies
Quinn

All night. I'd spent all night and all day scouring every corner of the city with no sign of Reina or Alesh. It was as though they'd disappeared into thin air. A passing thought flitted through my mind, a wonder if the Chaos Wielder hadn't already eliminated them, hadn't already won. I pushed the thought from my head. Bleary-eyed, I rode Aeros to the palace, the place I *must* find them. With so many people gathering, the Chaos Wielder was sure to be in attendance.

Would I know who he was? Would I recognize the child-like insanity we had witnessed on the ship those months ago? If I could make eye contact with every guest there, I felt sure it was possible. But how many? How many pairs of eyes would I have to search to find what I was looking for?

Finding a way in wouldn't be easy. I'd already learned the invitation was extended to one person per household. As I had no knowledge of the empire or the families within it, I'd have to resort to more creative methods.

"You're sure you know what you're doing?" Niles asked for the fourth time.

I tried not to be annoyed with him.

"Yes, Ingram. I have a plan."

I did. Mostly.

Find a place where there weren't many guards, and break in. What my plan lacked in detail, I made up for in confidence.

It wasn't difficult to locate the path to the palace entrance, given the throngs of impeccably dressed subjects heading to the hill at the center of the city, where the palace sat like a gleaming diamond atop the glittering sea of whitewashed buildings. The setting sun glinted off the colored windows, making them glow with an otherworldly iridescence.

"Looks like a damned rainbow prison," Niles grumbled as we approached.

I didn't respond. I nudged Aeros off the main corridor, to the right where we could circle wide before coming around to observe the back of the palace. The fact that the building sat on a hill was something of a concern. Any guards posted would have the added advantage of height, especially as the towers stretched high above everything else in the city. Judging by the smooth walls, there would be no climbing the bailey. Whatever the palace had been constructed of would not be so easy to scale as stone. Climbing was most certainly out.

I turned Aeros toward the palace again, angling her so we'd close in along the right-side walls before we reached the rear of the palace.

"All right. We're here," Niles said. "Tell me."

"The plan?"

He nodded. In the orange glow of the sunset, it looked as

though his ghostly form had been set aflame.

"For you," I began. "The plan is to go through the walls, see whatever you need to see, hear whatever you need to hear, and find me as soon as you possibly can. Go in early, start examining the guests. If you see a child who behaves as though he can't wait to throw the world into chaos, point him out to me."

"You still don't have a plan?"

"I have a plan."

I wanted to punch the doubt off his face… 'Twas a shame he had no solid figure.

I gave him a warning glare instead.

"All right. See you in there. I guess." Unprecedented worry etched on his face as he glanced upwards to the palace once more, he faded from sight, presumably to reappear again somewhere beyond the walls where he would proceed to do something useful.

Once he was gone, I rubbed my eyes, hating the grain in them, hating how very exhausted I already felt, loathing that I had no way of knowing if I would find Reina and Alesh, or even if they were still alive.

They were alive. They had to be. Reina wouldn't give up.

I dismounted, gave Aeros a long neck rub, and studied the palace walls, trying to decipher the layout and determine the best place to enter. The front gate was not an option. Obviously. Lost in concocting a plan, I stopped petting Aeros. She turned one large eye to me and pushed her muzzle into my arm.

I stifled a half-laugh despite myself. "Just like your girl, are you? Saints forbid I should focus my attention elsewhere. Oh, but you *are* a spectacular mare, aren't you? I always knew Reina had some sort of special bond with you, but I… well, I rather see it now."

I scratched her ears, and she stomped a hoof as she leaned her head into my side, knocking me off balance. I braced myself as she pushed her entire forehead up and down my side to scratch her face, leaving white and gray hair on every visible piece of my clothing in her wake.

"Thank you. This is why they have brown horses here, you know. This is—"

That's how I would get in.

I grabbed her muzzle to my face and kissed her nose. "Brilliant, Aeros. You're brilliant."

I pounded a fist on the large wooden door that barred entry to the palace grounds. It, too, was whitewashed to match the smooth walls around it. 'Twas a service entrance, used for the coming and going of goods and supplies as well as palace workers. Several minutes passed before a guard finally opened the sliding window. Two deep brown eyes peered out in suspicion, or maybe annoyance at having to answer the back door when no one was scheduled to arrive here.

"Etcharu?"

Of course he wouldn't speak my tongue right away.

"Hello!" I said, putting more cheer into my voice than I had felt in a very long time. "I have a present for the emperor. A present?" I held the reins aloft and pointed to Aeros, standing beside me, chewing the bit in her mouth.

The guard shook his head.

"Etcharu?" he repeated.

"Eh. From the north." I mimed north by holding my hand high in the air. Genius. "North? A gift, from the king of Castilles."

He shook his head, then slammed the window shut. I tapped a foot on the ground. I had anticipated disbelief, but I'd hoped I'd at least get *into* the courtyard first. I gave Aeros's muzzle another pat.

"*I* thought it was a good idea," I muttered to her.

The window in the door opened again, this time with more force. The face that peered out looked more annoyed than confused. A superior officer then.

"Your business, sir." It wasn't a question.

"Ah, good. Thank you. I come from the north, bearing a gift for the emperor from the king of Castilles." I pointed again to Aeros.

The guard's eyes flicked to Aeros. Hopefully, he was taking in her unusual coloring and anticipating what an asset she'd make to their stables. Hopefully.

"The…king?" he questioned. "Who…is…"

"King Eron Alexandre Morel," I supplied. "Settler of wars, peacekeeper of the north, and lone heir to the throne of Castilles."

"Of course," he replied, sliding the window shut. The

sound of metal sliding upon metal rang through the air as one bolt after the next was unlocked and the door was eased open.

Both guards were similarly dressed in gold and green, their uniforms shining as bright as the colored glass in the windows.

The second guard held out a hand to take Aeros's reins.

"You have a stable?" I asked. "I've been asked to see her to the stable, then relay a message to the emperor from the king, himself."

The guards exchanged glances, the superior seeming more annoyed by the minute.

"Emperor Gehtanan is occupied, as I am sure you can see."

I feigned stupidity, motioning to the front of the palace with one hand. "Oh! That's why the long line of people. I guessed there was something of importance tonight, but I didn't…er, well, I didn't want to chance stabling her in the city, not with her breeding. I'd have to sleep in the straw to keep her from being stolen away in the night, you understand? Her bloodlines are simply—"

"Yes, all right. Come. Come."

Excellent. When all else failed, flustering the opponent was always a good option. Given the current state of affairs and the sheer number of people pouring into the palace, it hadn't taken as long to succeed as I might have thought.

"I can set her up if you'll show me what stall is available."

Obviously done with me, the superior nodded to the guard who had originally opened the window to me and spoke to him in short, clipped words.

Something to the effect of, "Show this idiot to the stables, then get him out," I was sure.

The other guard motioned for me to follow as I led Aeros behind me. All the while, I scanned the buildings around us, the number of guards stationed, the entrances, the windows, anything that might give me an advantage now I was inside the palace's outer walls.

Through another gate, this time a large wrought iron piece with decorative swirls and artistic renditions of a herd of horses in its midst, then we reached stables twice the size of Irzan's with gleaming chestnuts, immaculate bays, and shining black horses of every size. I blew out a sigh. Not a single white or dappled gray, which is the only reason I'd made it through the doors.

The guard swung wide a heavy door to an empty stall, freshly bedded with a thick layer of soft shavings, as if they expected gifted horses to arrive on the regular.

I looked up as a stablehand led two horses through the opposite end of the breezeway. Of course they were expecting other horses tonight. Not everyone arriving would be able to arrive by their own two feet alone. There would be horses. And carriages.

I settled Aeros in the stall, removing her bridle and hanging it on a hook beside the stall door. She wasted no time before starting in on two large flakes of alfalfa stashed in one corner, paying me no attention as I removed her saddle and Reina's bag.

Motioning me to hurry, the guard pointed to a dark

corner on one side of the adjoining aisle where I could set the saddle. When the saddle was set on a stand and my hands were free at last, I turned and smiled my widest smile as I took in everything about our surroundings.

The stableboy had deposited the two horses and gone back to wherever he'd come from, probably the front gate to receive any additional horses. There didn't appear to be anyone within earshot, and not a soul was in sight.

I clasped my hands together once, gave a half-bow to the guard, and said, "Thank you! Thank you so much. I'm so glad I could deliver the gift to your emperor."

In response, he smiled and nodded along.

He wasn't much shorter than I, but he was stockier. His uniform would fit nicely.

"Please believe me when I say I am so, *so* very sorry for doing this," I said with a continued smile. I put one hand out to his arm, beckoning with the other, leading him to the saddlebag as though there was something inside to show him.

He followed me, smiling, confusion in his eyes as he didn't understand a single word I uttered.

"Em baro carutich?" he said.

"Yes." I nodded along. "Em baro carutich!"

He laughed. Then I dropped him to the ground.

He was unconscious before he had time to realize he was being assaulted. I didn't wait. I stripped him of his clothing piece by piece, stripping myself at the same time and donning his uniform just as quickly. I cinched his belt with its baton around my waist, fastening it two holes tighter than where he'd worn it. For comfort, I kept my own boots. I glanced around the stable for something to keep him subdued but saw nothing.

"It's a stable for Saints' sake. Where's the rope?"

I raced the length of the breezeway, skidding to a stop in front of a side room full of tack and supplies. Rope. Pulling a length of it from where it sat on the wall, I ran back to the near-naked guard who was already moaning on the ground.

Fiermi. He couldn't wake. Not now. Not before I'd stuffed him somewhere. I almost regretted my newfound reluctance to take a life. Killing him would have made my task a thousand times easier. Snap his neck and be done.

But then he wouldn't be home for breakfast tomorrow morning, and his loved ones would forever mourn him. I growled as I hit him one more time in the temple, ensuring he stayed unconscious as I tied him up.

Reina's bag. As a healer, she wouldn't travel without helsior bane in the event that she needed to perform a minor surgical procedure. A single dram of helsior bane would keep my new guard friend asleep for hours.

I shuffled through the glass vials, reading the labels, shoving them back again. "Vellowroot, proxide, plum basil, selaniac, gingerene, come on…ah!"

I pulled the vial from its spot in Reina's bag, unscrewing the cap as I moved back to the guard on the floor. I hauled him into a sitting position, then tilted the vial to his lips, dribbling what I hoped wasn't too large of a dose into his mouth. Reflexively, he swallowed.

I recapped the vial, returned it to the bag, and pulled the

guard into the darkest corner, where I covered him with a lightweight horse blanket. I tucked Reina's bag into a large wooden chest full of brushes and hoof picks, then made for the front of the palace, pretending I was meant to be here, was expected at my post. All the while, I prayed no one would ask me what I was doing.

By the time I found the entrance to the palace, the emperor's party inside was well underway. Guards were stationed throughout the hall leading to the large ballroom, and guards were inside as well. People packed the main room and spilled out into every hallway and every open door beyond.

I hadn't thought about the sheer number of guests who would be in attendance. If the Elorin Empire had a hundred-thousand families or more, and the emperor had invited a member from each of them to attend, I had already failed if even a mere tenth of the households showed up. There was no way to search ten-thousand people before the early morning hours when the eclipse would take place.

I scratched at the collar of the unfamiliar uniform, sorely wishing I could change out of it, but the last thing I needed to do was knock a guest unconscious, too. So, instead, I behaved as though I was on rounds, one hand on the baton at my waist, my gaze moving methodically over the guests as they mingled.

Provided I could avoid running into any of the superior officers, staying in uniform had its advantages. As long as I didn't speak, examining guests as I was appeared no different than any other guard doing what was expected.

"That is…*quite* the look."

I didn't need to turn my head to know who spoke. Only Niles would goad me on looks during a time like this. I *almost* smiled.

"Yes, well, the selection left something to be desired," I muttered beneath my breath in reply. "I'm here, aren't I?"

"Mmm." I made the mistake of glancing his way, noting the mix of laughter and disdain in his eyes.

"Don't," I warned, my voice just one more added to the din of the ongoing conversations around me. At least I could talk to Niles here. Unless I outright looked as though I was talking to no one in particular, it should be easy to converse without dragging much attention to myself.

"Or what? Haven't you learned, Quinn? Your threats mean nothing to me."

I huffed, then changed the subject. "What have you found?"

"Nothing yet. Most of the crowd is comprised of adults. There are very few children here and the children who *are* here are generally older. I haven't seen anyone younger than… Oh, fiermi."

"What?" I asked, but Niles pointed.

I followed his finger to where guards entered two by two in formation, splitting to line either side of the dais at the front of the room. In their midst, a girl-child draped in gold and pearls walked with confidence, her chin held high, a diadem on her head…and madness in her eyes.

"That's not… That can't be…" But I knew who it was. The girl on the throne was the one and only Chaos Wielder.

And Emperor Gehtanan.

Fiermi, indeed.

"At least you don't have to sort through tens of thousands of people?" Niles offered.

"No. I have only to go after the single one of them who's watched like a nuhawk by a few hundred trained guards at any one time." I cursed again.

"Quinn."

"What?"

Niles looked hesitant as he viewed the Chaos Wielder. He continued to watch her as he spoke his next words. "Just… be careful."

I shot him a look. "Of course I plan to be careful!"

"I…no. No time for an explanation. Whatever you do, do not touch the diadem."

I looked at him in alarm, no longer caring who might notice I was talking to thin air. "How do we get it from her if we can't touch it?"

"We don't get it. We don't touch it. We don't destroy it. We—I—bind it."

Niles finally met my eyes, looking anything but confident. I didn't like what I saw there—the uncertainty, the hesitation.

"This is what you meant about binding chaos when we were back beneath the mountain. This is what you were talking about." I dropped my shoulders, understanding. "*You* were the third item the mountain granted all along."

He nodded.

"I'm the only one who can bind the chaos," he said.

Pieces clicked into place. All the times Niles had

disappeared, and I'd assumed he was off being irresponsible, he was piecing together what he needed to do. How long had he known? Why hadn't he told me? Was he not confident in his ability?

"All those times…"

Now his eyes grew less uncertain. "Yes."

"And do you know? What you need to do, I mean?"

He nodded. "I can do it."

I nodded in return.

"Just…don't touch the diadem."

"I'll try to keep my hands off."

I continued to scan the guests around me, thoughts preoccupied with how I would get the Chaos Wielder alone, how I'd find Reina and Alesh, and how I'd do it all in the next couple of hours.

I licked my lips. "Niles?"

"Hmm?"

"What happens if I touch the diadem?"

He looked as though he debated answering. When he finally did, the solemn expression on his face told me more than his words ever could.

"Touching it pushes the clock forward. It seals the fate of all of Liron. The world descends into chaos and madness even before the eclipse with no chance at redemption."

I let the words echo through my mind, playing them over again and again. Finally, I asked, "Is that all?"

Niles snorted.

CHAPTER TWENTY-FOUR

Left Behind
Reina

They left me behind.

After all the planning and all the preparation, they actually left me behind. Alesh and Abigayle had gone to the palace, disguises in place, pseudonyms filed away. And I'd been left like an unused piece of luggage sitting on a closet shelf.

After weeks of noise and commerce carrying on all hours of the day and night, the streets below the window were eerily quiet, the vendors' stalls closed up, vacant. The vendors themselves were at the palace this very moment.

Nerves beneath my skin buzzed with anticipation. I kept searching for an escape but finding none. There was nothing for me to do. I'd been discarded as a liability.

Oh, I knew Alesh and Abi hadn't *discarded* me, not really, but it did nothing to ease the sting of being left behind when I could have gone with them. Doing something— anything—of use.

Instead, I stared out at the dark skies and the bright moonlight casting shadows on the quiet streets, making illusions out of buildings and carts, planters and garbage totes, even the few people who meandered the street after dark, not heading to the palace.

My breath hitched as I viewed a lone figure below. The man looked, *moved*, like Quinn. I pressed a fist to my chest, right where I'd been branded, pushing until the skin hurt, and I could barely draw a breath at all.

The shadow turned a corner, and I allowed myself to slide against the bed until I was sitting on the floor, overwhelmed by tears.

I was alone. Truly alone.

There was no one left to hide the pain and the sadness from, no reason not to let the tears flow, not to let my sobs sound.

Quinn was dead. Quinn was gone. And I was a fool for seeing him where he could not be, for wanting him when he could not be had, for wishing when wishes brought nothing but fresh pain. I'd once believed healers didn't sleep, but the lack of sleep had finally caught up to me. Though could I still call myself a healer when the only power I controlled was death, and my *control* was questionable?

Around the same time my tears were spent, someone pounded on the door, the sound startling me back to my feet. I held the talisman around my neck in my hand, pressing its comforting weight into my palm, fingernails biting into my skin with the intensity of my grip.

Ask or open? Did it matter?

I crossed the room, stood at the door, and stared at the wood, imagining who might be on the other side, knocking with such urgency. Finally, I put a hand on the knob, turned it, and flung open the door.

Mical nearly knocked me over entering the room before he slammed the door shut behind him. I backed away in surprise.

"What are you doing here?" I asked.

Mical should have been at the palace. At this point, he should have been inside, in one of the upper towers, waiting until the evening was winding down, until the guests were on their way home and Elodie was heading to her own chambers to sleep.

"I think the question is what are *you* doing here?" he growled.

"They said I couldn't be there. Alesh and Abi, they said she'd know." I pulled the neck of my tunic aside to show my terrible scarred tattoo once more.

Mical turned away, slammed a hand against the wall in anger, then turned back again, his face a mask of fury. "She knows anyway!"

"That's what *I* said!"

"Get changed. You can't wear *that* to the palace." He motioned to my tunic and breeches.

"We're going? You'll let me go?" I'd contemplated going to the palace on my own, but Mical's company would be a tremendous relief.

"It's a fool's move to leave you here unguarded, especially when we know she has someone after you! Now, go. We have no time to spare."

"But—"

He held up a hand. "Trust me on this. We cannot pull

this off without you *and* Alesh, no matter how much the old man would prefer to think otherwise. You don't know Elodie Gehtanan the way I know her. Now, change. Flare your magic however you must before we leave, so she senses it here, in the inn, across the city. Then keep it silent until the very second you need it tonight."

I didn't argue.

I raced to the washroom, grabbing my gown from where I'd thrown it over the back of a chair earlier and changed in record time, putting half of my curls into clips to keep them from my face. The fashionable high collar kept much of the brand on my chest from showing, but the very edges were visible if one examined the sheer fabric at the neckline for too long. I would have to make a point of keeping my spine straight and my shoulders back for the night, at least while in the public sphere until I could hide away in the library.

The talisman's chain was hidden beneath the dark strip of russet material at my neck, and two perfectly placed decorative, teal strips over the sheer fabric at my chest. The dress itself was made from panels of shining teal and russet, a mix of spring and autumn in a land that welcomed only the heat of summer, the sleeves sheer teal and slit along the outside edges in the popular style.

I spent only as much time as I could spare admiring the way the dress accented my waist before returning to the room. Would there ever be a reason to dress up again?

Mical's eyes took in the gown or, more appropriately, my *figure*, in the gown. He gave a wicked grin, one that sent amusement—or something else—right to depths of his hazel eyes. "Oh, but if the world weren't about to end, my dear, dear Reina," he muttered more to himself than to me.

"You shameless flirt."

"That I am. But I'd take you for a night in the city you'd never forget, and then a night in my bed you'd *also* never forget."

I didn't blush this time, merely gave him a scalding glare and smacked his arm. I'd almost grown used to Mical's suggestive behavior.

"Magic," I said.

"Flare it."

I looked around the room, but there was nothing to kill in a room full of inanimate, unliving things. Then my eye caught on a bouquet of wildflowers Abi had picked when we'd left the inn for the room "refreshening." The flowers, laid flat on the desk, had already begun to wilt. It took half a second to turn them into blackened ash.

The color drained from Mical's face. He swallowed. "That took much less effort than I thought."

I shrugged. "I pretended they were Elodie."

I hadn't. Not really, but Mical gave me an uncertain look, as though he hadn't anticipated I could be as deadly as Alesh as I had assured him days ago. I suspected he was currently rethinking his invitation to take me to bed. I laughed.

"Only a matter of time before she sends someone," I reminded Mical.

That broke the spell. "Right," he said. "Let's go."

Less than twenty minutes later, I was on my way to the front gates amid a thinning flood of late-arriving guests, and

Mical was, well, wherever he was, getting into the palace however he planned to get in.

I gawked at the enormous black iron gates as I passed through them, wondering at their towering height and impossible weight. Intricate designs swirled in the midst of the gates as though the very iron had been wrought of poetry itself. Against the sheer white outer walls, the design was more art than function.

"Natirá?" A mustached guard in green with a deep gold sash across his uniform spoke the one-word question Abi told me he would. He was asking my name. For half a second, I hesitated before spitting out the name I'd been told to use, the one I'd gone over again and again in my head.

"Ladia Eluvia Esmé Manyu." I spoke the words with a smile, pushing sincerity into my eyes, delight at being invited to this once-in-a-lifetime celebration at the emperor's palace. How lucky I was!

My performance, however lacking, was enough. Or the guard himself had simply had his share of the endless faces on his endless list. He smiled at me, marked off a name on the thick list of papers he held, then motioned me forward.

"Si etzi tu dola, ja?" He said with a laugh.

I smiled and nodded back as I moved with the swell of people onto the palace grounds.

"Natirá?" He asked the next man in line. Dozens of guards to either side of him were repeating the same motions, the same words. With a crowd so large, there was no other way to ensure everyone was admitted before the night was over.

I followed the crowd up the hill of neatly manicured

lawns, grass as green and fresh as any I'd known in Barnham, undeniably brought forth through Elodie's magic. The lawns and the palace were lit with beams of light also drawn from Elodie's magic. Women draped in jewels and scarves with glittering trim pointed out the thick carpet of green, and the brilliant pink birds adorning the lawn and the lake beyond.

I stared. Their tails were twice the length of their bodies, their slim necks in graceful curves, beaks eagerly searching the small pond for whatever fish might be their next meal. Long, lean legs held their bodies above the water, but none seemed to mind their fanned tails floating at the surface.

I'd never seen such a creature. Were they real? Or had they been created by Elodie's chaotic imagination? Was she as capable of creating beauty as she was of bringing forth decay?

One of the birds gave an irritated flap of large wings, then pointed its sharp, black beak upward to the starred sky above, letting loose an ear-piercing shriek. Like the guests around me, I reflexively covered my ears and pushed forward to the reach the palace. Laughter and music from inside the palace were far preferable to whatever sound that was.

The talisman hummed at my chest, as though sensing it would be used tonight, as though it had been waiting these weeks, storing up its magic, holding it until I would unleash it upon the Chaos Wielder.

I wouldn't, though. I swore to Abi I wouldn't. Not if it could be helped. Destroy the diadem, yes, but not the girl. I wouldn't take Abi's last remaining family member from her, no matter how much I longed to repay the vixen for what she'd put us through and who she'd taken from me.

Like the gates at the walls, the large glass doors of the palace were swung wide, their rainbow glass reflecting prisms on every surface reflected by the oil lamps and burning torches. The effect was mirrored a hundredfold, each lamp burning within rainbow-hued glass of differing shapes and sizes. The result was a beautiful, chaotic mess of color that distorted the entire entranceway, leading to an otherworldly feel.

I'd left Liron. I couldn't help but feel so as I made my way through the grand entrance hall and into the rooms beyond, and I wasn't alone in my perception. Guests around me pointed at the colors and shapes, their faces masked by the changing color of the lanterns.

The library. I had to reach the library, but the sheer number of people in the palace halls made the task nearly impossible. It wasn't that I didn't know where to find the library—the room was two halls, one turn, a stairwell, another two turns, and one long hall away—but walking through the palace felt like walking through the marketplace on the busiest of days. Worse. People were packed shoulder to shoulder, guards stationed every six or eight feet, depending on the length of the hall, and there was simply no way to move faster or slower than the whole of the crowd.

So I shuffled forward, like everyone else, marveling at one trick of chaotic magic after the next. Elodie had kept herself busy. I hoped that her use of magic here meant she was too busy to send her undead armies elsewhere on Liron.

At the end of the hall, the crowd was ushered into a

wide ballroom packed full of thousands of people dancing to a music I could feel thrumming in my very bones. I could find no source of the tune, no musicians in any corner of the room, no instruments, large or small, no crooning singer playing to the crowd. And yet, I heard it all the same. I *felt* the notes in my body, the music taking shape within me, a voice resonating in my ears. My fingers itched to dance along with the strange and foreign melody.

Many people around me did. They succumbed to their desire to dance, faces slipping into a blank contentedness as bodies began to sway, hands either moving into the air or reaching to pull a partner to dance with them.

I continued to move forward, pressing through the bodies, pushing aside the urge to join them. I didn't need the talisman to know the magic in this room was strong if it beckoned for *me* to dance. I was better suited to libraries than dance halls, even in the least serious of times.

I did my best to tune out the music in my head as I searched the crowd and moved to the end of the hall, where another set of doors led to the hall that would take me to the northeast corner of the palace.

Orange blossoms and something else—kissing blooms, maybe—scented the air as I crossed the threshold into the hallway, leaving the music and the dancing bodies behind. The crush of bodies was just as tight here as people picked their way through the palace's winding halls. The lighting, at least, was no longer a dim rainbow of color. Instead, bright, white spotlights were pinned on an array of entrees lining a sideboard that ran the length of the hall.

Guests pulled at various treats, sweets made to look like flowers and animals, chocolates crafted into coins meant to melt on the mouth, confections like snow that guests were catching on their tongues as pieces fell softly through the air and into their mouths. My stomach lurched angrily. I should have eaten earlier. If only I hadn't been too consumed by nerves. Still, I wouldn't—

A young woman beside me giggled as she grabbed my arm and shoved a small chocolate cake with orange icing into my mouth, her own mouth stuffed full of one.

"Issa baintchu, ja?" She held a hand over her mouth, hiding a smile as she chewed, as though it excused the fact that she'd just jammed a confection into my mouth.

But the grin in her eyes was unmistakable. I couldn't be angry at someone enjoying fineries they'd never before experienced, and Elodie had spared no expense when it came to tonight's treats.

The cake was also incredibly decadent, moist and chewy with just enough orange to keep the chocolate from overwhelming the more subtle notes. I smiled back at the girl, who gave an apologetic smile as she realized she had overstepped personal bounds in her enthusiasm.

"Ja," I agreed. Relief flooded her face and she moved down the hall, sampling bits of food here and there, turning to me with a suggestion from time to time.

Elodie wouldn't poison her own citizens, so I supposed the fare was safe enough. Still, I allowed myself only one more petite cake—a lemony custard this time, before passing through the rest of the hall, ignoring my stomach's rumblings and the appetizing fragrances emanating from the side table.

At the end of the hall, I followed the line of guests into another room, this one full of wondrous, soft white snowflakes falling from the ceiling. But, no, that wasn't quite true. The snow fell not from the ceiling, but from a space just below the ceiling, a thin layer of heavy gray storm clouds between the plaster of the ceiling and the chandeliers that hung throughout the room.

Soft gasps sounded in the room as guests entered and were surprised again and again. This far south, they had probably never seen snow, had never known its softness or its bite. A young man picked up a handful of snow from where it gathered along the floor and pressed it between his fingers, marveling at his reddened skin.

It caught in hair and on eyelashes. Guests lifted handfuls into the air, threw it over their heads, and let it fall down a second time. They made snow angels on the floor and aimed snowballs at unsuspecting visitors entering the room.

If Elodie's goal was to endear herself to her subjects further, she was certainly succeeding. The awe on the faces before me was a dreadful prelude to the ferocity they would use to protect her later. I was certain of it.

The next long hallway featured elaborate wallpaper with moving pictures that flowed across the walls. Illustrations of fish being pulled into ships, of embracing lovers watching a sunset from a cliffside beach, of horses racing with the wind. It was difficult to focus on any one image as each one blended into the next, forming a never-ending sea of ever-changing murals on the wall. Was this Elodie's magic, I wondered, or a spellbinder's charm?

The hallways and ballrooms continued, each more elaborate than the last in their magical offerings, each designed to delight and enamor the guests as they made their way through the palace. In one, the ceiling resembled the night's sky, but the stars seemed near enough to touch, the two moons already tantalizingly close to one another, as though Stellon had finally caught Andra in a lover's embrace after all.

In another, the floor had been transformed into a deep purple sea, large waves glittering with gold flecks. Guests were carried atop the crests of waves, laughing as they lost their balance and slid through the room, never getting wet, never dipping below the purple surface. The way the floor moved reminded me of childhood, when my mother requested my help in making the bed after the sheets were freshly laundered. She'd hold the corners, then flap the sheet upward, letting it drift downward.

When I was very little, I jumped in the center of the bed, below the falling sheet, just in time for the sheet to touch my skin and cover me with its silky softness. That's what the sea—the floor—made me think of. A rolling sea of freshly laundered purple sheets, the palace guests turned into playful children by the novelty of such a thing.

Eying two guards stationed at the stairwell to the second floor, I allowed the swell of the crowd to carry me forward into the largest ballroom yet. Abigayle said two guards would be stationed at the stair. I'd hoped I might take the stairs to the library, but Abi had laughed when I'd suggested it. Secret passage from the washroom, as originally planned. I just had to make it to the washroom.

The next ballroom was enormous, the largest room I might have ever seen. I put a hand to my face to feel with my fingers the change that had occurred on my cheeks as I crossed the threshold. My face matched those around me, a mask of glittering color across my eyes and nose, a shield on my cheeks. I joined dozens of guests occupying the space before one giant, mirrored wall to examine the color of the mask that had appeared when I'd entered the ballroom.

Russet and teal, like my gown, with a deep copper trim, the mask glittered whether I turned my head left or right, up or down. I ran my fingers along the smooth edges where the mask met, and melded into, my skin, but I could detect no seam, and so trying to peel the mask off was pointless, even if the idea of having a temporary attachment to my face made me exceptionally uneasy. Instead, I turned my attention to the room full of similarly masked attendees.

The ballroom was large enough for people to spread out. Couples danced to music—the regular kind this time, the type produced by bows pulled across stringed instruments and breath blown through reeded woodwinds. An orchestra, its members also masked in black and white to match their outfits, lined the front right corner of the room beside a dais where Elodie Gehtanan sat, pleased as a preening rufflefeather with shiny new plumage.

I fought the urge to run. She didn't know me. Yes, I still wore her brand beneath my dress, but I was different here. Alesh had changed my looks, and I'd flared my magic before we left the inn. If I didn't use my magic until the last possible moment, with any luck at all, she'd believe I'd been left behind.

Naturally, Elodie was the only person in the room who wore no mask at all. She was perfectly content to have everyone in the room gaze upon her in awe at the magic she'd put on display all throughout the evening.

Vain girl.

Even the guards bore green and gold masks to match their green and gold uniforms. I wondered if she required their undergarments to sparkle so, too.

As I pushed through the growing crowd, I kept my eyes open for Alesh or Abi, neither of whom I expected to see, especially among so many people, but still, I wondered if they knew I followed, if Mical had found and told them. Hopefully, they had already reached their hiding spots—where they would spend most of the evening waiting for the party to die down and Elodie to succumb to sleep.

My attention on the room around me, I was startled when the rough hand of a dark-haired guard in green and gold grabbed mine.

"Danzei," he said as he spun me into his chest and deftly began to move with the sway of the music.

"You presume too much, sir," I said, my words coated half with annoyance and half with mock-flattery. The last thing I needed to do was offend a guard and get tossed from the palace grounds for not feeding an ego, regardless of what language I'd spoken the words in.

The man across from me was hardly the only guard to

join in the festivities. There were dozens around the room also enjoying the celebration. Not the ones guarding Elodie, of course. They were stone-faced and serious, their eyes constantly watching everyone and everything in the room around them.

I half-pulled my hand from the grasp of the guard, stepping back and motioning that I intended to move onward to the next room, but he seemed offended, blue eyes flashing with annoyance that I hadn't been more inclined to spend time with him.

"I'm sorry," I muttered, turning away.

A hand landed heavy on my shoulder.

I turned back with dread, the talisman humming at my chest, begging to be used, my desperation nearly enough to entice me into using it…and met the dark eyes of a dead man.

CHAPTER TWENTY-FIVE

In Plain Sight
Quinn

The woman wasn't happy I'd cut in, but the guard who'd been dancing with her wasn't likely to give up his dance no matter how little his partner was enjoying it. So, when she stepped away, I took the opportunity to cut in, pointing the shorter guard in the direction of a dark-haired woman in a ruby gown and gold mask.

He was just as happy in her arms.

Unfortunately, my own prize was already attempting to get away, so I laid a gentle hand on her shoulder. I wasn't expecting the ferocity in her eyes when she turned around and her gaze met mine. Why should I?

Beyond having followed her all day and something about her being inherently familiar, I didn't know anything about this woman or her life.

When her gaze met mine, her lips parted. The fight left her body, and she gazed up at me wide-eyed.

"Apologies," I said. "You looked as though you could use rescuing."

Dolt.

Using the northern tongue here might get me somewhere

with some insignificant fraction of the crowd, but it was foolish to speak it in a guard's uniform.

She swallowed as she continued to stare.

I put a self-conscious hand to the ridiculous gold mask at my face. The monstrosity was welded to my skin, gold with a single horizontal slash of green through the center. I touched it as though I could peel it off, as though the magic might let me. Somehow, it seemed the right thing to do, to take off this mask and apologize fully, and yet, I could not.

Instead, I shrugged and gave what I hoped was a disarming smile. I bowed, then made to move away into the crowd. The woman was no concern of mine. Whatever she'd been doing, whatever reason she'd visited the spellbinder today, no longer mattered. All that mattered now was finding Reina and Alesh and helping in whatever way I still might.

"You speak the northern tongue," she said, her voice barely audible above the crowd and the swell of the music.

I turned back to her, tilting my head as though it might help me to hear better. A lock of hair fell into my eyes at the movement.

"I do," I answered as I brushed my hair back again. It had grown entirely too long for my taste.

She hesitated, toying with the neckline of her dress. Her dark eyes searched my face with a sense of desperation. There was an aching familiarity in the depths of those eyes I couldn't define. I wished I knew what it was she was looking for. How did I know her? Why couldn't I remember? Had Kufataba taken more than I'd realized?

"Will you dance with me?" I asked.

I had no time for dancing, and yet…

She bit her bottom lip to stop its quivering, looked into my eyes as though she knew them—knew me, then nodded as she stepped into my open embrace, her gaze never leaving mine as her soft hand slid into my own. I placed my other hand at the small of her back, curious at the familiarity beneath my palm, and we began to sway to the soft rise of the music.

"You're not from here," she said.

At the very same time, I said, "Surely, I know you from somewhere."

Our words tumbled over each other, the subsequent responses incoherent.

"No, I'm not."

"I don't see how."

She gave a shy smile, confused eyes working through a problem in her head. She *did* know me from somewhere. I was sure of it. But why couldn't *I* remember her?

When the music drew to an end, I released her hand. She stepped away reluctantly, her gaze pinned to my chest as though she could no longer bear to look at my face. Yes, she knew me. Somehow.

"Your name, my lady?" I asked in the brief silence before the orchestra struck up the next song.

Her lip quivered again. "Ladia Eluvia Esmé Manyu," she said before fleeing, pushing through the crowd.

Her voice.

Her eyes.

Esmé, she'd said.

My God, she'd been in front of me the whole time.

"Reina!" I called, but the rise of the next waltz swallowed my voice.

I fought the crowd to follow her, to follow Reina, who had somehow transformed herself into someone new entirely.

How had she managed such a feat? Had she seen the spellbinder to change *herself?* Was such a thing possible? Why was she alone? Where was Alesh? *How* had she not recognized me?

The questions flew through my head faster than I could think of answers to them. The simple reason as to why she hadn't recognized me was because she believed me to be dead. The less obvious answer was because I had a damn mask welded to my face, a mask that disappeared as soon as I left the room with its orchestra, its masquerade ball, the Chaos Wielder, and her jovial guests.

"Who was that?" Niles had followed me into the hallway outside.

"Reina," I muttered beneath my breath, craning my neck both left and right to see where she might have gone. The crowd pushed forward to the left, no one fighting against the flow to the right, so I followed left, leaving the Chaos Wielder behind me.

"I know you haven't seen her in a while, but"—Niles hesitated, cocking his head— "Reina doesn't look like that."

"You think I don't know that?" I snapped as I fought through the crowd marveling at some new magic at the end of the hall.

"Well, you were almost dead for a while, so I couldn't

say what might be going through that skull of yours. I mean, while you were under the mountain, you managed to forget about her entirely, so—"

I shot him a glower that stopped his tirade mid-sentence. Thinking my cutting glare was meant for her, the woman to my right gave me an uncertain glance in return and a wider berth. I didn't bother to mutter apologies.

"Can you find her?" I asked Niles, keeping my eyes trained ahead.

"I can try."

"Go."

There was no use in fighting the crowd. I would go where the Chaos Wielder meant for her guests to go, see what she meant for them to see.

Except…

I was still in a guard uniform. Pushing past other guards *might* land me in trouble, but it also might get me away from the crowd and better able to find the person I was looking for, especially now that I knew what she looked like.

Nerves rattled my chest. Something had drawn me to the blond woman, and now that I knew she and Reina were one and the same, it all seemed so obvious. She smelled like Reina because she *was* Reina. She moved like Reina because she *was*. She hadn't been fiddling with the neckline of her dress before we'd danced. She'd been touching the chain to the talisman that lay against her skin. How could I not have seen?

Of course, why would I have noticed? No one could have expected such a thing.

By the time I made it to the stairwell at the north end of the palace, I'd composed myself inside and out. Eying the stairs in front of me, I ignored the two guards as I passed between them, relying on protocol to keep them at attention.

I wasn't wearing the highest-ranking guard uniform in the palace, certainly. The guard outside who had let me in had rank over the near-naked man I left sleeping beneath a horse blanket, but it seemed the rank of whatever uniform I'd stolen was above that of the two men stationed at the bottom of the stairs, so I breezed past them without so much as a side glance.

I'd taken a gamble. This time, it paid off. I let out a sigh of relief after I'd reached the first landing, climbed the second set of stairs, and emerged in a hallway above as full as the one I'd just left. Two guards stood at the entrance to the stairwell here, too.

The throng of guests continued through the palace, pointing and laughing. One person per household, but they had formed groups, having been at the palace long enough now to strike conversation amongst themselves with whoever beside them might listen.

If Reina had followed the crowd on the predetermined path through the palace, I should theoretically be ahead of her, having taken a shortcut up the stairwell she wouldn't have been able to use.

All I needed to do was find a spot to wait, then let her come to me.

Wave after wave of guests came through the hall, turned right at the corner where I'd stationed myself and continued on, their incessant laughter carrying back to me as whatever surprised them in the next room continued to do so again with each newcomer.

I grew frustrated. Reina should have come this way by now. Had I missed her? I'd examined the face of every man, woman, and child who walked past me, but was it possible I'd been so focused on her that I'd missed the blond hair and the pointed chin?

No. *No.*

"She won't be coming this way."

My eyes turned to Niles briefly before I commanded my gaze back to the ever-moving, ever-changing crowd.

"Mmm?" I replied, watching a girl close to Reina's height turn the corner into the hallway. Too short. Too white-blond. Not Reina.

"The woman. *If* she's truly Reina, she's not in this crowd."

"Where is she?" I gritted my teeth, hardly raising my voice above the noise. Niles was dead. Surely, his ghostly hearing was more sensitive than human ears.

"She's stalled in the library. There's a number of people in there. The room is as large as the ballroom downstairs. The stacks take up half the space, but the remainder, a circular space at the center, has drawn a crowd for its display. She's there now."

"Care to lead the way?"

I could guess, of course. I'd been in enough castles and

palaces to know the general layout and would find the library in a few moments on my own, but as Niles had just come from there, it was far easier to ask him to lead me straight to it.

It was easy to see how many of the palace guests had gotten held up in the library. The large room was three times as high as it was wide, with an entire wall of rainbow-hued windows that stretched to the ceiling. Beyond the windows, firelight flickered outside, so the windows themselves came to life, projecting some sort of moving painting on the white marble floor of the library.

Guests gasped collectively as an image changed shape on the floor in front of them, then rose upwards to become what appeared to be a living, breathing being before it disintegrated into a puff of purple dust that found its way back to the window again, absorbing into the colored glass.

The crowd clapped and cheered. As some of them moved away to continue their palace escapade, I took a spot at the front of the display, where another picture was already taking shape.

I divided my attention between the glass on the windows and the floor beneath my feet. The colors on the windows had no definition, no specific shape or size, but on the floor it was as though all the colors had come together to paint a familiar landscape.

Ivirreh. An image of the city, then the palace itself as the swirling colors changed shape and reformed. Night above. The purple shadows of large birds soaring across the two moons, then landing on the lawns outside.

Then the diadem, an image as clear as cut crystal before me, as it rose over the palace, the entire image coming to life, upward through the floor as though it would take up the entire room. Startled by how quickly it moved upward, I stepped back. It wasn't as though I thought the larger-than-life diadem coming from the floor would throw me off balance, but the image had been so real, it was impossible *not* to react.

The crowd clapped again as the mirage fell into an orange dust this time, then whisked through the air to rejoin the glass in the window once more.

I moved to the windows, eyes drawn to the color and the flickering light outside. I had assumed the light was provided by a bonfire or flickering sconces just the other side of the glass, but I was wrong.

Up close, I could tell the light was *inside* the very glass itself. Shimmering reflections within the colored pieces glowed brightly, then dimmed again, in no predictable pattern. Despite my better judgment, I touched a hand to the glass and found it cool beneath my fingers. The heat of the night and so many bodies inside the room hadn't warmed the windows.

A collective gasp from the crowd drew my attention again, in time to see an alarmingly large, deep blue dragon with shimmering scales the size of my palm leap from the center of the floor outward toward the library's center chandelier. Squeals of delight and an appreciative round of applause sounded as the image of the dragon dropped into blue dust that headed for the rainbow-hued windows once again, swirling around one surprised man who held up one arm as though to deflect a blow.

I disregarded the subsequent awe at the new figures taking shape on the floor, instead closely examining each person who occupied the library's wide expanse. The crowd continued to change, but Niles had stationed himself at the door, so I expected he'd alert me if Reina traveled that direction. I slid a plush chair out from one of the many desks that lined the wall to one side of the windows, sat, and prepared to spend as much time as necessary to find the woman I loved.

CHAPTER TWENTY-SIX

Alternate Plans
Reina

Of course the guard would look like him. The entire palace was probably enchanted so at least one person took the shape of whoever guests loved the most. Had everyone else been dancing with someone they loved and missed, too?

I took in the hiding spot around me, a tight-quartered, specialized room where the most fragile books were kept. Abi had given instructions on how to turn the peculiar handles to open the seal so I could step inside and hide away until the night's festivities had ended.

As much as I had anticipated the dark and the quiet, I hadn't prepared to be bombarded by thoughts of Quinn, by *seeing* him not only in my dreams, but here, in the real world. Or, at least, seeing an image of him. Who knew what the guard I'd danced with actually looked like? Perhaps he was fifty-eight years old with graying temples and a receding hairline. Perhaps his nose was too big for his face and his teeth were yellowed with tobacco stains.

I put a hand to my chest, the rhythm of my galloping heart pounding away beneath my palm. The talisman glowed, bathing the room in a deep blue-green light. I clenched the stone, holding tightly, forcing breath in and out of my lungs.

No matter what physical form the guard may have taken, for that moment, for that brief time, he had *been* Quinn to me. A sob threatened to break loose. With a growl, I bit it, pushed it to the back of my throat, and swallowed to keep it from getting out. Then I slid to the floor, and rocked, repeating one remedy after the next in my head until the thoughts in my head ran clear again.

I winced as a sharp pain cut into my thigh in the very place I'd dreamed last night. Like wildfire, panic lit in my veins. I pushed aside the panels of the skirt on my dress, fumbling with the silk, my fingers slipping over the lustrous material. I pulled the talisman close, using its light to examine the skin.

The web of blackened veins was impossible to ignore. Had last night been a vision? A warning? Had it actually happened? I no longer knew what was real and what wasn't. The snake venom would soon be released into my system. Then it would no longer matter if the Chaos Wielder still held the diadem come the eclipse or not. At least, not to me. I'd be dead.

I wanted to howl in frustration. How could so many things go wrong at once? How could so much be stacked against us?

I winced again, then began to rub my leg, humming myself a tune that once belonged to my mother. I wasn't worried about the people on the other side of the door in the main library hearing me. The seal between the rooms was solid. Beyond a murmur of approval from time to time, I could hardly hear the commotion created by awe at the window display.

Calm. I had to keep calm. The more I exerted myself, the faster the poison would spread. If the sealed capsule in my body had a tiny leak, I might survive long enough to get the diadem from Elodie's hands, swap magic with Alesh, and save myself. I tried to ignore how much of my plan relied on both Alesh and me being alive at the end of the night, and that all the odds were monumentally stacked against us.

Slow. Slow the breathing. Ease the heart rate. In through the nose, out through the mouth. Just like I would tell any of my laboring patients. I hummed between shaky breaths, hummed and remembered simpler times.

My mother wouldn't have let this stand in her way. She would have stood up to Elodie without all the sneaking around. She would have scolded Elodie, demanded the diadem, and convinced the girl to give it to her.

I almost laughed. I wasn't my mother. I wasn't Quinn. I was only me, and this task was meant for someone greater.

A low roar of applause rumbled through the door, and curiosity got the best of me. The pain now subsided, I slid a few feet across the floor to look through one of the many small air holes in the door. I lined my eye up with several before I found one that gave me the vantage point I needed to see what was happening in the library.

A new crowd now, different faces than the ones I'd left behind when I slipped into this room, but still staring in awe at the center of the room where images from the window played out in various shapes and colors. From my position, I couldn't see what was being created, only the reaction to it afterwards.

I sat back again, then frowned. Was that—

I placed an eye to one of the holes again.

"Fiermi," I breathed.

The guard. The one I'd danced with. The one who looked like Quinn.

He was here, in the library, sitting at a desk beside the wide windows, sharp eyes focused on every person who entered the room. His tousled hair was longer than when I'd last seen him beneath the mountain, the dark stubble on his jaw a full beard now, but his face was as serious as ever. I grasped the door handle and pressed the lever.

It's Quinn!

No.

I released the handle as though I'd been burned. Then I pushed my desire away, reined in the excitement, the hope, and shoved it all back into the dark where it belonged.

Not Quinn. A trick. Magic.

I swallowed, my hands limp at my sides, and closed my eyes.

Elodie knew we were coming tonight. What better way to lure me out of whatever position I'd taken against her than to put forth an image of the very person she knew I loved? No one who had seen us traveling together could be fooled into thinking otherwise, so of course she knew I loved him.

Who better to dangle in front of me as bait than Quinn? There was probably a Quinn in every room of the palace, and in every hall, too. How many Quinns had I passed before I'd noticed the one in the ballroom?

Reluctantly, I pulled myself away from the door, ignored the single tear that fell from the corner of one eye, and refocused my breathing again. I had hours before the party would end, then a short window before the eclipse. I needed to conserve what little energy I still had.

Focus.

The warmth of the talisman pulsed at my chest, begging to be used, reminding me it had been weeks, that reserves of power were ready for my call. I swallowed again.

The talisman throbbed.

Soon, you wicked thing. Soon.

As there was no clock in the dark room and none visible through the tiny holes in the door, I had no way of judging the passage of time. What felt like an eternity could have been a whole twelve minutes. It was difficult to say.

I was exceptionally startled when the door was flung open to reveal Abi, her legs planted wide, in the costume we'd put together for her. We'd refused to age her, but that didn't mean we were ready to send her back to the palace with no cover at all.

We'd dressed her as a young woman from the immigrants' quarter, in the same elegant robes and head coverings many often used. As a result, both her telltale blond curls and the lower half of her face were covered in a sparkling emerald green sash flecked with gold and amber. Her striking Gehtanan blue eyes were heavily lined with charcoal we'd purchased from The Artists' Den.

"What are you doing here?" I cried in surprise, squinting at the bright light from the library beyond.

"She's announced a viewing for the eclipse."

"What?"

"Elodie. She announced there will be a viewing on the front lawn. Of the eclipse. Through scopes. I knew the scopes would be open, but I didn't think she intended to stay awake. I assumed she'd encourage our people to watch from the lawns."

"Fiermi."

She squinted at me. "I have only a mild idea of what that word means, but yes, fiermi. Come on."

I followed Abi into the library, sealing shut the door to the tomblike room behind me. I tried not to limp. Stiffness. Only stiffness from sitting for so long.

"What time is it?" I asked.

"Half-past midnight."

Her words struck like a spear. An hour and a half. We had ninety minutes.

"How did you know? Does Alesh know? How did you know to come find me?"

She shook her head in annoyance. "Mical located Alesh after he brought you. Alesh came to find me when he heard the news that the party wouldn't end tonight at all. And now I've found you, so hurry, let's get back to Alesh and Mical and get a new plan figured out quickly."

I rushed to keep beside her, the emerald fabric that made up the loose legs of her attire swishing behind her. Against my better judgment, I looked to where I'd seen the Quinn-look-alike sitting earlier, but there was no sign of him, nor any sign that he'd been there. Perhaps I'd been imagining—

Then he was in my line of sight, eyes focused intensely on mine as he barreled through the crowd in the room. I'd never felt more like prey.

"Run," I said to Abi.

"What?"

"Later. Right now, take me to Alesh, and *run.*"

She ran.

I followed, dashing between people, through the room and into the hall beyond.

We finally lost the Guard-Who-Was-Not-Really-Quinn when we turned a corner, then slipped behind a large tapestry that hid the opening to a passage that would bring us out above the laundry. I held my breath as we navigated the dark tunnel. Thin shafts of light shone through conveniently spaced air slits, enough to keep me from stumbling on the rough-hewn floor.

When we reached the laundry, I was almost disappointed the guard had not followed. I was relieved we hadn't been caught, but I would have given anything in the world to find that Quinn was alive after all. I bent and rubbed a stitch in my side as I caught my breath from running for the hidden corridor.

A stitch. No more, no less.

The veins there would show nothing if I looked. No web of black, no poison. Just a cramp from running.

"Are you all right?"

Abi's worried brow drew downwards. She put a hand on my shoulder as I stayed bent.

"Fine," I lied. "I'm fine. Just winded."

She studied me.

"You look pale, Reina."

"I haven't eaten much today." I admitted, giving a sheepish smile. "Too nervous."

I wasn't lying. I simply wasn't telling the truth, either.

As the pain in my side abated, I stood straight again, as if to convince her all was well. Aware of her scrutiny, I refused to wince with each step as I followed her through the empty laundry.

"Where is everyone?" I asked. I would have assumed the laundry to be busy day or night.

"Elodie probably has everyone working the kitchens. Laundry can wait a day, but with this many people? The food better keep coming! She wouldn't want her people to think her incapable, or worse—stingy. Come on, Alesh and Mical are up this way."

I swallowed. Hiding the pain from Alesh wouldn't be as easy as hiding it from Abi.

I willed the pain away, instructing my body to soothe whatever was being undone inside of me, whatever pieces were coming apart, whatever tissues were being destroyed. Less than ninety minutes now. I just needed to hold on for a bit longer.

Alesh nodded as Abi and I approached. "My stubborn Reina," he said.

I smiled weakly. "You're not mad."

He shook his head, a fatigue on his face I felt right to the core of my very bones.

"It is no use to be angry. I am always glad to see you, my friend. And you have done the noble thing to help your friends and do what needs to be done. How could I be mad?"

Tears pricked my eyes. "Plans now. Emotion later, Alesh."

I wiped the tears from my eyes with the back of one hand. He smiled and gripped my shoulder, giving a firm squeeze. In his other hand, he held his jewel-topped staff. Abi had snuck it into the palace through her secret passages, then given it to him after he passed through the front gates and reached his hiding spot.

"So how are we taking her down?" Mical said, bearlike arms crossed over his chest as he leaned against a wall.

I hadn't noticed him in the shadows.

"Why are you dressed as a guard?" I asked. I thought he'd come as a guest.

He looked down at his green and gold uniform, obviously pleased with the way he looked in it. "I've heard women like men in uniforms."

I rolled my eyes, prompting a deep laugh from him.

"For someone my size, it was the easiest way to blend in."

Alesh made a sound that could have been from frustration or from amusement. He waved his hands at the air. "Back to—"

"Yes," I agreed. "Back to the matter at hand."

"She won't sleep. Not tonight," Abi said.

Alesh gave a frustrated sigh. "We should have thought of this. Before the celebration. We should have realized."

We should have. Would I take the time to sleep if I knew I'd have control over the world as long as I could keep my enemies subdued a few more hours? Would I sleep if I knew my magic was strong enough to overcome anyone else's? No. I'd drink every jittery beverage if it meant I could keep my eyes—

"Spike her drink."

All eyes turned to me.

"Is there something we can put in her drink to make her fall asleep? Surely there's a palace healer, a medical room, a physician, something?"

"There's a physician, but you'll find no help from him."

I smiled. "I don't need help. I just need his medicine stores. And you to translate the labels."

Alesh held up a hand. "We get a drug to make her sleep, but how does she sleep? When? What does she drink? How do we get the drug into the drink?"

I gave a deflated sigh. With how highly guarded Elodie was, there was no way to slip anything into her food or drink.

"You forget I have friends here." Mical's eyes held a glimmer of mischief. "Yes, most of the guards would kill the first person to suggest such a thing, but there are a few who *might* have heard rumors about a younger Gehtanan still being alive."

I shook my head at the smirk on his ridiculously handsome face.

"You didn't," I said, pinching the bridge of my nose.

"Mical, tell me you didn't say anything."

Alesh regarded him with disdain. "Can you ever be trusted?"

"Of course I can be trusted. And I know who else to trust as well, including the very guard who will get whatever you want into Elodie's food or drink, so figure out what you need and get it done. You can thank me later for setting the rumor mill freely running and figuring out an alternate plan before you knew you'd even need one."

Slack-jawed, I stared at him.

He pushed off the wall, stood, took three steps toward me and grinned. Then, in a motion so fast I had no time to protest, he grabbed my face in both palms, and planted a kiss firmly on my lips, pulling back quickly with another mischievous grin.

I hadn't even had time to step back, to argue, to deny him the kiss.

"You cad!" I cried as he turned his back. There was a spring in his step.

"Can't blame me," he called over a shoulder. "I had to chance it where you wouldn't wilt me like you did that bouquet. Can't use your magic here. Not yet anyway." I couldn't see his face, but damn him, he was smiling!

I seethed, even as part of me was amused by his unpredictability. I searched for a reply, something to say that might put a damper on his arrogance.

"No time to waste!" he said. "Better get moving." Then he reached the door leading from the laundry and slipped through it.

I turned to Abi, then to Alesh with an expression of shock still on my face.

"Did he really… Did you see…" I couldn't seem to find the words to finish my questions.

Alesh shook his head and gave a tired sigh, but he was clearly amused. Abi grinned outright.

She shrugged. "*I* think he's handsome."

"Abigayle!"

She rolled her eyes. "I know, I know. Your heart belongs elsewhere. All I'm saying is that if your heart ever decides to give him a chance, he's not bad to have around."

"You're eleven," I reminded her.

She snickered in response. "Come. Let's go look at the physician's medical stores. We're running out of time."

As though I needed reminding.

CHAPTER TWENTY-SEVEN

Delicate Work
Reina

I didn't know who Mical's friend was or how he would manage to slip anything into Elodie's food or drink, but the ground dreamroot Abi and I located should have been more than strong enough to induce a persistent fatigue.

We needed Elodie to feel sleepy, not to pass out. We needed her to want a place to rest, not to cause alarm and fall unconscious in front of an entire palace full of people.

Mical, Alesh, Abi, and I were stationed in various locations in the crowded masquerade ballroom, each watching Elodie as intently and inconspicuously as possible. I danced with the other guests, dipping and twirling to keep from standing out. I smiled and threw my head back with laughter, though the poison in my blood had begun to seep into my lungs, and they burned with the exertion.

Through it all, I kept an eye on Elodie on her raised dais, the lone unmasked figure in the room, her dark hair crowned with the diadem we so desperately needed to remove from her possession. As always, it was woven into her dark bun, the pearls dripping from the gold swirls, the yellow sapphire radiating an almost otherworldly light. I began to wonder if her eyes would ever reflect anything but madness, and then, finally…a yawn and a rub of the eyes.

She leaned to tell the nearest guard something.

An hour. You have time for a nap. Take a short nap, Elodie. Just a few minutes. You'll wake for the eclipse.

I found myself willing the words into her mind, praying my will was stronger than hers. When she nodded to the guard and stood, I nearly wept with relief. Three of the nearest guards followed her from the room, out a side entrance.

Finally.

I caught Alesh's eye across the wide expanse of the room. He gave a single nod.

The fake smile fell from my face. I pushed against the pain in my legs and insides. I could press through.

An hour. If the poison didn't leak completely in an hour, I could still make this happen.

By the time I reconvened with Alesh, Abi was already there.

"You need to go," he told her. "Hide until we give the sign."

"I don't want to hide. I want to help!"

"You'll be no help at all to us if you're not here afterwards to take the throne," I whispered into her ear.

She huffed and crossed her arms.

"Fine, but I'm *not* happy about it."

I ran a hand along her back and squeezed her shoulder before she left, shooting us a single glance behind.

"Mical?" I asked Alesh.

"In place. He will take care of the guards. We have only

a short time."

I nodded and followed Alesh back into the hall, jumping at the sensation of the mask leaving my face again. The movement sent pain down my side, and I winced.

Alesh didn't miss the motion. He squinted. "You are not well."

I shook my head. "No, but we'll finish this, our magic will reverse, and then we'll have all the time we need for you to fix the venom in my blood."

He didn't look convinced.

"Alesh," I said softly as we turned a corner to a lesser used hall where the crowd was not directed. "My life doesn't matter. Not now. We save the world from chaos first. Then, if there's time…*then,* we worry about my life." My throat thick, I swallowed, then forced a smile. "Besides, if I die, I get to see Quinn again," I added.

Alesh shot an alarmed look my way and grabbed my hand, stopping me in my tracks.

"You must fight," he said. "Fight the poison with all you have. You must. Promise me this."

"I promise."

"You must mean it."

"I do. I promise." I did. Mostly. I couldn't succumb before we got that diadem from Elodie.

"Let us go."

I wasn't comforted by the fear and concern etched on Alesh's face. I wish I knew the thoughts running through his head and if they were as disjointed as my own.

Then we were in front of the door to Elodie's chamber,

unguarded, as Mical promised it would be.

We entered quietly, slippered feet falling on heavily carpeted floors. The decor in the palace, particularly in Elodie's rooms put the castle at Irzan to shame. The sheer number of gilded vases, frames, trinkets, and lamps was astounding. It was as though anywhere the eye could fall or the hand might touch was covered in shining, yellow gold.

The four-poster bed was intricately carved, and hand-painted with gold leaf at every turn. Gold lilies and frogs, golden cranes, golden koi, gold, gold, everywhere gold. It was a wonder Elodie rested on a thick duvet the color of deep red wine. I almost expected her bedding would be woven from spun gold, but the plush duvet and the dozen or so pillows on the bed were varying shades of wine and burgundy.

I winced and put a hand to my side as a particularly fierce pain stabbed my middle. Breathing through, I closed my eyes and forced the pain away with each beat of my heart. It was fine. I was fine. My body was fine. As the pain subsided, I wiped the side of a palm across my damp brow. An hour. I would survive an hour. I refocused my attention on the sleeping figure in the bed.

Elodie was small, lying in an enormous bed that was meant for two adults. She might have looked innocent were it not for the fact that she'd left the diadem on her head, even sleeping. So instead of the sweet picture her sleeping self might otherwise have painted, she still appeared an ever-looming threat. We'd joked about her weaving the diadem into her hair, but I never anticipated she truly *had.*

I questioned Alesh with a wide-eyed panic, motioning to the top of my own head, and mouthing "the diadem." He nodded, lips drawn in a grim line as he pulled our artificial diadem from wherever he'd hidden it on him before he came through the front gates.

Then he leaned close, whispering in my ear, "You remove the diadem from her head. Softly. I will replace it."

I gave a terrified shake of my head. "No," I whispered back sharply. "It's *woven*."

He looked back to Elodie, getting close, hovering over her as he worked out exactly how she'd twisted the diadem into her hair. I held my breath, terrified for every second Alesh's face was near hers.

Elodie gave a sharp inhale and murmured in her sleep, sending my nerves skittering, but Alesh remained unfazed. When he drew back, he leaned close to my ear to whisper again.

"She has…ties. Into her hair. We cut them. How deep in sleep is she? And for how long?"

I shook my head and gave an exaggerate shrug. "I can't say. I don't know how much dreamroot Mical's friend used."

The depth of her sleep all depended on how much of the dreamroot Elodie had ingested. I told Mical she needed a minimum of half a spoonful in her drink, but how much had she drunk before she'd begun to feel its effects? Without a full dose, it was impossible to say how much dreamroot might be in her system, how deep she would sleep, or how long her sleep would last.

I shifted, uncomfortable with standing so close to the

Chaos Wielder for too long, even with her eyes closed and her breathing deep and even. Already, we'd wasted precious minutes.

If I hadn't promised Abi I'd keep her sister alive, I might try to use the talisman's magic to kill her now. I was lying to myself, of course. Even without my promise to Abi, I was no good at killing anyone, and I knew it.

Alesh flashed a pocketknife pulled from Saints-knew-where. He slid the blade outward, then offered it to me. My fingers grazed the smooth wood of the handle hesitantly, my gaze falling briefly on the large clock in one corner of the room. We were out of time. Out of options. Every tick of the clock told me so. Every painful beat of my heart told me so, too.

I nodded, gripping the handle of the blade tighter, then stepped close to the sleeping figure on the bed and pretended she was a patient. She was a patient, and I was a Healer. Surely, I could use the knife to cut a few threads, and extract the diadem from where it sat, poisoning her. Adopting that mindset made it easier to steady my hand and draw breath.

The diadem was poisoning this child and I needed to remove it, just as I'd set a broken bone or aid with ingestion of spoiled food. I leaned over the sleeping figure, avoiding looking at Elodie's face, pretending she was someone other than the mad girl who'd tried to murder me outright.

Fingers trembling, I began.

Alesh crept to the other side of the bed, ready to place the fake diadem atop her head as soon as I freed the real one from its bindings. The work was frustratingly slow and tedious.

The raw power roiling from the diadem was palpable in the very air surrounding it, an unpleasant heat that reminded me of the talisman when I'd first donned it.

I had no doubt I'd receive an angry shock once I grabbed the diadem from her head, but there was no point in touching it before I absolutely had to, so I worked carefully on the threads that bound it to her coiffure. The work was not simple, as the binding threads were designed to match her dark hair, so distinguishing between thread and hair was difficult. The last thing I wanted to do was wake her with a tug on her scalp instead of a thread.

Who styled her hair? Who centered the diadem and wove the strands into the smooth, elaborate bun with all its shine and pearls? I wondered.

Then I accidentally cut one of the bound pearls I'd just been contemplating. I froze as it rolled from its place in her hair down one temple. My breath stuck in back of my throat as the pearl rolled downward across her skin.

When it reached the spot between her neck and the pillow, it came to a rest. Beyond a single flutter of Elodie's eyelids, she didn't seem to be aware that anything was amiss. I let out a slow breath between pursed lips, swallowed, then steadied my hands and began again. Locate a thread, slice. Locate a thread, slice.

Many tense moments later, the diadem was mostly free from its bindings, tilted dangerously far to the left, with a handful of threads remaining. I stole a glance at the clock. Another fourteen minutes gone.

I swore I could feel the eclipse in my bones…or maybe

that was the snake venom in my bloodstream. Whatever the case, sweat gathered at my brow and my temples. It trickled between my breasts and stuck thick, blond hair to the back of my neck.

I focused with surgical precision.

Three more threads conquered.

Four threads left to cut.

I halted as Elodie took a deep breath inward, then raised a hand to scratch her neck. No, not her neck. My body buzzed with anxiety. Eyes still closed, Elodie's sleepy brow furrowed as her fingers found, then clasped the pearl.

I looked at Alesh.

"Now!" he mouthed, urgency in his eyes.

I lunged forward with the knife before her eyes fluttered open, slicing two of the last remaining threads, but missing the final two as the girl came fully awake, startled by the assault.

Shards of ice-cold pain plunged into my chest, sending me backwards with the force of a dozen horses. I hit the wall beside the large clock, my teeth rattling with the impact. The fall knocked the wind from my lungs. In a daze, I struggled to stand, tripping and stumbling, not coherent enough to realize several panels of my skirt were wrapped around my legs.

Murder in her eyes, Elodie raged. She leaped from the duvet, putting the bed between Alesh and herself even as she sent her power hurtling his way. Held by two lone threads, the diadem flopped against the side of her head, no longer adding to a regal appearance, but instead making her look all the more crazed.

"You *dare*!" she cried. "You *dare* attack me in *my* home?"

Alesh didn't waste time crafting a response. When it came to the Chaos Wielder, words were pointless. Instead, he sent a surge of power racing across the bed, turning the golden images of marsh grasses, lilies, and frogs into real, living beings. The golden trim unwrapped itself from the bed posts, enlarging in size until the cranes were as tall as Elodie herself, their feathers losing their golden tinge as they shook their plumage into a downy white, their sharp beaks snapping at Elodie's face and body. She flung her hands upward to protect herself.

The frogs leaped across the lily pads that scattered onto the floor. All the while, Elodie had begun to scream. Struggling, I pushed myself to my hands and knees, forcing my eyes to focus, pushing away the radiating pain in my abdomen. I stood, fell, then stood again. Alesh had created a chaos of his own with the power of the staff.

Just as Elodie extended an arm, the wide double doors to her room flew open and the Guard-Who-Was-Not-Really-Quinn rushed into the room. Fiermi, she'd summoned the guards!

"Don't touch the diadem!"

CHAPTER TWENTY-EIGHT

A Taste of Chaos
Reina

Elodie shot another burst of power through the room, sending everyone back to the floor, including the Guard-Who-Was-Not-Really-Quinn. Why would she strike her own guard? Was she so terrified that she didn't care who was here to help?

"*You!*" she cried, her face morphing into a mask of fury when she saw the guard.

She sent a blast of wind at him again, but, with a growl, Alesh sent his own magic at the same time, and the floor that was now half marsh grew long, green cattails that wrapped around her ankles and pulled her off balance. Unhappy with the commotion, the cranes in the room squawked, nipping and biting at the frogs, the bed, Elodie, and anything in their path until they finally found the open door and flooded into the hallway beyond.

My head throbbed. I panted, dragging myself up again. This time, when I stumbled, I latched onto strong, familiar arms that caught me in a fierce grip, even though he, too, was on his knees. Terrified, I flung my gaze upward to meet familiar dark eyes. It couldn't be.

It *couldn't*.

Quinn was dead.

Quinn was here.

He looked at me as though he could communicate the seriousness of his words if he bored into my soul with his stare. "Did you touch the diadem?" he rasped.

"Quinn?"

"Reina, did you—"

But he didn't get to finish his sentence. The world split in two, and I was falling, alone, into nothingness. Falling, falling, until at last, I landed in the middle of a sunlit path amidst a lush jungle.

My head spun with vertigo, my eyes blinded by a white fog that was too slowly dissipating. Bending, I half-tumbled to my knees and waited for the feeling to pass. The venom.

Not yet. Not yet!

"Reina! What's wrong?"

Alarmed at the voice beside me, the hand on my back, I looked up with alarm, heart pounding beneath my ribs. That's when I realized where I was, *when* I was, and who was with me.

"You can't be," I whispered.

Quinn—real, firm, solid, and standing beside me. His hand moved from low on my back to grip my arm as I stumbled backwards. Concern flooded his eyes, his mind likely working to figure out why I would try to run from him.

"Reina?" His voice was soft, questioning, his brows drawn. "Are you unwell?"

I didn't answer, *couldn't* answer.

Instead, I looked past him, to Alesh and Niles. Niles Ingram, who should have been dead. Niles Ingram, who instead of being dead, stood, shoulders slumped in defeat, looking miserable and still mildly concerned at my sudden outburst.

Alesh stepped forward, his staff glinting with Kufataba's artificial sunlight. "You are ill?"

Saints above. We were beneath Kufataba.

"Alesh! She sent us back!"

Alesh leaned forward, confusion etched in his kind eyes, worry apparent on his face. He turned to Quinn. "Is she fevered?"

"I'm not feverish! I'm not sick. I'm telling you—"

I spun into the bushes beside the trail, ripping my arm from Quinn's grasp as nausea struck me. I vomited the few meager bites of food I'd eaten earlier, retching, coughing, then retching once more for good measure, as though my body wanted to be thoroughly sure I'd emptied it of Elodie's offerings.

"It's a dream. It must be. Another dream." I spat into the dirt twice, then wiped my mouth with the back of a hand.

I thought back to the dreams I'd had of Quinn over the past few weeks, all the thoughts I wasted wishing his existence back into my life, all the times his death plagued me, teased me, taunted me in my sleeping moments.

Then warm hands closed gently around my shoulders, helping to ease me back, supporting me as I stood. He turned me to face him, put a hand beneath my chin and forced my reluctant eyes to meet his as he examined me with a furrowed brow.

"You're most certainly ill. We stop here for the night."

"If there *is* a night in this place." Niles's voice was a slice to the gut. "I could be mistaken, but didn't you say time was of the essence? Wasn't that the whole point of taking this Saints-forsaken shortcut beneath the mountain?" He scowled as he crossed his arms.

It was hard to look at Niles, to look at Quinn, and not feel I was seeing dead men walking. But to hear them speak and watch them breathe? Niles, who had been crushed by a boulder, but…hadn't. And Quinn who had fallen into blue nothingness…and yet stood before me.

If I was here, really here, in my own body beneath Kufataba, then time hadn't yet grown short. We still had over a month to reach Ivirreh, to beat Elodie at her own game, to undo everything she'd done. She'd unwittingly sent me into the one place where I could change the outcome of all that had happened. The only element that could have made my task easier would be if Alesh had been sent back with me. It was clear he had not. The Alesh in front of me was the man who had existed those weeks ago.

I wondered where the Alesh from my time was. Was he still in the palace, fighting Elodie, protecting Abi? Or had the Chaos Wielder sent him tumbling backwards through time, too?

"Quinn." I finally looked at him, really let myself look, absorbing the dark chocolate eyes I wanted to fall into, the faint scar beside one eye from an arrow where he'd once fought to protect me from those who would have seen us both dead. Emotion swelled thick in my chest.

And I did the one thing that would help absolutely no one. I sobbed.

Like a newborn infant who'd been yanked from the warmth and safety of her mother's womb, I sobbed. I didn't miss the alarm and confusion on Niles's and Alesh's faces before Quinn pulled me into a massive embrace, shielding me from the world outside his arms.

I soaked the front of his tunic. "You're here, you're here, you're here," I muttered into his chest.

"Easy, easy." He brushed stray strands of hair away from my forehead, his other hand rubbing lazy circles across my back as he continued to hold me until the tears no longer flowed.

"I thought I'd never see you again, and I know that sounds crazy, and you must think I've lost my mind, but I'm not the same me I was a few moments ago, and I don't know how to explain what's happening or what happened or what—"

And like that, I was ripped out of Quinn's arms and spinning through a whirlpool of blackness and stars, catching flashes of images and places and people that made no sense before I landed in a spot that was all too familiar.

Panic flooded my veins.

Not here.

The canvas sides of the tent closed in around me, suffocating, shutting me in. I squeezed my eyes shut and forced an even breath out from my nostrils, trying to expel the lingering scent of cherry tobacco from the pipe on a side desk.

I knew exactly whose pipe it was.

I couldn't be here.

I couldn't.

I gave up on controlled breathing. I gasped, gulping down air, struggling to overcome the panic that welled within at the thought of the ropes that kept me tied to the chair. I couldn't do this again.

And then *he* walked through the flaps of the tent, that same dark hair with the graying temples, slicked back from his face, the same dark mustache and bushy brows. The same sick satisfaction on his face.

"I see I finally have the privilege of meeting the infamous White Sorceress," General Marcus Bruenner said, and, at the sound of his voice, I very nearly lost every last shred of sanity.

Then I was yanked from my body, hurling through blackness again, mercifully taken from that time with Bruenner, unable to make sense of where I was being thrown or why.

Was the world in full chaos now? Was this my future, to hurtle through random pieces of my past again and again until I went mad with it? Had we failed despite having thirty minutes before the full eclipse?

When I landed this time, I found myself lying on grass, the familiar smell of alfalfa on the breeze. Abruptly, I sat, blinking at the spindly arms and legs of the child I'd become.

A child. In a field I knew and loved, in a home I never thought to see again. The very smell of Barnham overwhelmed my senses, sending my heart singing with the familiarity of everything I called home.

"What now?"

I turned my head to the voice I once knew so well, to meet the dark, young eyes of a barefoot boy in a stream, whose nearly black hair had lightened to a burnished brown from hours beneath the summer sun.

Quinn—boy-Quinn—eyed me from the creek, his trousers rolled to his knees as he attempted to catch minnows with his hands.

I couldn't begin to imagine the look on my face. Seeing Quinn as the boy I once knew, before the Order had turned him into someone and something he resented becoming, was sobering. His hair was unruly, overgrown, almost covering the eyes that steadily watched me. Was he watching? Had he always been watching? Even then?

"Nothing." My child's voice surprised me, even though it was my own.

"You look like ye've seen a ghost!"

I didn't remember this interaction with Quinn. I didn't recall the specifics of a conversation or an experience we had together. We'd spent so many days—and nights—in this field, by this stream, they blurred into each other in one pleasant ache of a memory.

And now I was here.

When I didn't reply further, Quinn turned his attention back to the stream, the movement in his shoulders so familiar even in his child's body.

One moment, I was longing with the familiarity of the living memory, and the next I was taken from my home and being thrown through blackness again.

Then I was back in the palace for the briefest of moments, the Guard-Who-Was-Not-Really-Quinn holding my arms.

"—touch the diadem?" he was saying. He shook my arms. "Reina!"

"I…I don't know. I don't think so." Was that my voice? Were those my words?

I wanted to vomit again. What was going on? Why had Elodie attacked her own guard? Why did he look like Quinn?

He was speaking to me again. I tried to focus on his words, but my head was spinning. Everything was growing darker. What was he saying?

"Don't touch it. Whatever you do! Do you understand?"

I nodded. At least, I think I nodded.

"Niles is the only one who can bind the chaos." The words followed me into the darkness. I heard them, but they made no sense.

Niles was dead. Quinn was dead.

But not. Quinn was also here.

Then I was tumbling once more. Blackness and whirling, images, sounds, chaos. My eyes strained to focus, to make sense of *something*, anything that might help me stop falling. Then, when it felt as though it might never stop, there was sudden, complete, and utter silence.

I lay on the solid floor, panting, regaining my breath, trying—in vain—to push down the uncontrollable fear that welled deep in my soul.

Quinn. Real Quinn. He'd been here, at the palace, the whole night.

But had he? Was he real? Too many times I'd been taunted by the Chaos Wielder. Too many times I'd been teased by my own dreams. I no longer knew what was real and what wasn't. I'd assumed I was back in the palace, but maybe I'd never stopped falling through the endless chaos. Maybe I never would.

I sat slowly, gingerly placing a hand to the back of my head where I'd hit it on something at some point and wincing at the knot building beneath my fingers. Oddly, the pain in my body from the release of the snake venom didn't seem to persist here…wherever here was. The respite was a welcome one.

I rose to my feet and took in my surroundings, piecing together where I was and trying to determine the when. Rows and rows of books filled the darkened space. I breathed in the familiar, musty scent of leather and parchment and ink long unused.

Irzan.

The castle.

I was within the castle's library, the place I'd spent so many hours on research, where I'd uncovered the prophecy that sent us in search of Alesh those months ago.

But *when* was I?

I'd never fallen in the library, never hit my head on the shelves the way I just had. Although maybe the cause of such an injury had been due to my conscious being thrown into this particular time and not an actual occurrence that had happened to my body.

Still.

Something didn't sit right.

Quiet voices carried from beyond my line of sight. I followed the shelves, fingers lightly touching the spines of the books as I walked, more from habit than to maintain my balance after my fall, even if my head throbbed.

At the end of the stack, I halted.

Three women stood silhouetted with their backs to me, illuminated by a light source in front of them, a lamp on the table as they bent to review something together.

Three women. Illuminated.

I swallowed as I remembered the mural, overlaying the two scenes in my mind. The match was uncanny.

I'd never seen these women in the castle's library. I'd never seen them at all. Which meant, I was not—could not be—in the past.

And if I wasn't in the past, and I wasn't in the present, I must be…in the future. The realization shook me. There *was* a future.

Chaos hadn't won. Not yet.

The oil sconce beside me flickered with my sudden inhalation, drawing the attention of all three. They were close to my age, a bit younger even. They smiled in unison, not appearing even mildly alarmed that an unfamiliar woman had disturbed them.

"You're here."

The voice of the one who spoke was melodious, familiar in an unexpected way, and I wondered what that voice might sound like singing during winter festivities.

"We wondered when you'd come," the youngest of the

three said.

"Liana." There was a warning tone in that single word, in that name.

They were sisters, I realized, which explained why they looked so alike in both their mannerisms and physical features. Each had long, dark hair of varying shades of brown, half-twisted into braids, the remainder of their hair spilling down their backs and falling gracefully over their shoulders. The older two were near to my age, the youngest somewhere around Abi's age.

"You wondered…when *I'd* come?" I asked, placing a hand on my chest, my fingers falling around the talisman instinctively.

Nothing made sense about this exchange, but after my time with the Chaos Wielder, I was somehow no longer surprised that nothing made sense. The girl called Liana smiled wider but didn't speak again. She let the tallest of the three speak instead.

"We'd hoped you might come soon, but we didn't know…" She held out her hands and let them fall as if to show the uncertainty they'd had regarding my arrival. "You are Moreina, yes?"

I swallowed, my eyes growing wide as I studied them before nodding, a tingling in the back of my throat. "How… did you know?"

She smiled wider. "That's a longer story than we have time for, and you'll be leaving again soon, but before you go, before you leave us, know this. If nothing else, hold these words close to your heart and remember them. The most difficult moment to believe is the moment you must place your trust in him entirely."

I furrowed my brows in confusion, ready to confess I had not an inkling of what she meant by her words, when the world tilted beneath my feet again.

"It was good to see you again. I've missed you so!" Liana's words came from far away, even as her sisters hushed her, even as I was falling away into the blackness. "She looked so different!"

I had no time to contemplate the meaning of the words left echoing in my mind.

When I next found myself in my body again, I was falling to my knees in a wide grassy plain, fighting the urge to vomit once more. There was nothing left in me to vomit, but that didn't stop me from dry heaving into the grass. This time, when I was finished, when my sides ached from trying to push out what was no longer inside, I rolled onto my back and lay on the ground, catching my breath.

The stars were bright overhead, only Stellon visible above, but there was no eclipse, not in this time and place. Whenever I was, Andra had already set. I lost focus as I connected the constellations I'd known all my life, picking out the ox and the horse, the king, the jester, the cottage. Oh, the cottage. That one was my favorite.

And then there was something else in the sky. Something that made no sense. I sat, my head spinning with the sudden movement. Where was I? The constellations were familiar. I must be in Castilles, or somewhere in Liron's northern hemisphere. I stood slowly, one hand on the ground until

I was steady enough to stand on my own two feet. Then I stumbled through the grass, taking in the measure of my aloneness.

Something was different, changed. Liron didn't…sound right. The meadow birds I knew, the night beetles I loved? None of them sang. There was the occasional chirrup of a meadow cricket, and a singular hoot of an owl, but it was not the symphony of sound I had always encountered in my life, whether in Castilles or the Elorin Empire. Where were the creatures?

I returned my gaze to the object in the sky once more. A light that did not belong, a soaring, steady light, stable across the blackness, making its way through the night as though following in Stellon's light. But it wasn't following. No, it was moving much faster, and it wasn't long before it passed Stellon and disappeared, dipping below the horizon and out of sight.

I took a shaky step forward, hoping for a moment of rest before being thrown back into a spinning void of nothingness, but I was granted no reprieve. In moments, the soft, still night was left behind and I was hurtling through the blackness again until I was spit out at the palace gates.

The world flickered around me in and out of sight again, repeatedly. Women dressed in shining finery of all colors and textures, men in long, white coats and polished black boots, faux swords at their belts, guards in green and gold. All of it here and then gone. I'd been thrown into the past again, but this time, I'd been sent to the beginning of the evening, when the crowds had first arrived.

Did the Chaos Wielder know? Did Elodie know where she was sending me and how? Or had she lost all control of the stone and its power? Is this what was meant when the prophecy stated chaos would reign? Not the wearer of the diadem at all, but rather absolute chaos without a master at the helm?

With no warning at all, I was back inside a palace hallway, as though Elodie had snapped her fingers and simply decided it was where I belonged. I spun to find Mical beside me, looking every bit as bewildered as I felt.

"What the bloody hell was that?" he asked, his whisper a dull roar in my sensitive ears.

"You, too?"

He nodded.

I had no idea where Alesh or the Chaos Wielder or the Guard-Who-Was-Not-Really-Quinn had gone, but Mical's presence was a welcome one in the empty hall. The nearest window opened to the sprawling lawns, revealing thousands of people who looked upward to the sky.

"We're out of time," I choked, a blinding pain seizing the back of my skull. I doubled over as my vision blurred.

Elodie. We had to get to Elodie. If the guests were on the lawns, the eclipse was well underway. We had…minutes. Maybe. I couldn't do the calculations. I couldn't even trust my own mind to remember the way to Elodie's chambers.

I looked to Mical, pouring every bit of the desperation in my soul into my voice.

"Get me to her room, then get help."

CHAPTER TWENTY-NINE

Unlikely Reunion
Quinn

"She was supposed to join me! We were supposed to rule it all together!" the Chaos Wielder screamed.

The diadem hung limp in her hair, a shining beacon hovering over one ear, as though taunting me to tackle her and grab it. Instead, I ducked for cover behind the fallen clock as she sent another wave of frost over everything in the room. The frost in my corner was particularly thick.

"It was supposed to be *fun*. But because of *you,* she crossed me."

Reina had never crossed anyone. You couldn't cross someone if you never agreed to join them in the first place.

"The prophecy said. It said two girls!" she howled. She took the marsh grasses Alesh had made and turned them into thorns, shooting them across the air with enough speed to bury them in whatever lay in their path. The artfully papered walls, the clock, the paintings, the furniture, and my shoulder sported a barrage of buried thorns.

I hissed as I pulled two from where they'd sliced into the muscle of my shoulder. A third was buried too deep to withdraw, its presence a biting sting with every movement.

It figured the girl would go on about another damned prophecy. I wanted nothing more than to never hear the word "prophecy" again in my life, however long it might be.

I searched the destruction in the room, looking for something to use against her, searching for Reina or Alesh, who had been here one minute and gone the next. I couldn't imagine how she'd done it, but the Chaos Wielder had taken Reina and Alesh and somehow sent them…elsewhere. I hadn't immediately recognized Alesh when I crashed into the room. Like Reina, he'd been altered, but there was no one else who owned that staff, or who would dare to wield it with such confidence.

I dodged another round of thorns and cursed. Reina claimed she hadn't touched the diadem, but if that were the case, how was such chaos already in motion? Where had Reina and Alesh been sent? *Someone* must have touched it.

And where the bloody hell was Niles?

The clock exploded around me, splinters of wood and bent cogs flying through the air. Instead of running away from the debris, I shielded my face and ran directly through it, cursing the whole way, to the door that led to the hallway beyond.

I hadn't been taught to run. I'd been taught to fight, but how could I fight an opponent who was a thousand times more powerful than I could ever hope to be, who wielded magic like she didn't care about the consequences?

The only people she cared about, according to her devout following, *were* her followers themselves. I sprinted around a corner as the carpet behind me pulled up into a giant, burgundy hand the size of a horse, grabbing at me, grazing the back of my tunic as I made the turn before it lost its magic and flopped harmlessly to the floor again.

If I could find a few of her guests, I'd have a chance at keeping her at bay—

My thoughts came to a screeching halt even as I raced onward. How could I contemplate using her own people as leverage against her? The thought alone made me as bad as Niles all those years ago.

"Get her back to the dais in the main ballroom. It's where I can do what I need to without anyone getting hurt." Niles was suddenly beside me, keeping stride.

I hoped he hadn't heard my thoughts.

"Where have you *been?*" I berated him.

"Last minute preparations. Get to the ballroom."

Then he was gone again.

I followed the winding hallways, barely managing to stay out of reach of the angry magic on my heels. Finally, I made a turn that would take me to the main ballroom…only to run straight into six guards—real ones, guards who knew I was *not* one of their own no matter how I was dressed.

"Sietzu!"

I didn't need a translator to know what was said. Five of the guards rushed forward, gripping my arms before I could turn away. It wouldn't have mattered. An enormous ball of lightning crashed behind me, searing the painting that hung there, leaving a scorched mark down the length of the wall. I flinched at both the impact and the pain in my ears from the strike.

Thinking I was trying to escape, the guards tackled me, four of them holding me to the ground, knees digging into my back to keep me from rising. The carpet pressed into my jaw as my hands were yanked behind my back.

The Chaos Wielder rounded the corner at that moment, entering the hallway leading to the main entrance of the ballroom. I had done as Niles had asked. It was all that mattered now. Whether I lived or died was of no importance.

It was one thing to think such a thing. It was another to believe it.

I'd been willing to lay down my life for Reina's, but to die for no good reason was much, much harder. Still, I had to find a way to lure her to the dais.

"Studei enu," she said to the guards with a smile.

They hauled me upwards, holding my arms tight, wrenching them once to remind me they could dislocate both my shoulders anytime they pleased. Or if their mistress should request it.

The Chaos Wielder took a moment to rearrange the diadem, pushing it back onto her head, burying its corners into straggled dark hair that no longer looked as though she'd spent hours smoothing and sculpting it. With her wild eyes and mused hair, she looked more a peasant than an emperor. If peasants wore gold.

Despite the chase, she wasn't out of breath. She stepped close, her gown billowing behind her with a breeze she'd crafted, mad blue eyes widening as she approached me, chin tilted upward, a defiant smile on her artificially pink lips. I tried to back away, but the guards reminded me I had no say in the matter. I winced as the shoulder with the thorn still buried in it screamed in pain.

"She thought you were dead."

"So I've heard," I muttered.

She ignored my words. "So *I* thought you were dead. I thought I had a chance at winning her over. The prophecy said two girls to rule, bonded by magic. She's the other."

"You might have started with talk of horses or healing to win her over before pivoting to the whole chaos and death scene." I shouldn't speak. I knew this, but I would do anything to stall for more time. In response, she scoffed, somehow managing to look down at me even though she stood as high as my chest.

"Why don't you bring me into your great, big ballroom, and kill me in front of all your guests to prove your power, to prove the king of Castilles is no match for your power?"

She furrowed her brow as she examined me. "King of Castilles?"

I gave a slow nod in return.

One corner of her mouth tilted upwards, twitching in amusement. "I've never heard of him." She turned to the guards. "Priemtera inu itzi la waltzental."

I was hauled into an empty ballroom, stumbling as I was half-dragged. No masks formed on any of our faces now. The magic must have been needed for other things, like hurling frost and thorns and sending lightning shooting down the corridors.

The Chaos Wielder entered the room before me, extending her arms open wide, looking upward at the painted dome of the ceiling. "As you can see, the crowd has already gathered outside to watch the most important event in all of Liron's history, but I can still kill you, and I'll do it beneath the eclipse."

She nodded to a guard just inside the door, who pulled a lever on the wall downward. A grinding sound of stone against stone came from overhead. The dome of the ceiling split in half, both sides sliding downward to reveal the night sky above and the horrifying view of an eclipse well underway.

One moon was visible, Andra—no, Stellon. It only looked like Andra because of the pink hue projected by Liron's shadow. Andra was already somewhere behind Stellon.

Niles, where are you?

The Chaos Wielder kicked the skirts of her dress outward as she skipped to the dais, spun around to face me, and flopped onto the throne like the petulant child she was.

I tested the strength of the guards holding me, pulling forward again. They had not released even a hair of pressure.

"Níanli," one of them said sternly.

The closest one leaned in, hissing in my ear. "Still following my lady, I assume? I did warn you away."

I tried to spin to view the giant man holding my arms behind me. How had I not realized it was the same man I'd fought? Sure, he'd been standing behind me, but still…

Then, a young girl in deep emerald robes burst through the opposite door, pulling a sash from her face and dropping it on the floor in her wake. She was accompanied by another half-dozen guards. And…Alesh? Where was Reina?

"Elodie!" the girl yelled across the expanse of the room. "You murderous traitor! I won't allow this."

The Chaos Wielder went rigid at the voice of the blond-haired girl currently stalking her way through the room.

The bear of the guardsman holding my arms gave a sigh and shook his head.

"Here we go," he muttered beneath his breath.

At the same time, Reina, panting heavily, her skin covered in a sheen of sweat, stumbled through the door the guards had pushed me through moments before, one hand on the wall, holding herself up, as she entered.

Instinctively, I lurched to go to her. I didn't like the green hue beneath her skin. Was it part of whatever they had done to make her look different? Was that magic failing?

"Stop," she panted. "Abi, no!"

Maybe it was the shock of seeing *his* lady in such distress, but the guard behind me loosened his grip and I raced forward to Reina. Preoccupied with the young girl Reina had called Abi, the guards surrounding me didn't react when I ran to Reina's side to catch her as she stumbled. She held tightly to my arm, using me to keep herself standing.

"Reina, what can I do?" I breathed.

She looked into my eyes, pain written in her expression. She gripped one of my hands in hers with a strength she shouldn't have possessed. "Quinn. Real Quinn, my Quinn. Don't let her come to harm. Protect her. No matter what."

"Give over the diadem," Abi said, scowling at the Chaos Wielder. She stood in front of the dais now, her feet planted wide, hands on her hips in an obstinate display of stubbornness. Then she rattled off a slew of words in the Elorin tongue that I couldn't begin to understand.

"I thought you were dead," Reina said, putting a hand to my face.

I turned my head into the curve of her hand to breathe in her scent, and kissed the skin of her palm, skin that was colder than it should have been.

"I thought I was, too," I said.

"I'm sorry I couldn't fix this. I tried so hard, Quinn. I tried."

A tear squeezed from one eye and slipped down the side of her cheek, an unfamiliar cheek the shape of which didn't match my memory. I missed her smile. I missed her beautiful face. She squeezed her eyes shut and looked away, trying in vain to stop the flow of tears now that they had started.

"Shh, Reina, shh. You should know one thing by now," I said, brushing the tear from her cheek.

Her questioning eyes blinked as she watched my face.

"If this world's about to go stark-raving mad…there's no one I'd rather go daft with than you."

There it was. I'd elicited a smile—a small, sad smile, but a smile, nonetheless.

"We've done everything we could," I said.

"It's not over. The eclipse. Abi is the true heir to the throne. She shouldn't be here. Her sister killed the family. She'll kill her, too."

Then Reina leaned on me to push forward, a new resolve in her bones despite looking as though she wanted nothing more than to close her eyes and never open them again.

"Reina."

"Mical," she said. "Now!"

The guard, the one who'd beaten me into the ground yesterday, the one who hadn't liked that I'd been following Reina even though I hadn't known who she was, surged forward, baton pulled from his belt, to attack the Chaos Wielder.

Confused, his cohorts didn't know which sister to protect. Two of the guards with him attempted to grab him even as two others fell upon *them*. In a mess of confusion, the Chaos Wielder remained seated on the throne, untouched.

Reina reached for the talisman at her neck, closed her eyes, her lips murmuring something indiscernible, but whatever magic she was doing wasn't outwardly visible. In fact, the Chaos Wielder narrowed her eyes and raised both hands as though to send magic hurtling towards all the enemies before her.

I took in the scene, weighed my options. There were so many threats to her at once, if I acted now she'd never see it coming. With purpose, I moved across the room to the rear of the dais to approach from the side. I pulled the baton from my waist. Having restrained my hands earlier, the guards hadn't bothered to relieve me of its presence.

Now, I surged forward, baton in hand, just within the Chaos Wielder's peripheral vision, praying to the Saints above that she was too preoccupied to notice me, but my prayers had fallen on deaf ears. On guard, she stood, extending one hand outwards towards me even as she kept the other directed at the front of the room.

Then the air grew thick, difficult to pull into my lungs, impossible to move through. Everything in the room ground to a complete halt mid-stride. I strained against the invisible barrier…and barely moved a hair. The Chaos Wielder was draining herself, though. The sheer concentration on her face alone was proof she'd been using too much of the magic for too long. All night, in fact. The very effort to maintain the barrier was visible in the veins on her neck, in the sweat dripping down one temple.

The problem with the tactic she'd chosen this time was that she'd opted for a defensive move rather than offensive, which meant she was locked into utilizing her magic continuously to keep herself safe. Offense, magical or not, could be performed in short spurts, saving energy for whatever battle lay at the end. Defense, however, offered no such flexibility.

She *would* fail.

I struggled against the viscous air, pushing, forcing her to work harder to keep the wall in place. If she exerted herself for long enough, she'd lose control. When she did, I'd do what needed to be done.

The silence in the room was deafening. With the air so thick, no sound carried to my ears. So, even though a moment before, there had been yelling and a clashing of batons, the utter lack of sound in the air now was near-overwhelming. My heartbeat thundered in my ears.

I pushed again until my muscles quaked, sweat from the exertion gathering on my brow. Then I pushed harder.

She was close to failing now. The air had begun to thin.

The barrier was quickly falling. She was—

I lunged forward as the barrier came crashing down, and sound and motion resumed. My baton swung sideways at her head.

"Quinn, no!" Reina called, her voice weak, but it was too late.

My hit had found its mark, and the diadem was driven off her head as the baton made contact with it. The tiny crown sailed twenty feet through the air before landing on the polished marble floors with a clatter, sliding another ten feet and landing directly at Reina's toes.

The Chaos Wielder let out a howl of rage, then sent a strike of lightning towards the girl Abi, who was closest. Alesh grabbed her, spinning her away as one of the guards with them intentionally took the brunt of the impact to keep her from being hit. He fell to the ground in a heap, dead.

Fiermi. The Chaos Wielder could still use her magic. I had hoped she would be useless if we broke contact, but such was not the case. Just like Reina, she controlled the magic even without touching the stone.

Reina stared down at the diadem. I could almost see her thoughts taking shape.

"Reina!" I screamed from across the dais. "Let Niles take it!"

Then I prayed Niles had heard my plea and was ready to do whatever it was he'd been preparing to do all this time.

Reina bent, stooping as though to pick up the diadem.

No, no, no!

CHAPTER THIRTY

Trust Above All Else
Reina

I stared at the glittering diadem as it hit the polished floor, gliding to a stop at my feet. There it lay. The source of all our problems. So close. So small, it could fit in my palm.

My head was fuzzy, my knees weak. I bent to ease the pain in my chest, sliding to my knees to the floor. The diadem crackled with energy, the gemstone pulsing with an invitation to pick it up, destroy it, let it all be done.

"Reina, no! Reina!"

I knew that voice.

I searched through the haze in my vision for its source. Quinn. Quinn was calling me.

"Reina, it has to be Niles! You *must* leave it for Niles. Do *not* touch it!"

My hand hovered over the diadem. I should use the talisman's magic, the power of death to kill whatever horrible magic lay in the diadem. Elodie couldn't use the magic if I killed it first. I gathered the talisman's magic in my veins, panting with the exertion. Saints, but I was tired.

"It has to be Niles!" Quinn was still shouting at me.

What was he *saying?* What did those words mean?

And then, for no reason at all, I remembered the three young women I'd seen in Irzan's library when I'd tumbled chaotically through time and space moments ago, the women who looked exactly as the likenesses painted on the mural in Ivirreh.

The most difficult moment to believe is the moment you must place your trust in him entirely.

Had they known? Is this what they meant?

But Quinn wasn't of sound mind. He was babbling about Niles, and Niles was dead. Niles was—

Kneeling in front of me.

I blinked away the fog in my eyes and released the talisman's magic from my grasp, absorbing the glowing, translucent form of Niles Ingram that sat before me. He knelt on floor, the diadem between us.

Niles looked as he always had. His blond hair was neatly combed, and he was radiant with the light of his current form, the blue of his tunic matching the blue of his eyes, the tunic itself fitting across his shoulders and chest the way I remembered. The same glint in his eyes, the same smirk of his mouth. But that wasn't true. His expression held no anger, no loathing, no pain. It was…pure light.

His gaze met mine, and he gave a single slow nod, as though reassuring me he was truly here. I wasn't hallucinating, not even with the venom running wild in my body. My vision blurred. I fought to clear it again.

With a tight smile, he cupped his hands over the diadem on the floor until a glow emanated from the spaces between beneath his fingers. A loud crack startled me to my core.

Fracture lines in the floor zigged and zagged across the room, spidering out from beneath where the diadem sat under Niles's cupped hands.

I swallowed, then looked overhead to the sight of the eclipse above. Liron's shadow had shifted. Stellon was no longer tinted pink. Andra had begun to peer out from behind Stellon's face. The eclipse was no longer full.

I turned panicked eyes to Niles, but he didn't look up. He continued to focus on the light that was slowly growing within his hands, illuminating his face, turning him into the very vision of an angel.

I glanced to Quinn, to the others in the room. Did they see Niles, too? The awe on their faces confirmed my suspicions. He was not a figment of my imagination, nor a hallucination brought on by venom poisoning. Paralyzed, Elodie watched in utter fear. I wondered if she could no longer feel the diadem's magic in her blood, if the bond had been severed.

Niles stood and lifted his hands from the floor, the diadem rising within them, one of his hands moving to cup from below as the other stayed centered above. The crack in the floor crumbled further and gave way to an inky black chasm that had no business being in the human world, let alone residing beneath a palace.

Niles's practiced hands moved around the diadem in an intricate web of motions too complicated for me to understand. His fingers formed symbols in the air around the glowing gold and jewels one after the next. I wished I knew what the symbols meant, what he was doing.

Place your trust him entirely.

Maybe they'd meant Niles.

Then I began to see the pattern in Niles's actions, a pattern that produced and wove threads of light surrounding the diadem, threads that tightened with each pass of his fingers, as though he'd been tying the diadem with rope this entire time. Beneath the threads of light, the diadem itself had begun to dim.

When at last he was finished, his fingers splayed wide on either side of the glowing mass, the diadem confined in the middle of the web that hovered between his hands. His eyes met mine as he looked up, satisfied. Eyes shining, a content curl to his lips, he gave a single nod.

Saints, had I ever seen Niles look so happy, so proud. So…sad?

"What is it, Niles?" I barely had the energy to speak the words.

Niles shook his head at me, looked upwards, closed his eyes, then jumped into the black chasm below. My lips parted with shock, hands reaching for him even though I knew I could not stop him from falling. Still, he slipped beyond my reach, and I was left grasping the darkness that swallowed him whole.

The screams that shook the palace were near inhuman, but they did not belong to Niles. On Elodie's face was an expression of pure rage. Abi tried to speak, tried to say something to appease her sister, but her words could not be heard above Elodie's shrieking. Elodie raced across the floor and dove into the chasm.

Instinctively, I reached for her, too, as she slid over the

edge, my fingers brushing the billowing edges of her gown. Then Elodie disappeared into the darkness, too.

Dizziness struck hard, my head spinning. I pulled back from the yawning chasm, fearful it would swallow me, too, if I fell forward.

"Elodie!" Abi called as she scrambled on her hands and knees across the floor to the edge of the chasm. She moaned, then spoke in a long string of words in her own language, words I didn't understand, but the meaning behind them I understood all too well.

Abi had hoped we could save Liron *and* Elodie.

The room darkened. No, that wasn't right. The room hadn't darkened. My vision had. I clenched my jaw to keep my wits.

"Alesh," I called weakly, my voice hardly sounding.

But he was already here. He'd leaped across the narrowest part of the chasm to where I lay. Quinn was here, too. When had he joined me?

Alesh's face hovered over me, his concern unmistakable. I stared at the stars above the dome, at the clear white luminance of Stellon and the tiniest sliver of pink from Andra behind. I breathed. The eclipse was over. Elodie was gone. The terror of her chaotic reign was over.

I should have felt relief. Instead, there was numbness and pain. I marveled. How could I feel both excruciating pain and incredibly numb at the same time?

With his fingers, Alesh pulled open one of my eyes, lifting and lowering my upper and lower lids to fully inspect for whatever it was he was hoping to see. I didn't have the energy to flinch.

"I do not like her eyes," Alesh said.

I thought he was speaking to Quinn. I hoped he was. *I* had no answer to give him.

He tapped into the magic of the staff, the ruby at the top glowing a deep red as he sent it flaring. He put one hand on my forehead and urged me to close my eyes. "Be still," he said.

"Alesh?"

"Yes, my Reina?" He spoke the words as though distracted, as though already deep within his own magic and figuring out what path he needed to take to remove the venom from my blood.

But the venom was no longer in my blood alone, and no amount of magic would remove the venom in my body at this point. It had already dispersed into my organs, and into my nerves. I tasted the metal on my tongue, felt the ache of it in the marrow of my bones. My body had been soaking in it slowly all night.

"Can you…would you tell my father I'm glad I got to meet him?"

Alesh didn't miss a beat. He continued to work even as he answered, "You can tell him when you see him next."

Quinn tensed at my side, his grip on my hand tightening. Then his lips were against my ear, whispering all the reasons I should stay. He spoke the words as though I had a choice, as though I wanted to succumb to snake venom after so many weeks of keeping it at bay.

Yes, there were many reasons I would have liked to stay.

But my mother's voice was singing now, a lullaby from long ago. Behind closed eyes, I thought I saw her form—glowing, as Niles had.

I smiled, inside if not out.

I was going home.

Open your eyes, Little Me.

I groaned. I didn't want to open my eyes. I wanted to sleep. Nothing hurt when I slept. When my eyes were open, everything hurt.

It's time, Moreina.

Maybe if I ignored her, she'd let me keep sleeping.

Now.

Reluctantly, my eyelids fluttered. My insides felt like a pile of steaming horse manure. No, that wasn't accurate. They were more like a pile of steaming horse manure that had been spread over fields, then tilled, then sliced open for planting again.

There wasn't a single measure of my body that wasn't in agony from my scalp to my lungs to the tips of my toenails. I took shallow breaths to minimize the pain and licked at dry, crackled lips.

"She's awake."

I turned my head to the sound of the voice. At least, I *tried* to turn my head. Excruciating pain radiated through my scalp. In response, I whimpered.

"Don't try to move yet, Reina." Mical stood over me,

joined by Alesh a moment later.

"You are very weak," Alesh said.

Concern was etched on his face, but his expression no longer held the familiar worry of losing a patient, which meant I somehow, miraculously, had cheated death again. Alesh looked like himself, I noticed. His hair was no longer a starched white and the wrinkles around his eyes had relaxed into their usual number. He looked *right* again, even more right when he grinned his familiar grin with gleaming white teeth.

"How did you—" But I didn't have the strength to finish my sentence.

I struggled to draw a breath.

"Close your eyes, my stubborn Reina." Alesh's voice was soothing in my ears.

I wanted to sit up. I wanted to demand answers. I wanted to know why I was still alive and where Quinn was. There were so many questions that needed to be answered.

"I will remain with you. By your side. Sleep."

Alesh's hand repeatedly smoothed back the hair from my forehead, his touch surprisingly gentle despite callused hands. The motion lulled me back into a sleep that was all too easy to succumb to once again.

When I next woke, the room was dark, a single oil lamp burning low in one corner. The pain in my lungs had eased, though the burning sensation remained. Without moving my head, I glanced around the room, taking in as much as my line of vision would allow.

Along one wall, I recognized a long row of hanging

cabinets with shelving full of powders, pastes, and elixirs. I was in the palace physician's room, the infirmary Abi and I had raided for the bottle of dreamroot. A comfort to my senses, the room *smelled* as an infirmary should. Proxide and tumeria, vellowroot and yarrow, and dozens more scents I could identify had I the time and inclination to do so.

To my left, someone shifted. Gingerly, I turned my head. The pain still radiated from the base of my neck, but it was no longer so excruciating that I could not move. A small relief.

Quinn had pushed a cot beside mine and lay dozing on his side. His hands were tucked beneath one cheek, the beard that had been there now gone and replaced with a day's growth of stubble.

How long had I been sleeping?

I swallowed, my throat like scorched earth. Then I cataloged all the aches and pains, attempting to determine how I wasn't dead. All the while, my gaze lingered on Quinn.

How was he here?

I could imagine him fighting his way out of Kufataba's clutches, but I couldn't imagine how he'd escaped the death that had seemed so certain. I couldn't understand, even once he'd escaped the mountain's confines, how he could have traveled the miles to Ivirreh to be here. Alesh and I had taken weeks to arrive.

As though sensing he was under scrutiny, Quinn's breathing shifted and he opened his eyes, straightened his legs, and stretched his arms overhead in a full body stretch accompanied by a groan. Surprise flickered across his face when he realized my eyes were on him.

"Y'er awake." He shifted closer, propping himself up on an elbow, and smiling at me.

He reached out with his other hand to brush my fingers, the sensation sending fire shooting through my skin—and not the good kind. When I winced, he withdrew his hand with a grimace.

"I'm sorry. Alesh said you'd be in pain. I didn't think."

"What happened?" I rasped.

"Do you not remember?"

"Not yesterday. What happened with you? In Kufataba."

He swallowed. "It wasn't…yesterday. The other things, I mean."

My thoughts froze. "What?"

"It's been a week. Alesh and I have been caring for you, with some help from the palace physician, of course."

"A *week?* How did I eat? How did I"—I raised my eyebrows. Saints, that hurt— "you know."

"Liquids. We dribbled broth into your mouth, much like when you were fevered in that cave and I…"

"Fed me rabbit. Yes, I recall. Please tell me there was no rabbit in the broth this time."

Quinn met my eyes with an unamused stare. "There was *no* rabbit in the broth. Nor goat, nor chicken, nor any other living, breathing creature."

If it weren't for the burning in my lungs, I might have let out a sigh of relief.

"And then I tended to your…needs. I wouldn't let anyone else handle that part of your care."

"You…"

"I carried you to the privy and sat you on the pot. Your body did the rest."

Oh, Saints above, he'd set me on the pot like a child just out of nappies. Half of me was beyond mortified, but the other half was too grateful to care. Quinn had cared for me, had nursed me back to health.

"You would have done the same for me had our positions been reversed."

"I couldn't lift you."

He snorted a laugh.

"Thank you, for looking after me. Again."

He waved a hand. "Enough of that. I expect you'll pay me back a good ten times over in the next seventy-five years. I'll hold you to it."

A smile tugged at my lips as I marveled the meaning behind his words. "We're both still alive."

"We are. So you're stuck with me for quite some time."

Now it was my turn to giggle. Oh, my ribs!

"Don't make me laugh," I groaned.

"Apologies." Then he sobered, sitting up, eyes assessing me as though he was going through a mental checklist to assure himself I was still here and in one piece.

Finally, casting his gaze downward, he answered my question. "The sacrifice the mountain wanted was my pain. My guilt."

"What?"

"Kufataba. 'Choose your sacrifice,' it said. I thought it meant my life. I thought I was giving up my life, and I was all right with that if it meant you lived, if it meant you could go on and save the world from lunacy. But Kufataba didn't want my life. It wanted my pain."

I struggled to find something to say. I couldn't imagine what Quinn's words meant, how one could pay in pain. I didn't know if I *wanted* to know. I swallowed and lifted a hand despite the ache in my muscles. I laid my fingers on his arm.

"I'm sorry," I said softly.

"'Twas a gift, Reina. I faced the guilt, the pain I'd been holding onto, and I…forgave myself." He gave a hoarse laugh. "With Niles's help."

I blinked.

The vision of Niles hadn't been some fever dream. "But Niles is…"

"Dead, I know."

Quinn rose from the cot, ran a hand through his hair, and went to the counter where a pitcher and a few glasses had been set. He poured a glass of water, then came to my side.

"Do you want to try sitting?"

I nodded, then winced as he helped prop me against several pillows. He put the glass to my lips, and, as I'd broken into a sweat from the exertion of trying to sit upright, I let him hold it. I sipped, the lukewarm water a relief to my throat.

When he took the glass away, he set it back with the pitcher. Then he leaned, tucking his hands behind him against the counter as he considered his next words. He spent the better part of the next hour telling me about Niles's second chance, the Saints, and all that had transpired beneath the mountain.

When he reached the part where he relayed the three items he requested, I stopped him mid-sentence, breathless with hope.

"Aeros is here? You mean to tell me Aeros, *my* Aeros, is *here?*"

He smiled. "Let me get this straight. All of this, and you've focused on the horse?"

"She's not just any horse, and you know it! Is she here?" My voice cracked on the last word.

With a knowing smile, he nodded.

"Would you like to see her?"

My chest filled with a lightness that almost—*almost*—overtook the pain. "Yes!"

"I'll take you to the stables as soon as the sun rises. I promise. In the meantime, you should rest as much as you can. Alesh will want you to work with the talisman to heal yourself as much as possible. He was able to isolate the dead tissue and remove it from your body, but with the power of death restored to him, he couldn't help you…do whatever it is you do on your end." He motioned with his hands in the air.

"Grow new tissue?" I asked.

"Right. That."

"So Alesh was able to rid my body of the poison…" My mind reeled at how he'd possibly done it. "I didn't think I had a chance once the venom had broken free of the capsule we'd made."

Quinn titled his head. "About that. He did what he could,

but it turns out the palace physician has antivenin on hand."

Of *course* the physician would have Gohmi viper antivenin. They were native to this land. Would it have made a difference if I'd gotten a dose sooner? Or would it not have mattered since Alesh and I had encapsulated the venom for all that time anyway?

"It took three doses of the antivenin, Alesh's fine work with his staff, and my stellar bedside care, but here we are." He pushed off the counter, leaned in, and kissed me on my forehead.

"Am I still…" But I wasn't. The hair around my face was back to its deep brown, the single white streak at my left temple where it had been all my life. I put a hand to my cheek and the other to my chin, relieved to feel the bones as they should be, the shape of my face as I'd always remembered.

"Alesh reworked it all. 'Easy to undo what shouldn't have been done,' he said. Or something like that. You're as breathtaking as you've always been."

I gave him a reproachful glance. "I see spending time with Niles has turned you into a smooth talker, Quinn D'Arturio."

Then Quinn did something I would have given anything in the world to see. He threw his head back and laughed, a full-throated laugh I hadn't heard in so very long. It echoed off the walls of the empty space around us.

I sniffed at myself, then continued. "Beauty or no beauty, I smell. What must a girl do to get a bath around here?"

Quinn's eyes grew hungry, his smile turning from innocent to playful. He swallowed, the knot in his throat bobbing with the motion. "I think I can draw you a bath, but

I suspect you'll need help washing."

My cheeks heated.

"You scoundrel."

Still, I didn't oppose.

CHAPTER THIRTY-ONE

Anything is Possible
Reina

The sight of Aeros after so many weeks was enough to bring tears to my eyes. Or, perhaps the tears were due more in part to the fact that the prophecies had finally been fulfilled—in all the best ways. Soon, Quinn and I could return to live a life at Irzan doing nothing more exciting than speaking with local farmers about the price of grain day in and day out.

After the last year, I looked forward to the monotony.

In the late morning, I had done as Alesh instructed and healed myself to the best of my ability, but the talisman's magic was weaker than I remembered, as though, without the chaos to balance out the life and death equation, the power of life had begun to wane. I wondered if a day would come when the talisman would no longer hold magic within.

Alesh believed he and I were the last in a long line of magic-wielders. The thought evoked mixed feelings. Part of me was glad no one else would learn to use the magic I had come to think of as my own. Another part of me lamented that something so true and good would be lost to this world forever.

Yes, a person could heal with herbs and tonics alone—I

had, many times—but I'd learned to use the magic to do so much good so quickly, it was difficult to imagine a time going back to being without it. Quinn said I should open a school for healers, that while the king of Castilles should heal our borders, the queen should raise an army who could nurture life and heal the world.

The idea was not without merit. If nothing else, doing so would honor the memory of my first student and friend, Selena Mayst. I'd hardly gotten the chance to know her, but she'd opened my eyes to the fact that others shared my thirst for knowledge, my quest to find any way to heal.

I smiled to myself, a warmth in my chest that wasn't due to the aftereffects of the venom. There was hope for Selena. If Niles had gone on after death, then she had, too. Selena was well and smiling…somewhere just out of sight. I was sure of it.

Now, standing in the stable, I stroked Aeros's nose, then leaned over the stall door to kiss the velvet softness of a muzzle I'd missed so much. She nickered, which I took to mean she'd missed me, too. Then she nosed my arm twice, looking for treats.

I laughed. "I don't think they have applikens this far south. I'm sorry. I'll make sure you get one every day when we're home. Promise."

Beside me, Quinn laughed at my words.

"I assure you she's been well cared for," a familiar voice said.

I turned to see Mical striding down the center of the stable aisle, looking dapper as ever, the changes Alesh had wrought on his face now gone as well, his former looks restored.

"Mical," I greeted. "This is Quinn."

Mical's eyebrows shot upward. "Oh, I know."

"Right. You two would have seen each other while I was…attempting not to die."

Quinn's mouth stretched into a flat line, eyes growing hard. Had the air cooled?

"Sure, that's how we know each other," he said, no inflection at all in his voice.

Mical grinned, turned to Quinn, and gave him a tap to his shoulder. To his credit, Quinn did not flinch.

"Sorry about knocking you out, friend. If I'd known you were the love she'd gone on about, I would have brought you into the fold days before the eclipse instead of beating you unconscious." He shrugged, then gave a wolfish grin again. "Or maybe I still would have beaten you into the ground. Who's to say, really?"

"Mical." I stared at him until the grin faded from his face.

He huffed. "Fine. I truly am sorry, Quinn."

Quinn nodded, not looking entirely convinced that Mical's apology was genuine, but he was too diplomatic to say otherwise.

Mical turned to face me, his lips tugging into a side smirk. "Oh, and I'm sorry I kissed you. I mean, can you blame me? It was the end of the world. If we survived, I hoped I might have a chance."

"You what?" Quinn spoke like he'd practiced driving actual steel into words. His eyes drilled into Mical's.

I put a hand on Quinn's arm, my gaze never leaving

Mical's face. "Surely you must remember what I told you, Mical."

"Yes, yes, your heart was elsewhere. So you said. A few dozen times since we met, at least." But there was a teasing in Mical's expression, a smile in his eyes. He'd known all along I was not interested. He'd stolen a kiss for pure amusement. To see if he could get away with it. I could *almost* forgive him for it.

"Are you staying?" I asked, deciding a change of subject was well warranted.

Mical nodded. "I am. Alesh said I was worth keeping around—imagine that—and Abi will need someone who knows what's going on to help her keep things in order until her father's sister arrives from Jhalpa to rule as regent. I mean, Abi's a Gehtanan, but she's still eleven."

"And the guard?"

He shrugged. "Since Abi reinstated me as head of her personal entourage, it seems those I owe money to have become forgiving. I guess they assume I'll make enough now to pay off my debt."

I nodded. I hoped Mical had learned his lesson where gambling was concerned. At the very least, he understood the gravity of the terrifying future we'd barely escaped. It was unlikely any gamble involving coin could rival the one we'd already taken.

"Anyhow, I'm to retrieve you and escort you to the emperor's side."

I knew he meant Abi, but a chill still slid down my spine at the words. I nodded, hooked an arm through Quinn's, then said, "Lead the way."

Being back in the large ballroom was eerie, with its dais and its golden throne and the split across the floor. There was no black chasm there now, just a wild crack in the length of the floor as though the marble had sealed itself around the chasm to darkness. Still, I was almost hesitant to step near the jagged line in the floor, as though doing so might tempt it to reopen.

Abi sat in front of the throne, on the floor of the dais, feet resting on the marble of the main floor. She was no longer in the immigrant dress I'd last seen on her. Instead, she wore the royal white and gold robes that looked far less threatening on her than they had on her sister. Atop her head sat the diadem. I reeled when I saw it.

No, it wasn't *the* diadem. It was Djana's diadem.

Abi's face brightened when I entered. She rose and ran across the floor, unfazed by the crack in it. Then she slid across the polished marble and into me, wrapping her arms in a fierce hug around my middle. I hugged her back.

"You're alive! Reina! I didn't think we'd gotten you to the infirmary in time. I begged Alesh to tell me you'd make it, but he wouldn't promise. He said he couldn't. And then this one"—she gave Quinn a scowl— "spent so much time with you that it was impossible to pin him down for   an update."

Quinn smiled at her. "I told you everything I knew when

I knew it, your Highness."

Abi let her head fall to the side. She pursed her lips. "You're the king of Castilles. We can skip the titles."

"As you wish." I enjoyed watching Quinn interact with Abi. I'd never seen him banter.

Abi grabbed my hand and pulled me toward the dais, where several seats had been set in a circle before it. "Come, sit," she said.

I glanced upwards as we moved across the ballroom. The large dome remained open, blue skies and puffy, white clouds visible beyond.

Seeing my gaze, Abi said, "Oh, that. After that night, the door's jammed. The architects will have to fix it before we get rain, but that won't happen for a few months yet, so we have time. It's nice to have the breeze in here, actually."

"I like your diadem," I said, pointing to her head.

Abi curtsied before she sat. "Thank you. I rather like it, to be honest."

"Do the people…"

"Know? No. And they won't. All the guards there that night have been sworn to secrecy and brought into my personal guard so they won't be spending much time outside the palace grounds, and the pay they earn will ensure they have no qualms about keeping quiet."

"Probably for the best," I murmured.

"Indeed," Mical agreed.

Quinn and I took seats across from Abi, but Mical chose to stand behind her, his hands clasped in front of him.

A guard. He'd truly taken on the role and was behaving

as a guard ought.

"So, I'm sure you're wondering why I asked Mical to find you," Abi began.

I hadn't, actually. I'd just been glad to see the girl again, and to see her where she belonged. That night, *that* night, I thought we might have lost her. I thought we might have accidentally set the Elorin Empire ripe for a civil war. After Castilles having found her own peace not long ago, the last thing I wanted to do was set another land in turmoil.

"Elodie mentioned a prophecy."

Abi's words turned my veins to ice. My heart gave an extra thump.

Please, no more prophecies. Please.

Sensing my unease, Quinn grasped one of my hands and held it in his lap, sliding his chair closer to mine. Maybe he was preparing to catch me if I passed out.

"Yes?" I finally managed.

"A prophecy about two girls with power who should rule."

"Mmhmm." My voice was barely audible. I swallowed.

"I talked with the librarian, the records keeper, I mean. She was able to locate the book the prophecy came from. It was quite old and referenced our family a dozen times in prophecies throughout history, but this was the last of them.

"When it mentioned two girls, Elodie must have thought…well, who knows what Elodie thought." Abigayle paused to clear her throat. "What I mean is, there's nothing that implies it was about you. I think—the records keeper thinks—it meant me. I was the second girl come to power.

The two girls were Elodie and me. Just not at the same time. Anyway, I thought you should know."

Oh, thank the Saints. The sweetest words I might have ever heard had just come from Abi's lips. *Last prophecy. Not about you.* That was all I needed to hear to heave a giant sigh of relief, to let the stress of the last year fall from my mind. My body relaxed as though I'd slid the weight of a dozen stones from my shoulders.

"Imperial Majesty, Emperor Gehtanan, the craftswoman you called upon is here."

Abi stood, gave up the chair she'd occupied, exchanging it for the golden throne on the dais. She nodded to the guard at the door. Mical followed, taking his place beside the throne.

"Send her in," she commanded.

And my, how her very tone had changed. Suddenly, Abi was no longer Abi. She was Emperor Abigayle Gehtanan, who exuded royalty from every pore. The scrappy girl I'd come to know on the streets of Ivirreh had transformed into the leader this empire would someday deserve.

Djana strolled through the doors dressed in attire far more impressive than her work clothes and apron, wearing loose-legged yellow pants and a wide, sleeveless flowing robe with orange and yellow large floral print, feet bound in shining gold sandals. The bright colors accentuated the flawless dark skin on her toned arms.

Her long, black hair was fastened in multiple braids that reached to her waist and ended in festive orange and yellow beads. She tossed braids behind her that had fallen over one shoulder as she scanned the room, surprise on her face when her gaze fell on Quinn.

Djana didn't seem to care that protocol dictated she wait for the emperor to speak first. "You," she said. "I suppose you found your friends."

He grinned. "I did."

"I suppose you were telling the truth."

He gave a nod. "I was."

Djana turned her attention to Abi, who gave her a royal stare. Djana slipped to one knee, then rose, the closest she would probably get to a curtsy.

"De atzi du terro," she said in greeting.

"You know why you are here?" Abi asked, using the northern tongue so we might also understand what was being said.

Djana nodded. "I suspect I do, your Highness."

"I understand you crafted a replica of my family's diadem."

Djana's dark eyes narrowed as she took in Abi and the diadem atop her head. No doubt she was weighing the words she wanted to say. She knew the difference between citrine and yellow sapphire, and she was certainly familiar with her own handiwork. Wisely, she made no mention of it.

"I did," she finally answered.

"I would have liked to have seen it," Abi said. "My friends tell me it was a divine piece of work that had no equal."

"Thank you, your Highness. I'd like to believe my work is second to none." Djana glanced to me, surely wondering what game was being played, but she held her tongue.

"Regretfully, I heard it was destroyed," Abi continued.

Djana's gaze shifted from Abi to the diadem on her head, then back again. "A shame," she said.

"Regardless, that's not why I called you here. It's past time to retire this diadem. The crack in the gemstone makes the magic unstable, which my sister—may she be at peace—learned the hard way. Magic will no longer be used in the Elorin Empire. Neither for my pleasure, nor for public entertainment. I would not have my people made unsafe simply because magic is *fun*."

Oh, but how Elodie had loved the *fun* of her chaos.

Djana nodded in agreement.

I thought Abi's plan would be to wear the replacement diadem, but her words stuck in my mind. She was right. Her nonuse of magic would be obvious to anyone around her and would be cause for speculation. What better way to disguise the nonmagical diadem than to deem it unsafe due to the crack in the gemstone? Then no one at all would question the fact that Abigayle Gehtanan stayed far away from the magic that killed her sister.

"You wish for a new diadem?"

"I do, and I'd like you to craft it for me. For the empire."

"I am honored, and I will do my best to create a crown worthy of the strength and beauty in your empire."

"*Our* empire," Abi corrected.

Djana bowed her head. "Indeed."

I didn't miss the way Mical watched Djana with interest, nor the way Djana's own gaze slipped more than once from Abi to Mical at Abi's side. I bit my lip to keep from smiling at the ideas that took place in my head. A gambling, womanizing guard with a good heart and a morally questionable jeweler of unmatched talent would make for a *very* interesting match indeed.

When Djana was dismissed, Abi released Mical from her side and returned to the empty seat beside us. Sunlight from the open dome above played on her golden hair, setting it afire, giving her an angelic glow. Mical wasted no time in heading for the door through which Djana had just disappeared.

"There are four guards at each door, and I am among friends. I certainly don't need a personal guard hovering over me here. Let him have a try with the jeweler. She'll chew him up and spit him out," Abi said with a laugh.

"How did you know Djana?" I asked.

Abi smiled. "Artur was positively enthralled with her. She used to have a shop on the main street of Jeweler's Row. Then the rumors started. Artur tried to help, but she was angry, and he only made it worse. Probably because he was ten years younger than her. People can be so cruel. Anyway, she moved after that, set up shop in the alley, started taking on a *different* clientele. Artur always said—"

Abi paused, distracted as she tilted her head upwards and squinted. I followed her gaze to the blue sky, not seeing whatever had caught her attention.

Then I saw.

A butterfly, a beautiful orange and gold butterfly, wings delicately lined with black, and adorned with white spots, floated through the dome opening and into the ballroom.

It fluttered lazily in circles, catching a draft upward, then flitting downward again until it landed squarely in the middle of Abi's extended palm.

Her enormous blue eyes looked from the butterfly to me, then back again. Her mouth had fallen open as she stared.

A butterfly.

How fitting. It was her brother Artur, after all, who had—

I leaned closer.

The butterfly was made of folded paper.

"Is that—" But I couldn't finish.

She nodded, tears filling her eyes. Then she smiled at me and pulled the butterfly close to her middle, cupping it in both hands.

"It's Artur's butterfly," she breathed. She bit her bottom lip, then smiled through the tears that fell down her face. "Anything is possible."

The End and the Beginning

Yvonne Harris stood in the livestock stasis pen, carefully monitoring the different species she'd brought with them far from the Milky Way and clear across the universe. She'd be waking them soon, filling the air with a cacophony of animal brays and neighs and squawks. But for now, they slept on, unaware that when they next opened their eyes, they would not be in the home they once knew, or on the same ground they once grazed.

She checked off the list in the database on her handheld, the soft blue glow of the screen illuminating her face in the low light of the livestock room. Yvonne debated whether it made more sense to reanimate the goats before or after the horses. Before, she decided. Even if it meant they'd be trying to tear metal panels off the walls. The goats' presence would calm the horses. She'd chosen the hardiest individuals, but horses weren't made for space travel, and even though they'd be in transit a few days at most before landing, she'd prefer to make the transition as smooth as possible.

Naturally, most of the thousands of each species had been brought as fertilized embryos to be implanted and nurtured when the time came. You couldn't think to colonize a planet with sustainable livestock otherwise. Not without sending two, three, even five ships full of nothing but livestock.

Yvonne almost laughed at the absurdity. As though TransUniversal Habitation, LLC would have considered sending an entire fleet of ships for the population of animals. She gave a smile. At least the cryofreezer stocked with eggs from dozens of breeds of chickens would finally answer the question of what came first. On L.I.R.O.N., if nowhere else, the egg would definitely come first.

She'd been told the planet had an abundance of flora and quite a bit of fauna of its own, so she and her team had deliberately chosen not to bring species that might take over the natural resources, but only those that could be kept by humans for optimal survival in a world without technology. Horses for heavy lifting and pulling carriages, chickens for eggs, pigs for their meat, goats for their milk, so on and so forth.

No cows, though. For whatever reason, TransUniversal hadn't been able to adequately adapt cows to travel under stasis, which was why milk goats had become all that much more popular with each colonization mission. Cows were tricky, and they were entirely too sensitive to changes in atmospheric makeup and pressure.

"Attention L.I.R.O.N. leadership team, please report to the bridge. L.I.R.O.N. leadership team, report to bridge immediately."

Immediately.

Interesting.

Rana must be in a mood. The captain had a penchant for making demands when something wasn't done quite the way she expected. Naturally, this made her a difficult person to work under, but Yvonne had never met anyone who could command a ship better. She respected Captain Chandra Rana with all she had and more. Certainly, she wouldn't be traveling across the universe with her, never to return, otherwise.

She smirked as she clicked the handheld unit into its charger on the wall and pressed her hand to the small panel beside the door. The door slid aside, and Yvonne left the stasis pen for the long, slow bounce-walk to the bridge. Damn half gravity.

Rana making such formal announcements via the ship's comm system was utterly ridiculous. The captain could just as easily say, "Hey, everyone, get your asses to the bridge. We need to talk."

With a statement like that, at least there'd be a laugh among the crew. So far, the expedition leadership team and a few of the ship's engineers were the only reanimated humans on the ship, so it's not as though the passengers would have heard.

But no.

Rana had gone with a much more professional approach, which meant that something had gone wrong.

Yvonne was the last of the leadership team to arrive on the bridge, the livestock stasis pen located clear on the other end of the ship. Already the others were seated in their assigned spots.

So this was no small issue then. This meeting would be a long one. Yvonne's nerves twisted as she took her own seat beside Joe Faranzine, her fingers tingling with anxiety. Whatever Rana wanted to discuss would not be a simple matter.

"Good of you to join us, Harris."

Well, at least the captain still had some sense of humor. That soothed Yvonne's nerves a little.

"You know the pens are on the other side of the ship, and you know my rotations. I would have jogged, but *someone* insists on keeping the gravity core running at half g. If I didn't know any better, Captain Rana, I might think you planned the comm for when I was farthest away from the bridge."

Rana smiled and Yvonne took a breath, confident that whatever it was the captain was about to tell them was not life-threatening, at least. Not if she could still smile.

Captain Rana studied the notes on her screen for a long time before speaking. It gave the crew time to exchange dubious glances, which they did…in abundance.

The leadership team was small as far as colonization missions went, but the planet was also small, offering a slower lifestyle to the humans aboard who'd signed on to pursue a simpler way of living. They didn't need computer and technology sectors involved, which meant the crew was focused entirely on the startup of various colonies in three locations that had been deemed prime for human occupation. Not that they would branch out immediately, of course. But eventually.

"As you know, we were sent to L.I.R.O.N. because the planet was devoid of intelligent life, but offered the right conditions for humans to thrive," Rana finally said after clearing her throat. She paused, swallowing, her fingers gripping the sides of the console as she looked up and scanned the crew. She clicked her tongue against her teeth. "There's no other way to say this, so out with it, I suppose. The planet's occupied."

Beulah Abram, the mission's Atmospheric Science Director, leaned forward in her seat. "That's not possible!"

Yvonne blinked, suppressing her shock.

It was possible, of course. It had taken them two-hundred fifty-three years to make the journey, during which time they'd been in stasis, the ship's autonavigation system doing most of the heavy work when it came to cruising among the stars at near light speed. The crew hadn't been reanimated until two months ago, when they entered the edge of the galaxy L.I.R.O.N. called home, the galaxy that would soon be their home. Yvonne's head still swam from time to time with the stasis chemicals that hadn't yet been fully purged from her body. She'd been warned they'd remain in her bloodstream for up to six months and suspected that was why she felt woozy now. She folded her hands in her lap and rubbed one thumb across her knuckles.

"How many?"

The baritone belonged to Booker Jones, a tall, brawny man with skin darker than Yvonne's own and sexy, dark eyes she'd love to watch turn her direction with interest. Once they were on the ground, Yvonne had thought to ask Booker out. When things were settled, of course. Not while they were still in the first months of survival.

She suspected Booker had been thinking the same about her, but preparing the Interstellar Voyager III for its arrival came first, and there was no time for space trysts. But damn if the way that uniform stretched across his shoulders wasn't fine. She dragged her thoughts back to the matter at hand.

An already colonized planet.

As the Settlement Director, Jones was the first to concern himself with how many humans already occupied the planet. He was responsible for decisions about settlement locations and the instruction of crew and passengers alike on how best to succeed in their new establishments, so his question made sense.

"Rana, how many?" he repeated when she didn't answer.

Captain Rana rubbed her eyes with one hand, then pinched the bridge of her nose.

"Fully colonized." Rana pushed her screen to share, and an enlarged image of the blue and green planet so similar to Earth popped up on the large main screen that took up the wall behind her. A moment later, thousands of dots appeared, strewn across L.I.R.O.N.'s landmasses, representing every city detected by the computer.

Yvonne gasped, her own breath lost in the collective surprise of the crew on the whole.

"In two-hundred fifty years? That's impossible," Abram repeated. "Booker, you know as well as I do, it takes a hell of a lot longer than that to colonize a planet with no established technology or infrastructure."

"She's right." Amy Lukawicz, the mission's Natural Resource Director. "There's no way they could have colonized in that period of time. Not to that extent, not with what's available."

"We don't *know* what's available," Rana shot back. "Not really. We know only what the probes sent back. Landscape intrinsic to relative optimal incorporation. The planet has water, essential elements, established flora and fauna, and the right atmosphere for human occupation. That's it. That's all we know."

L.I.R.O.N. Landscape Intrinsic to Relative Optimal iNcorporation. Those were the words the computer had spat out for the planet before TransUniversal had sent them to embark on the journey, but if what Rana said was true, the landscape wasn't habitable at all. It was *already* occupied.

The implications were overwhelming.

"So what—"

The captain didn't let Lukawicz finish.

"I've already got the computer running every alternate scenario. There are two other options nearby—A.P.H.O 12 and I.S.C.O.P. 4, but either one will take two years minimum to reach and we can't reinitiate stasis, so it'll be a sacrifice on all our parts. With a skeletal reanimated crew, we have the supplies and the fuel, so it's not impossible, but I need the team to discuss both options thoroughly and make this a unified decision. This? This is up to you. It's up to all of us. Am I the captain? Yes. But you've already given over your lives and everything you knew when you signed on to begin with. The least I can do is give you a say in what quadrant of the galaxy your future home lies."

"So you're not even going to send a transport to check L.I.R.O.N.?" It was so rare to hear Jon speak that Yvonne's brows lifted in surprise at his suggestion.

Jonathan Tarrowburn didn't say much. If he needed to communicate, he did so via written comm sent directly to the computers in their quarters. Yvonne often thought TransUniversal should have chosen someone more vocal as Expedition Team Leader, but what did she know? She was a Livestock Engineer.

The captain licked her lips. "You think that's wise, given the occupied status of the planet?"

Yvonne could too easily picture what kind of chaos a transport capsule might bring to a planet of humans—or creatures of human-like intelligence—who didn't know or understand the possibility of life beyond their own stars.

Tarrowburn shrugged. "If someone managed to establish and occupy the entire planet in two-hundred fifty years, they're using tools we don't have on Earth. We should find out more before we decide on our final destination. Whoever they are, wherever they've come from, they may already have dibs on the other potential landing sites as well. It's unwise to pick a new destination without seeing the entire picture."

Rana breathed a curse.

Yvonne's head swam again. She hadn't thought about encountering alien life on this expedition. None of TransUniversal's orientation holos had prepared them for the possibility of an encounter. Their route had been carefully mapped to avoid any chance confrontation, and they were headed to establish human occupation on what was previously *unoccupied* L.I.R.O.N.

Did intelligent alien species exist? Sure, Yvonne supposed a few sectors of the universe were populated with intelligent life, but so far, she hadn't considered the possibility that anyone other than TransUniversal and a few smaller companies had sent out ships for colonization purposes. TransUniversal had explicitly stated that each area of every location prior to arranging the settlements had been thoroughly explored.

"I'm with Jon," Booker said after a long silence. "Who else?"

There was an uncomfortable silence before the rest of the team began to nod and utter their agreement. Yvonne nodded with them.

The devil you knew was always better than the devil you didn't. That's what her mama always said, anyway, and it was true. It would be better to know who was on the surface of L.I.R.O.N., and if L.I.R.O.N.'s occupants knew anything about A.P.H.O. 12 or I.S.C.O.P. 4 development.

"Fine. Tarrowburn, Jones, Lukawicz, and Faranzine, you'll go to the surface. Faranzine, how soon can you prep a transport?"

Joe leaned forward in this chair, the mental calculations in his head visible only by a subtle pursing of lips and an eye squint behind his glasses. "Should be able to have one ready to go in sixteen hours. Need to cycle the power a few times, give it a full charge from the IV3 before we take it down, though."

"What if you do a half-charge, and let it do the rest from the surface of the planet? How long then?"

"Nine hours, but the atmosphere at the surface will make for a slower charge. Better to have full power before going so we can get out quickly if needed."

Yvonne's heart stuttered, an uncomfortable thump in her chest. She'd signed on to engineer and help tend livestock. Not start a war against aliens.

And then her thoughts trickled to the three decks full of thousands of passengers inanimate in their stasis pods, waiting to wake again, and her pulse surged in her veins. *They* hadn't signed on for a war, either. They'd wanted to get *away* from that kind of life entirely.

"You think they're hostile?" she asked the ship's engineer.

Joe shrugged. "I can't say. They wouldn't be much threat if they were, given the transport's safeguards, but that's not the point. I'd rather take a few extra hours up front and get a full charge beforehand."

The captain closed her eyes and nodded. Yvonne didn't envy her the headache that was surely brewing.

"What's the status of the translation system update?" the captain asked.

"Almost complete," Faranzine answered. "Latest version fixes a few bugs in the mainframe. It'll be ready when we need it."

The translation system was built to translate any language, known or unknown, to the user via a thumbnail-sized pod that clipped around the ear and a soft silicone speaker that fit into the outer ear canal. The software used speech patterns and an array of complex algorithms to translate unknown languages into the user's preferred language.

Likewise, a handheld comm unit was available for reverse translation so a two-way conversation could be held among virtually anyone, regardless of whether they could speak other languages fluently.

Yvonne's gaze fell back to the image of L.I.R.O.N. on the large screen. The dotted overlay of all the occupied cities had disappeared. The planet now looked exactly as it had in the images she'd been shown when she signed on. A beautiful blue and green marble with swirling white clouds across its surface. It looked so silent from here, so peaceful. So welcoming. Who could have guessed it wouldn't be home after all?

Yvonne stood at the large viewing window before the bridge, as the transport capsule pulled away from the docking station and grew smaller in her vision. Then, one flare against its heat shields as it entered L.I.R.O.N.'s atmosphere and she could see it no more. She rolled her head from side to side, rubbing her tight neck, attempting to loosen muscles that hadn't wanted to release since Rana had broken the news.

Tarrowburn and Rana agreed on a landing site in a more populated region. Yvonne was glad not to have been involved in the decision. Had it been up to her, they would have avoided the mission entirely and headed straight for

A.P.H.O. 12.

Every minute that ticked by was decades-long. Even knowing they wouldn't receive an update for hours didn't stop Yvonne's body from burning with nervous energy. She took the long walk to the stasis pens, checked every animal thoroughly despite having checked them all this morning. Two hours later, she returned to the bridge and resumed pacing the shining metal floor.

"Sit down, Harris. You're going to wear a hole in my ship."

Captain Rana didn't glance up from where she sat in the captain's chair, examining the newest and most detailed images of L.I.R.O.N. the ship's computer had supplied.

"I don't know how you can just sit there all relaxed and carefree," Yvonne snapped as she flopped into the closest seat—Faranzine's.

Rana's eyebrows raised, two fine, dark arches on an intelligent light brown face. She pursed her lips once, as though weighing her thoughts, deliberating before speaking.

Rana was a good captain—the best. The woman had never made a rash decision in all the years Yvonne had known her, and they had worked together often, delivering cargo from one quadrant to another, from one sector to the next. So much cargo.

When Chandra had suggested a new venture, one that paid more than Yvonne could earn in two lifetimes hustling on the cargo ships, the answer was clear. She had no remaining family, no home, and no pets for all her love of animals. Depart to establish a new life on a new planet with mountains and pastures, oceans and lakes, air and space for miles and miles? *Of course* she'd said yes.

"Spit it out already, would you?" she snapped at Rana.

The captain finally glanced up and met Yvonne's eyes, but her fingers never stopped flying across the computer's holokeys, and her gaze soon returned to the task at hand.

"Spit what out, Yvonne?" she said mildly.

"Whatever you're thinking. You're wearing that face again."

"That face? My face? Unfortunately, it's the only one I have, my friend. I'm sorry, but you'll have to deal with it."

Yvonne leaned back in her seat, letting her arms and head hang over the chair's supports, sprawling her legs out in frustration. She let out a noise somewhere between a growl and a sigh and stared at the smooth white metal of the ceiling above.

"You know what I mean, Chandra. Don't screw around. This isn't the time."

Finally, the captain pressed a key and turned the hologram aside, sliding back into the projection desk. She swiveled in the chair, turning to meet Yvonne evenly.

"What do you want from me, Yvonne? Do you want me to panic? To scream and yell and stomp in frustration? I'm a captain. I didn't make this rank by acting like a four-year-old."

Yvonne's shoulders slumped. "That's not what I meant. You've earned your rank. If anyone knows it, it's me, but"— she rubbed grainy eyes from too little sleep— "Chandra, aren't you even a little worried about what they're going to find down there?"

"Of course I am," she bit. "I'd be a fool not to be. I have rank when it comes to the ship, but Tarrowburn outranks us all when it comes to the planet, and if he wanted to go, what was I supposed to do—say no? I hope he finds something useful. Because if not, we've just wasted days we could've spent prepping for travel to one of the other prospects."

Yvonne breathed a sigh. Chandra's outburst shouldn't have made her feel better, but somehow, it did.

"That's all I wanted. *Some* emotion out of you."

The captain laughed. "You have issues, Harris. I ever tell you that?"

"I think you might have mentioned it once or twice."

The two watched the observation window in silence, though the transport ship was long out of sight. The quiet Earth-like planet spun slowly before them, the larger of its two moons peeking from behind the planet and rotating into view, deceptively peaceful and quiet.

When the off-site comm finally rang through, Yvonne almost jumped out of her skin. She leaned forward, as though doing so would help her hear better.

"Chandra Rana, Captain, Interstellar Voyager III," Rana answered smoothly without a hint of the nerves that had Yvonne on edge.

"Jonathan Tarrowburn, Expedition Team Leader, Transport One, reporting L.I.R.O.N. findings." Tarrowburn's voice echoed through the speakers of the nearly empty bridge.

"Good to hear you, Tarrowburn. What's your status?"

There was a pause before Tarrowburn answered, during which the voices of Lukawicz and Faranzine could be heard distantly arguing in the background. Yvonne held her breath and bit a lip.

Finally, Tarrowburn spoke again. Slowly. "Captain, the general consensus is that you're going to need to see this."

"Tarrowburn, *what* is the problem?" Chandra had turned to full captain mode once more.

When the comm came through again, it was Faranzine's voice.

"Captain, you, Abrams, and Harris should fire up Transport Two. I charged it when I charged One. You'll need to program it with the identical flight path as Transport One. Then meet us here as soon as you're able. There's, uh…well, there's a lot to discuss."

For the first time since Yvonne had known her, Rana appeared flustered.

"Faranzine," she said. "Who colonized the planet?"

Faranzine's voice boomed through the bridge in two small words, and even while Yvonne heard his response, she didn't understand.

"We did."

She and the captain looked at each other in confusion, each trying to piece together what Faranzine could have meant.

Finally, Rana spoke again. "Humans?" she said. "From Earth?"

Impossible.

Tarrowburn took the comm back from Faranzine, but

Yvonne could still make out faint traces of arguing behind him. "He meant exactly what he said, Captain, and the only way you'll understand is to get down here as soon as you can. Leave the ship in orbit, put one of the engineers in charge, and take the transport."

"Did he just give you orders?" Yvonne asked, astonished.

Rana turned to Yvonne. "Ask Abrams to start up Transport Two and have it ready to go in an hour."

Yvonne nodded, stood, and went as fast as half g would carry her across the bridge, listening acutely to the last of the conversation before stepping into the hall beyond.

"Tarrowburn," Rana said, her voice a force to be reckoned with. "Who's on the surface? What did Faranzine mean?"

"He meant exactly what he said, Captain. We did."

The landing was nothing like what Yvonne had dreamed of for months on end. She was too preoccupied with the questions in her mind, the endless worries that had grabbed hold and didn't seem to want to let go.

After a bumpy entry into the atmosphere, the transport virtually glided to the destination coordinates Tarrowburn had given them. Yvonne kept her eyes glued to the scenery behind the glass panels that surrounded them.

She couldn't remember the last time she'd seen so much green, or even if she ever had. Once she'd reached adulthood, she'd signed up for work in space travel and hadn't looked back. The landscape that slipped by beneath them now was breathtaking, unmarred by factories and smokestacks, spaceport traffic and ground transport. The land was pristine.

Then the transport began to slide by homes, and people who stood in cobbled streets and pointed up at their transport. The very sight was a shock to the system. Anxiety churned in Yvonne's gut, but they were humans, just as Tarrowburn and Faranzine had confirmed.

Humans who didn't belong here, who weren't supposed to be here.

How?

How had it happened? How had it all gone so wrong?

When the transport finally landed beside its twin in the midst of a large grass field, Yvonne unbuckled and followed Rana and Abrams to disembark via the ship's ramp.

It was the smell that struck Yvonne first.

The scent of fresh, growing things. Of dirt and grass, trees and pollen, of flowers somewhere in the distance, perfuming the air with their fragrance.

That part was *exactly* as she had hoped, at least. Her closed eyes fluttered as she inhaled, reveling in the ecstasy of fresh, non-recycled air, of the warm breeze that blew across her face. It took everything she had not to throw herself to the ground and roll in the feel of the grass.

And then they were being welcomed by Tarrowburn, Faranzine, Jones, and Lukawicz, and ushered to a castle.

A castle!

Rana demanded answers as they walked, but Tarrowburn continued to put her off, spouting the history of the castle and the people who lived here, the people who were waiting to meet them. They traveled the halls of a stone castle that seemed as though it had jumped from the pages of medieval European history texts, their boots echoing across the stone floors and walls.

They passed few people along the way. Word of their arrival must have gotten out and occasional onlookers in simple dress peered at them from adjoining hallways and open doors. They were curious in their open stares but welcoming with their eyes and smiles. The body language alone helped ease the tension from between her shoulder blades. No open war with aliens, then. This was good. A step in the right direction.

Oil sconces lit the way between large arched windows that revealed rolling hills in one direction and a sprawling town in the other. Yvonne couldn't help but smile at the way the fire flickered gently. It had been so long since she'd seen open flame, she'd almost forgotten its mesmerizing allure. Fire. In a castle.

"It's not my place to tell you, Captain," Tarrowburn was saying as they reached the end of the hallway and turned. "It's bigger than I can explain, and you'd do best to see it on your own."

They descended a stairwell and passed through a stone archway into what appeared to be a library. The shelves were packed with ancient texts, the kind of books that looked like they belonged in the Renaissance—leather-bound, gold-leaf lettering across their spines. Thousands of books. The lettering, though…was familiar.

Was this what Faranzine meant when he'd answered "we

did" to Rana's question about who colonized the planet? The humans she'd seen from the window of Transport Two had left little doubt as to the genetic makeup of the intelligent species on the planet, but it was highly possible human-like species had formed in various locations throughout the universe.

But these bound texts with the Latin alphabet splashed across their spines? These humans were from Earth. The revelation was a punch to the gut.

They navigated the library, Tarrowburn and Faranzine keeping Rana's questions at bay even though the captain was growing visibly more irritated by the minute. Then they descended another stairwell within the library and passed through a second stone archway, this one engraved with letters she caught briefly as she passed beneath them. IV3.

The Interstellar Voyager III?

An absurd thought. The engraving must refer to something else. An odd coincidence at best.

But the gears in her head were turning, and she couldn't let go of the bizarre thought that the people here had known they were coming, that this visit was anything but a surprise.

"This," Tarrowburn says, "is why we needed you to be here."

Still standing toward the back as they approached whatever it was Tarrowburn was pointing out, Yvonne craned her neck to see. The group reached the end of the alcove where three women stood around a pedestal supporting an open book.

The women were in their thirties or forties, dressed in

the kind of finery Yvonne might expect from centuries-ago Europe, and they were related, their dark chocolate-colored eyes matching each other in both shape and the intensity of their gaze. Their long hair in varying shades of brown was swept back from their faces in intricate curls and braids, but for all their presence spoke of wealth and royalty, they wore no jewels upon their heads or on their fingers.

The woman in the center lifted the comm unit in her hand and spoke into it, her smiling eyes casting a welcoming glance to each of the newcomers in the room. The strange syllables rolling from her mouth were almost musical, a language that sounded foreign and familiar all the same. As the translation unfurled in the translator she wore, Yvonne began to realize why. The language wasn't so far removed from their own. Just…evolved.

"Welcome, new friends. I am Alenya Elise Morel. These are my sisters, Corrine Moreina, and Liana Mathilde." The woman held a hand to each side of her, motioning to her sisters as she named them. "As the royal family of the northern lands of Castilles, we are representatives of our people, but more importantly, we welcome you on behalf of all of Liron. Your arrival has been highly anticipated."

Yvonne looked to Abrams who returned her questioning glance with one of her own.

"Thank you for the kind reception," Rana replied. "We're grateful that our arrival is met with such enthusiasm. I am Chandra Rana, captain of the Interstellar Voyager III, which has traveled many millions of light years to reach L.I.R.O.N. With me, are Beulah Abrams and Yvonne Harris, both members of my crew. Of course, you've already met Jonathan Tarrowburn, Joseph Faranzine, Booker Jones, and Amy Lukawicz. I must admit, though, I am…puzzled by your welcome. Our arrival was anticipated?"

The three women smiled wider, obviously expecting the question. The one introduced as Corinne leaned to Alenya and spoke quietly, her dark eyes shifting across the faces of the expedition team.

Alenya nodded, then spoke into the comm unit again. "My sisters and I are the granddaughters of two of the most widely celebrated heroes on all of Liron—Eron Alexandre Morel and Moreina di Bianco.

"To you, these names mean nothing, but to the people of Liron, Moreina and Eron—better known as Quinn—were responsible for fulfilling foretold prophecies over a hundred years ago and saving our people from darkness and chaos.

"It is because of them that we're here to greet you today. And it is because of *you* that they were able to do what they did. Where your journey ends, ours begins." Alenya traced a circle in the air with her hands to further emphasize her words.

Visibly shaken by Alenya's words, Rana's breath hitched. Yvonne might not have noticed had she not been standing beside her friend and so attuned to her friend's demeanor. Alenya's words reverberated through Yvonne's brain.

Prophecies.

What madness had they descended to?

After a moment, Rana collected herself. "I'm sorry," she said smoothly. "I'm not understanding what you're saying.

I think we're experiencing a problem with the translation system. You referred to a…prophecy?"

Alenya motioned to the book on the pedestal.

"It is not the original Book of Keys, I regret, but we've compiled a history so far as we've been able to piece together. A history of Liron and the Tarrowburn Prophecies that saved us all. Magnus Tarrowburn provided only what was needed for all to come to fruition."

Rana, Abrams, and Yvonne pinned their gazes on Tarrowburn. This news was apparently not a surprise to the other crew members, as they gave no reaction.

"Magnus?" Rana asked.

In response, Tarrowburn's eyes widened as he pressed his mouth into a hard line. He shrugged, then cleared his throat. "Middle name."

"I see."

"That's as much as I was informed of before I called you," he said. Was it Yvonne, or did Tarrowburn look pale? Yvonne supposed she'd feel faint, too, if someone casually dropped her name in reference to a planet-saving prophecy.

Rana pointed to the book. "You're saying this is…a book of prophecies?"

"No," Alenya said, placing one hand atop the pages. "It is a book of our history. It contains multiple prophecies, which are key to understanding everything that has happened on Liron in the thousands of years since humans first came."

"I'm sorry. *Thousands* of years, you say?"

Yvonne was glad to hear Rana speak the very words she wanted to scream herself. None of this was possible.

Alenya and her sisters nodded as the translation of Rana's words echoed through the comm unit. "This is…a lot to absorb," Alenya said. "We can discuss further in the chambers above, but I—we—felt it was essential that you see the evidence for yourself, that you understand the beginnings of Liron and her people. We wanted you to understand that it is because of *you* that we exist. Our library seemed the best place to do that."

Yvonne thought back to the IV3 engraved in the stone archway they'd passed on their way. She shivered. Not a coincidence at all. But *how?*

On the ship once more, Yvonne regarded Rana carefully, trying to decide what her friend's marked silence meant. Shock? Yvonne certainly felt a sense of shock herself. It wasn't every day you traveled across the universe to find a supposedly uninhabited planet fully occupied by people who claimed you were their ancestors who should have arrived several thousand years prior.

Yvonne turned her gaze to the observation window. From here, L.I.R.O.N—er, Liron—was a peaceful, silent ball of blue and green in a sea of inky black nothingness dotted with pinpricks of light from stars millions of miles away. The solar system closely resembled their own, and if the planet hadn't been circled by two moons, Yvonne might have assumed she was looking down on Earth.

But that wasn't exactly true, either, was it? The

landmasses below the swirling white clouds made it clear the planet below was not Earth.

"How are we proceeding, Chandra?" Yvonne turned from the scene below and sat in one of the seats on the bridge, studying her friend's face for any sign of what she was thinking behind those carefully guarded eyes.

Rana ran the side of a finger over her lips twice. "I haven't decided."

"Okay, in that case, what are you thinking?"

"I'm wondering if A.P.H.O 12 and I.S.C.O.P. 4 aren't better options than the sheer lunacy that's down there." Rana hadn't even glanced up from the data she was currently scouring on the screen.

Yvonne was glad the others on the leadership team had either gone about their business or retired to their cabins until they were called for further input. Or maybe they were waiting for the captain to make her decision without their input. Either way, their absence meant Chandra was more likely to be candid with her thoughts. Yvonne appreciated the opportunity for brutal honesty.

"Did you backtrack the navigation?" Yvonne didn't want to seem overly eager, but she was dying to know if what the three women had said was true. Could the IV3 have brought them through a portal three-thousand-some years into the future by mistake?

"Mm." The best the captain could give her was a distracted sound as she stared once more at the holoscreen.

"Chandra."

"What?"

"*Chandra.*"

The captain's head snapped upwards, her attention fully focused on Yvonne. "*What?*"

"Did you backtrack the navigation?"

"I did."

Yvonne groaned. "You're doing this on purpose."

A hint of a smile graced her friend's lips. "I am. But see for yourself."

Rana swiveled the holo to face Yvonne. She watched the screen as a red dot representation of the ship tracked through space on its way to L.I.R.O.N., then disappeared just outside the solar system's orbit. It blinked back a moment later.

"What the hell was *that?*" she asked.

"That." Chandra stood from her seat and massaged the back of her neck with one hand, trying to dislodge the clear evidence of job-related stress. "That, my friend, is our error."

Yvonne waited, her gaze pinned to the holo.

Rana began to walk the bridge. "That's the wormhole our instruments failed to detect, the wormhole we traveled through, the wormhole that dumped us so far into the future, the planet we came here to colonize is already colonized."

Near speechless, Yvonne leaned back in her seat, the padding doing little to cushion her sudden movement.

"So, we have to…go back?" Yvonne swallowed, her throat dry with understanding.

Chandra nodded. "I need to run it by Faranzine. I'm not sure how else to fix this mess. If what they say"—Chandra pointed to the window behind her, and Yvonne didn't have to ask who she meant by "they"— "is true, then we can't leave for A.P.H.O 12 or I.S.C.O.P. 4 because then none of *that* happens."

"What if they're out of their heads?"

Chandra let out a hoarse laugh. "I'd like to believe that, Yvonne. I really would. But they knew we would be here. They were *waiting* for us to arrive. They knew Tarrowburn's name for God's sake! And Faranzine. You saw what they showed us."

The evidence was difficult to ignore, but it was still hard to believe the drive crystals would be used to craft jewelry that somehow ended up possessing…magic. This was far beyond anything Alice had ever encountered in Wonderland.

"Anyway, did you know Joe designed jewelry?"

"Not until he confirmed it after they told us everything. A hobby. Apparently." Chandra gave another dry laugh and rubbed her temples. "I did not sign up for this kind of crazy."

"And what about Tarrowburn? If what they say is true, he can't go with us. What do we do? *Drop him off on the way?*"

"I've been running that through my head nonstop. I think if he takes the transport unit through at the same time the IV3 goes through the wormhole, the difference in mass means he gets spit out first, and we'll keep going."

Yvonne nodded slowly, comprehending without fully comprehending at all. "He won't go back as far."

"Exactly."

She let out a soft sigh.

"And what's he going to do, show up and assimilate into an already-civilized society as a fully formed prophet of doom?"

Chandra screwed up her face into a mask of confusion. "You know? Is it wrong that I feel like he'd enjoy that?"

Yvonne burst into laughter. She laughed until Chandra joined in, until the two of them had tears streaming down their cheeks.

When she recovered, she stared at the planet, at the peaceful blue and green ball spinning out the window.

"Is it possible? Is it possible to go *back* in time through a wormhole?"

"I don't know. I *think* so—the science is there, tentatively—but I'm not positive."

Yvonne turned her attention from the window to her friend's face. "You know what my mama always told me? Well, she said a lot of things, but whenever she wanted to spur me in the right direction, or push me to challenge my situation, to step forward, to make my life what I wanted it to be, she always resorted to three little words."

Chandra viewed Yvonne, the curiosity genuine on her face. Finally, she said, "And what were the three words?"

"She told me, my dear friend, that anything is possible."

Chandra was silent for a long moment. Then, she leaned forward, tapped out a command on the holo, and looked back to Yvonne with a nod.

"Decision made. Let's go home."

THE END

ACKNOWLEDGMENTS

Wow—so, hey, I finished a trilogy. But the thing is? I couldn't have done it without the support and assistance of so many people. A gigantic thank you to all the readers who made Chaos Bound, and the entire Tarrowburn Prophecies trilogy, possible. Without your love of Reina, Quinn, and their various companions, I never would have given them the ending they deserved. (Unless you hated the ending, in which case, sorry about that. You have my permission to ignore the epilogue.)

To my immediate and extended family, I am so grateful for your support. I want to name you all, but I'm desperately afraid of forgetting someone. Regardless, let's give it a whirl. Thank you to Barbara and Frank (aka Mom and Dad), Dan and Jen, Jessie and Brent, Joan and Peter, Janet, Chris and Francis, Diane and Las, John and Maki, Denise, Kim and Justin. Plus, all "the kids"—Justin, Sam, Jack, Caelyn, Rebecca, Marisa, Lily, Abigail, Allison, and Sarah. And Mark, who might as well be a kid. Most of all, to my husband, Nate, who provides for our family every single day so I can play with imaginary friends on the page. Your belief in me is my world.

To my friends, critique partners, and beta-readers who have cheered me on and helped make my work stronger, thank you. Jean Grant, Mariah Ligas, Barbara Longo, Jess Rancatore, and Vanita Shastry, I appreciate all the time you've given to me throughout the course of this series. Your keen eye, your ability to steer me in the right direction, and your dedicated support is unparalleled. A big thanks to my SCBWI critique group—Cindy Mock, Alyssa Capel, and Clare Milliner. Meeting with you each month keeps me sane.

To my Twitter writing friends, thank you. That goes for both my #5amwritersclub and #8pmwritingsprint pals! Special thanks to Nikki Minty and to Mariely Lares, who read on an itty, bitty screen to get me a blurb in time for release. There are far too many of my Twitter friends to name, but thank you to Jackie Bahas, Jonathan Bing, Jason Coleman, Gail Gilmore, Jay Heltzer, Melanie Hooyenga, Lakshmi Iyer, Virginia Jacobs, Joe Martin, Shanah McCready, Suzanne Miller, Maggie Moris, CM Rother, Margot Ryan, Maria Stout, Rachel Strayer, Katelyn Botsford Tucker, Ralph Walker, EJ Wenstrom, and so, so many others. I couldn't have continued writing without your encouragement. 100% sure I missed naming some *very*important*people* here. If your name isn't listed, I'm still so thankful for you! Thank you. All of you.

A special thank you to my cover artist, AK Westerman, who made the cover of book 3 as beautiful as books 1 & 2. Lastly, a thank you to my talented editor, Sorchia DuBois, who has helped make these books shine from start to finish.

ABOUT THE AUTHOR

L. Ryan Storms is a writer, photographer, traveler, and dreamer. She's a member of the Eastern Pennsylvania chapter of SCBWI who enjoys working PR & Marketing for her local library. She has written articles featured on the front page of local newspapers, but mostly she writes novels near and dear to her heart. She hold's a B.S. in Marine Science from Kutztown University of Pennsylvania and a Master's in Business Administration from Marist College, but writing young adult fantasy has always been her true passion. Her first young adult novel, *A Thousand Years to Wait,* placed first in the Young Adult category in the 2021 Royal Dragonfly Book Awards and was an award-winning finalist in American Book Fest's 2019 Best Book Awards.

Storms lives in Pennsylvania with her cancer-survivor husband, two children, and a "rescue zoo" featuring two dogs, two cats, chickens, and an ex-racehorse. When she's not writing, reading, or keeping her kids in line, she enjoys hiking, photography, and planning the next big adventure.

L. RYAN STORMS
(Photo credit: Laslo Varadi)

Find out what L. Ryan Storms is working on & visit her blog at www.lryanstorms.com. You can also find her frequently tweeting about writing (and parenting) on Twitter (@LRyan_Storms).

Also in this series:

A Thousand Years to Wait
(The Tarrowburn Prophecies, Book 1)

The Heart of Death
(The Tarrowburn Prophecies, Book 2)